An Insubstantial Death

There is nothing so greedy as the grave

Hilary Creed

instant
ap□stle

First published in Great Britain in 2017

Instant Apostle

The Barn
1 Watford House Lane
Watford
Herts
WD17 1BJ

British Library Cataloguing-in-Publication Data

A catalogue record for this book is available from the British Library

This book and all other Instant Apostle books are available from Instant Apostle:

Website: www.instantapostle.com

E-mail: info@instantapostle.com

ISBN 978-1-909728-58-5

Printed in Great Britain

Disclaimer

This is a work of fiction. Names, characters, businesses, places, events and incidents are either the products of the author's imagination or used in a fictitious manner. Any resemblance to actual persons, living or dead, or actual events is purely coincidental. For the purpose of the story, some details, such as ferry timings, have been fictionalised.

Bible references

'Let the little children come to me' (Matthew 19:14, NIV UK).
'An enemy hath done this' (Matthew 13:28, KJV).

Other references in the text

'The woman I love' is a quote from Edward VIII's speech on the day of his abdication, 11th December 1936.

With thanks to Cherith, and to the members of my local writing group, without whom these characters would not have lived, breathed and briefly coexisted somewhere along the south coast of England over one memorable Easter weekend.

Contents

Part I
Dangerous Undercurrents

Thursday

Chapter 1

Barely 20 hours before she found the body, Dame Emily was walking down the old path through the Lime Walk. She turned abruptly at the sound of squealing rubber at the entrance to Seascape House, and watched as an extremely long, pink limousine swerved through the main gates, narrowly missed a large furniture van on its right, and skidded off the tarmac drive onto the beautifully manicured lawn.

Gripping her stick tightly, Dame Emily hurried towards the limo, unable to see the occupants through the darkened glass. As the two front doors opened simultaneously, she just had time to notice the peaked cap and shocked face of the chauffeur, before being confronted by a red-faced man, whose ample width abundantly compensated for his shortness of height.

'What do you…?' Dame Emily began, but was immediately interrupted.

'Bloomin' 'eck! What's that blinkin' van doing 'ere?' he demanded.

Dame Emily's stick twitched and then wavered more decisively around the newcomer's paunch. She ignored his rudeness and said, as a headmistress to a pupil who has overstepped the mark, 'I live here. I think it is you who should explain yourself.'

The little man, finding himself trapped between the flank of the car and the rubber tip of the walking stick, seemed to be at a disadvantage and was breathing heavily. ''Ere, put that thing down. This 'ere ancient pile's mine, and nobbut spiders live 'ere.'

'Ah!' Dame Emily's eyes gleamed. Far from being put in her place, she seemed to grow a couple of inches. She looked down into the upturned face. 'I need a word or two with you.'

Her challenger's face turned an explosive pink, not dissimilar to the paintwork which was now supporting his back. Dame Emily, enjoying the encounter, thought of a chameleon; even the bulging eyes, double chin and little stubby fingers running through the last remaining strands of hair on his head helped to complete the ridiculous image. If she had not been so angry she might have laughed.

'I,' she said firmly, 'am Dame Emily Hatherley-Browne – with an "e". And you are?'

The bulbous figure swelled a little and the voice became more refined, the language grander. 'I am James Wedderburn, originator of Wedderburn's Pork Sausage Empire and now owner of this whole estate.' He tried to wave a hand to indicate the extent of his property, but was too aware of the proximity of the weapon pointed at his stomach to be effective.

Dame Emily lowered the stick and leaned on it heavily. Two removal men dressed in overalls came out of the porter's lodge behind the van.

'We done the settee, like you said,' reported the older one. 'The fridge-freezer's in, but there's no power and the food in them cool bags is on the kitchen table, ready.'

'Well done, lads,' Dame Emily nodded, looking at her watch. 'I know it's only 11.30. What about an early break for lunch? We'll reconvene in 45 minutes.'

A relieved smile came over both faces and the older man doffed his cap. 'Right-oh, Dame Em. See you later.' He clambered up into his cab and was opening a pack of sandwiches before Dame Emily could respond.

She turned her gaze on the rotund man in front of her. 'Right, Mr Wedderburn,' she said briskly. 'We'll walk together to the chairs on the lawn at the front of the house and have a little chat. I haven't long.' She caught sight of the chauffeur's smirk as she turned her back on him and led the way. James Wedderburn, breathing heavily, followed her, his footsteps squelching on the sodden grass.

'Now,' said Dame Emily, using one finger and thumb to remove a decaying leaf from a chair and seating herself. 'I shall explain myself, and then I shall expect you to do the same.' She sat with a perfectly straight back, trim in her old but very respectable tweed skirt and green parka, ignoring the fact that a few strands of her white hair had escaped from the comb and pins which held it back, and were being blown across her face by the very cool breeze.

James Wedderburn sank onto the chair opposite her and drew his camel coat closer round his wide frame, enabling, for a brief moment, the scent of cigar smoke to waft from it. James had turned pale at the mention of Dame Emily's name; now he looked decidedly uneasy. No doubt, she thought, he was unaccustomed to being ordered about by a woman. The novelty certainly seemed to have knocked his confidence.

'I,' said Dame Emily, leaning dangerously near his face, 'as you now realise, am the previous owner of this wonderful Elizabethan mansion.' She nodded towards the gabled brick and flint building behind James. 'When you bought this house, you agreed that I should continue to live in the Lodge here, until the contents of the house were sold and I had found myself a bungalow locally. I have it in writing. You, however, thought that you could evict me, despite our agreement, and decided that I should rent, from you, a town house in Roostings, at the back of Eastbourne, nowhere near the sea and seven miles from my friends here. Seven miles!' The horror in her voice made it sound like exile in the snow-covered wastes of Siberia.

James Wedderburn thumped a podgy fist on the imitation wrought-iron table; his Yorkshire accent vanished completely as he attempted a genteel but forceful response. 'I couldn't wait for ever. It was extraordinarily generous of me to find you somewhere to live – added to which it was a brand-new, purpose-built house.'

'Precisely! It was indeed a house, and definitely not a bungalow,' Dame Emily continued. 'This mansion has been my family home since the sixteenth century! You think you can condemn me to one of those new faceless buildings, which looks as if it has been made out of children's plastic interlocking building blocks, in the middle of an estate, on the edge of a less than charming village, spoilt by the new motorway into Eastbourne! No character, no garden to speak of, and no space for my dog to run free. It's hardly a place to recuperate from a serious hip operation. You showed no consideration whatsoever.'

James shifted in his seat. 'It's been nine months since I bought this place,' he argued defensively. 'It wasn't convenient to have the Lodge occupied. Besides, the house I offered you had become available, and I needed to begin work on the mansion.'

But Dame Emily was warming to her task. She had been longing for this moment for several weeks. 'I'm not stopping you beginning work. It was you who ignored my letters and my explanations about my broken hip and the two operations which kept me in Australia; your secretary insisted it was impossible to reach you, though I doubt that very much.'

James sat bolt upright. 'You're mistaken,' he objected loudly. 'Martin would never have said such a thing!'

Dame Emily snorted, but let the remark pass.

'So,' she said with deliberate emphasis, leaning a little nearer the sweating face, 'on my return I moved to your so-called "attractive home", despite the fact that it was totally unsuitable. I had chosen my belongings with infinite care when I first transferred to the Lodge. There was so much I wanted to keep.' She fought to keep her voice from shaking as she continued the tirade. 'When I arrived in Roostings, I discovered a small yellow digger in the back garden, where a large hole had been dug across the whole width of the lawn, there were piles of soil on the rest of the grass, it was highly dangerous and smelt very unpleasant.'

James took a breath, but Dame Emily held up her hand to pre-empt any interruption. 'I had been in your dreadful, characterless house two weeks,' she almost spat out the words, 'when the wiring in the loft caught light. In the middle of the night the whole roof went up. If it hadn't been for the neighbours, I doubt whether I or my beloved Cavalier King Charles spaniel would ever have been seen again. Neither you nor one of your minions replied to my letter telling you what had happened. I assume you didn't care!'

James' eyes were wide, his breathing laboured. 'Of course I did...' he began, but Dame Emily had no interest in his answer.

'The fire brigade came quickly – but then there was water damage to the upstairs rooms and the furniture.' She omitted to tell him that she was not using the stairs, to avoid aggravating the newly repaired hip, and had settled into the downstairs rooms only. There would be time enough to go into details when absolutely necessary.

A finger waved in front of James' face, making his eyes cross. 'I hold you responsible,' Dame Emily insisted. 'Did you employ anyone to oversee the building work? Did you have the house thoroughly checked afterwards? Did you even go to see it?'

James' face resembled a goldfish now. His mouth moved, allowing a few words to escape. 'Now, just a minute...'

Dame Emily ignored him. 'It was obvious what I should do. I could hardly live in a house with a flapping, ill-fitting, bright blue tarpaulin for a roof. In the last six months you have not acknowledged my messages from Australia, nor replied to my solicitor's letters, neither did you come down to visit me in my temporary home when I came back, so naturally I couldn't give you my set of keys. As I still had them, the most practical course of action was to return to the Lodge at Seascape House. I am moving in today and intend to remain here until we can resolve this satisfactorily.'

James' eyes were wide with horror, and Dame Emily enjoyed the images she felt sure were playing there – the previous owner now reinstalled in the place where he himself should be sole proprietor; the headlines on the front page of the local newspaper: 'Heiress in fire tragedy now denied small home on ancestral estate'. She could almost see him shudder.

He waved a finger in her direction. 'Now look here,' he began. 'I shall be contacting my solicitor; he'll be staying here this weekend. I really can't allow this.'

Dame Emily leaned back in her chair, allowing its intricate metal design to prop her upright. 'Please do. I'm sure he will see the wisdom of my decision. He can always pop into Eastbourne and discuss it all with my own solicitor; I will arrange a meeting at the earliest possible date.' She paused and James Wedderburn, no doubt realising that this was checkmate, glared at his enemy.

Dame Emily smiled – a stiff, formal smile. 'That's settled, then. The removal men will finish in a couple of hours; they're good, solid workers as long as you keep an eye on them. The van will turn in the old exercise yard, so please make sure there is room for it. They should be out of the way by…' She looked again at her watch, '2.30 at the latest.'

She stopped, waited, and was finally rewarded with, 'Well, now you're here, I suppose you'll have to stay – for the time being.' James looked badly shaken. Dame Emily could see he was struggling to resume his Lord of the Manor image. 'I am expecting several guests and members of the family from about four o'clock,' he said, in a futile attempt to regain control. 'We have a… a conference for the whole of the Easter break.'

Dame Emily had no interest and no sympathy. 'Perhaps we can talk after your family have met,' she said. 'I hope you will be staying for rather longer than the Bank Holiday weekend; I shan't be able to contact my solicitor to tell him you are here until Tuesday, of course…'

James gulped, obviously unable to think quickly. 'I should be moving into the converted barn later next week,' he murmured. 'There have been a few, er, complications.'

Dame Emily stood and James Wedderburn, supporting himself on the edge of the garden table, raised his body, which obviously had no desire to move, and began to make his way back to the limo. The Dame glared at his back and then walked across the lawn, her stick swinging in easy time with her movement.

She glanced back just before she disappeared inside the Lodge. One of the removal men was pouring something hot from a flask into his mate's mug, and she caught the new owner of Seascape House looking gloomily at the muddy tyre tracks on the bright-green grass. He lowered himself carefully into the front passenger seat as the chauffeur held the door.

'Round to the back of this pile,' she heard him growl, 'and watch how you park. Your dad needs his pride and joy back in one piece next week. Now, let's 'ope Martin's fixed a good lunch. I'm fair famished.'

Dame Emily stepped through the Lodge doorway and shut the door with a suddenness that made the knocker rattle. She marched into the kitchen, waking the sleeping dog, and offered her a biscuit from her pocket.

'Finlandia, we are at war!' she announced.

Chapter 2

Samantha Wedderburn sighed as the car braked yet again and her husband's long, elegant fingers tapped a repeated, rhythmic pattern on the rim of the steering wheel. He stared out at the cavalcade of small children trooping over the zebra crossing in front of them, a never-ending stream, wearing outlandish bonnets and carrying large Easter cards. More harassed mothers, with pushchairs loaded with assorted shopping bags, dragged disconsolate toddlers and the occasional dog on a shortened lead, towards the kerb, putting defiant feet on the painted stripes, daring a single car to move.

Samantha looked at Philip anxiously. 'I'm sorry,' she said for about the fifth time.

Philip's tense shoulders relaxed. 'It's not your fault. They obviously break up from school later in this part of the world.'

'The last sign said ten miles to Eastbourne,' she said. 'I think we should still make it in time.'

Philip nodded, quickly lowered the handbrake and eased the car over the crossing, managing to beat the next frantic mother, who was a good three paces from the kerb.

Samantha sighed. The day seemed to have lasted for a week. Up at 5.15, they had left Cornwall at six o'clock and watched the sun rise ahead of them, a pale golden disc, scarred by grey March clouds; an indistinct compass point directing them towards an unfamiliar destination.

Samantha had been driving then, and their talk had been of whether their tiny flat over the launderette was secure, if the temporary staff would be able to manage without her in the little café in the main street, and how her father would cope in his first-floor flat above it with his new live-in carer. As the distance from home increased, they had been able to relax a little and enjoy the scenery in a strange no-man's land, where time hung like a stationary pendulum. But now, five counties and 300 miles later, as the distance to Eastbourne decreased on the road signs, the tension had returned.

'Philip, you will be patient with your dad, won't you?' Samantha asked after they had wound their way through the streets of Newhaven, and had begun to catch glimpses of the dull, platinum sea between the red-brick bungalows of Seaford.

Philip grunted.

'He can't be that bad,' she persisted. 'He was pleasant at Clara's and Archie's wedding, and fine at ours, and when we first met, when you came on that family holiday to St Ives, he seemed jolly and good natured then.'

Philip repositioned his glasses on his nose. 'You know, that was the only happy childhood holiday I remember. Dad had only been married to Cassidy for two or three years, and was thoroughly taken up with her. He ignored Clara and me, so whenever we could, we would escape. Clara was 13 and all she wanted to do was to go and look at the teenage clothes in the shops. I pretended I was 18 and hung round all the art galleries and talked to artists. Then we'd go to the beach and Clara would swim – she wasn't so conscious of her weight in those days – and I'd paint.' He paused, 'I wonder,' he said thoughtfully, 'if it would have been different if I'd met you early in the holiday instead of on that last afternoon?'

Samantha smiled, thinking back to the day when a stocky, middle-aged man and a slim, elegant young woman in her twenties had come into her parents' café. She remembered them being followed by a tired, rather sulky Clara and the tall, ungainly Philip, his foot slipping as he stepped down into the shop from the pavement, and the crash as he'd grabbed at the table nearest the door, before collapsing onto the floor. It had been some entrance.

They stopped at some temporary lights and the fingers began their tapping again. Samantha ran her hand, fingers splayed, through her long blonde hair and pushed it back from her face. She looked at Philip, with his deep brown eyes and mass of dark curls, aware of the thinning patch on the top of his head.

'It was your hair I noticed, when I first saw you.'

Philip's face showed the flicker of a smile. 'Handsome, eh?'

'No,' returned Samantha. 'I was jealous of it – no man should be allowed to have such gorgeous hair – nor curly eyelashes.'

She looked out of the window; the long rows of shops and houses had given way to countryside, soft woodland beginning to show green, and fields dotted with sheep. She watched a couple of black-faced lambs gambolling, racing up a small mound and playing king of the castle like excited children. 'Philip, it is going to be all right, isn't it?'

'It's never all right with Dad.' Philip scowled. 'I'm never flavour of the month. I'm a disappointment to him and always will be. We shouldn't have come.'

Samantha glanced across at him. Desperate to dispel the lurking fear in the pit of her stomach and in an attempt to keep him happy and restore a positive attitude towards his father, she said, 'But he wants you and the rest of the family to be with him and enjoy celebrating his special birthday.'

'It's a smokescreen.'

'What do you mean?'

'You read the invitation when it came.'

'Only quickly.'

Samantha bent down and found her handbag. Pushing a brown, folded envelope to one side, she pulled out a white card and read aloud:

Dear Philip and Samantha,
You are invited to celebrate my 60th birthday
in my recently acquired Elizabethan mansion
set in a large estate by the sea,
to discuss our partnership
in my new and exciting venture.

Arrival time: 4.30pm. Thur. 24th March
At: Seascape House, Long Dean, Eastbourne.

Fri. 25th and Sat. 26th March
Family conference and meetings with my solicitor

Sun. 27th and Mon. 28th March
Planning for the Future

Tues. 29th March Depart

PS Bring your own sheets, duvets, towels and swimming gear.
Dad

Samantha sighed. 'Well, he's not too hot on writing a friendly, chatty letter – it's brief and to the point.' She glanced again at the opening lines. 'But what does "my new and exciting venture" mean?'

Philip accelerated a little too fiercely up the hill. 'I'll tell you what it means. It means he's suddenly got a new money-making project to work on. He's not interested in us, except to get us onside. If he's blown all his finances on this…'

'Surely he wouldn't. What can he do with an Elizabethan mansion that would make money?'

Philip shrugged. 'I don't know. Turn it into flats and live somewhere else on the estate? Invite campers and caravanners to enjoy the south coast and feed them breakfasts of bacon and sausages?'

'Surely not?'

Philip's knuckles showed white. 'If this is a "venture", he's in it for what he can get. He knows how to handle money and speculate. Look how successful he's been. All his life he's worked all the hours God sends. He's progressed from pig farmer's son to pork butcher, to an empire of several farms, as well as 14 or 15 shops, and the last I heard he was supplying local supermarkets. It makes sense to sell the lot before the small shops are squeezed out of the market – and before he gets too old to cope.'

'He must have more money than he needs.'

'No doubt, but he also takes risks. I know what you're thinking, but I can't imagine us persuading him to give us another loan – not when we haven't paid back the first one.'

Philip's shoulders tensed again and Samantha's stomach churned; she sensed his anger rising. 'Phil, we can't go on like this. The flat is so cramped and the rent is eating into our money, and there's my dad to support. How will we ever save?'

'We can't. As it is, you work far too long hours in the café, and then there's the extra time you put in at the pub. I still can't afford a decent studio, and I can't be sure the summer visitors will go for my paintings with all the others that are out there for sale. Added to all that I'm away from the gallery for the whole of this Bank Holiday weekend. Steve will try to encourage buyers, but it's not the same as me being there – I could lose hundreds over the next few days. I know I shall have to go back to accountancy and I can't bear it.' Philip's voice became unnaturally high as he hit the steering wheel viciously with a clenched fist.

Samantha knew there would be tears in his eyes. He was so passionate about painting, and he loved his woodturning that occupied most winter evenings, but it didn't bring in the money they needed.

'Please try,' she begged. 'Please, be nice to him and ask him for money. Last week you said you'd try. Surely you can find some time to see him over the weekend on your own?'

Philip said nothing.

Samantha stared at the back window of the car in front. 'Little princess on board', it stated in bold pink letters. Had Philip noticed it too? She rested her hand on her stomach. Perhaps she'd know by the time they came home…

Samantha tried to push the anxious thoughts out of her mind as the little car sped on. It wouldn't be long now. She opened her bag to return the card and instantly the greater worry returned. The brown envelope seemed to have grown, filling the space: an unexploded time bomb ticking with the same ferocity as her heart was beating now. Had she been too reckless? Could it, would it, destroy their marriage?

'That's the eighth lot of roadworks,' observed Clara, unnecessarily. 'Five on the M1, two around Gatwick, and now these.'

Archie swerved the little car from the outside lane into the middle and grunted as a royal blue MG tore past at well over 80 miles an hour. 'You don't need to remind me,' he snapped. 'Anyway, we turn off at the next junction, so let's hope the minor roads are clear. We've wasted enough time today; if we get there by 4.30 it will only be by the skin of our teeth.'

Clara bit back the tears. They'd argued from the outset. First about Archie wearing his torn jeans and uncoordinated khaki fleece, and then they had continued on and off most of the way down. The morning rain and leaden sky hadn't helped, and she had found it really hard to appreciate the scenery as the wipers complained and squeaked. It was bad enough to give up a Bank Holiday; she really didn't want them to fall out on top of it.

She wriggled in her seat and looked down at her new size 18 jeans – there was a mark on them. She fiddled with it. Pickle she could scratch off; cheese would leave a greasy mark. She decided to forget it. Perhaps her pink top would be long enough to cover it. She pulled the sun visor down, made a face at herself in the mirror on the back of it, and tried to comb her matted, brown hair with her fingers.

'My hair looks more like dreadlocks than ever,' she remarked, 'and my double chin's growing…'

'Clara,' the name came out like a growl. 'Stop it. I love you as you are, and so do the rest of the family. Leave it.'

'Sorry,' she whispered, pushing the sun visor back in its place. She tried to enjoy the countryside and the small signs of spring which were increasing in number the further south they drove. She'd been silly to look in the mirror – Archie had said a couple of months ago that he'd remove it; he'd obviously forgotten.

She waited until they were safely on the Newhaven Road where, rather belatedly, the sun was making a pathetic attempt to shine. 'Archie, I'm really sorry it's turned out like this. The breakdown service will be so busy this Bank Holiday and you could have done with the extra overtime. Was your boss cross when you said you were going away?'

Archie grimaced, sighed and leaned back against the headrest. With his short brown hair standing on end and his baby blue eyes, he looked younger than his 31 years.

'He wasn't exactly pleased – a relative's birthday bash is not much of a reason for letting them down.' He broke off to swing out to overtake a local bus. 'It's not your fault. You can't help having such an odd father; I knew I was marrying into the whole package.'

Clara didn't have the energy to take offence. 'Dad's just got this fixation.'

'A fixation with pigs.'

Clara ignored the contempt in his voice. She propped her elbow up on the car door and rested her head on her hand. 'It may have been pigs at first, but I think it's the money now. He's just wanted to get more and more. He found if he worked hard enough he could get more farms, more shops, more local fame, and much more money.'

'And less of his family!' Archie retorted. 'Have you forgotten that he even went to the office on our wedding day, and only just got to the church in time to walk you down the aisle? What was all that about?'

'I don't know, he was pretty upset about something. At first I thought he was angry and then I thought I saw tears in his eyes. He's not one to get emotional about weddings. Maybe a deal had gone badly wrong. I've not seen him since and I could hardly question him then.'

'I suppose.'

'Please don't rake it up, Archie. He is my dad, after all, and he does love Philip and me, really.'

'After he loves Cassidy.'

'Please leave it, Archie. She's not been much of a stepmother, but she was never nasty. Just preoccupied, rather like Dad, and busy…'

'Oh yeah? Going abroad for weeks on end to visit her exclusive scuba-diving schools! That won't have been necessary. I bet she's got other people managing them.'

'Archie, please don't be like that. We need to give Dad a good birthday this weekend.'

'He'd better not upset you, that's all.' Archie leaned on the horn as a car cut in from a left-hand junction, and glared as it accelerated rapidly away.

'Perhaps he might be feeling generous,' said Clara, only barely aware of the other car, 'now he's sort of retiring.'

'I doubt it. He's bought this place in Sussex, which will have cost a fortune. He's not exactly generous; he won't even run to providing the bed linen! The next thing will be that he'll charge us to stay there.'

'That's cynical.'

'You didn't bother to deny it.'

'Archie, be serious. Do you think we can persuade him to loan us some money – even give us some?'

Archie scratched one of the half-dozen spots on his face. 'We can try. I know he loves you, Clara, but there's something funny about that invitation – it makes me feel uneasy.'

Clara glanced at him. 'What do you mean, funny?' she asked as she leaned backwards and retrieved her bag from the back seat and pulled out the bent, dog-eared invitation.

Archie was too busy negotiating the large roundabout to reply. He pulled out to find himself behind a removal van. 'Come on, come on,' he muttered. 'We haven't got all day.'

Clara glanced to her right. 'Oh, the sea,' she exclaimed, almost bouncing in her seat and allowing the invitation to fall at her feet.

Archie grinned. 'You baby!'

'You know I love the sea and we hardly ever see it. Archie, can we try to enjoy the weekend for Dad's sake, and for ours? Maybe something good will come of it. I'll be the dutiful daughter and try to charm some money out of him. You know we can't manage on what we've got coming in.'

She glanced at the strong hands on the steering wheel and wished, for the hundredth time, that they could be settled and happy. 'Archie, I'll go mad if I have to live in that little flat any longer; and if you really are going to set up on your own as a car mechanic, you'll need tools and your own van, and a lock-up garage, and then we need the deposit for a place in a better part of Leeds…'

Archie snorted. 'And pigs might fly.'

'Archie!'

He turned and smiled at her. 'Pax,' he said.

'Pax,' she replied, returning his smile.

Chapter 3

Dame Emily seemed to be in her element that afternoon. Perhaps it had something to do with scoring points off the new landlord, and thereby achieving her prime goal: to return to the little home she had occupied so briefly, but happily, before her Australian trip. She supervised the removal men with great efficiency, and thanked profusely the two ladies from the church who had come to 'sort out the little things'.

Every box had been intricately labelled with its destination and precise area of floor or shelf. For Emily, flitting between rooms and the back of the removal van, there were no decisions to make; everything was to be returned to its rightful place in her cluttered but homely house. Family heirlooms and large pieces of furniture were stored in their accustomed places upstairs, while her bedroom was reassembled in the little annex, built as a granny flat for the mother of the last porter to inhabit the Lodge.

She watched the ladies remove and fold the newspaper for recycling and flick a duster over each item. On the whole they could remember between them the correct position of each ornament, item of crockery, and cutlery. They had brought flasks of hot water and had the knack of knowing when tea (Indian) and biscuits (chocolate) should be provided for the men, and Earl Grey and Dundee fruit cake for Dame Emily. One had even put a bowl of sweet-smelling paper-whites, her favourite bulbs, on the dining room table.

Dame Emily came out of the sitting room, sat on the hall chair and put a piece of paper next to the phone. She gave herself a moment to catch her breath and heard voices coming from the kitchen.

'She's a case, that one,' she heard Dorothy remark.

Violet's all too audible voice reached the hall without problem. 'She's one of those eccentrics, right enough. Mind you, she's got a heart of gold. All that trouble she went to when our Lily was took ill at choir practice. The nurse at the hospital gave one look at the Dame and went straight for the doctor – no messing.' The friends laughed.

'It's good to have her back; we might even persuade her to play the piano again for the women's get-together,' Dorothy went on. 'She's been treated real bad, and I don't know what'll happen to her in the end. She's getting on and it won't be easy finding a new place to live. Let's hope the new chap will let her stay for a bit.'

'The new chap' had vanished from the scene. Emily had seen nothing of him since their earlier encounter, but her first task was to ring the electricity people to check that they were coming to put the power on. The lights seemed to be working, but not the power points – perhaps it had something to do with the thunderstorm last night. Not a very helpful woman at the other end. She doubted they'd come; she couldn't get in touch with the men once they were on the van. Emily raised her eyes to the heavens, put the phone down and went outside.

Well wrapped up, Emily sat and watched and issued her orders from one of her dining room chairs which Charlie, one of the removal men, had left for her beside her front gate, near the parking space where her little yellow Nissan glowed faintly in the grey afternoon.

It was just before one when the main door of the mansion opened and a slim man in smart trousers and a black blazer emerged, accompanied by a younger man in a navy hooded jacket and scruffy jeans. An envelope exchanged hands and then the younger man left, stuffing the envelope into his jacket pocket. Emily watched with interest as he strode down the drive, bent under the weight of his backpack. It was only when he was considerably nearer that she recognised him as the chauffeur – without his cap.

He nodded to her as he drew level with the little white fence which guarded her property. His bronzed face looked out of place on a cool March afternoon; she wondered at his necklace of brown beads, and as for the wedge of reddish-brown curls adorning the top of his closely shaved head, Emily could only think of a cockerel and speculated about its appeal to teenage girls.

He looked up and his eyes met hers. 'Er, Brighton bus?' There was a slight hint of a query in his statement.

Emily was amazed by the ability of the young to be so succinct these days; it hardly amounted to interesting conversation. She smiled at him. 'I'll show you,' she said, and got up and walked with him the couple of dozen steps to the main gate. 'Oh, I'm sorry, how rude of me. I'm Dame Emily. And you are?'

'Fraz,' he said.

'Well – Fraz – are you doing anything special this weekend?' Emily queried, and then remembered the young didn't like giving any information which might pin them down.

To her relief he grinned. 'Got a few gigs in Brighton. Mate's bringing the drums down in the van.'

Emily wondered what a gig might be; jogging around to their so-called music, she guessed. 'I hope they go well,' she said, knowing that she sounded like an out-of-touch spinster reaching the point of extreme antiquity. She rested her hand on one of the flint gateposts, and caught her breath. 'You want the bus stop over the road. The Brighton bus is due at 1.05.'

'Cheers,' Fraz said, adjusted the backpack into a more comfortable position, and crossed the road without a backward – or sideways – look. Emily left him to it.

She was thankful that a watery sun was shining and that the early morning's rain had vanished over the horizon, but the air was still cold. As Emily retraced her steps, a small van came from behind the mansion and backed into position by the front entrance. Two men flung open the van doors and struggled to lift out two strangely shaped pieces of stone, before placing them carefully on either side of the front door. Dame Emily blinked. The newly positioned boulders strongly resembled very large pigs. What was the world coming to?

She turned away, trying to control her rising anger at the disfigurement of the front entrance, waited for the van to drive past her, and then glanced into the removal van. She sighed – it was barely half empty. A few large boxes and a standard lamp were poised ready for lifting, but the rest of the clutter, covered in grey blankets, she found hard to distinguish in the dark interior. She moved to get a better view and was startled when a blue, low level, expensive-looking car came speeding down from the rear of the mansion. Quickly she stepped back, almost overbalancing, and desperately clutched the end corner of the van. The driver seemed oblivious of her, braked hard at the gates, indicated left and sped away.

Dame Emily walked over to her chair, hoping that this latest upheaval in her life would soon be over. However, her optimism was misplaced. In the end, the upright piano proved particularly difficult to manoeuvre, and it was almost three hours later that the last box made its way out of the van.

Emily stood, holding the back of her chair, watching Charlie and his mate, Keith, as they eased the battered box up the path and though her front door. Without warning, the first car of the afternoon came through the gates and halted just beyond the removal van. A tousled head appeared out of the driver's open window. Emily grabbed her stick, limped the couple of yards and bent to ask, 'Can I help you?'

'Ah. Er, yes, please.' The black curly hair belonged to a man in his early thirties, she guessed. 'I'm Philip Wedderburn,' he said, pushing his glasses higher up the bridge of his nose, 'and this is my wife, Samantha,' he added by way of explanation as Emily smiled at them both. The young woman in the passenger seat leaned towards Emily, brushing a mane of straight, blonde hair away from her eyes, and smiling with the practised confidence of one who, Emily thought, had never been camera-shy. Dame Emily smiled back, straightened, and looked at Philip again.

'Er, can you tell me if this is Seascape House? The sign was a bit overgrown.'

'It is indeed.'

'It belongs to my father. Can you tell us where to park? We've not been here before.'

Dame Emily enjoyed her moment. 'You'll find some parking spaces just in front of the stable block, which is straight ahead, just beyond the house.'

Philip smiled politely and nodded. 'Ta, muchly.'

The engine revived and the car took off with a jolt, leaving a puff of exhaust mushrooming in the air in front of her. Emily turned away, raising her eyebrows. Two down; how many more to go? she wondered.

By the time Dame Emily emerged from the Lodge again, following the removal men to the now empty van, the two new arrivals were walking round the front of the house, carrying a collection of bags and a couple of suitcases.

'Charlie, Keith, thank you again,' Emily said, pressing a £20 note into each upturned palm. 'I really hope I shall not have to call on you again, but...'

Charlie, whose mind, Emily guessed, was probably focused on a swift pint at the Snail and Shuttlecock, nodded. 'No worries – you know where to find us, Dame Em; it's been a pleasure.' He doffed his cap and made for the door of the van.

Keith stopped as his mobile rang. 'Tom? Yeah, we just finished. You what? Never 'eard of it. New'aven-Brighton road and up towards Gatwick? On the evening before a Bank Holiday? You must be joking. OK, OK, you can't 'elp it.' He struggled to find a pencil and scrap of paper in his pocket. 'Say it again. Yeah, got that. OK, then, cheers.'

He opened the door on his side of the van. 'Piano to pick up somewhere near Hope Street Village and bring back to Eastbourne. Tom's got a flat. Need to turn the van round

31

sharpish.' He pulled himself up to join Charlie in the cab and slammed the door.

Emily waved her stick as the van revved noisily into action, and headed for the exercise yard. At the front of the mansion, Philip and his wife put their luggage down, mounted the steps between the two stone pigs now guarding the entrance, and knocked loudly.

The rotund figure of James Wedderburn appeared in the doorway. Emily watched as Samantha zipped up her pale blue fleece and slipped her arm through James'. She gently nudged him down the three steps onto the path and then across the damp lawn. Her voice was unnaturally loud and high-pitched; nervousness, Emily diagnosed.

'James, what a wonderful place! And so close to the sea – I love it!'

James smiled, a podgy smile, and patted her hand. 'Aye. It's grand all reet, lass.'

They stood and watched as the removal van completed its five-point turn and headed down the drive past Emily at the Lodge gate. It stopped at the road, but although the right brake light seemed to have failed, the offside indicator appeared to be working.

Emily sighed and turned back to her little wrought-iron gate. She had just lifted the latch when the blue Mazda swept back into the drive. It had only just passed her when it came to a controlled halt. A petite figure, in a shocking-pink suit, almost fell out of the car and tiptoed cautiously on very high heels across the lawn, as the car continued round the back of the mansion.

'Weddy, Weddy, I thought I'd never get here! The wind was against us, you've never seen such queues at Gatwick, and it all took such ages. Darling, I've missed you!'

Emily stood transfixed as the woman skidded and almost fell into James' arms, her ash-blonde hair covering his face and her capacious handbag crashing into his ribs.

Emily was suddenly conscious of a figure standing at her side, and started.

'So it's all sweetness and light,' the stranger said, with a hint of sarcasm.

Emily fixed her gaze on him. He must have been in his mid-forties. His hair, which was becoming peppered with grey, had already begun to recede, while his dark-green anorak and slightly worn, olive cord trousers gave him the air of someone who was rather tired. Definitely a bachelor, Emily decided. He must have got off the 4.20 bus.

The man put down the laptop case he was carrying and eased a rucksack from his shoulders. 'I do apologise, I didn't mean to give you a fright. And don't worry about watching the pantomime over there; the vision in pink, who's just collapsed into my brother's arms, is Cassidy, his second wife. I'm Edward, by the way.'

Emily shook hands and was relieved to find he responded with a firm and definite grip. Not as wishy-washy as he appeared, then.

'Dame Emily Hatherley-Browne,' she said briskly, 'the previous owner of Seascape House.'

'Oh,' said Edward, with a look of surprise. 'You've been invited…?'

'I've returned to the Lodge for the moment,' said Emily, interrupting him. 'There was a fire in the roof of the place where I was staying. Now I'm nicely settled here, thank you.' She was aware that she sounded curt, and 'nicely settled' was a slight exaggeration. She hoped that he hadn't noticed the removal van – it was unlikely, as he'd have been getting off the bus as it turned out of the gates.

'Well,' Edward seemed uncertain. 'I'm really sorry about the roof, but so glad my brother has been generous enough to house you here.'

Emily warmed to this newcomer and relaxed a little. He seemed genuine and considerate towards her – quite unlike his brother.

Edward turned and looked at the old building. 'What a magnificent place! I love brick and flint, and the three gables, each with those little spires, give it so much character.' He paused, tilting his head back. 'Then there's the symmetry of those old windows – and the tall chimneys which aren't symmetrical at all! It must have broken your heart to leave it.'

Emily smiled, finding that for a moment, she was unable to speak. 'Yes,' she said, at last, brusquely. 'Well, I mustn't stop you joining the others.'

Edward picked up his rucksack with one hand and his laptop case with the other. 'I suppose not. I must say I'm not a family person, really, but at least I can enjoy the building and escape for a walk by the sea.' Edward took a step towards the lawn and his hugging relatives. 'Goodbye, Dame Emily – it was good to meet you.'

———

Chapter 4

For James Wedderburn, standing on the top step, framed by the old wooden doorway of a 400-year-old house, this was his finest hour.

The sun had once more disappeared behind grey clouds, and the cold dampness of the late afternoon was beginning to bite. He adjusted his coat, which he had flung round his shoulders. Behind him, dwarfing his large frame, was the three-storey, elegant building, which had been prepared to receive the members of a new dynasty. The next chapter of its variegated saga would soon begin. The waiting was nearly over. As James paused – a rare and fleeting pleasure in his busy life – he rather regretted the lack of press attention. He had asked his secretary to inform the local paper a week ago. Never mind, the family would soon be assembled. He licked his lips, savouring this latest triumph.

James Wedderburn, pork sausage empire magnate, was satisfied. Decades of hard work: from the day his father had found him as a four-year-old in his grandparents' pigsty, with his arms round the neck of a sow who was larger than he was; to the early days of scattering sawdust in his father's shop in Huddersfield, and then learning the trade as a gangling 16-year-old; to taking on the business following his father's premature death. He had worked for this moment. He no longer had the energy to go round checking on the 15 shops he'd seen open all over the north of England, but his pride in them remained, and in the quality of the pork his farms had produced. What had been his catchphrase? 'Everything but the squeal' – that was it.

And now he had exchanged that empire for a new and exciting project, and he stood on the threshold, quite literally, of a new era which would bring happiness to himself, his wife and, of course, to his family too. This was not retirement, but preparation for the last decades of his life, when he would surely receive the rewards which were due to such a lively and beneficent man.

James shivered slightly; the wind had turned and was coming in from the sea. He had waited, dreamed of this moment for so long, and he wanted his wife and two children with their spouses to enter their new family home together – the rifts between them would be magically healed and old age would be welcome and comfortable.

He watched the figures in front of him, restlessly walking the paths and talking, looking like children waiting to be let in to school on a bitter winter's morning. He couldn't remember when they'd all been together last. Not that it really mattered; now, together, they would all experience the fulfilment of his dream.

He hadn't expected to begin his new life in Sussex, but it put distance between him and his past life in the north. Before him lay his front garden – was that the right term for this area, large enough to contain an estate of ten or more houses? In a couple of months it would be summer; they would have Sunday tea by the sundial – he could almost taste the strawberry jam and feel the smoothness of the cream on his tongue.

He looked across the wide lawn, with its graceful cedar of Lebanon, to the avenue of skeletal trees beyond, which followed the line of the old brick wall bordering the road. Cassidy was there, walking towards the Lodge on the other side of the drive, by the imposing entrance gates to Seascape House. She was laughing with Philip and Samantha, flicking her long hair back over her shoulder as she had done that first day he'd met her and had known he wanted her and no one else.

He watched his brother Edward wandering down the path to his right, looking at the early tulips in the newly dug border, on his way towards the old summer house in the far corner where the boundary walls met. It was a pity Edward was distant and ungrateful – strained relations so often made for a bad atmosphere.

There were just Clara and Archie to come. A pale sun made a feeble attempt to create faint shadows on the lawn, and the wind gusted a few leaves left from autumn, but James, warmed by his full-length camel coat, was determined to wait. They knew better than to be late, but it was approaching 4.25 and even James' resolve was waning.

The sound of waves breaking on the beach was just audible now. He watched Cassidy, who had finished talking to Samantha and Philip. She left them huddled together as they walked back up the drive, and tiptoed over the grass, trying to avoid getting her heels caught again, skirted a flowerbed and reached a square of stone slabs, where she inspected the sundial. She appeared to be attempting to read the Latin inscription. Edward, having completed his circumnavigation of the lawn, joined her and greeted her with a kiss on the cheek.

A single gull screamed into the wind from the gable top, as James gazed absentmindedly between the bare branches of the trees at the roofs of cars that sped intermittently to and from Eastbourne. One green one braked suddenly beyond the gates, backed rapidly and turned left into the drive. James lifted one arm high and indicated the exercise yard. The car disappeared round the side of the building and, after a brief pause, two doors slammed. The waiting family members, looking hopeful, turned and made for the front door as Clara and Archie appeared round the corner of the building, Archie staggering under the weight of two heavy suitcases.

Clara came up to James and allowed herself to be kissed. Panting, Archie arrived at her side and dropped the suitcases by all the others.

James mounted the top step, pulling Cassidy up with him, and cleared his throat. 'Welcome to your new family home,' he said, waving his arms in what he hoped was an all-embracing movement. He paused, but there was no cheering, no ripple of applause.

'This ancient building will soon be home to many delighted guests, as I am having it converted into a luxurious hotel,' said James, grandly. 'It isn't quite ready yet – ' he paused, aware that they would soon find out just how much was still to be done, and then continued, 'but our family home is almost ready; you may have noticed the magnificent Old Barn, close to where you parked your cars.'

The stunned silence was marked. Eyes stared at him, uncomprehending, minds shocked. The seagull took off from the gable top, brilliant white against the dark clouds, and wailing like some lost soul, fighting its course against the strengthening wind.

James looked at the upturned faces. 'Now, everyone,' he continued brightly, 'while we are still wearing our coats we shall do a brief circuit of the grounds, then we shall have tea followed by the grand tour.'

Cassidy pulled her thin jacket closer round her and folded her arms; her face looked pinched and tired. Her earlier bounce was fading. James put his arm round her shoulders and led the company back along the front of the house to the main drive.

They turned left past a semicircular, castellated tower which had been added to the east side of the mansion, and soon found themselves facing a beautifully converted stable block. On their right and at right angles to the stables was an enormous flint and brick barn. 'I haven't got the right set of keys on me, but I shall show you the inside of the barn over the weekend,' said James with the air of a conjuror, enjoying his power to increase his audience's sense of anticipation with every alluring word. 'This is where Cassi and I shall live, and where you will all be welcome to come and stay. It comprises…'

'Come on, James, you're not an estate agent,' Edward chipped in, shivering visibly.

James paused long enough to glare at his brother and repeated, 'It comprises a vaulted lounge with split-level study, dining room, fitted kitchen and breakfast room, a family room, a master bedroom with en suite, five bedrooms, two further bathrooms, and a double garage.'

Despite the cold, the little group paused and gazed in wonder. 'You're not going to live in the main house, then?' Samantha asked.

'No, I don't want to be surrounded by workmen now, nor the guests in future. We shall be cosy in the barn, but have the whole estate to enjoy and a small garden of our own at the back.'

He turned and led the group away from the barn, past the stables to another large building. 'I believe this was the old coach house,' said James, pausing by the door and ignoring the heap of rubble piled up outside. 'The lower floor has been turned into a gym and upstairs there will be a sauna or Jacuzzi or something of that nature. They've still got a lot to do up there.'

The group murmured words such as 'very nice', and 'oh, yes', as they huddled together. The wind was bitter this side of the house, facing north as it did.

Clara went ahead of the group and glanced down the far side of the coach house. 'Where does this lead?' she asked.

James had no time to reply as the group followed her quickly down a very short passageway between the coach house and another building. At the end they peered through intricate wrought-iron gates at a beautifully laid-out rose garden, which extended along the back of the stables and old coach house. To the left was an untended field, whose grass was already spilling through the fence into the formal garden.

'I thought we would have a children's play area in the field,' said James, addressing the backs of his family.

'That's nice,' said Clara brightly as she turned and marched back the way she'd come, like some bandmaster leading his troops on a parade ground. She paused, looking through a window into the dilapidated building on her right.

'What's this place? Looks a bit chaotic inside.'

'This back part was the old dairy,' said James, proudly. 'It has two doors, so I thought we could turn it into a small shop selling pork products as well as sweets and ice cream. Visitors will have to go through it to get to and from the play area, so we shall have double the chance of selling our products. Smart thinking, even though I say it myself! The men haven't started in there yet. There's a lot of rubbish from the coach house in there, it needs sorting. The front part of the building was once the old laundry – it's being modernised. The machines have been delivered and are being plumbed in. The upstairs is being converted into two small flats for staff on duty.'

'Now where?' said Clara, glancing hopefully at the back door of the mansion opposite.

'Just one more special place,' said James, passing the old laundry and pointing to a very high, ancient wall, which continued from the laundry to the western corner of the property. 'This is the old kitchen garden, where I've built a covered swimming pool.' He walked over to a black, wooden door and grasped the round metal handle. 'It's locked at the moment.' A brief look of annoyance passed over James' face, then he smiled. 'I forgot to collect the keys from the pantry, but the heating has been tested today and it'll be ready to use tomorrow. I'll be there to see Cassi, when she's the first to dive in!' The group turned to look at Cassidy, who smiled faintly.

To the obvious relief of the whole group, James then walked smartly down the west side of the house and led them back to the front door. It was made of rough-hewn wood, bleached with age, and was studded with old nails. James stood on the steps and fiddled in a pocket. He wasn't just going to lift the latch and open the door. He pulled out one very large and ancient key and inserted it into the old lock. It turned smoothly enough.

Cassidy shivered and Clara snuggled up to Archie for warmth as, at last, James Wedderburn opened the front door of Seascape House and welcomed his family over the threshold. Collecting their belongings, they stumbled in, relishing the warmth and the smell of furniture polish overlaid with woodsmoke.

They deposited their suitcases in the corner behind the door and removed their jackets, while James put the key in his pocket and shrugged off his camel coat, tossing it onto one of the hooks of the coat rack above the cases. He went to stand at the bottom of the elegant wooden staircase. Holding the round, intricately carved newel post, he watched beatifically as, one by one, his children and their spouses gazed around.

The very large, square hall was panelled in dark wood, and on their right an enormous fireplace, with stone surround, was host to a smoking log in a pile of ashes. Their feet echoed on the black and white tiled floor as they turned to gaze at a dozen or so portraits of previous owners, in gilded frames, hanging from chains on the walls. These ancestral worthies sat with their families, tastefully arranged in grand sitting rooms, fanciful scenery, or surrounded by favourite horses and dogs. Behind the Wedderburn family, the stained-glass windows on either side of the front door let in a little cold light, as the belated spring sunshine faded with the coming of early evening.

Cassidy teetered over to James and put her hand on his arm. 'Oh Weddy… it's so… big.'

James beamed. 'Of course it is, my love. My pork empire has provided a veritable treasure trove, with a delightful, private residence for the master and his little wife, and a beautiful building to renovate – I bought it with you in mind, because I knew you'd love the whole exciting adventure!'

Cassidy removed her hand and took a step back. 'Well, we've seen the hall,' she said brightly and rather obviously. 'What happens next?'

She was interrupted by the rattle of an old metal tea trolley, advancing from the back of the building and turning left round a corner as it headed towards them. A plump, homely lady in a pink overall was pushing it, still wearing her white kitchen hat over her grey hair. She was followed by a girl in her late teens carrying a large teapot. Her head was almost totally shrouded in a tight-fitting hat, a few inches of her chestnut hair just showing under its maroon and grey stripes. Her pink T-shirt proclaimed the message, 'Don't blame me, I'm only the bottle washer'. Below her rolled-up jeans, her flip-flops tapped on the polished floorboards, out of rhythm with the squeaking wheels of the trolley. A tall, slim, smartly dressed man headed the party.

'I'm so sorry, James,' he said. 'I'd wanted to get this into the sitting room before you came in, but there was a slight delay. I'm sure you won't mind beginning your celebrations a day early.'

'Certainly not!' said James, beaming. 'I expect you all remember Martin Chumleigh, my secretary-cum-personal assistant?'

There were faint smiles and Clara said, 'Hello,' then all eyes turned to the trolley.

James looked at the top shelf. A cake fashioned into the shape of a pig lying on its stomach, and whose icing was coloured a vivid pink, was bordered by six large, red marzipan flowers, each bearing a gold candle. The writing on one side of the pig's stomach declaimed: 'Happy birthday James, 60 hammy years', and on the other, 'Another of Weddy's Wonders'.

James bent to read the writing and then laughed loudly. 'It's reet champion, Mrs…?'

'Mrs Summerfield, sir – and Jayne here did the icing.'

'You're the first to give me a present.'

The guests shuffled awkwardly; Edward leaned over the cake. 'Weddy's Wonders?' he queried.

James looked surprised. 'Aye, lad. Surely you've seen our logo, specially designed by Martin and myself, for the wrappers of our pork pies?'

'Er, no, I'm afraid not.' Edward shook his head and did not look overly impressed.

'We shall have some Weddy's Wonders over the weekend. Isn't that right, Martin?'

'There's a row of them sitting in the fridge as we speak,' said Martin, with a smile.

'There you are then,' said James.

'Would you like tea now?' Martin asked.

'How can I refuse?' said James, as Martin moved to open the drawing room door. 'Lead on, my good man, and we will follow.'

The group stood dutifully in the generously appointed room, while Cassidy led the singing of 'Happy Birthday', and hastily produced phones recorded the moment when James managed to blow out the candles at the third attempt. He inserted the knife into the stomach of the pig – no need to wish, hadn't his wishes come true? – and Cassidy was left to cut it into suitably sized pieces.

The kitchen staff left, and soon the guests were helping themselves to tea from the enormous teapot, and piling up generous platefuls from the selection of scones, sliced chocolate cake, muffins and doughnuts which were filling the lower shelf of the trolley.

Gradually the company spread out, balancing steaming cups and overflowing plates.

James moved to the far end of the room, put his saucerless teacup on the mahogany surround of the bookcase, and raised his plate containing a slice of birthday cake and two doughnuts to chest height. As he pondered its delights he found himself cornered by his wife.

'Weddy, what is going on? I don't understand. When you said you'd bought a "little place by the sea" last year, you said nothing about buying an old mansion! I thought it was somewhere we could pop down to at weekends, once we'd bought a place for your retirement in Yorkshire. What do you mean by all this? You've kept it very quiet! No wonder you didn't show me any photographs of the place!'

James, having taken the opportunity of his wife's short speech to find the jam in the doughnut, found himself unable to utter a word. He placed his sugary hand on his wife's arm, swallowed hard and with still bulging cheeks said, 'It was a secret I've been keeping for months, and I did it for you, Piglet. You will love being near the sea, and there's so much you'll be able to do to get the hotel off the ground. But I'm not going to explain any more till everyone's here – at dinner,' he added licking the sugar from round his lips.

Cassidy lost none of her anxious look. She glanced round the room. 'But everyone is here.'

James followed her gaze. 'Not quite everyone. We're still waiting for my solicitor and Ian, the activity centre supervisor.'

'What activity centre supervisor?'

'The one I've engaged to work here. He's in charge of the pool, gym, Jacuzzi and all the rest of it. Now, don't pester me, Piglet, you know I won't tell you any more until I decide to. Go and talk to Clara and Archie. It must be several years since you saw them.'

James took another large bite from the doughnut and red jam bounced down his pink and blue tie, leaving two distinct blobs. Cassidy turned away and made for the tea trolley and poured herself a cup of black tea, keeping her back firmly towards her husband.

James smiled to himself – he'd never been able to give her a present like this one. It would bond them together, curb her wanderlust and keep her at his side for the rest of their days. He had given her all the freedom she had longed for over the last 15 years, and now for their crystal wedding and his sixtieth birthday it would be her turn to give to him the next 15 years of their life together – if not 25 – at the very least. Her figure was still trim, though not quite as it had been when he had first fallen for her beauty, on that day when she had walked gracefully in her turquoise swimming costume across the stage of the Prince Albert Ballroom in Huddersfield...

He looked round the room. While he knew Cassi would conform, he wasn't so sure about his children. They had turned out all right, despite all the things people had said at the time of the divorce. He'd been right – Cassidy and the series of au pairs had got them through it all, when he'd been so busy building up the empire. He hadn't seen much of Philip or Clara since they had married and moved away, but after all, he was their father. He could count on their support for that reason alone.

Then there was Edward. Well, his younger brother owed him everything, really. A home, a good education, financial support.

Edward must have a reasonably comfortable bank balance these days. It would be all right. He would tell them all at dinner, and if he played his cards right, they would go to bed delighted, and the solicitor would finalise it all tomorrow. Today he was on the brink of a new, fulfilling life, and tomorrow – on Good Friday – they would plan its details and make his dreams a reality.

James realised with a shock that his plate contained only a scattering of crumbs and smudges of jam. Without any concern for the ring of spilt tea left on the mahogany bookcase, he lifted his cup and drank the cold contents.

James walked back to the trolley. The pig was no more and dirty cups were piled up on the second shelf. He would use every moment of his finest hour to the full. He banged on the side of the trolley with a teaspoon and waited for silence. 'Now, before we do anything else,' he said, 'I have a present to give.' He clicked his fingers towards Martin, who reached behind the piano and promptly produced a parcel wrapped in pink tissue paper and tied with pink shiny ribbon. James took it and held it out to his wife. 'Cassi, my dear, this is a token of my esteem on our fifteenth wedding anniversary.'

Cassidy, who had been sitting sideways on a chair talking to Samantha, stood and slowly walked towards James. Her fingers shook as she pulled at the paper. All eyes were on the box inside. 'Oh, Weddy, how lovely!' She lifted the lid and carefully held up a crystal pig which nestled in her hand.

'Read the inscription!' James said impatiently, snatching the paper and the pig from her.

Cassidy lifted out the base, squinted at it, looked up at the intrigued company, gulped slightly and responded, 'It says: "To Piglet from Porky on our crystal wedding. You are the sparkle in my life."'

There was a pause. Then a polite, gentle ripple of applause.

James smiled benevolently.

45

Chapter 5

'Now, ladies and gentlemen,' announced James, positioning himself strategically in the drawing room doorway, every inch the proud owner, 'we have the grand tour. We'll all sleep in the house over the weekend, so now you can choose your rooms.'

He led the way to the foot of the imposing staircase which filled the back part of the entrance hall. He ascended as far as the turn in the stairs and paused on the small landing, watching his straggling followers, his breath coming a little faster now.

'From here,' he pointed a stubby finger upwards, where a row of portraits in oil adorned the wall of the second flight, 'you can see more of the old ghosts! They'll have to go, of course.'

Below him the front door flew wide open, crashed into a suitcase and juddered to a halt. The whole group turned, in one synchronised movement, and looked down into the entrance hall. Below them a tricoloured Cavalier King Charles spaniel pattered across the tiles, peered short-sightedly through the banisters and began barking loudly. It was closely followed by an elderly woman waving a stick and panting with exertion. Her wrinkled face was surrounded by a halo of tangled white hair, and she looked, as James' mother would have said, as if she'd been 'dragged through a hedge backwards'.

'Quiet, Fin!' she said, pointing the stick at the dog. It glared at her reproachfully and sat with a resigned sigh. Its owner realigned the point of the stick upwards and proclaimed, 'Mr Wedderburn, you've lit the entrance hall fire!'

James stared down. 'Aye, and it's nowt t'do wi' you, Mrs…'

'Dame Emily Hatherley-Browne,' the authoritative voice reminded him. In a couple of strides she had reached the fireplace and bent down for the tongs. Expertly she removed the small log from the grate and used the poker to spread the ashes.

The tour party stared in fascination. 'You seem to have forgotten what I wrote about this part of the house,' Dame Emily continued. 'I said that the chimneys had not been swept for a couple of years, and that it would be unsafe to light any fires until they had passed their safety checks. I have no desire to see this place a blackened ruin; you've done enough fire damage already.'

She gave the dying embers a quick rake, restored the tongs and the poker to their holder with a considerable clatter, and looked up at her audience once more. 'Good day,' she said firmly. 'Come, Fin!' Ushering the dog into the front garden, she left, pulling the old door shut as the knocker rattled a final salute. There was a stunned silence.

'Daft old witch!' muttered James, as wafts of smoke hovered around the suitcases and bags.

'Who on earth was that?' asked Clara.

'Previous owner,' growled James. 'Interferin' old bat.' He grasped the banister rail firmly and resumed the role of master of the house. 'We'll continue our adventure and begin at the very top of the house.'

Behind him Samantha sighed as they reached the first landing. 'I do find big buildings confusing,' she murmured to Philip.

Edward overheard. 'You need to concentrate on the stairs,' he said. 'We came up the main stairs in the middle of the building, now we've reached a long corridor running the length of the house. At the right-hand end, you can see more stairs which continue to the top floor; I guess at the other end there will be the back stairs which are much narrower and go all the way down to the kitchen.' He looked at James, who was listening. 'Am I right?'

James turned away. 'You allus was a clever clogs,' he said over his shoulder.

The group plodded onwards and upwards to the second floor and trooped after James in an excursion through what must have once been the servants' rooms.

'These will all be en suite,' he announced unlocking the three doors on the left-hand side of the corridor, whose rooms overlooked the front garden and the sea. The rooms were mainly totally empty of furniture and musty, but there were piles of removal boxes in each. James watched eagerly for signs that his family had caught his enthusiastic vision. However, as the following pack dutifully inspected dusty fireplaces, torn wallpaper and damp patches on ceilings, he was vaguely aware that a collective gloom had descended and the earlier cheerful chat had subsided.

James smiled at them encouragingly. 'Cassi will choose the colours for each room,' he announced. 'We shall go round Eastbourne and Brighton at the end of next week and begin planning. I think a different colour in every room would be jolly, but the decision will be wholly yours,' he said, putting his arm round his wife's shoulders. 'I'll have to return to Huddersfield on Tuesday to get the solicitors moving on selling the last two shops, but I'll be back and we can do it together.'

Cassidy said nothing, but slipped from his grasp and wandered towards the window. 'I suppose that's the sea,' she said. 'It's so grey.'

'But think of it in summer, Piglet,' said James, following her. 'Blue, with little white horses, and you shall go down onto our little beach and swim as often as you like.'

'Our beach?' Cassidy looked a little more interested.

'Well, anyone can use it; it's just across the road. You go down a few steps and you're there. I'm told not many people use it because there's nowhere to park.'

'Sounds nice,' Cassidy said.

James frowned slightly; he felt she lacked conviction. Eager to distract her, he ushered the family out and relocked the doors.

'Now we'll go to the rooms that look out over the countryside. We'll start with this one,' he said, opening a door by the back stairs. The room was quite a contrast to the rest. The pink rosebud wallpaper was matched by pink rosebud curtains and a pink candlewick bedspread. Both ceiling and floor sloped at different angles. There was a washbasin in one corner, and a very large dark wood wardrobe and matching chest of drawers took up most of one wall. Two pink slippers stood to attention at the bedside and a pair of overgrown, blue flannelette pyjamas and dressing gown had been flung onto the bed together with a wash bag. A single bed behind the door had a vermilion duvet thrown carelessly over it, while blue and white checkered shorts and a shapeless T-shirt adorned the matching pillow. In the middle of the floor was a small zip bag with various items of underwear, a make-up bag and an iPod spilling out of it.

'Oh!' Clara couldn't control the exclamation. 'Someone lives here?'

James felt decidedly nonplussed for a moment. 'It must be Mrs What's-her-name… the cook… and the girl,' he said at length. 'Martin said he'd arrange for someone local to be here over the weekend, but I can't see why they can't go home at night.'

Cassidy had walked over to the small casement window. 'It's all roofs and green grass,' she said, 'I can't even see any sheep.'

James followed her. 'But, Cassi, love, I've bought a couple of fields that back on to the garden, just over there. I thought we might have a few Gloucestershire Old Spots – just like the old days.' He turned his head. 'Remember, children?'

Clara looked at him, horror on her face. 'Dad, they smelt! They were disgusting.'

James tipped his head on one side. 'I seem to remember my lass enjoying the odd slice of bacon with her egg every morning of the school hols.'

Clara's head shot up. 'That was then,' she began, and then suddenly stopped as Archie put his hand on her arm. 'I was little then,' she added lamely.

Archie steered Clara towards the door. 'Come on, let's choose a room. Do you want to be up here or on the floor below?'

'I'd like one of these little rooms,' Clara suddenly decided. 'I like the sloping ceilings and the creaky floors.' She pushed through the doorway, past the open door of the bathroom and down the corridor as the rest followed her.

She opened the last door by the main stairs, saying, 'Shall we have this one, Archie?' and then stopped.

Archie looked over her shoulder. 'Seems you want to be with another man?' he remarked.

Clara giggled. 'I don't think much of his taste in shirts,' she commented, looking at the open wardrobe where a blue striped shirt and its mauve companion hung above three smart black suitcases.

'I'd look good in that silk dressing gown though,' Archie rested his chin on his wife's shoulder. 'Shall I borrow it for the night?'

James hurried them on. 'I forgot the staff would have put their things in the rooms,' he blustered, 'Martin, of course, being so efficient again. I did tell him to leave good rooms for you all. We'll look downstairs.'

The first floor was in better condition.

'Cassi and I will have this room,' said James opening the door of the tower bedroom nearest the staircase.

'Oh, James, it's lovely,' cooed his wife. 'What an enormous room! Look at those huge wardrobes – and so many windows!' She hurried across the room and looked out. 'Oh, I see,' she said, peering to the right. 'There's the entrance from the main road, and the drive goes under this window and turns into the yard below the window on the left. What about those trees opposite? Are they yours – ours?'

James shook his head. 'A Christmas tree firm,' he said briefly.

Cassidy turned to leave. 'Oh, look, another window overlooking the back. We've only got to open this window and we're onto the fire escape! Now, that doesn't mean you can smoke in bed, Weddy!'

Philip cleared his throat. 'Dad, can we go and choose our rooms now?'

Instead of answering, James pushed his way through his family, crossed the bottom of the stairs and opened the next two doors on his right. 'These two rooms have a connecting door, so you can choose whichever one you like, Philip.'

Philip walked through the second door, and Samantha through the first.

'Pity you didn't bring all your clothes, Sam, though even you couldn't fill these wardrobes!' Philip called loudly, opening the connecting door to join his wife.

She put an arm round his waist. 'Thank you, Mr Wedderburn, we'll take it!' She smiled, but seemed too tired to laugh.

'That's settled, then,' said James contentedly. A brief sense of fatherhood had reminded him of distant days, when he had tucked his children into bed and said goodnight.

The family crowded through both doors, eager to see the view.

'Just fields,' reported Archie.

'No, Archie, look.' Samantha was craning her neck downwards. 'Below us is the car park, you can see the roof of the stables and the garden behind them. Do you own any horses, Mr Wedderburn?' Her eyes shone. 'I loved riding as a child, but my parents couldn't afford to let me have more than a couple of lessons.'

James followed her gaze. 'They don't mix with pigs,' he said briefly. 'You were all supposed to be sleeping in the converted stables this weekend, but the bloomin' electricians said they couldn't join up the wiring in time, so we'll all be staying in the main house.'

Samantha's smile faded a little. 'What a pity,' she said, 'it would be sort of romantic to sleep in a stable. I wonder if horses have ghosts.'

Philip looked up from testing the mattress on the bed. 'If you're sleeping in a stable, I'm not keeping you company.'

Clara called out from the second room. 'Down there on the left, it's all walls and more roofs, I can't make it out.'

James joined her at the window. 'That's what we looked at before tea. There's the old coach house at the end of the stables, then the path to the garden and on the other side the old dairy and laundry. The front wall of the laundry continues to become one side of the walled garden, Cassi's special place.'

Cassi, who had been gazing at the blue and white tiles round the tiny Victorian fireplace, became aware that her name had been spoken.

James went over to her, took her hand and led her to the window. 'I told you, Piglet,' he beamed. 'I've had the garden dug up, except for the border each side, and there's a heated pool with a diving board. It's covered in glass, with floodlights at night, so that you feel you're swimming in a magical garden. Martin gave me some of the ideas, and he's assured me the men got the heating system working perfectly this afternoon. You can't see it from here, just the high wall of the old garden.'

Cassidy swallowed. 'Weddy, you think of everything. It's... lovely! Now let's see the rest of the rooms.'

She hurried ahead to the top of the backstairs. 'Perhaps this would suit Edward,' she said, opening the final door. 'What do you think, Edward?'

The door creaked as it opened and Cassidy stepped back hurriedly. 'Oh, I'm so sorry,' she said, and closed the door quickly. She tottered back to the others, bent double, with her hand over her mouth, desperately trying not to laugh.

'Weddy,' she said in a shocked whisper, 'who is that woman you keep in there, in nothing but her underwear?' Then she broke into uncontrollable giggles.

James felt the redness creeping up from beneath the collars of his pale blue shirt, his shiny navy-blue suit, and through his thinly striped tie. Nothing prevented it from colouring his neck and hastening towards his cheeks.

'Woman,' he said, 'I don't know any woman.' But the family clustered round him, like a group of teenage bullies.

'Come on, James,' said Edward, brightening for the first time on the tour. 'Who is she?'

James paused as the door at the end of the corridor creaked again. A medium height, well-built woman emerged, neatly dressed in a navy-blue suit with a pale-pink woollen jumper under it. She carried a smart briefcase, black to match the sensible shoes. She smiled at the group. 'Hello, Mr Wedderburn, I'll see you downstairs...' she extended her arm to look at her black and silver watch, 'in 15 minutes?'

She turned, and holding the tall wooden banister, began to descend the steep staircase to the kitchen area on the floor below.

'She knows you!' Samantha broke the silence and dared to stare her father-in-law bravely in the face.

'Oh,' said James shrugging it all off, 'she's just the woman dealing with the upkeep of the house. Been a bit of a thorn in the flesh, but we'll get over that.'

'What do you mean?' Cassidy asked sharply, the giggles forgotten.

James took her by the arm. 'Nothing to worry you, my Piglet. We'll get Clara, Archie and Edward settled and then we'll go downstairs for a sherry.'

He stood in the middle of the corridor and waved an arm towards the remaining front rooms, catching the gist of a brief conversation behind him.

'I'd like to unpack and go to bed!' It was Samantha.

Over his shoulder he caught sight of Philip stroking her hair. 'Be patient! It's only half five. I'll sort something out when the old man's finished playing Lord of the Manor. He's no concept of how far it is to drive from Cornwall to here, and to arrive in time. He wouldn't know five o'clock in the morning if it hit him in the face, so he'll have no sympathy.'

The group's enthusiasm was obviously waning. 'Clara!' snapped James. 'It's time you chose.'

But Clara was not to be hurried, and delayed them all. She danced between the three front-facing rooms, while Archie stood with arms folded. 'Clara, make up your mind. We're only sleeping here. You won't even see the place, you'll have your eyes shut.'

'I won't when I wake up. I'll want to open my eyes and see a big room and hear the sea, and run to the window and look out.'

'It's winter,' said Archie, 'even if it's supposed to be spring. If you're lying in bed you'll see the grey sky.' He followed her over to the window.

Samantha and Clara sat on the window seat and stared out. 'The front lawn looks so much smaller from here,' Samantha remarked. 'I love those daffodils, especially the ones with orange centres; they seem to glow, even on a gloomy day.'

'Look!' said Samantha kneeling up. 'Isn't that the old biddy who put the fire out in the hall?'

The question brought the whole group and James to the window. Dame Emily was walking away from the Lodge, along the avenue of limes, her little dog pulling ahead on its long lead, well aware, it seemed, of where it wanted to go. Dame Emily, in a tweed skirt and sensible shoes, had the hood of her green parka up, was carrying what looked like a cool bag, and was limping a little.

'She's a game old bird,' Edward commented as Emily and the dog continued down the path towards the west side of the mansion.

James snorted. 'Silly old bat who can't leave the past behind and doesn't know when she's well off.'

Edward shot him a wary glance. 'James, we've all come a very long way today. I for one could do with a comfortable chair. Some may enjoy your promised sherry, but I really would like to unpack and get settled in first. If Clara's decided on this room, I'll take the one next door.'

The family had left the room by the time James remembered they had not toured the ground floor. Well, they would see the dining room at dinner, and he would surprise them all with the grandeur of the music room when they met in the morning. He paused, looking at the gathering gloom outside the window. From this height the sea was visible, but inextinguishable from the grey sky which merged with it.

The outlook was ill-defined and unpromising.

Chapter 6

By the time James had reached the drawing room in his new navy suit, pale-pink shirt and bow tie, the family had settled with drinks and were toying with dishes of nibbles as they chatted. He felt slightly disappointed that they had not dressed for the evening meal. Too late now. This was just the beginning of the weekend, and in the morning there would be presents to look forward to… He seated himself in an armchair, sherry in hand, the Victorian father surrounded by his brood.

Cassidy, who had put on a warm jumper under her jacket, came in, filled her glass and walked over to the blue-suited lady in the bay window. 'I'm so sorry,' she said. 'I didn't realise…'

'Please don't apologise,' laughed the woman, moving her glass to her left hand and holding out her right. 'I'm Stella Harrington. Mr Wedderburn has engaged me as the manager here.'

Cassidy took the proffered hand. 'I'm Mrs Wedderburn, but please call me Cassidy.'

Stella smiled. 'It's good to meet you. Mr Wedderburn said you were coming from the airport today. Were you on holiday?'

'No,' said Cassidy with a small laugh. 'I've been on a business trip to Greece and then Barbados.'

'My dear, you must be exhausted,' said Stella indicating a chair. 'The weather here must be quite a contrast.'

James turned away from the two women.

Outside, the world was retreating into the gathering darkness, and judging by the rattle of one of the windows, the wind was stronger. James decided to leave his children to chat. Philip and

Archie had pulled up a couple of battered armchairs and seemed involved in some deep and meaningful conversation with Clara and Samantha, who were sitting on the old brocade settee. No doubt they had several years of news to catch up on.

Cassidy was still talking to Stella, but Edward was alone in the second bay window, staring out into the darkness of the wet night. He turned as the floorboards creaked under James' patent leather shoes.

'This is a beautiful room, James.'

James looked around as if seeing it for the first time. 'That faded stuff will have to go,' he remarked.

'James, the tapestries? You can't throw those out, they must be worth a fortune! They've got to be really old, and think of the work that went into them.'

James looked interested. 'Could I sell them?'

'James, you must have paid for them, you know what they're worth.'

James made a face. 'I haven't bought anything in here, yet. The old witch wouldn't come to any agreement, she said, till she saw me face to face. Technically it's all hers. She says I wanted things to move too quickly and she didn't have enough time to clear the house and move out, as well as have everything valued and sold to museums and stately homes and what-have-you. She'd better get a move on now – I don't want her grisly ancestors staring at me for the next quarter of a century!'

Edward surveyed the contents of the room. 'James, what are you doing, robbing this beautiful house of everything that gives it character? Why don't you buy some of it from her? You could keep the old-style sofas and chairs and give them new covers, and the baby grand piano over in that corner – it makes it seem like home – and the brass coal scuttle, and the little marquetry tables and those magnificent gold curtains… James, there's so much! You really need to get advice before you talk to her.'

James pushed back the single lock of hair which was falling into his eyes and carefully placed it across his bald pate. 'It's really not the first thing on my agenda at the moment,' he prevaricated. Edward sighed and shook his head. 'You never could see the whole picture, only the bit that interested you.'

'I see a very big picture, Edward. But the details will have to wait until the end of dinner, so don't ask me any more.'

He stopped as Martin entered the room and walked purposefully up to him. 'There's a lady in the kitchen, sir; says she's Dame Emily from the Lodge…'

'What does she want now?'

'She hasn't said anything herself; it's the cook. She says that Dame Emily popped into the kitchen for a chat – used to know her, apparently – and she's worried that Dame Emily won't get a proper meal tonight. Her lights are all right, but there's something wrong with the power points. The electrician has said he can't come this side of the weekend, so could she stay for dinner?'

James glared. 'There's nothing to stop her having it in the kitchen.'

'James!' Edward butted in. 'You can't treat her like that! She deserves some respect – and anyway, you may want to give a good impression,' he said, glancing at the tapestries.

James scowled. 'All right, Martin. When there are so many, what's one more? The activity centre chap doesn't seem to be here yet, and then there's my solicitor.'

Martin almost bowed. 'The activity centre supervisor is in the hall as we speak.'

James nodded. 'I'll come and have a word.'

James followed his secretary out into the hall, where a man in a smart tracksuit was taking off his outer jacket.

'Evening,' said James shortly.

Martin rescued the coat while effecting the introductions.

The stranger stepped forward and shook James warmly by the hand. 'I am so grateful, sir, for this opportunity to work for you. At my interview Mr Chumleigh explained that it would not be possible for you to be present, in view of the distance involved. So I'm very pleased to meet you now.'

James looked at him hard and nodded. 'And I am very glad to meet you at last, Ian. Martin consulted me, of course, but he seemed to think you could do the job. I trust you've got your presentation ready for this evening? You'd better come in.'

He led the way into the drawing room and looked around helplessly. He caught Stella's eye and she came up to them. 'Hello, Ian,' she said. 'We've both been so busy this week we haven't had the chance to chat. I hope we can make up for that now. But first, please do grab a drink, and then I'll introduce you to a few of the family. It looks as though Edward, Mr Wedderburn's brother, is on his own. Why don't you meet him first?'

James left them and escaped into the hall. Why didn't this place have mirrors like a normal house? He wanted to check his bow tie. He fumbled with his collar and once more adjusted the position of his remaining lock of hair. There was something in his briefcase he must check. He took it from the cupboard under the stairs and was just opening it when there was a loud knock at the front door. He jumped nervously and, as he went to answer it, quickly put the briefcase under the settle, out of sight.

No sooner had James lifted the latch, than, without warning, the door crashed against his chest. As he struggled to regain his balance, the visitor turned away from him, shook his umbrella and then entered the house backwards, wiping his feet thoroughly on the threadbare mat. James fought to close the door behind his solicitor.

'What a night, James! The traffic was dreadful on the last stretch coming out of Eastbourne, a coach and car were having a confrontation and all the Bank Holiday traffic was snarled up behind... Sorry I'm late.' The little man leaned his dripping umbrella against the blue and white Delft tiles of the fireplace, deposited his battered case in a corner of the hall, and shrugged off his raincoat.

'It's all right, George,' said James, taking his coat. 'It's nearly time for dinner, so you'd better join the rest for drinks. We're in here.'

James opened the door and ushered the final member of the weekend party into the drawing room.

Chapter 7

At 6.30 promptly the gong sounded. A gentle rumble at first, getting louder and louder until the final crash could be heard in the furthest corner of the house.

Emily felt hungry now that the smell of roast dinner was penetrating the mansion. She walked along the passage from the kitchen, reproving herself for being nervous. She had heard that Edward had insisted that she join the family for dinner, but she felt awkward, and would far rather have stayed in the warm kitchen with Grace Summerfield.

She paused as James opened the drawing room door, summoned the troops and led them past her into the vast dining room. She joined the end of the line and watched James as he looked around the room. He nodded approvingly at the perfectly laid places, the shining glasses and the neatly spaced bottles of red and white wine. He moved to the head of the refectory table and grasped the sides of the carver chair.

'Cassi – here next to me,' he said, pointing to his right. 'Philip on my left, Clara on my right…' He waited to check that his children had heard, and then pulled back the beautifully carved chair. He seated himself heavily, his family grouped around him, and the other guests took the remaining seats, leaving Dame Emily the only vacant space, in the other carver chair at the far end of the table facing James. Edward sat on her right and next to him an elderly man, whom Emily guessed was the solicitor. Opposite the solicitor sat a man in a tracksuit. As Emily pulled in her chair, she glanced at the lady on her left, and suddenly recognised a familiar face.

'Stella!' she exclaimed. 'What are you doing here?'

Stella looked delighted. 'Emily! I thought you had left the area! How do you come to be back here?'

There was just time for brief explanations and a promise to have a proper chat after dinner. Over a number of years, Emily and Stella had met at local Elizabethan Heritage Association meetings and they got on well. Emily felt enormous relief; she needed an ally just now. They were interrupted by the rumbling of the old metal trolley being wheeled in from the kitchen.

'Stop!' called James, in a booming voice, startling Mrs Summerfield who was entering the room backwards, having just manoeuvred the wobbling wheels through the doorway. Surprised, she halted, causing Jayne, who was pushing, to overbalance slightly.

James stood suddenly, his chair scraping on the wooden floor. 'Rise and salute our heritage!'

With one accord the family rose, lifting filled glasses shoulder-high. Hurriedly the guests scrambled to their feet, confusion on their faces. Edward quickly poured wine for those nearest him as James beckoned the trolley to approach, the dishes and their covers bouncing slightly as the trolley wheels twisted and turned over the uneven wooden floor.

James pushed his chair back, stepped forward, lifted the lid from the roast meat, gave it to the open-mouthed Mrs Summerfield, and then held the silver dish aloft for all to see.

'Pork with crackling!' he cried and the response echoed back: 'Pork with crackling!'

Glasses clinked and there was a moment's silence as everyone drank; then the chairs scraped again as the company sat and normal conversation gradually resumed.

Emily and Stella both looked at Edward expectantly. He glanced up and laughed. 'Don't worry – a family ritual. It doesn't happen at every meal, just special ones, and I guess James thought his birthday weekend was special.'

Emily watched as James tapped the crackling to test its quality, nodded his approval, and then took the steel and expertly sharpened the carving knife.

Emily leaned towards Edward. 'I can guarantee it will be superbly cooked. Mrs Summerfield is a gem; she cooked for my sister and me for 20 years. That's Jayne, her granddaughter – why she has to wear that extraordinary woollen cloche hat I can't imagine, but she's a delightful girl.'

Edward smiled and introduced Ian, a fitness trainer, George, James' solicitor, Stella and Emily to each other, before identifying the rest of the family members, and Martin, at the other end of the table. Soon generous servings of pork were being passed down the table, the potato and vegetable dishes quickly emptied, and a contented silence took over.

From time to time, Emily glanced down the table and watched as James surveyed the gathering with a certain air of satisfaction, though the slices of meat left on Samantha's and Philip's plates drew a frown. Emily felt for them. Had Philip become vegetarian since leaving home? That wouldn't please James. She wouldn't like to be in his shoes.

Emily watched Ian as he mopped up the remainder of his gravy with a particularly crispy roast potato. As a fitness trainer he didn't seem to mind eating well. He'd hardly lifted his eyes from his plate during the meal, but he was probably feeling awkward among strangers, Emily decided. He looked smart enough in his grey tracksuit and brand-new trainers, even if she wouldn't have recommended such an outfit for dinner. His brown hair, framing the sallow skin, had been cut in a conventional style, and was beginning to recede. She guessed he was in his late thirties or very early forties. She leaned forward. 'Ian, forgive me for asking, but what is all this about a gym?'

Ian looked up. The hazel eyes smiled and he seemed relieved to be asked to speak about something he enjoyed. 'The coach house at the end of the stables has been cleared,' he said.

'Has it?' said Emily. 'I wonder what's happened to the things I was storing in there? Take no notice; please go on.'

'I have the post of activity centre supervisor,' Ian replied. 'That's involved planning the layout of the gym and changing rooms and so on, and hiring equipment. We shall open the gym and the pool, which I am also responsible for, to the general public from next Wednesday. I have put adverts in all the local papers and will offer personal fitness plans for people of all ages, who we hope will come regularly. There's plenty of parking and we hope that people will appreciate the personal help of someone who has been professionally trained. And I shall be here should any of the family want a session this weekend,' he added.

Emily, whose idea of fitness did not extend further than a twice daily dog walk, found it hard to comprehend. 'It seems so purposeless,' she said. 'All that effort on a machine and getting nowhere. I can't see the point.'

Ian laughed, and as he leaned forward, Emily could feel the enthusiasm oozing out of him. 'The point is to provide the most suitable kind of fitness training for each person to keep them healthy and happy. A balance of activity, without the interference of the weather.'

'And you believe in this?' Emily was amazed.

Ian smiled. 'Yes, I found it so beneficial, I decided to become an instructor myself. I enjoy working with people, and it's great to see the difference in performance and attitude at the end of a course.'

George, sitting opposite Ian, put his knife and fork down with a satisfied sigh, the buttons on his sombre suit straining. 'Don't expect to see me over the weekend. I shall get my exercise chasing a golf ball, if the weather permits, and I don't drown in paperwork. I'd like to get it all finished tomorrow, and leave on Saturday afternoon at the latest, but knowing James, it won't be that straightforward.'

Stella cut her last potato into two neat pieces. 'I hope I'm not speaking out of turn,' she said, 'but Mr Wedderburn had told me you would be staying for the whole weekend.'

George looked up at her and shook his head slowly. 'The wife won't like it; it's our daughter's birthday tomorrow, and our grandson reaches double figures two days later. I need to be back for the special celebration lunch on Easter Sunday.'

Edward drained his glass. 'I would say you hadn't a chance, knowing my brother. Always gets his own way.'

Emily looked at him sharply. Why was he so sarcastic about his brother? Was he going to have this attitude throughout the weekend?

Laughter came from the other end of the table. Emily looked up to see Martin leaning across the vegetable dishes, pouring more wine into Cassidy's and Archie's glasses. For a secretary, he was really quite suave, she decided. His light-brown hair was cut short, just beginning to grey at the temples. He'd probably had his fortieth, then. He was dressed immaculately, with a pristine blue shirt and black blazer with gold buttons on the sleeves, but he seemed to have relaxed, losing the formality he had displayed in the kitchen when he'd invited her to join the family for dinner. Emily wondered how long he'd known James' children. They all seemed to be getting along happily enough.

As the last mouthfuls of dessert were being eaten, Mrs Summerfield wheeled the trolley in. 'Is it all right if we clear away now, sir?' she enquired.

'No,' said James, swallowing the last of his second helping of syrup pudding. 'I need to talk to everyone. Leave it for now.'

Cassidy leaned forward. 'Thank you, Mrs Summerfield. Perhaps we could have coffee and tea in the sitting – er – drawing room later?'

Grace took one serving dish and put it rather heavily on the trolley. 'Very well, madam,' she said, before wheeling the trolley to the side of the room and leaving, wiping her hands on her apron as she did so.

Martin poured himself another glass of wine and stood, holding it at shoulder height. 'I know James wants to speak, but first, if I may, I would like to propose a toast.'

There was a shuffling around the table as glasses were hastily topped up. 'To James and to the future of Seascape House, and to the family, may you enjoy your time here as you stay awhile amid its ancient charms. To James, the Wedderburns and Seascape House!'

The whole company stood and raised their glasses. 'To James, the Wedderburns and Seascape House,' they chanted obediently.

As Martin had been speaking Emily had been aware that Edward had stiffened. Now, as everyone settled back into their chairs, he leaned across George and attracted Martin's attention.

'What's your connection with Ripon?' he asked, somewhat bluntly.

'Ripon?'

'That's the city whose welcome sign invites you to "stay awhile amid its ancient charms".'

Martin looked surprised. 'So it is. I'd completely forgotten. The phrase just came to me. As a matter of fact, I went to school there.'

'Really?'

'St Petrock's and St Wilfred's.'

'I went there!'

'I think I vaguely remember you as a prefect in the sixth form when I first went.'

Edward frowned. 'I didn't mix much with younger boys – well, only in the drama club.'

'I didn't belong to that – not my scene at all! I was a swimmer and won the diving cup for several years.'

Edward shook his head, 'Sorry, I've no recollection, and as I've never been to…' He was interrupted by James as he rose unsteadily to his feet and, forcing his chair back behind him, banged loudly and unnecessarily on the table with a spare serving spoon.

Emily grasped the arms of the carver and made to get to her feet. Edward put out a hand to prevent her. 'Don't go. You can see this isn't exactly a private family affair. He'll just make one of his lengthy, welcome-to-the-family-pile speeches; we shall be bored stiff and all too glad when we can get to our rooms and sleep. It's been a long day.'

Emily sank back in her chair. It would have been impossible to leave the room without attracting attention, and it seemed rude to go just as James was beginning his speech. She looked at the new owner of Seascape House as he smoothed back his limp hair and, not for the first time, wondered how it was that some men could dress immaculately, while others looked as if they had literally taken their clothes 'off the peg', regardless of size or suitability.

'This is a very spesh, special night,' James began. 'Tomorrow begins a new era for the Wedderburns. You 'ave a new 'ome and new opportunities.'

All eyes were fixed on James. The guests looked politely interested, but the family exchanged puzzled glances. Edward leaned back in his chair and clasped his hands behind his head.

'Here we go,' he commented. 'Thinks he's opening a village fete – wonderfully beneficent; he fools them all. Next he'll turn on his posh voice.'

'Now what I am going to say affects you all, except…' James turned his eyes to meet those of Dame Emily's, some 12 feet distant. But the remainder of his words were lost in an almighty crash of thunder overhead. James seemed satisfied he now had everyone's attention. 'This is an exciting project, which will fill my time over the next five years or so, when I shall retire fully. However, we have made an excellent start.'

'Get on with it,' muttered Edward, balancing on his two back chair legs and resting his feet on the wooden bar of the table. He stared past Stella to the portrait of one of Emily's not-so-smiling ancestors, complete with a sleeping Cavalier King Charles spaniel.

'This will be a most successful hotel, once the rooms have been redecorated and modernised and en suite bathrooms are in place.'

Emily's eyebrows shot up and her eyes widened in horror. She looked at Stella, who shook her head and smiled. 'Not just yet, if the Elizabethan Heritage Association have anything to do with it,' she whispered.

'Now, we have with us,' continued James, feeling for one arm of the carver as he swayed gently, and waving vaguely with the other hand, 'our activity centre supervisor, Ian. I've asked him to explain – briefly – what we shall offer our guests in the future.' He nodded to Ian and sat, Emily thought, rather more suddenly than he had intended.

Ian got to his feet slowly and smiled uncertainly. 'Yes, well, ladies and gentlemen. Er, thank you. We have quite a large heated, covered swimming pool in the old walled garden, which will be available from tomorrow morning. We hope that from next week people from the nearby villages will want to drop in and avail themselves of the opportunity to enjoy a quiet swim,' he glanced at James, 'for a small fee, of course.

'The plans for the old coach house are in place, but the new floor upstairs has yet to be completed before the Jacuzzi and sauna can be put in. Downstairs we have a small gym; the equipment was delivered this week, and that too will be ready for use tomorrow.'

Emily kept one eye on James, who was smiling benignly as he looked down the table. He had made an enormous effort to make his future hotel really impressive. Ian continued to speak, twisting his serviette between his fingers as he did so.

'These facilities will be a great attraction for guests and the general public, and I'm sure all this will contribute to the health, well-being and happiness of all those who come here. Mr Wedderburn also has plans to set up a bowling green, repair the tennis courts and introduce crazy golf. We will soon welcome the contractors to start work on the adventure playground in the field at the back of the proposed sweet shop.'

Emily's hand went to her mouth and she turned to Stella, slowly blinked her eyes and then opened them wide. Stella responded with a slight shrug of the shoulders.

'Thank you,' James interjected. 'That's quite a good summary; now let's hear from the house manager, Mrs…'

Martin leaned forward, 'Stella Harrington.'

James waved vaguely in the direction of the bottom of the table. 'Speak!' he said.

Edward sniffed. 'Without hesitation, deviation or repetition,' he murmured.

Stella rose quietly as all heads turned in her direction. 'Good evening,' she said. 'I'm responsible for the running of the mansion this weekend, so please let me know if there is anything you need. I am based here in an advisory capacity and have also been in charge of the refurbishment of the newly converted stables and Old Barn. I shall be overseeing the changes to the dairy and laundry. When the hotel is ready, as joint manager with Martin, we will take on local staff and run the enterprise between us for Mr Wedderburn.' She paused and looked up the table to James, 'As for the refurbishment of the main building...'

'That'll do,' James cut in. 'You see,' he smiled magnanimously round the table, obviously enjoying the uncomprehending faces in front of him, 'I have sold the Wedderburn Pork Empire and invested in a gold mine.' He turned to Martin. 'Anything else?'

Martin rose to his feet. 'I'd like to congratulate you. I think there's been remarkable progress over the last few months. There are just one or two other local attractions we could mention for this weekend: the golf course, accessed from the grounds here; the local stables just a mile from Long Dean village; and of course the small beach, on the other side of the road, which will provide hours of enjoyment for young families in the summer. As you've heard, I will liaise with Stella in the day-to-day running of the whole exciting enterprise, and will continue as Mr Wedderburn's personal assistant and accountant.'

As Martin sat, Edward began a slow handclap which echoed off the walls. 'Well done, James! You exchange one empire for another. Who's going to benefit this time? Not the guests, we can be sure.'

Emily, taken aback, stared at Edward. The friendly face had become hard, the eyes showing dislike, the tone sarcastic.

James eased himself to his feet once more. 'Brother Edward, not so fast. It is the whole family that will benefit.'

'Are you sharing the profits, then?' Philip pushed his dessert plate towards the middle of the table, folded his arms and waited for a reply. His wife, looking alarmed, put a restraining hand on his shoulder.

Cassidy responded sharply. 'Philip, what an attitude! Let your father explain. None of us knows what he proposes yet.'

Philip glared at her, but fell silent.

James smiled at his wife and continued. 'This is to be your house,' he announced to the family. 'Your inheritance.'

Emily caught a muttered conversation between Archie and Clara. 'In how many years' time?' he murmured.

Clara looked at him. 'I don't know what he's going on about,' she whispered back.

'When you have worked as hard as I have,' continued James, 'you deserve the rewards. But, as in all worthwhile work, we meet obstacles. That is the case with this house, but I have come up with a wonderful solution which involves every one of you.' He looked down on his wife and children as though offering some expensive Christmas treat. 'We have found that the refurbishment now comes under… What heading was it?'

Stella spoke up. 'It should be called restoration work.'

James glowered. 'Someone in this room decided to involve the Elizabethan Heritage Association or some such organisation because this is a listed building.' He looked hard at Stella. 'We can't just mend bits of wall or remove old bathrooms or install new ones – we have to use materials which are the same as the original. They keep rejecting my plans and this has caused a lot of delay and money,' he paused and glared again. 'I'd wanted it all finished by now. We're a good four months behind and consequently I need another £50,000 pounds for the first phase. When I sold the empire, I invested money very wisely in bonds, the shortest of which will not mature for ten years, so I have no ready cash. However, I have the solution.'

In the old panelled room not a muscle moved. James smiled brightly at his family, 'Your money will bring us through. This is why I have gathered you all together. In the morning you can each tell me how much you will be able to loan or give me over the next couple of months. Martin and George will write it all down in a legal document and the basic facts will be recorded in a new will, so that after my death you will have the same proportion returned to you – that's only fair. You understand that will only be after my beautiful young wife has – er – been provided for.'

James waited. There was no clapping, no murmur of excitement, no vote of thanks; the whole company, all breeding forgotten, stared at him.

James sat.

Cassidy smiled at him and patted his arm. 'That sounds like a remarkable solution,' she said weakly, looking round at the future heirs.

Samantha had her head in her hands, her long hair brushing the table and dipping into the sticky crumbs on her plate; her shoulders shook.

Philip glanced at the top of her head and then turned to James. 'We haven't got any money to give you,' he protested. 'You know we haven't!'

James eyed his son. 'I kept you, when your mother couldn't cope with you...' A gasp went round the table. James seemed remarkably oblivious to his own insensitivity. 'I told you to train for accountancy – it was about all you could do. I gave you support then.'

Philip got to his feet, his eyes blazing. 'How dare you bring our mother into this? You know why she left. She was ill! When I had to leave her and come and live with you and Cassidy, you didn't want to know me. In those two years you made my life a misery. I didn't want to do Maths; I wanted to do Art, and all the extra Maths I had to do meant I nearly didn't pass in Art. For your information I'm not an accountant; I'm an artist. I do other work too, to get money, but it isn't enough, and Sam, she works

71

all hours and nights in the café and the pub – and we've her father to support. I've got nothing to give you.' He sat abruptly and glared at his father.

A wailing sound came from Samantha as she pushed back her chair and fled, sobbing loudly, through the dining room door. Her feet could be heard pounding up the main stairs till, somewhere on the upper floor, a door banged. In Emily's mind she could be clearly seen flinging herself onto the bed and crying in despair and agony.

Philip made no attempt to follow her. He fixed his eyes on the remaining slice of sponge pudding in the serving dish and fought to control the twitching muscles in his face. The silence deepened.

Archie shot a worried look at Philip's hunched shoulders, and turned to James. 'We haven't any money either. We both work hard, but there's rent to pay and overheads…'

James looked at him. 'When I was your age I was about to buy my third shop,' he said. 'Don't talk to me about work; I know what hard work is. No doubt our Little Podge has been mooning around as usual, worried about her nerves, or her weight or something.'

Archie's face reddened as he clenched and unclenched his fist. For a moment he was speechless.

Clara's head shot up. 'Why can you never say anything nice? You've never understood me! I've never been good enough for you and nothing I've ever done has pleased you! When I needed you, you were never around. I wanted to stay with Mum, but you made me come with you. Cassidy was young enough to be my sister, but she never got to know me. She stayed in her little room at the top of the house, writing articles for her precious Spanish water sports magazines for hours on end; then for the last few years she was abroad, setting up scuba-diving schools and generally having a good time! Cassi never took me with her, even in holiday time, and we were left with some au pair or live-in housekeeper!'

Cassidy, reddening, fiddled with the fragile necklace that hung over her pale blue jumper. 'Clara, dear, I needed to earn some money to help your father...' she began.

Clara turned away from Cassidy and looked across the table to Philip's bowed head. 'Remember, Philip, that holiday in Cornwall?' Philip looked up wearily and nodded. 'That's all we had, Dad, one or two holidays at the most. I loved the little shops in St Ives, the beach, the sand, but it was too late to make it up to us. When we went back home I still didn't belong.' Clara paused, fighting tears. 'You couldn't even be on time for our wedding. I was left at home, totally alone, on the most special day of my life. Cassi and the bridesmaids had gone to the church and you had gone to the office! I had to go to the church in the car on my own.'

Emily watched the redness creep up James' neck, turning his face to puce. 'I was delayed!' he shouted. 'I met you at the church, I walked you down the aisle! I was there the whole time!'

Clara ignored his protests. 'And you smelled of drink – at 12 o'clock on a Friday morning! And you made a mess of your speech. You were all over the place and you couldn't even be bothered to smile for the photos. You failed me, Dad. I think you were literally glad to give me away that day!'

James fingered his collar. To Emily, he looked like a first-class candidate for a heart attack. 'Don't be ridiculous! I'm your father,' was all he managed to say before Clara began again.

'Well, at least Archie loves me. We work really hard to pay the rent on the flat, but one day Archie will start up as a mechanic on his own, we'll get a bigger place, in a better part of town, and we'll have somewhere that's our own and we'll have done it by ourselves. I don't owe you anything – you failed as a dad, and I hate you!'

Archie looked at Clara in horror, then buried his head in her hair as she sobbed on his shoulder.

'What did I do to have children like these?' James raised his eyes to the beautifully and intricately moulded ceiling. 'You're pathetic, both of you, just like your mother. You can choose to

73

reject my offer – but you'd better think it over before the morning, or it'll be too late.'

Cassidy glanced from her husband to her stepdaughter's head. 'Clara, dear…' she began again, but stopped, aware of Archie's angry eyes. She looked across the table to Martin, then George, then Edward, but no one met her eyes or offered support.

Ian poured himself a glass of water. The sound was a brief distraction.

'Well, brother, the birds are coming home to roost at last.' All heads turned to look at Edward. 'Shall I add the final family comments at this jolly meal?' Edward's voice carried clearly and Emily knew that James could be in no doubt as to the tone and strength of feeling. 'Seeing as I won't be giving you any money either.'

'Edward, be reasonable. We may not have met for a number of years, but we are brothers.'

'Brothers!' Edward launched himself to his feet as Stella and Dame Emily flinched.

'Edward, is this wise?' Emily murmured, unable to remain silent and uninvolved.

Edward ignored her. 'James, it's time everyone learned the truth. You're a manipulating, thoughtless old man. You care for no one but yourself – except occasionally for your second wife.' He paused and took a long look at Cassidy before he resumed. 'Before Dad died, when we were boys, I thought you were wonderful, the older brother so much wiser than me; I was sure I'd always be able to rely on you.'

James remained seated. 'So you could,' he said loudly and defiantly from the far end of the table. 'Who comforted you when our mother died? I did! Who worked all hours to raise the money for your privileged education? I did! I'd already left the local school at 16 – no higher education for me! You owe me your life, your training, even your teaching job.'

'Oh, no, James!' Edward's eyes were blazing. 'It was a relief to get away; away from the pig farm, from the talk of butchery, the price of feed, the prize sows, the little flat over Dad's shop. Boarding school was a haven. The boys in my form were more like brothers to me. There were good teachers, competition with the other boys to excel, the drama group...' His voice softened. 'They were the good years. Jonathan, who joined the school when I did, became a good friend. He invited me to stay on his parents' farm every summer holiday. I was welcomed and treated like another son; they became my family. You had no sympathy when I found my first two teaching posts so tough, it was the Wests who kept me going.'

James stirred in his chair. 'Your little setbacks have nothing to do with this present enterprise,' he said, thumping the table so that the spoons rattled on their plates.

Edward ignored him, his eyes flashing dangerously. 'Do you remember, James, how you took advantage of my friendship with Jonathan? Without a word to me, you went to his parents and offered to buy their pig farm, promising them a fair price. And what happened? You did the dirty on them! You undercut the price and they had barely enough left to buy a new home. Jon's dad never recovered. Within a year he'd died and his mother two years later. And Jonathan, you know what happened to him, don't you?' Edward's voice was unnaturally high. 'He took his own life! His wife was devastated; I've watched his children struggling to adjust, tried to help them get through exams, find worthwhile things to do in life. You've murdered two men, James, and destroyed a family! Now you are trying to squeeze your own family dry. I hate you! You are no longer my brother – get lost!'

Edward turned, knocking his chair onto the floor. It crashed and rocked gently as he strode from the room.

There was a lengthy silence. James, visibly shaken, looked to Cassidy for help. She flicked her hair back and said, 'I think we are all tired. I need to unpack and have an early night – if you'll excuse me.' With quiet dignity she moved her chair away from the table and left the room.

James, breathing heavily and his face scarlet, took a final gulp of wine. 'Martin, my pills, I need them now.'

Martin looked up and hurried from the room. No one moved as they heard his feet lightly ascending the stairs and then returning. With practised ease he pulled back the plastic lid covering the day's dose and tipped a couple of pills into James' outstretched hand. He moved down the table and picked up a jug of water, but James in one quick movement threw the pills down his throat, heaved himself to his feet, walked four or five unsteady paces, then put his hand out and grasped a wine bottle securely by the neck, raised it to check its contents, and finally turned and walked uncertainly towards the door. Once there he paused and glanced at his watch. 'George, we'll meet in the music room at 9.45; I need some fresh air first, and the rest of you – think on!' Without waiting for a response, he left the room.

Martin shrugged, returned the jug to the table and, mobile in hand, made his way out without glancing up, his mind clearly fully occupied with some other matter. Archie, his arm round a pale and shaky Clara, followed him out together with Philip, red-eyed and sombre, his head down and eyes on the floor.

Emily reached for her glass. Her hand shook; she realised her heart was beating a little too fast. She felt as though she had crashed into an enormous, invisible brick wall, and the magnitude of the whole complex situation horrified her.

George leaned back in his chair and stretched his arms. After a pause he sat up and checked his watch. '8.40 – it feels more like 11.40. I'm longing for my bed – which I gather I have to make myself. Why does he have to demand a meeting so late tonight?'

Stella forced a smile, avoiding the question. 'We took delivery of a number of new beds this week, with brand-new mattresses, so I trust you will enjoy yours, when the time comes. I'm so sorry we haven't yet bought any sheets.'

As George left the room, Ian stood up. The earlier excitement had left his face and he looked tired. 'I don't really like to mention it,' he said to Stella, 'but I had expected my salary to be in the bank the day before yesterday. I checked again today and there's nothing there.'

Stella smiled at him. 'I expect the move has put it out of Mr Wedderburn's head. He had to divert all his belongings into storage because of the problems with the workmen – it's been quite a week. But anyway, I think it's Martin who deals with that side of things. I'm sure you can ask either of them tomorrow. Honestly, I don't think Mr Wedderburn's that short of money. Hopefully the gym and the pool will bring in some cash which will ease the situation a little for now. Don't worry. Everyone seems to be very overwrought at the moment – this must have been a shock for the family. They've travelled long distances and were tired and one thing led to another. Let's wait and see. You get home, now – things always look better in the morning. Goodnight! Drive safely.'

Ian shrugged, grimaced, and said, 'OK. I need to do some paperwork in the gym first, then I'll be off. Goodnight.' He turned less than happily and walked slowly from the room.

Chapter 8

Emily and Stella remained sitting at the long table as Mrs Summerfield came in to clear the remnants of dinner. Emily looked up at the portrait of her great-grandfather, Bartholomew Hatherley-Browne, whose disapproving demeanour dominated the end wall of the dining room. Even though he had been reputed to rule the family with a rod of iron, Emily could almost wish he had been present in the room to maintain order in the most recent gathering.

She sighed as she stacked the dessert plates that were within reach and handed them to Grace to put on the trolley. 'Oh, Stella, what a family! What an awful man! Has he put any money aside to pay for the things I was going to leave in the mansion? Will he even be willing to negotiate?'

Stella did not reply. She was staring absentmindedly at the reflected light patterns on the polished table. 'What do I do, Emily?' she asked. 'If Mr Wedderburn can't find the necessary money to turn this place into a hotel, he won't employ me. I can't manage without this job. Frank gets a reasonable salary, but I've needed so much money for Alex since her accident.'

Emily shot her a quick glance. 'You still cope with her at home?'

Stella shook her head. 'No. She's 17 now. I can't lift, wash or dress her any more. She's made really good progress, though. She lives just half a mile away in her own ground-floor, purpose-built flat, and has a rota of carers who ensure she's never on her own. She can use her hands now and enjoys working with her computer; she even does a little cooking, with help. She's got a new lightweight wheelchair, and next week will take delivery of her own specially adapted car. After that it's a driving test and out into the big, wide world.'

Emily smiled. 'You must be proud of her. When you think of the early days when she couldn't move at all...'

Stella passed some glasses to Grace and sighed. 'Yes, of course I'm proud. And delighted, and frightened... I still wonder at night what will happen to her, and whether the compensation will ever come through, and whether I can hold everything together until then.'

Emily touched her lightly on the arm. 'I think you need to take your own advice! Forbid yourself to think about any of it at night and wait until the morning.'

Stella sat up a little straighter. 'You're right. I just hope I can sleep. She smiled. 'Mr Wedderburn took the family round the house before supper and his wife barged into my room while I was changing. She was somewhat embarrassed!'

Emily laughed. 'I must find Finlandia. Last time I saw her she'd found her nice warm patch in the kitchen, by the hot water pipes, and was fast asleep. I expect she's pestering Grace for the leftovers – and she's soft enough to give them to her!

'And I must check that the coffee has gone into the sitting room,' said Stella. 'You go on ahead.'

Emily made her way to the kitchen. Mrs Summerfield was busy with a mop and bucket, and Jayne was sitting on a high stool by the table, drying her feet with a paper towel. Emily paused in the doorway. 'The Forever-Reliable up to its old tricks?' she enquired, glancing at the dishwasher, which had been past its best years ago.

Grace Summerfield looked up and nodded. 'I told Jayne not to worry. That rinsing hose is always the same. Turn the tap a little too far and the water spurts out, bounces off the plates in the rack and all over the floor in no time. I said the floor needed cleaning but, well, I did swear when I first saw the whole place awash, and told her off for wearing flip-flops in the kitchen. I think it's only her pride that's hurt.'

Jayne smiled ruefully and Emily smiled back. 'Do you remember when the Courtney-Blighs came to dinner?' she asked Grace.

'Do I not!' Grace twisted the mop with practised ease as the grey water swilled into the bucket. 'Must be 20-odd years ago. The kitchen helper managed to spray the whole room while trying to turn the tap off. It even flowed down the corridor to the back door. It took me an hour, with I don't know how many goes with a mop and bucket, to get it under control.' Both women laughed.

Stella appeared in the doorway. 'Emily! I should have known you'd be chatting. Mrs Summerfield, as well as tea and coffee, do you think we could have a large jug of hot chocolate for the drawing room? We have one or two of the family who are in need of comfort drinks, I think. I can take it in for you.'

Grace gave the mop a final, vicious twist and nodded. 'Jayne, put a couple of pints of milk in the microwave and the small kettle on, while I throw this water down the drain outside,' she ordered. 'Then you can put those silly flip-flops to dry with the other shoes by the back stairs. And then, for goodness' sake, go and get your trainers from upstairs – without getting splinters in your feet!'

Jayne gave her grandmother a hard look, then finally did as she was told, and vanished.

Emily wandered over to the old larder and took out the tin of chocolate. 'It looks tempting,' she said, thinking of her cold little home without electricity, and glancing down at the sleeping Finlandia, who had one white paw over her nose and was dead to the world.

Stella smiled. 'I'm sure we could stretch it to six or so,' she said as Grace reappeared.

'I'll double the amount,' Grace said, going to fetch the milk, 'and we'll have some too, before we turn in.'

Soon Emily was wheeling the rattling trolley along the passage and across to the drawing room, while Stella carried the jug of hot chocolate, not trusting it to the rigours of the old wooden floors and uneven marble slabs of the hall.

'Let's stay in the drawing room,' she whispered to Emily as they paused at the door. 'I think they need some "ordinary" people around to diffuse the situation.'

Emily whose hip ached slightly, and who relished the thought of a few minutes in her comfy, old chair by the piano, gave in to the smell of chocolate and her friend's insistence.

Edward was sitting in the far corner of the room by the bay window, accompanied by his laptop. He held a mobile in his hand. He did not look up when the trolley bounced over the edge of the carpet and rolled in front of the fireplace. Philip was sitting in an armchair near the back of the room, staring into space, ignoring the open book on his lap, while his wife and sister-in-law had taken a settee each, facing him. Clara was lying full-length, gazing at the carpet, while Samantha, presumably brought downstairs by Philip, was curled into a ball hugging an old tapestry cushion.

In silence, while Emily poured, Stella held the mugs and then distributed them together with a box of chocolates. There were muted murmurs of thanks. Stella settled herself in the nearest bay window while Emily, with a sense of relief, sank into her favourite chair. Was normality beginning to be restored, she wondered?

A pattering sound heralded the entrance of Finlandia, who squeezed herself through the partly open door and, tail wagging, made straight for the occasional table by Clara and sat expectantly watching every movement Clara made, as she absentmindedly waved her chocolate in the air.

'Oh, you darling!' Clara sat up and turned to Emily. 'May I give her a piece?'

Emily, who had very strict rules on chocolate, but who felt even more strongly that something must be done to change the atmosphere in the house, said, 'I'm sorry, no chocolate, but I think I've got a biscuit in my coat pocket.'

She was soon back and, closing the door behind her, walked over to Clara and gave her a small dog biscuit. Clara patted the seat next to her and Finlandia bounded up. She watched Clara's hand intently, gulping down the biscuit in a split second the moment it was offered. Clara stroked her, but Finlandia was not prepared to stay. She jumped down and trotted over to Samantha and patted her knee expectantly. Samantha looked up and swallowed the last mouthful of chocolate before uncurling, bending and lifting the small dog onto the settee next to her.

Clara held her mug in both hands, warming them. 'How old is she?' she asked Emily.

'She's seven now,' said Emily settling back in her chair. 'When I first brought her here she was so tiny I could hold her in one hand. I made the mistake of bringing her into this room and putting her in the middle of the carpet. The excitement was too much for her and we were soon mopping up a puddle!'

'We had a puppy once,' Clara said. 'I was ten and Mum bought her for me. She came from a local farm. I only had her three years and then we went back to live with Dad. He wouldn't let me keep her. I don't know what happened to her. I've always wondered. Do you know, Uncle Edward?'

Edward glanced up. 'The collie? After you'd left, your mother asked me to take her to the local animal rescue centre; they'd had a request for one and she fitted the bill,' he said shortly, looking back at his screen.

'You never told me.'

Edward ran a hand through his hair. 'I expect it was a long time before I saw you again. A lot happened that year.'

Philip suddenly focused on the conversation. 'Clara, don't start again, we can't rake up the past any more.'

'It doesn't hurt asking about a dog.'

Philip shrugged and went back to his book.

Clara looked over her shoulder towards Edward. 'Please explain, Uncle Ed.'

Edward sighed, slipped his phone into his pocket, walked across the room and straddled the arm at the other end of Clara's settee. 'What do you want to know?'

Clara glanced across at Philip, before curling up in her corner of the sofa and sipping her drink. 'Well, not just about the dog. I want to know about Mum.'

'Clara,' Philip warned.

'It's no good, Philip. I've got such odd memories and I always think the worst.' She turned back to Edward. 'I've got a right to know. Did dad get drunk and hit her? Did he hate her? Did she do something to upset him?'

Edward turned to Philip and spoke quietly. 'Philip, I think she's right. I don't know very much, but it's only fair she knows. I've taught enough children who've been worried about things at home to know that it's better to deal with the truth than half-imagined fantasies.'

Philip shut his book. 'I suppose so. I don't think any of us have any emotion left after tonight, and I haven't the energy to go to bed yet. Go on, then – as long as Dad and Cassidy don't come in.'

Emily looked across to Finlandia, who was sleeping contentedly on the settee, her head on Samantha's leg. Samantha looked exhausted and there was still redness around the eyes, but she was showing interest in the conversation. Emily met Stella's eyes and raised an eyebrow. Stella gently shook her head. No matter how tired they were, this was not the moment to leave.

Edward moved to an armchair, crossed his legs and leaned back against the cushions. 'You must remember that I didn't see much of my brother – there are 14 years between us. Dad died when I was seven, so James and Mum had to manage the business. By the time he married Sharon – I mean, your mother – I was at boarding school in Ripon and spent the holidays on Jonathan's parents' farm near Flockton. I went to James' and Sharon's wedding, of course, and they were very much in love. I think she'd been a customer in the shop and it was love at first sight. I was in the sixth form when you were born, Philip, and I did come and see you one day in the holidays, but babies weren't really my thing then.'

Philip grinned. 'I don't hold that against you. I'm not keen on them myself.'

Emily glanced across at Samantha, who was gazing with undisguised dismay at her husband, before she bent over the sleeping dog, letting her hair fall over her face.

Edward resumed his story. 'I was up at Oxford when you were born, Clara, but again I came to visit you. Being an uncle twice over was quite something, even though you weren't exactly real people to me then. I was happy to send you birthday and Christmas cards and presents over the next few years, but I went into teaching and neither of my jobs was easy. If I'm honest, I didn't think much about my own family.'

Edward paused. There was no sound in the room apart from the gentle snoring of the dog. Tired eyes focused on him with some vague and distant understanding, waiting for the revelation to come.

'When I was at my second school, your mother asked me to come and see her. Our term finished before yours and James was, as ever, doing overtime with the office paperwork. Sharon was desperate. She was sure that James was involved with someone else, but I didn't believe her. James had always been a workaholic and so intent on amassing a fortune – he'd got three or four shops by then – I didn't think he'd have time for anything like that, and I'm afraid I didn't take it at all seriously.

'I went to stay at Jonathan's parents for a week or two in the next school holidays, and they'd kept the local Huddersfield paper for me, and enjoyed teasing me about the large photo of James presenting a silver cup to Cassidy, who had just become "Miss Pork Chop 1999". It had been taken eight weeks before, about the time your mother had started to feel uneasy. Then I began to feel anxious too.'

'Miss Pork Chop?' Philip echoed, disgust written all over his face.

Clara put her mug down on the table rather too heavily. 'So that was it. I've seen his picture of Cassi in the office. She's wearing a turquoise bathing costume and has this sash across her. I never got near enough to read the writing on it.'

Edward leaned forwards, his hands clasped between his knees. 'I'm sorry if I failed you, but I never saw it coming. I gather Sharon finally had a breakdown over it and James demanded a divorce. At first Sharon managed to look after you, but the strain was all too much; she didn't get enough money from the divorce and couldn't go out to work with the two of you to care for. She tried to end her life, but a neighbour found her in time and eventually she was sectioned.'

'Sectioned?' Samantha had clearly never heard the word before.

Philip remained still, staring into some distant time zone. 'I remember,' he said slowly. 'I cried for her so much someone took me to see her in hospital. It was awful. They kept all the patients behind a locked door. You could see her through the glass, and I looked at her and she looked at me, but she didn't recognise me, there was nothing there in her eyes. They were sort of empty, blank. When we were allowed in, I sat next to her, but she didn't speak, just stroked my hair and my arms, as if I were someone else's pet cat. She was a stranger.' Philip stopped and fiercely brushed his cheek with the heel of his hand.

'That was the kind of detail I wanted to spare you,' said Edward, 'and I'm sorry if that is your last memory of her. When I did enquire after her, years later, the neighbours said she'd improved and eventually met and married a widower she'd known when she was younger, and really seemed to be happy again. They didn't know where she'd gone to live.'

'Dad didn't care about us.' Clara looked accusingly at Edward. 'I hate him.'

'All he wanted was to build up his pork butchery empire,' Philip added. 'What a jerk.'

Edward kept one eye on the door, obviously aware that either James might drop in before his meeting with George, or Cassidy return from her unpacking.

'Well, that's...' he began when the door was flung open. Archie marched in, threw his damp coat onto a chair, and looked round at the sombre group. 'Well, that should teach him a lesson,' he remarked going over to the trolley. 'Is this hot chocolate?'

'Probably tepid,' said Clara. 'What do you mean? Teach who a lesson?'

'Your dad,' said Archie. 'Forgotten how to keep his chin covered.'

Clara sat bolt upright. 'Archie, what have you done?'

Archie poured himself a chocolate, letting the jug rise and fall to make the mixture froth more. 'I wasn't letting him insult your mother – or you, come to that! I told him what I thought of him and followed it with a right hook.' He grinned. 'Gave him a bit of a shock. He staggered across the lawn into the sundial! Kept his feet, though. I thought I'd have another go and floor him, but the rain started again, so I left him to finish his cigar and think about it, while I went and battered the punchball in the gym instead.

'Is he all right?' Clara enquired anxiously.

'Well, he was upright when I left him, so he must be.' Archie was quick to change the subject. 'So what have you lot been up to, then? Uncle Ed, I thought you were leaving.'

Edward had turned his attention to his phone again. 'I intend to go first thing in the morning, if I can find the information I need.'

Archie wandered round the room, mug in hand, staring at the tapestries.

Edward glared at him. 'For goodness' sake, if you can't sit down in a civilised manner, go somewhere else, Archie.'

Archie gulped down his chocolate. 'Well, what do you suggest?' he said. 'It's too early for bed.' He turned to Emily and

Stella. 'What else does one do around here? Why isn't there a television?'

'It's in the Old Barn, where you would have joined James and Cassidy after dinner each evening, if the electricians had finished,' replied Stella.

'No cards, I suppose?'

'There are some in the drawer of the bureau, and there's a snooker table,' said Stella quietly. 'Turn right out of here and down the right-hand corridor. It's the last door on the left, just before the music room.'

Archie turned back to Edward. 'What about it, Uncle Ed?'

Edward looked less than thrilled. 'Archie, I can't come right now.'

'I need to unwind.'

Edward groaned as he was interrupted yet again. 'Then for goodness' sake go to the snooker room and get warmed up. I'll meet you there in about ten minutes, and I'll give you just one game. I've got an early start in the morning. Oh, and when I beat you, don't expect a return match tonight.'

A faint smile flickered across Archie's face. 'Who says you're going to win? And don't be late or I'll start without you,' he added as a parting shot.

'And don't you be late up to bed!' Clara called after the disappearing figure as she got up. 'I know it's not late, but I'm shattered, and I'm going to bed.'

Samantha unwound herself from the settee and replaced the cushion. 'I want to go to bed too. Philip, are you coming?'

Philip, staring into the empty fireplace at the far end of the room, his hands clasped behind his head, didn't bother to look round. 'Give me ten minutes, love.'

After the girls had left, the room was silent. Emily knew she should move, but that required effort, and it was a little early for Fin's walk. Perhaps James would come in after his meeting with George, but would it be a good moment to ask him about her furniture? She doubted it. She leaned back in her chair and allowed her eyes to close.

She woke with a start, conscious that her head had nodded forward. She looked around. Stella had her eyes closed. Philip was still staring into space, while Edward was now studying the screen on his laptop intently. The information he needed appeared elusive.

Philip made a groaning noise as he got up from his chair. 'Well, I'd better go up before I fall asleep here.'

Edward was still intent on his screen. 'Oh, at last,' he said to himself more than anyone else. He pulled out a notebook and pen from his pocket and copied a few details. He shut the notebook and proceeded to send a brief message before closing down. 'Stella, what time is breakfast?' he asked.

'8.30,' Stella responded.

'Could I have mine at eight o'clock, do you think?' Edward spoke calmly and politely. Perhaps, thought Emily, he was happier now that he had found the times of the trains home. If that was what he'd been searching for.

Stella paused. 'Yes, of course. I'm sure Mrs Summerfield and Jayne will be in the kitchen in plenty of time. I think they're on their way to bed now, so I won't trouble them, but do ask them in the morning.'

Philip watched him wearily. 'I wouldn't mind going home tomorrow,' he said wistfully.

Edward looked at him, 'Nothing to stop you,' he said, as the two of them left the room together.

Emily sank back in her chair. 'What a day!' she said very quietly, as the door clicked shut. 'I shall need to see Mr Wedderburn in the morning about his intentions towards my furniture, which fills most of this house. He promised me time to have it valued and sold. Let's hope he doesn't include it in his new will!'

Stella smiled. 'I'm so glad you're back. I wouldn't want to face this all on my own. I feel as if I've been through a hurricane tonight.'

They sat in companionable silence, occasionally reminiscing about the past. Emily sighed. 'I really must get going. It's fatal to sit so long.'

Stella glanced at her watch. 'It's nearly 10.30,' she said. 'If you'd like to get your coat on, I'll take the dirties out to the kitchen and meet you back in the hall.'

As Stella pushed the noisy trolley towards the kitchen, Emily collected her parka, put it on and then sat on the wooden settle, looking at the grey ashes in the grate. What a lot had happened since she'd remonstrated with James for lighting the fire earlier that evening. She shivered; the hall was cold without it.

Emily gazed at the large black and white marble tiles covering the entrance hall floor. She smiled as she remembered her father setting up a chess game one winter's evening, around Christmastime. The hall fire was blazing and the tree, with its many coloured lights, had stood in the well of the stairs. Everywhere was full of flickering reflections.

Her father had been competing against her uncle and they had used enormous pieces from a chess set her father had been given – of course, it had been Boxing Day she recalled – and she and her sister had to move the pieces to whichever square the men had chosen. Perhaps that's where her love of puzzles and strategy had come from; that first realisation that to win did not mean instant confrontation, but from carefully planned moves, anticipating the opponent's thinking, tempting him into a place where he could be trapped…

Her thoughts were interrupted by Cassidy, in her night things, clattering down the main stairs. 'Oh, hello, Dame Emily. I was looking for a hot drink.'

Emily smiled. 'Stella's just taken the trolley to the kitchen. I'm sure she'll find you something.'

'Thank you,' said Cassidy and disappeared down the kitchen corridor. A few minutes later Emily heard the ping of the microwave and Cassidy returned, warming her hands on a steaming mug. 'Goodnight,' she said briefly, and went upstairs.

'Good night,' Emily responded, and then looked across at Finlandia, who was sitting as close to the front door as she could. 'Soon, Fin,' she said. The dog gave a snort and lay down on her stomach on the rough doormat, gazing at Emily with big brown eyes.

There were more footsteps, this time on the back stairs and then along the kitchen corridor. Emily looked up as Martin strode towards her. 'You haven't seen James, have you?' he asked.

Emily shook her head and looked at the grandfather clock near the stairs. 'I thought he was meeting his solicitor about half an hour ago,' she said.

'He wasn't there 15 minutes ago,' said Martin. 'Never mind, the morning will do. Have a good night.' He turned and walked lightly up the main staircase.

'Thank you,' said Emily. 'Oh, is it still raining outside, do you know?'

Martin touched the back of his head. 'Just a little. I did put my head out when I locked the back door.'

'Thank you,' said Emily. 'Goodnight.' She took a long lead from her pocket and, calling the dog to her, attached it to Finlandia's collar. The tail wagged hopefully. As she was bending down, she caught sight of a briefcase under the settle.

Stella was soon back, carrying a couple of flasks. 'Just in case you want a hot water bottle and a cup of tea in the night,' she said handing them over. 'Here's a spare key to the back door in case there is any kind of emergency. And make sure you're here for breakfast!'

Emily zipped up her jacket. 'Thank you so much, that was really thoughtful,' she said, as she slipped a flask into each pocket. 'I've just noticed a briefcase,' she said, pointing to it. 'I don't know if it's safe there.'

Stella bent down and pulled the briefcase out. 'I've no idea who it belongs to,' she said. 'I suppose I'd better put it out of sight.' She looked round vaguely.

'The cupboard under the stairs,' suggested Emily. 'Just in case burglars come in through the kitchen.'

Stella chuckled. 'I go round and check the windows and lock the doors really carefully each night, but those old sash windows in the kitchen – well, the little plastic wedges in them wouldn't deter a child.'

Emily grinned. 'We got rather lax over the years. I've been meaning to get new locks for so long now,' she said. 'I presume all my valuables are still locked away upstairs?'

'All safe and sound,' said Stella. 'James and I have the only keys.'

'Then I'll get out of your way so that you can lock up and get to bed.'

'Oh,' said Stella, as she took a step towards the door. 'The key. It's not in the lock, and it always is.'

Emily frowned, thinking. 'Would James have moved it to let the family in? I saw them collecting in the front garden this afternoon. I imagine he would have brought them into the house this way.'

'Now what do I do?'

Emily looked at the coat stand in the corner. 'Isn't that his camel coat? He might've left the key in the pocket.'

'I feel dreadful, looking, but I suppose I'll have to.' Stella glanced over her shoulder before plunging her hand into the right-hand pocket. 'Clever Emily!' Stella smiled with relief as she drew out the old key. 'Now I shall sleep peacefully!'

Emily smiled back. 'Let's hope the rain has stopped for the moment. See you in the morning. I will pop in for breakfast, but I may have it in the kitchen. Goodnight, Stella!'

'Goodnight, Emily!'

Dame Emily felt an enormous sense of relief when, at last, Finlandia led her out of the Elizabethan mansion. The day seemed to have lasted a week and her body complained of extreme tiredness, but the cool air began to clear her mind.

It was good to be settled in her home again, but for how long? In the darkness she could hear the distant breakers of the sea – the tide had been going out for about three hours now. She loved watching it at full tide best, the waves cascading onto the beach, and breaking in spumes of spray against the rocks at the cliff edges on either side of the bay. Then it was like rhythmic thunder and it lifted and excited her.

The rain had stopped and the wind was lighter now. Dame Emily allowed Finlandia to lead her back to the Lodge by the right-hand path and the summer house; she knew better than to try to change the pattern of Fin's short lifetime.

She was home again, but this was not home. Strangers lounging on her furniture, the whole house waiting for its internal organs to be ripped out, and the outbuildings and dear walled garden changed forever. She shuddered; it was not always a good thing to return to somewhere one had been happy in the past. At least for tonight, in the dark, she could pretend it had not happened, but in the morning... then she would have to face reality.

She walked beside the lawn and down to the summer house. The full moon showed fitfully, which was a help, and nearer the road the yellow streetlights shone in patterned patches between the limes.

She took deep breaths of the cold, damp air and wished she could lose the voices which played and replayed the dreadful accusations thrown at James Wedderburn that evening. How could she have become involved with him? But then it had all been done through others: estate agents, solicitors, that secretary – Martin. If she'd met James Wedderburn earlier, perhaps she'd have sensed what he was like. No wonder he hadn't attempted to meet her himself. Would she ever get the correct value for the contents of the house? That wretched little man had betrayed her and broken his promise, but he would not get the better of her – there were ways and means...

Part II
Ocean Surge

Good Friday

Chapter 9

On Friday morning the door of the porter's Lodge opened at five minutes past seven and Emily stepped out, warmly clad in an olive waxed jacket and sturdy boots. Her white hair was cocooned in a red, light woollen scarf, a pair of binoculars was slung over her left shoulder, and she gripped her stick firmly with her right hand. The dog, hurrying ahead and straining at the end of her long lead, waited at the little gate in the fence, while her owner closed the front door with a quiet click. Emily headed for the wrought-iron gates of Seascape House and crossed the road into the empty morning.

She was back in routine. She could not bear to go and look at the changes James had made to the estate – yet – though she felt she must see what had been done in the last six months, if only to satisfy her curiosity.

But now she returned to the early morning routine she had established decades before, crossing the road immediately outside the gates and, turning a little to her left, she walked diagonally across Seascape Drift, a wide expanse of grass leading to the distant cliff edge, from where, in good weather, it was possible to see Beachy Head lighthouse.

Her walk skirted a small bay which lay to her right; it was flanked by sheer, crumbling chalk cliffs, the lower white strata stained brown. She glanced down at the tiny remaining patch of sand, littered with pebbles and surrounded by a scatter of white and beige boulders, still shiny from the drizzle of the grey morning; it reminded her of a bald patch on a well-worn sheepskin coat. Less than an hour to high tide, she guessed. She watched as the waves rose, each curved in a perfect arc, and then fell, pounding the beach and sucking at the pebbles, making them dance and chatter. A few gulls were combing along the tide line and turning over the seaweed, looking for a pre-breakfast snack, while a crow was pursuing a drunken course along a large boulder, fighting to remain upright in the windblown seaspray.

It had been a few years since she'd managed to get down the old wooden steps onto the beach. Now she dared not risk her hip. She had suffered enough at the hands of hospitals to last her the rest of her life.

Undeterred, she walked to the extremity of the Drift and turned east, taking her binoculars out of their case and adjusting them quickly. The light was increasing over the horizon and a pewter sea reflected it dully. The wind, with a hint of drizzle in it, stung her face and brought her to life. She could never survive at the back end of a horrid little village, on a cramped and airless estate, without the cry of the gulls and the smell of fresh seaweed. This was home; this was where she felt complete.

She put the binoculars to her eyes and noted again the familiar red and white stripes of Beachy Head lighthouse, the spray licking round the untidy white-beige chalk debris at its foot, the empty silver sea and a few white horses. She swung the binoculars with practised ease through an arc of 150 degrees. The Dieppe ferry had not left Newhaven then. There would be another half an hour or so before it emerged from the harbour and she could inspect its brilliant white and blue paintwork, and try to decipher the name on its bow, before it gradually became a toy boat on the hazy horizon.

Her gaze rested on the small headland on the other side of Seascape Bay. Its days were numbered. The sea lashed at the chalk day after day, night after night, and often there were fresh rock falls. The council had been at work and large, off-white cubes of concrete had been deposited in the sea, extending the curve of the bay. It was like a futile offering, an angular maiden given to appease a furious dragon, but how long before the monster tired of small prey and attacked the cliffs again?

She trained the glasses onto the ugly concrete; already the reinforcing rods were exposed, rusting and disfiguring, sealing off the very large rock pool which had formed between two landslips. There was something black there too. Surely the council would not dump black rocks at the base of white chalk cliffs? But it wasn't rock, it moved with the ebb and flow and swell of the water as successive waves spilled into the pool; it floated, a giant plastic bag, bloated, breathing its last and marring the beauty all around.

She refocused the binoculars and looked again. The plastic bag was not black, but a dirty navy blue; it divided into two leg-like parts at one end, and then she saw that its two bent 'legs' had feet. Emily gripped her stick more tightly and struggled to control the nauseous sensation that rose into her throat. She breathed deeply, calming herself, and studied carefully. The body turned in the swell and she saw the back of its head, shiny and bald, while its right arm reached out, as though attempting some ineffectual swimming stroke, searching to find a secure grip. The waves seemed powerless to pull this new prey out into the silver depths of annihilation; something below the surface held it fast.

Emily gained control over her shaking legs and checked her watch. If she were right and the torso were trapped in the rocks at the far point of the bay, the incoming tide would soon crush it mercilessly on the council's concrete blocks, or the swell from the Dieppe ferry would lift it free, toss it carelessly in the foam and suck it back into the greedy ocean current.

Emily had always told visitors to read the warning signs on the beach, and she remembered all too well the day she had grabbed a child to safety, pulling him roughly by the arm from the strip of sand to the wooden steps. He'd yelled and his mother, momentarily distracted by packing away their picnic, had been furious with her, until the mighty wave, stirred up by the giant ship, had crashed onto the place on the quiet beach where the boy had been playing, and sent its ripples almost to the steps, within inches of their feet.

Emily pulled her mind back to reality. She could not desert this stranger, if he were alive, which she doubted, nor abandon his body to the mercy of the sea; she must get help.

Suspending her binoculars round her neck, she hurried with a limping gait across the wide expanse of grass, dragging her uncomprehending dog on a short lead, her mind beginning to react to the horror of the scene. She must hurry for the sake of the victim's family, one of whom would have to identify the body. For a brief second she remembered that moment in the mortuary when she and her sister... No, emotions must be kept firmly under control.

Emily reached the road and stepped off the pavement. A small red car was coming, but it was far enough away, she judged. She waved her stick at it and struggled on. A second wave of thanks as she reached the other side did nothing to appease the driver, who swerved slightly and hooted long and loud as she sped on. Emily turned in at the gates and, holding her side, where a stitch threatened to bring her to a halt, and with her binoculars thumping against her chest, she reached the gate of the Lodge.

Emily fumbled clumsily with the catch and stumbled up the path, feeling for the key in her pocket. With considerable relief she fitted it in the lock at the first attempt and almost fell into the little hall. She had no idea where she had put her mobile phone. What a mercy her landline had been reconnected the day before. Panting, she grabbed the phone, and letting her stick fall, she pressed 999 before collapsing onto the upright chair by the hall table. Fin pattered past her into the kitchen.

'Police and coastguard, I want them both,' she announced to the woman at the other end. 'They must come to Seascape Bay instantly, there's a body in the water and the Newhaven ferry is due to pass in 30 minutes.'

Thankfully the woman seemed to have a measure of common sense and sympathy, but she did ask Emily to repeat the information in the order required by the computer.

Emily sniffed. 'Are you one of those call centres in India?' she demanded. Once reassured, she finished imparting all the necessary details and put the phone down. What now? She felt quite shaky.

Emily walked slowly into the kitchen. There would be enough hot water in the flask Stella had given her the night before for a cup of coffee – she couldn't abide tea made with water which had gone off the boil. She took a clean cup from the cupboard and found the drink quick to swallow and remarkably comforting. Her mind cleared a little.

This was no time for sitting still, she decided; she needed to be outside, directing operations. She picked up Fin's trailing lead, and, suitably armed with the front door key and her binoculars, she left the Lodge.

She walked across the Drift to the place from which she had first spotted the body. It was still there, but on the incoming tide it seemed to move more helplessly, rising and then vanishing briefly under the breaking waves, its arm still reaching out, searching for some means of purchase in the turbulence which rocked it repeatedly.

Emily gave herself time to catch her breath and lifted the binoculars to scan the horizon. Was that the bow of the ferry, just leaving Newhaven? She kept watching until she could see half the ship, before she turned to scan the visible, but completely empty, segments of the main road, which snaked its way down little valleys, over the undulating low hills and round a couple of wooden copses towards Eastbourne. She looked at her watch. How long would it take for help to arrive? There was nothing more she could do – only wait and dread the outcome.

Emily looked back again at the helpless body, its shape vaguely familiar, and suddenly turned away, her hand to her mouth. She spoke to herself firmly. This was no time to be sick. With her mouth set in a firm line and her head held up high, she regained control. She must not jump to conclusions. But even as the command entered her head it was dismissed; that instinctive, sinking feeling of dread told her she knew this man, and as she turned back to train the binoculars on the foot of the cliff, she was almost sure that this was the body of the latest owner of Seascape House.

But, she argued with herself, why should it be James? She only thought that because she hadn't been able to get him out of her mind since last night. Surely he hadn't decided to end it all? Had the family's response to him last night dashed his hopes? But somehow she felt he wasn't a man to give in to his family or grasp at suicide as the only way out. He had seemed so strong, determined to make his ideas work. Surely despair had not overcome him that quickly? It must be someone else.

But in her heart of hearts Emily knew it was James floating there. In death his bloated body was even bigger than it had been in life. She'd only met him for the first time a few hours ago… and for all that James had treated her so appallingly, his body must be rescued.

She shook her head in an effort to concentrate her mind – she needed the coastguards there first. They'd have to go down over the cliff edge to reach the body; at the moment there was no way round from the beach, there was too much water surging into the entrance to the bay. But the risk of falling rock and the wake of the ferry made her shudder. If only she had stayed in bed longer – just half an hour longer – she wouldn't now be putting other lives at risk.

As it happened the coastguards did arrive first, swerving onto the Drift as they saw her stick waving wildly, and stopping close to her. She raised her hand to prevent them getting out of their Land Rover.

'You'll need to drive round to the other side of the bay, across Seascape Heath,' she said, 'but you can see him from here. I'll show you where he is.'

The man in the front passenger seat jumped out and she led him to the vantage point, from where he could see the body caught at the edge of the deep rock pool. Quickly she explained the height of the tide and the danger from the ferry, which had now disentangled itself from the coastline and was embarking on its journey. She smiled as he thanked her politely and agreed with her assessment of the situation. He ran back to his companions and soon they were speeding round the bay and up across the short cropped grass to the clifftop.

She watched as the three men and a woman jumped out and then held their leader's legs as he crawled cautiously on his stomach to the edge of the cliff. Emily, like some eccentric conductor of several combined orchestras, waved her stick dramatically until he moved further to his left and at last located the position of the body. She lowered her stick and watched through the binoculars as he wriggled back and conferred with his teammates.

Emily gave a sigh of relief and made her way back towards the road and the edge of the Drift. It was there that the driver of the police car spotted her frantic waving, veered onto the grass and braked decisively.

An older man and a younger woman, casually but smartly dressed, got out of the car and walked across the grass to meet Emily.

'Dame Emily Hatherley-Browne?' enquired the man. 'I'm Detective Chief Inspector Drummond, and this is my colleague, Detective Sergeant Pollard.'

Chapter 10

Emily looked grimly at the two police officers. 'He's down there,' she said simply, 'and the coastguards have arrived.'

She turned and pointed, first at the prostrate figure still gently bobbing at the foot of the cliff, and then to the four tiny figures of the coastguards, some 50 feet above the encroaching waves, who had already harnessed themselves and were lifting a stretcher in readiness.

The chief inspector's formal politeness vanished. 'What on earth is going on? We need to see the body in situ. Pollard, go and tell them to wait.'

'I'm afraid that would be most unwise, Chief Inspector.' Dame Emily was at her most forceful. DS Pollard paused briefly, apparently aware of the authority in the older woman's voice.

'Pollard,' the chief inspector almost yelled. 'Go now!' DS Pollard ran for the car.

Emily shifted her balance and waved her stick vaguely towards the sea. One of the coastguards lifted an arm in her direction and turned to ease one of his comrades over the edge of the cliff, his abseiling harness glinting a brief reflection from the pale sun.

Emily, satisfied that the detective sergeant would be too late, tried ineffectually to disguise a smile.

The chief inspector swung round to face Dame Emily. 'That looked like a signal to me. How dare you interfere with police procedure?'

Dame Emily was unperturbed, and after a glance at the chief inspector's face, which barely controlled an explosion of anger, she decided to take the plunge. 'I would like to explain the problem facing the coastguards,' she said with the utmost politeness and dignity. 'In about 20 minutes,' she said, glancing at her watch, 'it will be high tide. That alone would be enough to dislodge the body from its position at the edge of the rock pool, but what you probably do not appreciate is that the Dieppe ferry left Newhaven about ten minutes ago. Like Seaford, we can get the occasional large wave pounding onto the shore from its wake. Such a wave, I can assure you, Chief Inspector, would cause untold damage to the body in the water, or even sweep him away altogether. He may be dead, but I believe his body should be protected at all costs. And of course I would not want to encourage you to go down to the beach in such dangerous circumstances.'

Drummond frowned as he cleared his throat. Emily could almost feel the anger shaking his body. Perhaps she had treated him a little like a schoolboy.

'Thank you for explaining that,' Drummond said shortly and less than graciously, as his eyes focused on the coastguard and stretcher which had now reached the bottom of the cliff. Already a second man was on his way down. Emily put the glasses to her eyes. The waves were breaking over the first coastguard's feet and he was finding it hard to locate a flat area for the stretcher. The second man landed, detached himself from the ropes and, leaping from rock to rock, hurried to the aid of his comrade.

Emily and DCI Drummond watched, motionless. The men, standing at either end of the body, lifted one side and eventually dislodged it from whatever had caught the clothing. The man who was holding the foot lost his grip as a larger wave crashed around them. The first man, who still held an arm, staggered and almost fell, while the body, rejoicing in new-found freedom, bobbed and twisted, and nearly escaped into the deeper water of the pool. As the wave retreated, the second man hurried behind the first. Swiftly he bent down and grabbed the other floating arm as it drifted past him.

Emily gazed as the two men froze in position, no doubt recovering their balance. If they didn't move, she thought, her mind racing, there would be three bodies in the water. Then, just as the next wave broke, Emily realised they had been waiting for the water to lift the lifeless James. She watched as, working as one, they pulled the body by the arms towards the stretcher and, using the momentum they had gained, heaved it onto the taut canvas.

As a rope snaked down from above them, Emily realised that the two on the clifftop had moved along to be nearer the rescuers. At the cliff base, other ropes were being used to secure the body to the stretcher. A shout, a wave and slowly the stretcher and one man were winched up the cliff. Emily glanced out to sea. The Dieppe ferry, getting smaller with the passing minutes, was well on its way to France, and the wave that Dame Emily had so much dreaded was approaching; a hump, just slightly bigger than the other watery mounds on the surface, showed with dreadful certainty. She let the glasses drop, jerking her neck as they swung above her waist. She cupped her hands and shouted, but the wind took the sound away.

Chief Inspector Drummond glanced at her quickly, then suddenly seemed to realise the danger for the man at the cliff base. He roared a message across the bay, but the rescuers showed no indication that they had heard. DS Pollard had left the car and was struggling up the remaining yards of the slight incline to the cliff edge with her back to them. Emily put the binoculars to her eyes once more as she and the chief inspector watched helplessly.

'God, help the man!' The chief inspector put his hand to his mouth and Emily held her breath.

At that moment the man at the cliff base turned and looked out to sea. Emily could only imagine his horror at the sight of the wave, now some ten feet high and at the point of breaking. For one brief fraction of a second he stood looking, and then with speed and incredible agility he covered the remaining couple of yards to the base of the cliff and leapt onto a tiny outcrop. He clung with one hand while the other searched for any small hold in the white chalk. He seemed to find it and for a moment was still, a minuscule, ant-like figure, flattened against the white of the cliff. Then the wave broke, making the familiar boom against the rocks, and there was nothing but spume and spray – white droplets rising high and triumphant – and then came the sucking sound as though the whole of the ocean were trying to swallow the base of the cliff at one gulp and bring the whole edifice down, together with its tiny morsel of drowning flesh.

The flying spray fell away. The cliff face was white and empty. Emily gasped. The chief inspector almost grabbed the binoculars away from her as he leaned over her shoulder to look for himself. 'I can't see him!'

Emily unhooked the binoculars from her neck and left him to search. Her keen eyes had glimpsed the crumpled figure, not far from where James' body had been removed.

The people above had placed the stretcher away from the edge of the cliff and left it with DS Pollard on guard beside it. As Emily had presumed, it was obviously too late for James. One coastguard was lying on her stomach looking over the edge.

'It's all right,' the chief inspector said, relief in his voice. 'The man at the bottom's waving. I can't tell if he's injured, but at least he's alive. I must go over there now.' He handed the binoculars back. 'We'll check with Missing Persons, but if our victim jumped off the cliff or waded from the beach during the night, I doubt if anyone will have missed him yet, especially if he's someone who's travelled from a distance.'

Emily held up one hand in the style of an old-fashioned policeman stopping London's traffic. 'You don't need to contact Missing Persons,' she said quietly. 'I think I know who he is.'

The chief inspector paused mid-stride and ran his fingers through his hair. 'And?' he said with an ill-disguised attempt at patience.

'He is, was, the new owner of Seascape House, just across the road. He arrived here yesterday with his family.'

'You knew him?'

Emily leaned on her stick a little more heavily. 'I only met him for the first time yesterday, but the – er – build looks remarkably the same.'

'Ah. I had better drop in to see them. And where can I find you?'

'I'm living in the Lodge at the end of the drive,' Emily waved her stick in the vague direction of her temporary home, 'but I will be in the mansion for breakfast.'

'And you are one of the family?'

'No, the previous owner of Seascape House.'

'I see.' The chief inspector, by the tone of his voice, didn't see, but Emily realised it was the easiest way for him to conclude the conversation. He looked her full in the face. 'I would prefer it if you didn't say anything to the family, no need to make them anxious. I'll sort things out here and come over. We shall need a formal identification – oh, and a statement from you, please.'

Emily nodded. She felt indescribably exhausted. As the chief inspector left her, striding round the edge of the bay and making his way up to the little group on the top of the cliff, she looked again through the binoculars.

It was almost high tide, and the little figure at the base of the rock had uncurled and was sitting, one leg caught under him, the other stuck straight out. The waves broke a couple of feet from him and lapped around him, but he was not in immediate danger of being sucked under.

The coastguards had found a second stretcher in their Land Rover and were lowering it and another man down the cliff. 'Thank God,' murmured Emily as she paused long enough to see the latest rescuer reach the base of the cliff before she turned away.

Finlandia had sat on the grass for long enough, her short sight preventing her from watching the proceedings with any interest. Even the newly arrived police car and ambulance, with their flashing blue lights, and the following mortuary van had left her unmoved as they had ascended Seascape Heath and parked by the coastguards' battered vehicle. Now that Dame Emily had taken a couple of steps, the dog was pulling at her lead, eager to scour the ground for interesting smells.

Emily glanced up at the clifftop, where police were stretching out blue and white tape, and allowed the dog to drag her to the road and on to the Lodge. Suddenly she realised she was shaky and hungry – and then remembered she had drunk the contents of the flask before taking Fin out. What a relief that the restorative breakfast that she longed for was, at that moment, being prepared in Seascape House.

Chapter 11

Emily allowed Fin to go past the Lodge and head straight for the back door of the mansion. The dog had obviously remembered that Grace Summerfield had been in the kitchen last night, and Grace was the one who would spoil her unfailingly. Emily recalled her parting conversation with Stella, and thought favourably of breakfast in the kitchen. Food would give her new energy and she'd be nowhere near the family. If the police needed her, they would have to come and find her.

Halfway down the drive, Emily paused to catch her breath. A weak sun was creating pale shadows on the lawn, and the great cedar tree, with a circle of bright-pink cyclamen at its foot, looked magnificent. Emily wondered at the vision of her ancestor who'd brought it to Seascape and planted it with such loving care. Several hundred years had passed since then, but the tree enhanced the building, which was still as beautiful as it must have been then. It was perfectly symmetrical, its three-pointed gables containing the small bedroom windows of the servants' rooms, below them the wider diamond panes of the family rooms, and on the ground floor the dining room and sitting rooms. She had always loved it and now it was no longer her home. But then, neither did it belong to the man whom she had seen so lately, standing on the top of the steps between the recently positioned stone pigs, and proudly showing his family his latest acquisition. Who owned it now? She felt protective and possessive – but she had no right to.

Emily was sure the front door would be locked, so she continued across the stable yard to the back of the mansion.

Signs of change were all around her. She sighed. Her mind acknowledged the need to live in the modern world; her heart longed for the carefree days of the past.

Emily paused by the back door. As far as she could see, the gate to the walled garden was firmly closed. It was just as well, she had no desire to see what she imagined to be an enormous greenhouse covering a ghastly blue-tiled swimming pool. These changes would help her to release her grasp on Seascape just a little. She would have to let go – eventually.

Emily tried the back door but it was locked. Forgetting that the key Stella had given her was still in her pocket, she rang the bell and soon heard the key turn in the lock as Grace opened the door. 'Dame Emily! Stella said you would drop in for breakfast, and I knew you and our lovely Fin would be here early, but I've been that busy I didn't give the back door a thought. Come in!'

Emily let Fin off her lead and she went ahead of them, scuttling into the kitchen, from where Emily could hear her thirstily gulping down the water that Grace had put out ready.

'Let me take your coat, Dame Emily, and then you can go into the dining room,' said Grace as they reached the kitchen door.

Emily undid her coat, eased it off, and allowed Grace to hang it on one of the pegs at the bottom of the back stairs, alongside a couple of coats the gardeners used. 'If you don't mind, Grace, I'd like to eat in the kitchen, I think.'

Grace looked at her hard. 'Stella said I should lay you a place with the rest.'

'Thank you, Grace, but not today.'

Emily walked into the kitchen and pulled back a heavy wooden chair from the nearest end of the old, scarred, pine table. It was as she sat that she noticed a figure seated at the far end of the table, a half-eaten full English breakfast in front of him.

'Oh, I'm so sorry,' she said. 'I didn't intend to intrude.'

Edward looked up from his newspaper, his fork halfway to his mouth. 'It's all right,' he said. 'I'm only avoiding the family, and James in particular. As soon as I've finished this, I'm off.' He returned to his paper.

Grace returned with a mug bearing a yellow smiley face, with the slogan 'Good Morning World' curving round it. She placed it in front of Emily and poured a steaming cup of tea.

'If you've been out walking the dog, you'll need this,' she said. 'Forgive me, but I need to get the rest of the breakfast onto the trolley and into the dining room. Jayne's checking the cereals and then she'll sound the gong. Last night Mr Wedderburn said he wanted breakfast at 8.30 prompt and I daren't be late.'

Emily, who had been momentarily distracted by normal life in the house, suddenly remembered what had happened just half an hour earlier and felt her stomach drop violently as if she herself, in a moment of terror, had lost her footing and fallen from the cliff edge. She steadied herself and looked across at Edward, who had almost finished shovelling the food into his mouth, and was buttering toast at great speed.

'Are you going far?' she enquired in an effort to slow him down.

'Where they won't find me,' was his brief reply.

Emily swallowed a mouthful of tea and wondered how long the chief inspector would be. She felt caught in some kind of time warp; nothing was real. The outside world seemed like a scene from some kind of horror film, the saturated body some oversized prop, the police robots playing out their parts automatically; only the rescue team, covering for one another, communicating, adapting their skills, seemed real people doing something practical, while she merely watched the drama being played out. And now she was inside preparing to watch another, possibly more terrible, scenario.

The kitchen was warm and comforting, the house full of early morning sounds: feet going to and fro to the bathroom above; the old floorboards creaking; footsteps on the stairs; the murmur of voices; the aroma of bacon and smell of browning sausage skins. Just briefly the house was living, but the moment which would change the lives of the whole family was approaching, and she could do nothing but watch…

She sipped her tea, cupping her hands round the mug, and watched Edward deftly organising pieces of orange peel around his piece of toast, while Fin sat as close to his left knee as she could, appealing eyes fixed on his face. Emily had no strength left to tell her to stop.

Along the corridor she heard Archie's voice. 'I made a real effort to get up on time. He'd better not be late. I could have done with a lie-in.' Then came the sound of the gong. Emily smiled to herself. Grace had done a good job and taught Jayne well. The throbbing sound grew louder and filled the whole house before gradually subsiding and ending with one loud crash.

Edward swallowed his last mouthful and stood. Emily stood with him. She could think of nothing to say, but at least she could walk ahead of him to the door and slow him down a little. The echo of pattering feet on the stairs was followed by a calm which settled over the mansion; the only sounds were from the dining room: a chink of cups and spoons on china.

Emily walked slowly down the corridor from the kitchen. She had just turned left towards the entrance hall when the old knocker on the front door crashed three times against its metal base. With an excited bark, Fin tore from the kitchen and rushed past them to stand on the front doormat, her tail wagging excitedly. Edward hurried past Emily, grabbed Fin's collar and pulled the dog forcefully away as he opened the door.

On the top step, grave and impassive, stood the chief inspector, while Edward, bent over in an effort to hold Fin with one hand and the door with the other, stared in disbelief.

'Good morning, sir, I'm Detective Chief Inspector Drummond,' the tall figure announced, waving his identity badge. 'I wonder if I could have a word.'

Speechlessly Edward opened the door wider as the inspector, followed by DS Pollard, wiped his feet carefully on the mat and paused on the tiled floor in front of Emily. He raised his eyebrows and Emily shook her head silently as Edward shut the door. As the door closed, she caught sight of a laptop case and a rucksack with an anorak casually thrown across them in the corner by the coat rack. Edward really was going to make good his escape. Above them a clattering of feet could be heard and then a dishevelled figure appeared at the turn in the stairs.

Cassidy, her minuscule nightdress almost hidden by a very thin negligée, continued her erratic progress downwards. 'I can't find James! I don't remember him coming to bed and... Oh!' She came to a sudden halt halfway down the staircase as she spotted the two strangers, the police inspector still holding up the proof of his identity.

'Oh!' she repeated as her hand went to her mouth. Edward went white.

Loud footsteps heralded the appearance of Martin. 'I heard the knocker,' he said. 'Is there something wrong?'

Archie appeared behind him. 'What's all the fuss about?'

DCI Drummond held up his identity badge once more. 'Perhaps if we could all sit somewhere?' he said firmly.

Archie said, 'We're in the middle of breakfast, except Dad's late.'

Drummond looked at the puzzled faces. 'I think I probably need to speak to you all. Would you show me to the dining room?'

Archie turned and led the way, announcing in the doorway, 'The police have come for breakfast!'

Martin offered to help Cassidy, whose breath was coming in short, sharp gasps, but she waved him away. The small procession made its way into the dining room and the participants sat, like obedient children, in the seats they had occupied the previous night. Just George and Ian were missing.

Emily sat in the furthest carver as before and observed DS Pollard as she propped herself against the panelled wall by the trolley, looking around at the portraits. She appeared to be fighting a battle between curiosity and solemnity.

Emily watched as the chief inspector went to stand behind James' empty chair. He glanced at the small heap of colourfully wrapped presents on the plate in front of him, took a deep breath and smoothed his hair with his hand. In his dark suit and tie he had a quiet presence, Emily decided, and was verging on handsome – perhaps it was the dark-brown hair greying at the temples. He regarded the group through rimless spectacles as he waited patiently.

Drummond cleared his throat and the whole company fixed their attention on him, Grace forgetting to put down the teapot she was holding, and Jayne replacing the lid on the bacon tray with an unexpected crash.

'Good morning. I am Detective Chief Inspector Drummond,' the policeman began. 'I do not want to alarm you in any way, but this morning the body of a well-built man in late middle age was found near here. As this is the only house in the vicinity, we need to ask if everyone here has been accounted for this morning, and whether you were aware of any stranger walking along the cliffs yesterday, or early this morning.'

A moaning sound came from Cassidy who was staring, wide-eyed, at the inspector. He turned to look directly at her. 'You are… madam?'

Martin spoke up. 'She's Mrs Wedderburn, the wife of the owner here.'

Cassidy continued to stare wildly. 'My husband, I couldn't find him, I had a sleeping pill, I've only just woken…'

'Your husband could have gone for a walk, madam, we don't want to jump to conclusions.' Drummond was obviously trying to be reassuring.

Martin leaned forward. 'Had his bed been slept in?'

Cassidy looked at him, panic in her eyes. 'No, I don't think so. No.'

'So he probably decided not to disturb you, if he stayed up late,' Martin smiled at her. 'He could have overslept, and there are any number of rooms where he could have spent the night.'

Cassidy wailed again, a little-girl-in-distress sound, and began to shiver violently. Clara pulled off her own lightweight fleece and put it round her stepmother's shoulders. 'Martin's right,' she said, reassuringly. 'This is just a terrible coincidence.'

Philip, who was sitting bolt upright, swallowed hard. 'Where was this body found?' he demanded, glaring at the chief inspector.

The detective's face softened. 'At the base of the cliff, across the road, sir,' he said more gently.

There was a barely perceptible intake of breath from the transfixed figures round the table.

'I am aware,' Drummond continued, 'that there are people who come from long distances to end their lives here. We cannot presume that this is a local person. However, I needed to ask you because the member of the public who found the body thought that Mr Wedderburn was the most likely person.'

'What?' said Philip. 'No one here knows us. My father only moved in yesterday. The place is still being renovated, and...' he broke off.

'Yes, who is this person,' added Clara, 'upsetting us like this and jumping to conclusions?'

'I found him,' Emily said quietly. Every eye turned to look at the speaker.

'You found him?' Edward confronted Emily. His loud voice filled the room. Yesterday's friendly attitude had vanished. 'You've wheedled your way back into this house with that silly dog. You think you can be part of our family weekend, and when you find a body, you decide it's my brother's? How dare you suggest such a thing?'

Emily had no easy response to give. She had sat opposite James for the whole of the evening meal; the contours of his body were etched into her mind. She was increasingly sure of what she had seen that morning. It was not the moment to defend herself. With an enormous effort she controlled her words.

'I'm sorry to cause you all such distress,' she said, looking down the length of the table. 'There was a distinct resemblance,' she added rather lamely, hoping that the inspector would not remark on the fact that she had seen the body from a considerable distance and the face not at all.

Drummond spoke decisively, but gently. 'So I'm afraid, I do have to ask that one of you,' he glanced round at the upturned faces, 'should come with me to formally identify the body or, of course, to confirm that it is not Mr Wedderburn's.'

There was a horrified pause.

'I'll do it.' The voice was Edward's, now calmer and more controlled. The whole company turned to look at him as he stood. 'I'm his brother, Edward Wedderburn. The sooner we put an end to this ridiculous charade the better.'

'Thank you, sir. Perhaps you would like to come to the mortuary later this morning?'

'I don't have transport. Would it be possible to go with you? I'd like to get this settled as soon as possible. The sooner we know that it is not my brother the better.' Edward glared at Emily.

'I could take you, if that would help,' Martin offered.

'Thanks, Martin,' said Edward. 'I would be grateful. Inspector, this is Martin Chumleigh, my brother's secretary.'

DCI Drummond nodded. 'I'll give you directions, Mr Chumleigh. You may come now, if you wish, but I think you may have to wait quite a while at the mortuary.'

'Now,' said Edward firmly, as he pulled his phone out of his pocket. The two men followed the chief inspector from the room.

Chapter 12

'It's not true, it can't be him,' wailed Cassidy, her head in her hands.

Archie, who had just taken a large mouthful of cold bacon, put his fork down. He glanced at Cassidy over the top of his wife's head. 'Of course it isn't! Look at the amount he had to drink last night – he'll have wandered off and lost consciousness somewhere.' He swallowed some tea and stood up. 'We'll go and look for him now,' he said decisively. 'He can't be far. Come on, Clara. We'll search the grounds.'

Philip got up. 'I'll do the house and get Ian to go through the outbuildings.'

'Philip, wait!' Stella pulled a bunch of keys from her jacket pocket and separated out three. 'James had keys to Emily's store rooms upstairs. You may like to search them, though I doubt he'd have locked himself in.'

'Thanks.' Philip pocketed the keys, and before he left the room he leaned over Samantha. Emily only just caught his words. 'You've got to make that phone call,' he said quietly between clenched teeth.

Samantha flinched and turned her head away. 'As soon as I've helped Cassi.'

As Philip strode out of the room, Samantha walked round the table and bent over Cassidy. 'Let me get you a hot drink; you've had a terrible shock. They can do the searching and we'll let you know as soon as we've found him. As Archie said, he's probably still sleeping off all that wine he drank last night. Come on, I'll help you back to bed.'

As Samantha and Cassidy left the room, Stella heaved a sigh and reached across the table, putting a sympathetic hand on her friend's arm. 'Emily, you poor dear. You must be so shaken, and then to have Edward go for you…'

Emily smiled faintly. 'It was a shock and I'll tell you about it, but… I suddenly feel so hungry. Is it dreadful to eat?'

Stella patted Emily's arm and looked across the room to where the kitchen staff were talking quietly. 'Grace, could we have a fresh pot of tea and some more toast, please?'

Grace and Jayne left the room and gradually Emily told Stella the awful events of the morning. She was a good listener, and food, familiar surroundings and sympathy helped a great deal.

At 9.15 they were still there when George came into the room. 'Where's James? I really need to talk to him before this meeting gets underway,' he said settling himself at the table.

Emily waited until he was seated. 'George, I'm afraid something dreadful's happened. There won't be a meeting.'

George scanned the debris on the table. 'What's happened to change his mind after all this preparation? While you tell me, I'll help to tidy the toast rack, if you ladies have finished with it, that is.'

'By all means,' said Stella, pushing the butter and marmalade in his direction.

George stabbed the butter with his knife. 'Something dreadful, you say?'

'I think you should know,' said Emily carefully, 'that a body has been found at the foot of our cliffs.'

George crunched a large mouthful of toast and frowned. 'Is that so? A drunk, I expect, probably wandered from a nearby pub. Nasty way to go, though.'

Emily took a sip of tea. 'The other problem is that James has not been seen this morning.'

'Sleeping off the evening's excess of wine, no doubt. I suppose that could explain why he didn't turn up for our meeting last night – he'd been so insistent that he wanted it.'

'He didn't turn up?' Emily said, looking thoughtfully at Stella. 'What did you do?'

'Well, nothing, to be honest; I didn't want the meeting anyway. It had been a very long, hard day. I gave James 30 minutes or so, then put my papers away and went to bed. Come to think of it, Martin dropped into the music room before I left and asked if I'd seen him.'

'The family are searching for James now,' Stella said.

'Well,' said George placidly, helping himself to another piece of toast, 'he can't be far away, and he likes his food.' He spread butter thickly and reached for the marmalade. 'He'll be back.'

'You don't think the family could have driven him to do something silly?' Stella asked.

George looked at the imprint of his teeth in the thick butter and considered. 'No, I don't think so. The family may have been difficult last night, but he's tough. Having invited the family here, he wouldn't throw away this perfect opportunity to get his finances sorted out and to draw up the new will. Anyway, he seems delighted with this place.'

Emily said quietly, 'I was the one who found the body – I'm almost certain it was Mr Wedderburn's.'

'Ah.' George poured himself a fresh cup of tea and absent-mindedly took another piece of toast. 'You mean that James and the body are one and the same. That does put a fresh complexion on things.'

Emily wondered both at the calmness and at the mental ability of the solicitor sitting so close to her. How long did it take to add two and two and get four? But perhaps she had been the one to jump to conclusions. She had been so sure at the time.

'The police have been,' she added, 'and Edward and Martin have gone to the mortuary to see if it's James' body.'

For the first time George's eyes rested on her face. The word 'mortuary' had apparently jerked his mind into full wakefulness.

'Is that so?' he said.

They were interrupted by the sound of feet hurrying down the stairs. Philip came into the room. 'I can't find Dad anywhere.

I'll join the others outside.' He returned Stella's keys and left as quickly as he had come.

Emily got up and walked over to the window which overlooked the front lawn. 'They're searching every inch, poor things,' she reported, watching as Archie peered through the windows of the summer house, while Clara pulled back the branches of the laurels by the front wall. Why was it that the human mind, faced with some dreadful news, so often refused to believe it, and accelerated into some alternative activity? Her heart ached for them; she wanted to put her arms round them and explain gently what had happened. She dreaded the moment when Edward would return with the devastating news.

Stella turned in her chair. 'You're really sure, aren't you Emily?' she said. 'So what happens next?'

Emily abandoned her morbid thoughts and decided she must be practical. 'I suppose I must get a statement written before the police return,' she said. 'It'll take me hours – my hands complain so when I have to write. The arthritis is always bad in the winter.'

'If you like, you dictate and I'll write,' said Stella. 'I can bring the laptop down to the snooker room – there's a small table there. I put the printer in the car in case I needed it, so there's no problem.'

'That would be wonderful,' said Emily. 'If you will excuse us, George?'

George reached for the final piece of toast and shrugged. 'I'll await developments,' he said. 'I'll be in the music room,' he added as an afterthought. 'If what you say is true, I'll need to think things through.'

Emily spent the next hour thinking, dictating and refining the details of her story. She was thankful for Stella's listening ear and helpful questions; somehow the horror of it all faded as the words settled on the page. It seemed to give her permission to forget, to relax her hold, knowing that she could always return to what Stella called 'the hard copy' whenever she needed to.

'Thanks, Stella, I really feel better for that. I'll leave you to print it whenever you have time and then Chief Inspector Drummond can have it.' As the grandfather clock in the hall chimed 10.30, Emily automatically glanced at her watch. 'I can't believe it's so early, it feels like lunchtime to me.'

Stella smiled. 'It looks like a grim day ahead. Emily, please do stay here. I know the family is antagonistic at the moment, but I think they are going to need both of us, in one way or another, when the news finally breaks. You know you're welcome, and you need to be in the warm.'

'Thanks, Stella. I think I will; I personally feel better with people around me after this morning's shock, and besides, this place is big enough to be able to find a bolthole if I need it.'

They went straight to the drawing room, where Archie was pacing backwards and forwards, anxiously looking out of the window into the garden. Clara was standing, leaning folded arms on the back of one of the armchairs, gazing towards the driveway. Did they still expect James to lurch towards them, with some story that he had been hiding in the grounds of the golf course, or the pub up the road? Emily hoped not.

Philip was there too, apparently oblivious to all around, sitting in an ancient armchair, sketching on a large pad, while at the other end of the room Samantha sat on the further settee, hugging a cushion and keeping her back to them. Fin lay at her feet.

Stella walked slowly over to Clara. 'I presume there's no news?' she said quietly. Clara shook her head. 'We've searched everywhere; I just don't understand.'

Emily moved over to her favourite armchair near the piano, aware of hostility but determined to ignore it with quiet dignity.

There was an awkward silence and then all eyes turned to the door as Cassidy entered. She looked a little better, and had put on blue jeans and a thick white jumper. She stared vaguely at the assembled company and then at the mobile in her hand, as it played some jolly tune Emily did not recognise.

'Business matters,' Cassidy said briefly, 'they follow you everywhere.' She read the message on the screen and then put the phone in her pocket.

Clara went over to her. 'I'm sorry about what I said last night,' she said.

'It's all right, Clara. You were understandably upset.' Cassidy raised her hand as if to forbid any further mention of the outburst, and went to sit on a chair near Philip. She shivered. 'I don't seem to be able to get warm. This is such a barn of a place and there's no hot water.'

Samantha turned and glanced over the back of the settee, looking almost relieved at the distraction. 'I was frozen last night; it felt as if someone had left a window open. This morning my bath was tepid.'

Stella shuffled uncomfortably. 'I'm so sorry,' she said. 'We'd originally planned to use the en suite showers in the stables, before the electricians let us down. Perhaps it would help to have coffee early? Or... there is one other, rather unusual solution; the swimming pool has four new showers which are working, or you could use the pool itself. Ian had special orders to have it ready for this morning, I know.'

Cassidy seemed to revive a little. 'I would love a shower... I think that would help.' She shivered again.

'I'll come with you,' said Samantha, brightening up and relinquishing the cushion. 'A swim sounds really good and we can have coffee afterwards. Anyone else coming?'

Clara stood in front of Cassidy and, offering both hands, helped her out of the chair, while Philip crumpled up his picture and threw it in the direction of the wastepaper basket. He stood slowly and stretched his back, yawning. 'It's something to do,' he said listlessly, 'Come on, Archie.'

'We'll let you know as soon as Edward gets back,' Stella reassured the group gently. 'Now, if you'd like to get what you need, I'll collect the keys from the pantry and meet you by the door to the pool area.'

Emily hesitated before joining the family; they had been politely hostile, but then perhaps a little air would do her good – and she badly wanted to know what James had done to her beloved walled garden. She found the group with Stella, who was about to unlock the battered black gate. Fin pattered past them into the walled garden, the family followed and Emily brought up the rear.

It was worse than she had feared: a few skeletal plants were clinging to the brick walls which surrounded a sea of mud. The two branches of a wide, stone-paved path led to the twin doors at either end of a large glass conservatory-type building, whose walls were opaque with steam. The glass structure appeared to be attached to the wall of the old dairy by a brick-built extension.

Emily shuddered – what an insensitive man! A brief flashback to the sight of his body that morning checked her invective feelings, but she still felt alienated in this war-torn piece of ground, with a few odd rose bushes leaning at rakish angles, giving just the merest hope of beauty in the future.

Fin busied herself padding through the mud, nose down, ears becoming increasingly glutinous, checking every area of the garden she had once known. Emily, watching her, thought gloomily of an enforced bath in cold water in the Lodge, and the effort it would be to lift her dog and to towel her down thoroughly afterwards. Suddenly Emily found herself at the fork in the path and turned to follow the others through the right-hand doorway into the brick extension.

Wiping her feet thoroughly, and shutting Fin out, Emily stepped over the threshold and found herself in an airy lobby. On her left, beyond glass doors, was the turquoise-blue tiled pool, its water still and glassy. On her right Stella, facing the pool, was standing in front of the doors of what Emily guessed was a large cupboard. She was holding up a small bunch of keys.

'These,' she said, 'unlock the doors to the changing rooms, toilets and showers: men's on your left, women's on the right. On the walls on either side of me are the drinks and snacks machines. And you'll need a couple of these…' She turned and unlocked the door behind her. Emily caught a glimpse of chlorine containers, garden chairs and refills for the machines, as Stella pulled a couple of black sacks out of the cupboard and inserted them into the flip bins, before switching the drinks machine on. She handed the keys to Clara, who happened to be nearest. 'Put these on the small table just inside the entrance door for Ian to collect later, when he cleans the pool. What time shall I tell him you'll be finished?'

Cassidy glanced at her watch. 'I think 40 minutes would be plenty of time; we need to be back in the mansion when Edward returns. Surely he can't be much longer?'

As the family disappeared to change, Emily and Stella removed their shoes and went through the glass doors to the shallow end of the pool area. Stella wheeled one or two plastic loungers into a more tidy position and lifted a garden chair onto the low white platform by the long wall. 'Just in case they want someone to act as lifeguard,' she explained, 'but I doubt they will.' Briefly she perched on the edge of the platform, and looked around approvingly.

'It was a good idea to suggest coming here,' Emily said. 'They need to be warm and occupied, and they're not going to behave in a frivolous kind of way.' She looked round, taking in the size of the pool area for the first time. 'He'd thought of everything, hadn't he?'

Stella glanced at her friend. 'Let's say he was quite demanding. Even so, I'm sorry the garden isn't finished,' she said, touching Emily briefly on the arm. 'James had intended to get at least the borders restored, and the little patch of grass with the fountain put back...'

Emily raised her hand to stop the flow of words; she couldn't bear to hear any more. Stella led Emily to the far end of the pool. 'Let's leave them to it. There's not much more I can do here,' she said.

At that moment Archie and Philip appeared, striding down the gentle slope into the pool. Soon their heads were under water and they came up spluttering and smoothing their hair down.

Samantha came next, almost pulling Cassidy by the arm, and Clara soon after. Cassidy wrested her arm away from Samantha. 'Really, Samantha, a shower would have been quite enough to warm me up, but now you've got me here, I'll get some lengths in.'

She walked along the side of the pool, her pale-blue costume contrasting with her tanned skin, her hair tied neatly back. She went straight to the low diving board at the deep end, close to Stella and Emily. She paused, bounced slightly and executed a perfect curve, as she entered the water with barely a ripple. 'Beautiful!' exclaimed Emily.

As the two friends opened the door to go, the round figure of Clara and the slim, tall figure of Samantha were making their way into the water and Cassidy was completing a length of effortless front crawl. She paused with her hand on the side of the pool, encouraging the two girls to join her. 'It's beautifully warm!' she called.

As they set off, Clara with a reasonable crawl, Samantha with backstroke, Stella and Emily collected the dog, left the old garden and walked together to the back door of the mansion. There they parted, Stella to see Ian, and Emily to find the scullery, where, with Grace's permission, she heaved the mud-clogged Fin into some welcome warm water in the large sink.

It was almost 11.30 when Emily returned to the sitting room. The swimmers had clearly finished early. Heads looked up and turned quickly away; no one spoke. The trolley, its top shelf spattered with coffee, was in its usual corner, and empty coffee cups were scattered across the room on low tables and on the mantelpiece, where James' crystal gift to Cassidy had been placed the evening before. Emily glanced at the pig balanced on its base, and wished she had thought to remove it to somewhere less obvious.

It would seem that Grace had been to the local wholesalers and had brought several magazines back with her. Samantha and Clara were occupied with a couple, Cassidy was sitting near the fireplace, staring into space, while Philip had resumed his attempts at sketching. Archie was once more standing looking out of the window.

Emily went across the room to join Stella, who was reading an article in the local Sussex magazine, while Archie moved closer to the window and craned his neck. 'A small blue car's just coming through the gates,' he reported.

'That's Martin's,' Stella said. She stood up. 'Philip, would you mind if I round everyone up? I think we would all like to know, but if you would prefer that the family heard first, I quite understand.'

Philip shrugged his shoulders and looked at his sketch with his head on one side. 'Whatever,' he said shortly. 'Might as well get it all over in one go.'

'Philip, what a thing to say!' Samantha lifted her eyes from her magazine. Her husband ignored her.

Stella looked at Emily. 'Would you mind finding George?' she asked. 'I expect he'll still be in the music room. I'll tell the kitchen and ring through to Ian in the gym.'

By the time Emily returned with George, everyone had gathered in the drawing room. Clara had moved to sit with her arm round Cassidy on one of the settees. Ian was perched on a chair right at the back of the room, on his own. The only sound was the slight scratching of Philip's pencil on his pad, but even that stopped when the door opened.

Edward stood there, with Martin behind him. His face looked grey and much older; he lifted his head with an effort as he looked at the expectant faces. 'It's him,' he said with scant regard for grammar.

Stella turned slightly to face Edward. 'I'm so sorry,' she said.

Edward chose not to respond, but looked straight at Emily. 'I want to apologise to you, Dame Emily,' he said, his voice quavering slightly. 'Earlier today I said some regrettable things, but I've discovered from the police just what an important part you played this morning, and I'm grateful.'

His audience looked puzzled. Edward glanced round at them.

'This morning, Dame Emily was walking on the cliffs and saw James' body in the water. She alerted not only the police, but the coastguards. Their rescue team was able to reach James before high tide, and before a large wave from a local ferry could dislodge him and sweep him out to sea. One of the coastguards was caught by the swell and is now in hospital with a broken leg – he could have lost his life. In this terrible business people did what they could.' He ran his fingers through his hair before sitting rather suddenly on the nearest armchair.

Meanwhile Martin moved from the doorway to the side of the piano, and stood with his back to the wall. He looked pale and tired, as if the strain of supporting Edward and losing his employer so suddenly had taken a lot out of him.

There was a brief, profound silence broken by a sob from Cassidy, and then the questions began. Had James walked into the sea and kept on walking? Had he jumped? When had it all happened? Why had it happened? Emily looked round the room as she listened to Edward's oft-repeated answer, 'I don't know.' But she guessed that in all their minds must be the fear that one, or all of them, had driven James to a fearful and literal edge. The unspoken question, 'Was it me?' would remain unspoken.

A gloom settled on the room. Cassidy was shaking from head to foot. She had moved away from Clara, her body slumped against the arm of the settee and her head buried in the crook of her arm. In every face disbelief was being replaced by numbing shock. Grace nudged Jayne and nodded her head towards the door, but before they could leave, Archie spoke.

'What now?' he said to the gathered company. 'And it's no good frowning at me. Where do we go from here?'

Eyes turned first to Cassidy and then to Edward.

'We need to think about a funeral,' he said slowly.

'A funeral?' Cassidy suddenly sat up. 'A funeral?' Her hands twisted together, elegant fingers constantly on the move. 'I've never been to a funeral – I don't want anything to do with it.' With sudden decisiveness she said, 'Perhaps you would make the arrangements, Philip?'

Philip's eyes widened in horror. 'Why me?'

'Because you're the elder,' Clara said, the relief in her voice showing a little too much.

Edward looked from Philip to Cassidy with a mixture of disbelief and sympathy. He paused and, putting his shoulders back, said, 'I would be prepared to do that if you all want me to.'

Nods and murmured agreement came from different areas of the room. 'If you need any help,' said Emily, 'I know the local vicar well. He's a very approachable man and will help you sort out either a burial or a cremation. You may prefer to make arrangements in Yorkshire, of course.'

'Thanks,' said Edward. 'I don't know what James would have wanted, do you, Cassi?' He obviously took the horror on Cassidy's face to be a 'no' and continued. 'I suppose we need to look at his will to see if he made any provisions for a funeral, and if he left any instructions. Whether it's in storage with everything else, I don't know. I expect the solicitors in Huddersfield have a copy. What should we do, George?'

George, dwarfed by the large armchair in which he sat, leaned forward and steepled his fingers. 'As it happens,' he said, 'I have his will with me. I would have needed to take certain particulars from it to put in the new will he was proposing to make. I can look at it and let you know.'

Emily looked at him sharply. So that was what he'd been doing in the music room while waiting for James. Going through the will. Nobody would know that, of course, so he could be economical with the truth. It was certainly a good thing that he had the will with him, but what would it contain? She doubted the family would mind whether James had opted for burial or cremation, but his legacies could arouse considerable emotion. Pandora's box had nothing on this.

George looked round the room and adopted a kindlier tone. 'May I suggest that you leave the reading of the will until later this afternoon? I think people need time to absorb what has happened.'

Edward nodded. 'Yes, that will be fine,' he said, glancing at Cassidy's pale face. She nodded slightly. 'I think we all need some space now.'

'If I could interrupt,' Martin stepped forward from where he'd been leaning against the wall. 'I'd like to say how shocked I am, and to express my deep sympathy to the whole family, and especially to Cassidy.'

There were nods of sympathy from Grace and Jayne, a murmured 'yes, indeed' from George, and 'I'm so sorry' from Stella. Emily found to her amazement that she could say nothing. The enormity of the distress and overwhelming nature of the changes that this would bring the family made her sick at heart.

'Thank you, Martin,' said Edward. 'This will have been a great shock to you, too. You've worked closely with James for so many years, and you were a great support this morning. Now there is just one other matter,' he continued. 'I've been told that the police will be here later in the day to take statements. They will want to know about James' frame of mind last night, and when each of you saw him last. There will have to be a post-mortem and...' he paused and added more gently, 'they have to consider the possibility that there may have been someone on the cliffs who helped him to his end. Part of the cliff has been taped off and there were white-coated police on their knees doing a fingertip search when we came back just now.' Without waiting for a reaction to his words, he turned briskly to Grace. 'Mrs Summerfield, what time shall we have lunch? I know some won't feel like food, but others will.'

Grace glanced at the clock on the mantelpiece which showed it was midday. 'I think we can manage 12.45, sir. The jacket potatoes will be ready by then and it doesn't take long to prepare the different fillings. The soup will be quick to heat and the pudding is almost ready to go in the oven.'

Edward looked round the room and gained a few nodded assents. 'We meet at 12.45 in the dining room,' he said.

As Grace and Jayne left the room, Stella began to collect the dirty mugs. Cassidy, picking up the plate of remaining biscuits from a table with one hand, reached for a couple of mugs on the mantelpiece with the other. Emily looked up to see the biscuits begin their slide towards the floor, and Cassidy, as she turned to glance at the crooked angle of the plate, with her other hand misjudged the position of the mugs, and caught the back end of the crystal pig. The pig, knocked from its base, began a slow-motion slide towards the edge of the mantelpiece; once there it half-somersaulted, with very little grace, and fell heavily onto the tiled hearth below. Hearing the crash, Cassidy gave a little cry, dropped the biscuit plate and ran from the room.

In silence everyone moved to look at the scattered remains of the crystal body, while the head of the pig, its grin intact, returned their gaze, sightlessly staring back at its horrified audience.

Chapter 13

After an emotionally charged morning, Emily was conscious of the need to be out in the fresh air. She decided to break the habit of a lifetime and take Finlandia out for a walk before lunch rather than after it. Once round the front lawn would do.

She wondered how things would turn out in the afternoon. She wanted to find out who owned the mansion now, and who therefore was responsible for the safekeeping of her special belongings before they went to auction and, more worryingly, with whom she would have to negotiate. For the twentieth time she wondered how she had ever got mixed up with this family.

As she was about to go out of the front door, Clara emerged from the drawing room and came to pat the dog. To Emily's surprise she asked to go outside with her. They walked in silence for some time, but halfway down the drive, Clara turned to Emily and asked, 'Will you show me where you found Dad?'

Emily was caught off guard. Startled, she said, 'Are you sure?'

They walked together, heads down against the biting east wind, across the road to the place on the Drift where Emily had first spotted James. Emily was relieved to see that the police had finished their search of the clifftop. They were grouped round a police van while one of their number rolled up the blue and white tape. As she watched, a member of the public in a light-brown jacket was turning away from them and was making her way down towards a red car parked at the bottom of the Heath.

Under the pallid sky, with its grey and white clouds casting long shadows, the tide was beginning its return journey, unhurriedly stalking up the beach with a deceptive innocence.

They watched the grey-blue sea, intent on reaching the pebbled foreshore, steadily swallowing the wide expanse of sand. The crashing breakers of early morning were replaced by medium-sized waves, spreading and retracting their tentacles, lapping round the broken body of a seagull as it lay lifeless and forlorn. The smell of seaweed wafted up to them. It looked a bleak and intensely lonely place.

They stood in silence as Emily gently pointed out the place at the base of the cliff opposite, where the retreating tide had left exposed the rock falls and the council's concrete blocks. Emily knew that low tide had been in the early hours of the morning, and it seemed fortuitous that James had not fallen straight onto the rocks, but had landed in the deep pool between the two landslips, and his clothing caught on some jagged object under the water. That would explain why the body had not been dragged out to sea. Again she wondered at the remarkable rescue by the coastguards.

Tears streamed down Clara's face. 'It's horrid, horrid,' she sobbed as Emily put an arm round her shoulders. Emily felt for her, just a young girl really, setting out on married life, probably wanting a family. Had she hoped that in retirement James might find the time (and money) to guide and encourage his daughter in her plans for the future? Now Clara found herself fatherless. Emily sighed; she doubted whether James would ever have displayed any paternal instincts.

'Clara, we don't know what happened,' she said, desperately clutching at straws. 'Perhaps your father walked round to the cliff base from the beach and, overcome by drink, he slipped and got caught by the tide; perhaps he walked too close to the cliff edge and stumbled, or had a heart attack, and fell. If it happened in any of those ways he would have known nothing at all; but it is certain that he doesn't have to live with terrible injuries. I know it's no comfort now, but hang on to that, and don't let your imagination run away with ideas that just may not be true. Nothing can hurt him now.'

Clara wiped away her tears and sighed as they turned to go back. Emily called Fin, shortened her lead and thought that her favourite clifftop walk would never be the same.

'If only I hadn't got so upset last night,' Clara said, wrapping her scarf more tightly round her. Emily said nothing, giving the girl time to think. They crossed the road together, scaring away a single magpie as it attempted to snatch a piece of flattened carrion before it flew off.

Clara was startled by the flapping wings. 'One for sorrow,' she said, then, 'Oh! I didn't think; we used to say it as children.' The tears began to flow again.

Emily struggled to find some kind of reassurance. 'I don't think men realise how much young girls worry about their weight and appearance,' she said at last, thinking of the previous night's conversations. 'I suspect your father was a very busy man and didn't realise how much you struggled.'

Clara looked at her and then at the ground. 'I've never told anyone this,' she said hesitantly, 'but I think it was my fault my parents split up. I just got in the way, or was bad, or something.'

She glanced quickly at Emily's face and Emily made sure that she remained calm and thoughtful. She made no effort to comfort the girl or deny what she had said. She would come at it from a different angle.

'Clara, you're an adult now. Then you thought as a child. Tell me, if your husband worked long hours and you missed him dreadfully, and you couldn't talk to him about problems because he was tired and hungry when he got in – can you imagine what it would be like?'

Clara made a face. 'I did have a really bad argument with Archie one night. It was awful and we said some horrid things to each other. He'd had to take the recovery vehicle out very late at night. It took him ages to get the stranded woman and her car to her home. I remember thinking how awful it would be to have a husband who was always out late or who was having an affair. Archie needs his sleep. He was crotchety for days, and I was really miserable.'

'Then,' said Emily gently, 'keep that feeling in mind and add into the mix: financial worries, elderly relations and two children to feed and clothe. There's plenty for adults to worry about, as you know; and they often think they keep it all from the children, but the strained atmosphere in the home always filters through to them. From what your uncle said last night it sounds as though your father was a workaholic. He probably didn't see much of your mother, and then Cassidy came on the scene.'

'So,' said Clara slowly, 'I didn't cause my mother to be ill, or them to break up? Dad was buried in his work and distracted by Cassidy, so he didn't give Mum the support that she needed to run the home. Her batteries sort of ran down and she didn't know how to recharge them, so she ran out of the energy she needed for me, even though she loved me really. And Dad was so taken up with Cassi, he never thought that I needed his approval. I didn't cause the break-up, I was just caught in the middle.' Clara stood still halfway down the drive and took a deep breath. 'I never looked at it like that.'

Emily patted her on her shoulder. 'Parents love their children, but they forget that the child needs to have the reassurance of hearing or seeing that love in action, whether it's shown in caring discipline or having fun times together. Just feeling love isn't the same as loving.

'And as for your looks, you don't need to be concerned about those,' said Emily with a smile. 'Your husband obviously loves you for the person you are, and you're lucky to have him. He's quite the knight in shining armour.'

Clara smiled faintly and rubbed her cheek roughly with the back of her hand. 'He's good to me. Sometimes we fall out – but we make up. Now it's too late to make up with Dad.'

Emily remained silent. She had always been fiercely against platitudes, and secretly agreed with Clara that it was indeed too late – although she was sure it was never too late to confess and be forgiven by the Almighty – but it didn't seem appropriate to say so at that moment. On an uncharacteristic impulse, she took a few steps across the lawn and picked a daffodil, still in bud.

'Ask Grace for a small vase,' she said, 'and watch the petals unfold. I think you'll be surprised by the colour of its trumpet.'

Clara murmured a thank you and they continued towards the back of the mansion. It was as they rounded the corner by the stables that they almost bumped into a young woman hurrying towards the front gate. She was wearing a sheepskin body warmer over a thick olive-green jumper, with beige trousers and long boots, and her long brown hair flowed below her shoulders. Her head was down and her hands busy with a mobile phone; she dodged past them with a quick 'Sorry!' and was gone.

Clara and Emily looked at the departing figure and then at each other.

'Who was that?' Clara asked.

Emily looked puzzled. 'Her face was vaguely familiar. I think I may have known her as a child, but I can't think for the life of me who she is. Now, if you don't mind, I'll just drop in and see Ian in the gym. I'll see you at lunch.'

Emily paused in the doorway of the gym and took time to gaze around at the old coach house. Where the old farm carts had rested since her childhood was a spotlessly clean and shining floor, the walls were decorated with fitness posters and there were various mechanical contraptions lined up along each side of the room. She gazed in amazement at the technology which was designed to strengthen and tone innumerable muscles in the human body. She was glad that her legs were still capable of going on a twice daily walk and keeping her fit by more 'normal' means.

'Hello, Dame Emily, can I help you?' Ian emerged from a side room and came to stand next to her. 'I was just about to lock up before lunch,' he said by way of explanation.

'I'm afraid I'm not looking for a "personal package" or whatever it is you offer,' Emily said.

Ian smiled. 'I could offer you something gentle. A pleasant alternative to the cold, wet clifftop.'

Emily shook her head and laughed. 'You're very persuasive, but no thank you.'

Ian sighed. 'I've just been talking to a local student who wanted one of our packages – the "work out and swim" one,' he said. 'She made enquiries early this morning and came to the pool just now to sign on the dotted line. I had to put it all on hold.'

'Oh,' said Emily. 'Clara and I almost bumped into a girl just before I came in here. I thought I recognised her. What was her name?'

Ian looked vague. 'Mandi something, I think. Yes, Mandi Jones.'

'Mandi Jones,' repeated Emily, gazing into space. 'That's right! I used to teach her the piano – years ago. We abandoned the attempt by mutual consent! Her parents run the Fox and Pheasant in the village. Pretty girl, but ever since she was tiny insisted on writing her name with an "i" at the end, and instead of dotting it added some kind of halo! She was quite fun as a small child. Loved inventing stories. I wonder what she does now?'

Ian shrugged. 'I don't suppose we'll see her here after this,' he said gloomily, staring around the empty gym. 'What do you think will happen, Dame Emily? It's taken weeks to set all this up. I suppose I shall lose my job.'

Emily sighed sympathetically. 'It's going to be a tough time for everyone,' she said. 'We'll have to see what happens this afternoon when the will is read.'

Ian grimaced. 'It's so embarrassing; I'm just an outsider caught up in a family tragedy – I need to know, but I just can't bring myself to ask whether I'm going to be paid or not.'

Emily leaned against one of the walking machines. 'It's the same for Stella and Martin,' she said. 'I know how you feel. I am an outsider too, and I may be talking out of turn, but I can only suggest that you join us for meals when you are here, and begin to feel part of the organisation, although it may not be for long. It really will depend on whether the place is inherited by Cassidy, or whether it is split between the whole family. None of them seems to be keen on the idea of a hotel.'

She paused and in the silence she glanced sideways at Ian's face. Could she detect tears in his eyes? She remembered the boyish enthusiasm with which he had spoken at dinner last night. This project was 'his baby' – perhaps his first – and suddenly its demise seemed imminent.

'Let's go to lunch,' she said brightly, consulting her watch. 'Food is a great help on occasions like this.'

Lunch was a sombre affair. Although the family largely ignored her, Emily was thankful that the atmosphere had become less frosty since Edward's brief speech and her walk with Clara.

Once everyone had gathered round the lunch table in their allotted places, Emily allowed her mind and eyes to wander over the assembled company. She was seated, as before, in the single chair facing the empty one at the head of the table, which no one had thought to remove. Perhaps they preferred not to face reality.

The food was distributed quickly. Cassidy kept her eyes on her plate as she picked at her meal, Samantha gave herself a second helping, while Philip idly chased a piece of lettuce leaf round his plate with a fork. Archie's appetite was unaffected, and even Clara was making an effort. Emily leaned towards Stella. 'Whose idea was the pizza?' she enquired with a slight smile.

'Samantha's.' Stella grinned. 'James had pork pie and chips on the menu. Early this morning I asked for jacket potatoes with toppings instead, as both Philip and Samantha are veggies, then she requested pizza and I decided to splash out! I'm afraid I rang and ordered the pizzas just half an hour ago; I couldn't ask Grace to make them at such short notice. I hope the funds run to it,' she added in a whisper.

Emily glanced across at George who had opted for the cheese and beans with his jacket. 'Money is going to be quite a problem, if all James' assets are frozen.'

Stella looked horrified. 'I had already thought that I would lose my job, but to be unpaid for the last month as well…'

Emily made a face. 'You won't be the only one,' she said quietly, glancing at Ian and Martin. 'It's quite a mess.'

At the end of the meal, Edward rose to his feet. He shuffled awkwardly, the words coming out like some over-rehearsed speech. 'I've had a phone call from the police. They won't be able to come until later – "unavoidably delayed" was the phrase DCI Drummond used – so we can forget them for the time being. I have talked to Cassi and to George. We know that it is not normal to have the formal reading of a will so soon after a death, but we are aware that you all want to know how things stand. The children and their spouses have jobs to return to on Tuesday, Cassi has to consider her responsibilities overseas, my school term starts in just over a week, and those of you who have been employed to work here need to know who is now responsible for the proposed hotel. Bearing all this in mind, and with Cassi's permission, we shall have coffee in the drawing room and then move to the music room. It's the semicircular room at the far end of the passage, if you haven't found it yet – the one that looks like a castle turret on the outside.

'Every one of you here is invited to be present for what I am assured will be a very short reading of the will. However, we would be grateful if you would keep the information confidential. You will obviously have questions about your own situations, but I would ask you to refrain from asking them just yet; the family needs time to grieve and to plan the funeral. Thank you.'

There was a general scraping of chairs and Stella slipped out to make sure that Grace and Jayne in the kitchen were aware of what was happening. In 20 minutes the dirty coffee cups had been left in the drawing room and Stella and Martin had prepared the music room, bringing some of the dining room chairs to supplement the settees and armchairs. They formed a wide semicircle facing George, who sat behind a large mahogany desk. The family settled in the comfortable chairs, leaving the staff and Emily to take the rest.

As Emily paused in the music room doorway she felt Stella's hand on her arm and caught her hurried whisper. 'Grace says it's on the local radio. Breaking news. Unconfirmed that the new owner of Seascape has been found in the sea…'

Emily looked at Stella, her eyes wide with horror. How had the news got out? Surely not the police? An army of journalists would not be welcome. How much worse could the situation get? Emily took a deep breath. She must keep her emotions under control, find a chair and concentrate on the matter in hand.

From her vantage point near George's desk, Emily could see everyone in the room. The staff, anxious and slightly embarrassed by the whole situation, the family unsettled, looking hopeful and uncertain by turns, husbands and wives exchanging glances, Cassi sombre-faced and passive. It was strange what inheritance did to families. Would James have divided his wealth fairly? From the little Emily knew of him, she couldn't be sure, and by the restlessness of the family they were decidedly uncertain too.

As everyone settled down, Edward stood briefly. 'I've asked George to cut out the legal jargon where possible; I hope that's all right?' He received a few acquiescent nods and sat down.

As everyone watched, George metamorphosed into the stereotypical solicitor – perhaps it was a characteristic of the breed when faced with the reading of a will, mused Emily. He coughed, tried clearing his throat and took a sip of water from the glass on the table. He held a single piece of paper and looked solemnly at the company over the dark rims of his glasses. Stillness filled the room. George read ponderously from the paper:

"'I, James Alistair Wedderburn of 47 Highgrove Gardens, Huddersfield, being of sound mind etc., etc., hereby bequeath my present residence and any other residences and property that I possess, the contents of the same and the whole of my estate to my brother Edward, who has been the only member of my family to be concerned for my welfare.'"

George returned the paper to the table and looked over his glasses once more at the family. Not one muscle moved, not one eye flickered and there was a profound and horrified silence.

'Well, finish it off!' Philip said. 'Don't keep us waiting.'

'There is no more,' said George quietly.

'Uncle Edward!' came Archie's protest. 'Uncle Edward gets it all? What about his children? What about his wife?'

Every head in the room turned to look at the new heir to Seascape House. Edward seemed paralysed. His mouth was open, his eyes, which looked both startled and frightened, were fixed on George.

'What's all this about, Uncle Ed?' demanded Archie. 'You've known all the time and you've said nothing!'

'How could you, Uncle Ed?' Clara's eyes blazed. 'You hated him, you said so!'

Edward, seated in an armchair near the door, on the other side of George, blinked. He had the look of a desperate, hunted beast, trapped by wolves. His hands gripped the arms of the chair, knuckles white. He glanced desperately at George who remained impassive, then he turned to face the whole company. 'I'm sorry. I didn't know, I really didn't,' he stammered.

The group sat, stony-faced, silent, waiting.

Edward protested again, 'Honestly, I…'

At last George took pity on him. 'To my knowledge, no one knew,' the solicitor said. 'James did not even want to keep a copy of this will himself. It has remained in our office ever since he signed it.'

'But what about Cassi?' repeated Archie.

George lifted his shoulders and let them drop. He glanced at Edward, who ran his hand through his limp hair and looked around helplessly, as if hoping for someone to jump up, wave some new and more rational will, and assure them all that this was some kind of joke. No one waved anything.

In the pause Philip leaned across Stella, who was next to him, and glared at his wife who sat on her other side. 'You stupid, stupid woman!' he said, slamming his hand down on the arm of the settee, making the dust rise. 'Now do you see I was right all along?'

Samantha gave a strangled cry, got up and ran from the room. As the rushing footsteps faded, Emily glanced at Philip. He was bent over, fiddling with his shoelaces. What was this argument that was forcing the pair apart so conclusively? Emily worried for them.

'What did that last bit mean?' Clara's voice cut across the awkward silence. 'Something about being the only one concerned for his welfare.'

George looked at Edward and raised his eyebrows. Edward took a deep breath as if desperate for more oxygen and shook his head.

Emily felt they were getting nowhere. 'George, what was the date of the will?' she asked. She felt the tension mount in the room. Nevertheless, interested eyes turned back to George, who glanced down at the paper.

'4th April 2006,' he replied.

Edward frowned, obviously thinking hard. 'Was he ill about then?' he asked the room in general.

'Yes, he was.' All heads swivelled to look at Martin. 'I'd been working for James for a year or so. He suddenly felt unwell one afternoon and was rushed to hospital. He asked me to contact the family and his solicitor.'

George's face suddenly cleared. 'I remember. He had a heart problem. He was terrified he wouldn't come through the operation and his previous will was very out of date – made soon after he married his first wife and before the children were born – so he asked me to draw up a new will to take into account his changed situation, and all his recently acquired shops and farms and so on. I'd forgotten until now. It was when I was sitting at his bedside just half an hour before the op that he said something to the effect of: "I asked all my family to come and see me and they didn't, only Edward. I shall leave him everything. There isn't time to make a complicated will now. I can always make another later, if I come through all this." But of course he never got round to making another. That was what he'd planned to do today.'

Cassidy sat up straight. 'I'd forgotten completely, it's so long ago. I was in Barbados when Martin rang me with the news – I would never have got back in time to see James before the op and it didn't sound serious. It was only a bypass.' She glanced across at Martin who nodded in agreement.

Clara frowned. 'But I must have been around. I'd have been 17 then.'

'I seem to remember leaving a message for you both,' Martin said, glancing at Philip, 'on the answerphone.'

Clara stared at him for a moment. 'I know,' she said, looking relieved. 'I was at my best friend Imogen's eighteenth birthday party. It was a Friday and I went straight from school and stayed the whole weekend, and then went to school from there on Monday morning. I found the message at teatime on Monday. I went to see Dad that night and by then he was sitting up in bed and seemed fine. Do you remember, Philip? You'd gone to Cornwall to stay with Sam. I suppose Martin didn't have the phone number there.'

Martin, tight-lipped, nodded his assent. 'I didn't know either of your plans. I thought at least one of you would be around to pick up the message, that you'd contact the other and both go to see your dad.'

Edward had listened in silence. 'Yes,' he said slowly, 'it's coming back to me now. I was in the middle of a drama lesson, when the school secretary came into the hall to tell me James had been admitted to hospital. It sounded urgent, so I rushed over after school, as soon as I could get away. I just took him some grapes and tried to reassure him. I think I had to get back for a school function in the evening, so I didn't stay long. I'm sure he didn't mention a will, though. This was several years before the trouble with Jonathan. I've not spoken to James since Jonathan died – not until this weekend.'

'I must have arrived after you'd left the hospital,' said George thoughtfully. 'I think James said you'd been, but it didn't mean much, as I didn't know you by sight then.'

'So that's it?' said Archie again. 'Uncle Ed gets the lot. Thanks, Dad-in-law. Thanks very much.' He stood and, deliberately knocking Edward's foot as he walked past, left the room, slamming the door.

Edward winced and, still clinging to the arms of the chair, looked at the family. 'I'm so sorry,' he said. 'Really I am, I had no idea; no idea at all.'

Chapter 14

As Emily sat in the warmth of the drawing room that afternoon, with Finlandia at her feet, she could feel her eyelids drooping. The house was totally silent following the aftermath of the new bombshell which had rocked and blown apart a whole family.

Reaction to the unreality of the situation came in different forms: Archie had retired to the gym, Clara had offered to go to the kitchen and roll out pastry for Mrs Summerfield, and Samantha had slipped away on her own.

Before she had left the music room, Emily heard Ian saying that he would use the time before the police came to finish cleaning the pool area and go for a workout in the gym. When Martin checked with Edward that it was all right for him to go to the off-licence for the purpose of topping up the drinks cabinet, nobody had wanted to stop him. Edward had remained with George, talking through the implications of the will, and as Emily went to the drawing room she found Cassidy sitting at the bottom of the stairs sending a text message. She said she was going to bed and would, no doubt, take refuge in another sleeping pill.

Emily found the drawing room empty, except for Philip, who was sitting by one of the windows sketching the cedar tree in the front garden, and Stella who was sitting in an armchair near the bookcase in the far corner of the room. The book she had taken so recently from the shelf remained closed in her lap, her head had fallen forward and her mouth was slightly open. Emily smiled to herself, eased her feet onto a footstool and allowed unconsciousness to drift over her.

She was woken by quiet, insistent voices. Instinctively she kept her eyes closed, but was unable to shut out the sound. Samantha had obviously come to find Philip.

'Well, did you make that phone call?' Philip demanded in a loud whisper.

'Yes.' Samantha's voice was subdued, with a hint of tearfulness.

'Did you speak to the estate agent?'

'Yes.'

'Any problems?'

'No. He was really understanding. He'd still got the details of someone else who was interested.'

'You're a fool, Samantha. I don't know how you could be so stupid.'

'I did it for you, for us. I thought when you saw the pictures of the place you would love it.'

'You nearly threw away the little money we do have. And now Dad... and the will...' Philip hissed the words.

Emily felt stiff. She longed to return her feet to floor level and didn't dare. Or perhaps she should – it might stop the conversation from getting even more heated. But then again it might prove she'd heard the beginning of it. She practised her even breathing and tried to ignore the pain in her hip.

'I'm sorry, I'm sorry, I'm sorry.' Samantha's whisper reached Emily's ears.

Philip snorted. 'So you should be. Don't ever do anything again without consulting me – and just so that you know, I'll sleep in the nurse's part of the nursery again tonight.'

Emily was aware of a muffled sob and then of heavy footsteps walking towards the door. The door shut with a loud click and Emily allowed herself the luxury of being woken up. She eased her feet from the footstool and sat up. She turned and looked across the room. Stella was still asleep and Samantha was mopping her eyes with a distinctly damp tissue.

Emily launched herself to her feet and walked across the room and sat on the other end of the settee where Samantha had curled into a ball. For a moment she said nothing. Samantha looked up and smiled weakly. 'I'm sorry,' she said.

Emily leaned across the gap between them and patted her arm. 'It's a day for tears,' she said. 'No one minds. You need to grieve.'

Samantha hung her head. 'It's not that,' she whispered. She looked up at Emily, who tilted her head slightly and raised her eyebrows.

'I've been such an idiot,' Samantha said quietly, looking towards the closed door. 'If I tell you, will you keep it to yourself?'

Emily glanced over the top of the settee at the still sleeping Stella. 'I can't guarantee...' she began.

'I'll stop if she wakes,' Samantha responded.

'So...?' Emily prompted.

'I did it for Philip,' she began and then stopped.

'What did you do?'

'A week ago I was delivering one of Philip's paintings to a customer. While she was writing out the cheque, she happened to mention the painting was to remind her of St Ives, as she was moving to be nearer her daughter and was selling the house. She showed me the whole place and I fell in love with it. It was old and quaint, with wonderful views out to sea, and the extension would make a perfect studio. There was even an extra bedroom, so we could have Dad to live with us. On the way home I called in at the estate agent's and got the details. I did a lot of sums while Philip was busy displaying his pictures in the shop for the Bank Holiday tourists, and I decided that, if we could let out Dad's flat over the café, and borrow money from Philip's dad, we might be able to afford it.'

A tear squeezed its way down the side of Samantha's nose as she continued. 'I couldn't bear to think that someone else would snap the house up this weekend while we're away, so I took the risk. I took some time off work and sorted it all out with the estate agent on Wednesday afternoon and made an offer.' She broke off and wiped away a stream of tears with her sleeve.

'I was sure Phil's dad would lend us the money, he's got – he had – so much. Then everything would be all right, and we could have a baby. And now…' she sniffed loudly, 'Philip's made me ring the estate agent to withdraw the offer, and he's furious that I did it all without asking him. Last night, when I told him what I had done, we had a terrible row, and he wouldn't even sleep in the same room.' Samantha broke down, hiding her head in the cushion she was clutching, and sobbing uncontrollably.

Emily waited till Samantha was a little quieter. 'And the baby?' she queried softly.

Samantha pushed her hair back from her face. 'How did you know? I was feeling sick this morning, but I didn't think anyone noticed. It could have been reaction to everything that went on last night. I've got the test with me, but I daren't use it.'

Emily glanced over the back of the settee. Stella had opened her eyes, quietly moving her shoulders. She looked at Emily who shook her head gently and indicated with her eyes the weeping Samantha. Stella gave an almost imperceptible nod and closed her eyes.

Emily turned back to Samantha and then felt in her cardigan pockets and pulled out a clean tissue. 'Have a good blow, dear,' she said, leaning forward and pressing it into Samantha's hand.

Samantha obeyed and gradually the sobs subsided. 'I'm sorry,' she said. 'I don't know why I should tell you all this.'

'Because it helps,' said Emily gently but firmly, and then, remembering that she had been 'asleep' when Philip was in the room, said, 'Now, tell me, have you rung the estate agent?'

'Yes.'

'Is there anything else to do?'

'I'd like to explain to the lady selling the house; she was so understanding, and really wanted us to have it.'

'Then,' said Emily, leaning back against the arm of the settee, 'that's next week's problem, and can be safely left. You've done all you can for today. It will take time, but I'm sure Philip will come to see that you wanted to be generous for his sake, but with everything that's happened, he can't see anything clearly at the moment.'

'It's just that I like to get things done and he's the passive one. And he feels everything so deeply. It's being artistic, I suppose. If he could only get out now and paint and be on his own it would help, but he can't in this weather.'

'Mmm... Now, let me suggest that you go and give your face a good wash, it always helps...' Emily paused. Had she just caught herself being motherly? Heaven forbid! She really mustn't get emotionally involved. 'Can you find something to occupy the time before tea?'

Samantha nodded. With difficulty she uncurled and put her long legs out straight in front of her. 'Thank you,' she said. 'You're right, it does help to talk, and yes, I think I might walk up the road to the village – Long Dean, isn't it? I could look at the church or something.'

She ran her splayed fingers through her hair and sighed as she got up. 'I'll see you at tea.'

As the door shut, Stella opened her eyes. 'What a mess,' she said quietly.

Emily sighed. 'It's just so dreadful for all of them.'

'How's Cassidy?' Stella asked, returning her book to the shelf.

'She was sitting at the bottom of the stairs when I came in here. She looked so young and so lost. She was doing something with her phone – said it was to do with business... Perhaps she was replying to an email. She really shouldn't have to bother with work at a time like this.'

'If that's what it was.'

'What do you mean?'

'Come on, Emily. She doesn't just look young, she is young. Well, compared with James, anyway. I wouldn't be surprised if she didn't have a man friend somewhere. Why does she fly off to Barbados and Greece so regularly? I don't want to besmirch her character, but she is attractive, and some bronzed Greek will have noticed that, you can be sure!'

'Stella!'

'Times have changed, Emily. It's not beyond the realms of possibility. Now I must go and check that everything is all right in the kitchen and there are no problems with the dinner menu. Grace and Jayne need to have some time off.'

Emily eased herself out of her chair. 'I really should be going to visit my sister in the nursing home,' she said wearily. 'Do you think it would be all right if I got back soon after tea? I suppose I have to be around in case the police come.'

'I'm sure it'll be all right,' said Stella. 'I'll tell them where you are.'

'Thanks,' said Emily. 'Oh, dear, I nearly forgot. I do need a quick chat with Martin before I go. Any idea where he might be?'

Stella glanced at her watch. 'Edward said he was going to the off-licence; if he's back he might be in the small room between the hall and the dining room, opposite the corridor down to the kitchen.'

'Ah,' said Emily. 'The butler's pantry – I'll try there first.'

Preparing to follow Stella out of the room, Emily paused by the baby grand piano. She lifted the lid and looked at the old familiar keys. Perhaps she'd better resist temptation. There was Martin to see, and Fin to shut in the Lodge before she could drive to West Dean, and she shouldn't be away too long. She took a deep breath and turned her mind to Martin. It didn't take long for the anger to rise within her. She had a strong feeling that Martin was partly, if not wholly, to blame for her present situation.

Deep down, she knew that insecurity was wearing away at the foundations of her capable lifestyle, but she buried her feelings under practical facts – these, she told herself, were the things that needed to be dealt with. Without knocking, she pushed open the door of the butler's pantry and marched in.

Martin was standing with his back to her, tapping his mobile phone fiercely. His ramrod back told Emily he was definitely not in a good mood. He swung round as the door opened, and frowned.

'Martin,' Dame Emily said brusquely, without an attempt at an apology. 'I need to talk to you.'

'Please excuse me a moment...' Martin continued tapping, pressed a final key, walked round behind an old oak table and sat on a swivel chair, straightening his tie. Emily couldn't be sure whether he felt like a schoolboy called to account for his misdemeanours, or an executive preparing to be suave when dealing with a slightly troublesome customer. He glanced at his watch. 'I have ten minutes,' he offered, getting to his feet again. 'Let me find you a chair.'

The walls of the old butler's pantry were lined with piles of neatly labelled boxes. With an effort, Martin removed a couple from a plastic chair and dropped them under a small table supporting a large photocopier. He then placed the chair by the table, opposite where he'd been sitting. 'Please sit down,' he said. 'I'm sorry it's so cramped. We had to bring all the office paperwork down with us, and there hasn't been time to set up a suitable room for it. Now I shall have to get it all ready to hand over to Edward, with the details of the unsold shops.'

Dame Emily glared. It was always difficult to be cross when the other party was polite; she'd often used the same tactic to her advantage and was suddenly aware that she had been caught by someone playing the same game. She needed to take back the initiative.

'Now,' she said, leaning her arms on the only empty space between the orderly piles of files on the table and clasping her hands together. 'I really need more information about the house James provided for me. I wrote and told him the roof had caught fire and heard nothing. Now I need to know the background to the arrangement we had, so that I can proceed.'

Martin closed the file in front of him and removed a piece of white fluff from his pristine navy jacket. 'This is quite a complicated matter,' he said slowly.

Probably playing for time, Emily thought. 'Then make it simple and straightforward,' she heard herself saying. 'You're an intelligent man, it can't be that hard. I'm about to go and see my sister and report the situation to her.' She stared at the top of his head, willing him to look up.

Martin loosened his tie and looked at her. 'Perhaps James wasn't quite straight with you,' he said.

'James?' repeated Emily. 'You were the only one I heard from!'

'Well, I was only following his instructions.'

Emily sniffed. She did not approve of those who tried to apportion blame where it was not due. 'Cut to the chase, man!'

Martin sighed. 'When James first considered buying the mansion, he planned living accommodation for the staff. I could have had part of the stable block or a flat above the old laundry. That would have been fine for the times I was on duty at the hotel, but I have a wife and two children and I felt it would be too restrictive for them. There was the possibility that my wife would be able to work in the laundry when the hotel was up and running, or possibly be in charge of the shop or adventure playground. However, if we had a house nearer Eastbourne, the children could finish their education in the town, be near their new friends, and we could drive here to work.'

Emily kept her eyes fixed on Martin's face. She began to suspect what Martin was about to say, and also started to realise why he did not wish to say it outright.

Martin took a deep breath and continued. 'James was kind enough to buy a house on a new estate. He had agreed that I could rent it from him – with a view to buying it, once I was able to sell my own place in Huddersfield. It was a sound investment for him and security for me. I could start to find schools for the children for the autumn term, while they finished the present academic year in familiar surroundings.'

Emily had little interest in Martin's domestic arrangements and was not prepared to hear more. She leaned forward in her chair. 'And this was the unfinished house you both dumped me in?' Emily's grammar went to the wind and her eyes flashed. Let him admit it and she'd pull him apart bone by bone…

Martin moved his shoulders restlessly. 'No, of course not. Well… that is to say…'

'That is to say what exactly?' Emily's eyes hardened and her voice resembled the sound of the old steel her father had used for sharpening the carving knife.

Martin winced visibly. 'We didn't know how long you would be detained in Australia. You didn't give us much notice of your return, so it wasn't easy to find a suitable place so quickly.' He added peevishly, 'And the house provided the ideal solution.'

'So you admit that although you were determined that I should not have use of the Lodge, you had put no effort into finding an alternative place in the months I was away,' Emily summarised. 'Not only did you not care that the house you offered me had stairs and I had been having my hip repaired, but you thought it was all right to dig the most enormous hole, covering the width of the back garden and nearly half its length. That was hardly safe, either for myself or Fin.'

Martin seemed to be getting more uneasy. Let him! Emily had a number of complaints up her sleeve yet.

'I explained,' Martin repeated. 'There just wasn't time to find alternative accommodation, and the arrangements had already been made for a company to install a swimming pool – just a small one.'

Emily snorted derisively. 'Well, I suppose I should be glad the roof caught fire. You can deal with the insurance! And should you think of evicting me from the Lodge here, I am writing to my solicitor explaining the situation fully and will be prepared to do so again, should the circumstances warrant it.'

Martin leaned across the table towards her, charming and reassuring. 'I am absolutely certain that no one will ask you to leave in the short term,' he said quietly, 'and I am sure Edward will help you to find a suitable alternative.' Emily stared at him; his words sounded as hollow as a drum, and as militant.

'Well, I shall expect you to sort it out with him,' she said firmly, with a sudden and unaccountable wave of sympathy for

Edward. 'And now, if you will excuse me, I need to report on all this to my sister. I am sure we shall speak again.'

She pushed her plastic chair back as she rose and it knocked noisily against a metal filing cabinet, just as some strange tune began playing on Martin's phone. She nodded briefly to Martin as he half-rose from his chair, and she walked from the room making sure the heels of her shoes made maximum impact with the floor.

Little upstart! Now that she knew what she thought were probably the correct facts, she had rather more leverage. How she would use it, though, she was not quite so sure.

However, her interview with Martin flew from her mind as she opened the front door of the mansion. She was suddenly confronted by four or five men and the young woman who had appeared earlier in the day. She blinked as cameras flashed and voices hurled questions at her.

'Can you confirm the news?'

'Dame Emily, can you tell us what's been happening here today?'

Emily raised her stick and advanced down the steps as Fin inspected the trousers and several pairs of shoes in front of her. Emily concentrated on the girl with the notebook.

'Mandi Jones!' she said loudly. 'You should know better! Now, if you will all excuse me, I have my elderly sister to visit. I don't have time for questions, and before you say any more, I have no comments either.'

The men stood their ground and Emily was very relieved to hear Martin's angry voice behind her. 'We have nothing to say to the press. Now, leave before I call the police. This is private property. And don't you dare hassle an elderly lady!'

Reluctantly the men parted and Emily walked between them, her stick still held at waist height, every inch the Dame.

After all that had happened, Emily arrived later than usual at the West Dean Nursing Home for Retired Gentlefolk – known locally as 'The Deanery' – and the postprandial game of bingo

152

was in full swing. No one as much as looked up as she entered the room. Fourteen elderly ladies and a couple of carers were bent over pieces of paper, markers at the ready, with forgotten, half-empty cups of coffee scattered on the occasional tables.

Emily walked over to her sister, but Margaret Hatherley-Browne was rather intent on winning a prize. Emily knew she could hardly do justice to the drama at Seascape House in a few snatched minutes between games. The bingo caller broke off to swallow a mouthful of tea.

Margaret glanced up. 'Move all right?' she enquired.

'Fine,' said Emily.

Margaret acknowledged the reception of this news with a nod and returned her gaze to the bingo sheet. She clearly had other priorities for that afternoon. Emily planted a perfunctory kiss on the top of her sister's head, received a wave in reply, and left them to it.

On her way out, Emily grabbed the opportunity to have a quick chat with the manager, who confirmed that the Parkinson's disease was not any more advanced and that Margaret was eating well. She explained to Emily that her sister's mobility scooter would have to remain at Seascape for a few more days, after which it could be stored in the newly redecorated Deanery garage. The Home would provide a wheelchair for going into the garden when the warmer weather came. The manager managed to combine sympathy, efficiency and a cheerfulness that put Emily at her ease every time they spoke. What a blessing Margaret had found such a lovely home from home. At the moment, Emily the Homeless rather envied her sister.

Twenty minutes later Emily parked at the Lodge, collected Fin and set out for the mansion. She let Fin off her lead and trusted the dog would not be in any danger from anyone driving around the mansion so late in the afternoon. Fin, nose down, tail flowing, and obviously delighted at her freedom, hurried around the lawn like an amateur historian let loose with a metal detector. She followed an erratic path and then crossed the drive and, opposite the curved outer wall of the music room, disappeared between the laurel and a rhododendron bush.

Emily reached the place where Fin had vanished. 'Come on,' she said. 'It's too cold to stand around. The fox has long since gone.' There was a rustling, a clink and Fin's head appeared. Emily frowned. The clink had sounded like Fin's name tag hitting something hard. She turned her stick and, using the handle, gently encouraged Fin across the flower bed to the path. As she did so, she moved one of the branches of the rhododendron. Lying underneath was a wine bottle. Emily held back the branch and stared at it. It was made of green glass with a drawing of some French chateau on its white label – just like the bottles they had had on the table for James' birthday dinner. Fin, evicted from her place of favourite smells, continued her impression of a bloodhound as she followed a zigzagging trail of her own towards the newly converted barn.

Emily left the dog to her own devices and, leaving the wine bottle where it was, she walked thoughtfully back round to the front door, her eyes scanning the path. Archie had said James was smoking after dinner. As she neared the steps, Emily turned and moved slowly across the grass to the sundial. Yes, there in the grass was a cigar butt, contorted as if it had been stubbed out, but not flattened underfoot. So if James had come from the front door to the sundial, it seemed likely he had smoked a cigar to calm his nerves, and then, if the wine bottle really were the one he had been carrying, he must have come back towards the stables and discarded it under the rhododendron. In that case he had not headed straight out to the clifftop. Who or what had persuaded him to turn back? And where did Archie's famous right hook fit in?

Chapter 15

Emily let herself in the back door of the mansion. As she opened the door, Fin pushed past her legs and hurried ahead. Emily was just in time to catch the sound of the 4.30 tea gong. She threw her parka on one of the gardeners' coat pegs, and bent to reunite a pair of shoes left on the bench under a grubby coat. Then she made her way to the empty drawing room, conscious of how thirsty she was.

As various individuals arrived they seemed to perform some silent, ritual dance, collecting teacups and plates, moving around the room without eye contact, sitting in disparate seats and fixing their eyes on some part of their surroundings. Only Samantha and Cassidy sat together. Samantha tried to put her arm round Cassidy, but she pushed it away impatiently. Gradually the conversations began as jam tarts and scones worked their soothing magic.

With discordant suddenness the front door knocker banged loudly three times. Fin leapt from the settee where she had been sitting opposite Samantha, and shot through the half-open door and barked frantically. Stella motioned to Emily to remain seated and went to restrain Fin and open the front door. A man's voice reached the listening ears. Soon the drawing room door opened and Detective Chief Inspector Drummond stood there, with DS Pollard behind him.

'I am so sorry to intrude at this very sad time,' he said, looking at the serious faces focused on his own. He spoke gently. 'I would find it most helpful,' he said, 'if, as a group, you would give me a picture of the events leading up to Mr Wedderburn's disappearance. Later I will interview each of you, asking for more details to add to the overall picture. You will appreciate that it is important to ascertain Mr Wedderburn's state of mind last night.'

Drummond's words appeared to fall on stony ground and Emily felt some sympathy for him. There was not a flicker of change in the expressions facing him. Was this merely shock? Were they mentally incapable of realising that this kind of death had to be investigated, or was this the beginning of resistance to questioning, a fear that something would be uncovered? 'Did he fall or was he pushed?' The age-old question had to be answered, but Emily felt that the time had not yet come to reveal details about the wine bottle.

Drummond tried again. 'Perhaps you would explain how you all came to be here – Mr Wedderburn?' He directed the question at Edward.

'Well,' he said, 'my brother sold most of his businesses in the north and moved down here this week. The manager can explain.' He glanced at Stella.

'The furniture vans arrived on Wednesday morning, but there were complications,' she explained. 'The Old Barn, where Mr and Mrs Wedderburn were to live, was not ready, so, on Mr Wedderburn's instructions, everything went into storage. Mr Wedderburn drove down later that day, after concluding some business. He stayed in St Albans on Wednesday night and arrived late morning yesterday.'

Edward took up the story. 'James had invited the whole family to be here this weekend to see his new home and to celebrate his sixtieth birthday. He wanted to tell us his plans for turning Seascape House into a hotel.'

Drummond remained impassive. Emily wondered how many stately homes he had visited and whether he knew that listed buildings were not easily converted. Would he think James remarkably foolish, or would he believe that James knew exactly what he would be able to do and that he had the means to do it?

Edward continued, 'The family arrived yesterday afternoon: James' son, Philip, with his wife, Samantha, sitting in front of you; his daughter, Clara, with her husband, Archie, by the window; Mrs Wedderburn here and myself.'

'Mrs Wedderburn didn't arrive until yesterday afternoon?' Drummond looked surprised.

'I'd been on a business trip abroad,' Cassidy explained.

Pollard clearly couldn't control her curiosity. 'Did you leave Mr Wedderburn to manage the move without you?' She gave the impression that no man could manage to move house without his wife heading up the arrangements.

Drummond glared at the interruption, but still listened to the explanation offered.

Cassidy smiled faintly. 'James and I planned the move before I left. Martin, his secretary, was to oversee the final packing up of the office and come down earlier in the week. James was going to stay in the flat above the original shop, tying up the last of the paperwork before coming down here for the weekend.'

'I see,' said Drummond. 'Now, perhaps Mr Wedderburn would introduce the other people in this room.'

'Of course,' said Edward, indicating the different individuals with a wave of his hand. 'I think you've met Dame Emily, who is living in the Lodge, and this is Stella Harrington, a local representative for the Elizabethan Heritage Association, who has been acting as planning advisor for the future hotel, and is the housekeeper for the next few days. Ian Matthews, sitting at the back, lives in Eastbourne and is employed as a personal trainer, overseeing the gym and the swimming pool, which were to be opened to the public next week. Finally, this is George McFarland, James' solicitor, who was also invited for the weekend.'

George nodded as if to agree with Edward. 'There were one or two papers which needed to be drawn up, once the family had discussed the future of the proposed hotel,' he said, as if to justify his presence.

'And, of course,' added Edward quickly, with a glance at DS Pollard who had been making notes, 'we have Grace Summerfield and her granddaughter, Jayne, who are working in the kitchen.'

Drummond acknowledged the information with a nod of his head. 'Thank you for your help,' he said to the room in general. 'Now, Mr Wedderburn, I wonder if we could have the use of a room where we might interview everyone. We do need to make further enquiries to ascertain the deceased's state of mind and, of course, find out who was the last to see him alive. I would be grateful if each of you would make yourself available for interview from now on.'

Edward swallowed hard. 'Of course,' he said politely. He looked round the room and located George. 'May we use the music room?'

'Yes, I won't be needing it and I've already cleared my papers away.'

'Then we shall begin as soon as I have looked at the deceased's room,' said Drummond.

Edward stood and walked to the door. 'I'll show you the way,' he said, as he led the two officers from the room.

Emily eased herself from her chair and went to pour her second cup of tea.

'I don't understand!' The voice was Clara's. 'Why do they want to talk to us? Dad said he was going out for fresh air. He must have got too near the cliff edge after all that drink... That's what you said, Dame Emily.'

'It was just a theory,' Emily reminded her.

Briefly Clara was quiet, then she looked round at the glum faces in the room. 'What if it was all of us?' she whispered, with an anxious glance at Cassidy. 'What if we were all so horrid he decided to end it all?'

There was no response. Emily suspected that like herself, everyone in the room was wrestling with the same problem.

'I know I only spoke to him briefly when he first arrived,' Emily said, forgetting that the present company had no idea of her initial meeting with James, 'but from what I saw of him at dinner, your father seemed to be a strong and determined man. I don't think any family argument would have driven him to end his life.' She didn't dare say the word 'suicide'.

Appraising eyes turned on her; the old hostility was mixed with relief that she had spoken as she had, almost absolving them of collective responsibility.

'But there is another reason the police need to talk to us all,' Emily continued gently. 'Whenever someone dies without witnesses, they must find out if a passer-by tried to rob or attack the victim.'

'That's horrible,' Clara burst out. Then she looked at Cassidy, sitting impassively on the settee. 'Oh, I'm sorry,' she said simply, but the new widow continued to stare at the swirling blue and old-gold patterns on the carpet and did not respond. There was a brief pause.

'So what do we say to the police?'

Emily sighed. Clara was like a dog with a bone.

Archie shuffled his feet. 'Clara, do give it a rest. If we all tone down what we said to him last night, and what each other said, that should be enough. After all, no one here physically pushed him over the edge – so the police should be satisfied with that.'

Philip suddenly sat up, as if his brain had engaged for the first time since the events of the morning. 'How do we know that?' he said. 'And what about you?' He turned with vicious suddenness to Archie. 'You went out soon after he did. You punched him – you told us yourself – and none of us saw him after that.'

Archie went pale. 'We were just outside the front door, in the garden. He was standing by the sundial with his back to me. When I shouted at him he turned and took a step towards me. I only gave him a bit of a jab, to teach him not to speak to Clara like that. He didn't fall over – he didn't even hit his head… After that, I told you, I went straight to the gym.' Archie's voice grew louder, but he also seemed to be pleading as he stood and held the back of his chair.

'What about Ian?' said Philip abruptly. 'Did you see Archie?'

Ian, sitting in the far corner, looked blank. 'No.'

'Come on!' Archie insisted. 'I wouldn't have told you about the punch if I'd done something terrible to him. How could I have time to persuade him to walk to the cliffs and leave him to fall over? I wasn't out there long enough, it was too cold – I told you, he was standing in the garden when I left him.'

'I don't believe you!' Philip got to his feet and faced his brother-in-law, his fists clenched, but Samantha went over to her husband and pushed him back into his chair. 'Sit down, both of you. This isn't helping.'

At that moment the door opened and all heads turned, seeming to be glad of the distraction. Edward came into the room followed by DS Pollard. 'They would like to see Cassi,' he said.

Cassidy stood. 'Thank you,' she said. Her voice wavered, but she moved with dignity. Emily decided that she had begun the long adjustment to widowhood, and was beginning to display that quiet courage she herself had seen in a number of her friends. She felt for Cassidy as she went to answer the painful questions the police were bound to ask.

Edward went to a chair by the window. He sat with a sigh and pulled out his mobile phone.

'Well, what did they ask you?' Clara demanded.

Edward shrugged his shoulders. 'Just when I saw him last, what sort of mood he was in, how I was feeling.'

There was a pause. Edward's dramatic exit had been the most highly emotionally charged departure of the evening. Clara persisted. 'Did you see Dad later in the evening?'

'No!' Edward's voice was becoming dangerously sharp. 'You know he was out in the garden with Archie. I certainly didn't see him.'

Archie half got out of his chair and was pulled back again by Clara.

Emily glanced across at Stella for some sort of support; some oil was needed for these troubled waters, and she had none to offer.

One by one the guests at Seascape left the room, gave their statements in the music room and returned. On the whole they agreed the police gave the impression that the interviews were a mere formality. Family members seemed to have managed to soften their accounts of the evening's events, referring to 'a slight disagreement', or 'confusion', about James' intentions for the weekend at the mansion, and a certainty that James would not wish to end his own life. Would the police accept that this was a tragic accident which had befallen an inebriated man? Emily suspected they would be less than satisfied.

When it came to her turn, Emily gave the bare facts of the case to DCI Drummond, mentioning her meeting with James when he had arrived, her short exchange with him in the hall, and a brief but accurate summary of the conversation at dinner. Like the others, she denied having seen James from the moment he left the dining room. Drummond listened carefully.

'Oh, I nearly forgot,' Emily leaned towards the chief inspector, 'there is a wine bottle hidden at the base of the rhododendron bush opposite this middle window.' She glanced towards DS Pollard, who seemed distressed by a small cough. 'I've left it there. I presume James discarded it after he took it from the dining room.'

Drummond smiled and made a brief note. Dame Emily was thanked and politely dismissed.

Martin was the next to be summoned, and Stella followed. She had almost completed her statement when she remembered something.

'I can't imagine this is important,' she said, addressing DCI Drummond, 'but last night, I locked the door behind Dame Emily and as the hall clock was striking 10.45 began to walk up the main stairs. I heard a door bang on the floor above, but thought nothing of it. There was no sign of anyone on the first floor, but I was concerned as I began to walk along the corridor.

On the right is a pair of rooms with a connecting door. I could see light under the left-hand door, but there was a sound of sobbing, which I thought came from behind the right-hand door. I did not feel it was my place to interfere, so I went on to my room.'

'Thank you,' said DCI Drummond. 'It is always worth passing on even the tiniest details. Perhaps you would be kind enough to ask George to come to the music room.'

George was followed by Grace Summerfield and Jayne, and last of all, Ian Matthews. When each returned to the drawing room they all seemed to have the same impression – that the police had been polite and methodical and seemed to be treating James' death as suicide, or possibly an accident although, of course, they would not admit to it. George told everyone that he had reported to the police that James had not come to the music room at any time for their planned meeting.

Ian had been given permission to return to his home in Eastbourne, so he merely dropped into the drawing room to check with Edward that he could leave. The police left soon afterwards and the family found themselves back together in the sitting room. Gradually they drifted away, taking pre-dinner drinks into the dining room, until only Emily and Stella were left.

Stella came to sit opposite her friend. 'Oh, there's something else,' she said. 'I thought you ought to know – we've had the press on the doorstep.'

'Well, that's Mandi Jones for you,' said Emily.

'Pardon?'

'Mandi Jones, whom I once taught, was here this morning to book swimming sessions for next week. She must have found out from Ian that James had gone missing. It looks as if she's a local reporter. I guess she saw the police out on the cliff and realised there was a story in it. Come to think of it, she may have been the driver who nearly ran me over, when I was hurrying back to ring the coastguard before breakfast. I met her and her cronies on my way out this afternoon, but refused to say anything. Martin must have heard me arguing with them. He came out, gave them short shrift and sent them packing.' Emily grinned. 'He virtually rescued me from them. He has his good points.'

'What about this Mandi? Will she sensationalise the story?'

Emily looked gloomy. 'I've no idea, but she could suggest it was other than suicide – and perhaps it was.'

'Emily?'

Emily shook her head. 'I can't work it out,' she said. 'Something's not right. Angry as he was last night, I can't see James marching out on to the Heath and falling by mistake – although the drink must have had some part to play in what happened.'

'He'd just swallowed some pills as well,' Stella pointed out. 'Martin gave them to him.'

Emily suddenly remembered the wine bottle and told Stella her thoughts. 'It almost confirms James came back round the side of the mansion,' she said, 'but it doesn't really seem to get us nearer a solution.'

Stella leaned forward. 'Emily,' she said quietly, glancing nervously at the door, 'are you saying that, because James came past the rhododendron bush, he did not go out to the cliff edge of his own free will, but someone encouraged him to go back on to the Heath, and that this is not suicide, but – and I can't believe I'm saying this – actually murder?'

'I think it could be.'

'But who?'

'I don't know. Archie seemed so natural when he bounced back into this room last night. He'd probably had a few too many, but he didn't behave like a man who had lured another to his death. He was almost proud of that jab to the chin. And why hit a man near the house if you want him near the cliffs?'

'We've only his word for it,' Stella pointed out.

The two friends were silent, pondering.

'There's Martin. He gave James his pills. Could he have given him the wrong ones or upped the dose?'

'And then led James back to the cliff?' Emily sighed. 'I can't see why he should – unless Archie ran to find Martin before James had returned to the house, and they took him there together. He'd just have time, I suppose.'

Stella shook her head. 'But they don't know each other, do they?'

There was a long pause. Stella idly picked up a newspaper from the chair next to her, tidied its pages and folded it in half. 'George said this morning that James didn't turn up for the meeting,' she said. 'For a solicitor, he seemed to take a very long time to realise it was James' body you found; but then, if he knew already that James was dead, you would think he'd have put on more of an act. Anyway, he would hardly gain from James' death.'

'No,' said Emily absently. 'I don't think George has a reason or the necessary initiative to attack James. As far as I know, Edward is the only one with a motive for wanting him dead, but he was with us, and then he went to play snooker with Archie. Though I suppose he and Archie might have colluded. Archie could have left his father-in-law dead or unconscious outside, and they could have removed the body together. Or they could have persuaded James to go for a walk before his meeting with George.'

Stella looked solemn. 'I suppose you could be right. The hatred poured out of Edward last night, and he is the only beneficiary. But he seems to be so shocked by the whole thing, and is taking responsibility for all that needs to be done. But that could be a way of putting the police off the scent, or even an indication of remorse for what he had done.'

Emily frowned at the potted plant in the window. 'Edward really seemed surprised by the will, though I suppose he had time to plan his reaction.' She shook her head, as though trying to force her disparate thoughts to slot into some kind of logical order. 'It wasn't any of that that was worrying me, though now we've talked about it, it is a big concern. No, there's something else. It's been niggling at me ever since I saw James' body…'

'Do you want to look at a copy of your statement for the police? It might jog your memory.'

'No,' Emily said slowly. 'I think it's something I didn't put in my statement. Give me a minute or two.'

Stella obediently sat back in her chair as Emily closed her eyes and replayed the sequence of events. She saw again the bloated corpse, the rescue teams, the two men waiting for the wave and lifting James' body free, and then, for a split second, the deceased of Seascape House lying on the stretcher.

'Stella,' she said, 'what do you know about rigor mortis?'

'Nothing really,' came the reply. 'I think it sets in quite quickly, but it depends on the temperature of the place where it is. Why?'

'The body,' said Emily slowly, 'wasn't just lying straight, it was, well, curled a little, with the knees bent. He couldn't possibly have been asleep, could he? Could he have walked round the beach and sat on the rocks, overcome by pills and drink, and then been caught asleep by the tide and knocked against a rock? No it doesn't fit. There is something strange, but for the life of me, I can't work out what it is.'

Chapter 16

Dinner was an awkward meal, and coffee in the drawing room even more so.

Edward had reacted badly to the information imparted by Grace that James' death had been confirmed on the local six o'clock news, and Martin had become furious when, on answering the door during dinner, he had found himself instantly photographed, seconds before being questioned by three eager reporters. Slamming the door in their faces had not relieved the tension.

Everyone had expressed shock; no one could think how the press had got hold of the story. Emily and Stella did not enlighten them. Ian had left for home and they could not test their theory that he was inadvertently responsible. Emily sighed deeply. She could not bear the thought of reporters storming the mansion and maybe the Lodge. It was more than she could face. She was relieved when, by common agreement, the family decided to have an early night – all except Archie and Edward, who went off for their return snooker match.

By 9.15, Emily was glad to be saying goodnight to Stella. She stood in the entrance hall, stooping to put on Fin's lead, when suddenly she was wide awake; the memory of last night clear and sharp. When Stella brought her coat she waved it away. Minutes later she and Stella were seated at the kitchen table with a second cup of hot chocolate each.

'Emily, you can't!' Stella watched in horror as Emily plonked a battered briefcase on the kitchen table and rested her hand on the catch.

'They're all in bed or in the snooker room, aren't they?' Emily retorted. 'Anyway, I couldn't resist looking at it! You can just see the indentations where James' initials were originally stamped into the leather on the front. It's too late to contact the police without a very good reason. Much better to see if there's anything important in here and then decide whether to inform the authorities or not.'

'Emily, you're dreadful!' complained Stella. 'Wait – there could be evidence – you might destroy fingerprints! There must be something.' She searched the kitchen desperately with her eyes. 'I'll look in the scullery.' She returned, waving a pair of yellow rubber gloves. 'At least put these on.'

Emily glared, but unwillingly acknowledged that she might have been about to put herself in a compromising position. Encumbered by the gloves, she found it hard to undo the catch of the briefcase. At least it hadn't been locked – perhaps James had lost the key in the intervening 30 years or so since it had been fashionable.

The main compartment was almost empty, apart from a selection of small oddments at the base. A big, black desk diary took up a sizable amount of room. She pulled it out and allowed the ribbon to open it at the present week. Untidy phrases jostled at varying angles. Tuesday's entry: 'Furniture van leaving' had been amended to: 'Furniture van to storage unit – Wed.' Below it, under Wednesday, in a neater hand, was written, 'Limo ordered for 2.30.' Across the sections for Friday, Saturday, Sunday and Monday was written in an untidy scrawl: 'Family birthday bash! Retirement!'

The previous pages were covered in neat writing, noting meetings and committees, usually prefixed with the word 'last' or 'final' or 'farewell'. Conveyancing dates for shops and for contract signing were also there, some changed to future dates and some written more than once, where the sale had clearly been held up.

Emily put the diary on the kitchen table. 'That will take some concentrated reading,' she remarked, 'a bit too much for now.'

She pushed her arm, elbow deep, into the depths of the briefcase and fiddled around. Eventually she gave up and turned the briefcase upside down, allowing an assortment of things to fall onto the table. There seemed to be nothing of consequence: an old biro, a couple of cigars, a hip flask, a front-door key, a dirty tissue, a couple of small suitcase keys tied with thin string, and three draft copies of the invitation to James' retirement weekend in Eastbourne.

'Well,' said Stella, sounding relieved, 'that's hardly incriminating.'

Emily didn't reply; she was fiddling with a tightly fitting, inner side pocket and endeavouring to pull out an old foolscap envelope, roughly folded in two. Broken sealing wax still clung to it.

As she fumbled, the rubber gloves bent at the fingertips and Emily muttered darkly, until at last, with the aid of a knife, she managed to ease open the envelope, and tipped the contents onto the table. In the main it consisted of folded newspaper cuttings and a small coloured photo of a fair-haired woman in a turquoise swimming costume, sporting a wide sash across her chest and posing like a model.

Stella had lost her disapproving look; curiosity was obviously beginning to win. She reached for the knife and, using its rounded blade, gently pulled the photograph nearer. Emily craned towards the snap so that their heads almost touched.

'Is that Cassidy?' Stella asked. 'She's no more than a child! This must be the photo Clara referred to the other night, the one she said was in the office.'

'I imagine so,' said Emily, as she carefully unfolded one of the newspaper cuttings dated 2001. '"Well-known local butcher weds Miss Pork Chop 1999",' she read aloud, glancing up at Stella's disbelieving face. '"James Wedderburn, of Wedderburn's Pride of Choice Retailers, married his youthful sweetheart last Saturday. Miss Cassidy Weeks, who has won several beauty titles, as well as being a Yorkshire swimming champion, drew all eyes and a ripple of applause as the couple walked from the registry office to the nearby St Clement's Hotel for the reception. Mr Wedderburn's daughter, Clara, made a charming bridesmaid. The bride's parents…'" Emily's voice faded as she skimmed the rest of the article before pushing it across to Stella, who read it carefully, and then placed it, together with Cassidy's photo, in the middle of the table.

Another cutting looked much older. It was clipped to a rather battered photograph of a village hall full of young people. Emily positioned the paper where the dim glow from the central kitchen light made reading easier.

"'An enjoyable evening was had by all those who attended the 'Water for all' disco last Saturday",' she read. "'A considerable sum was raised, which will go towards a well-digging project in a drought-ridden area of central Africa.'"

Carefully, Stella picked up the photo by its edges. A slightly smudged arrow pointed to a long-haired youth laughingly holding his hand out to a slim teenage girl. 'That photo looks ancient!' she remarked. 'When do you think that was taken?'

Emily shrugged her shoulders. Stella turned it over and read out loud: '"George dancing with Gloria while his Doreen was in hospital giving birth – naughty George! 27th March 1978." What's all that about? Is it solicitor George?'

Emily shook her head slowly. 'It could be – the build is the same. If James kept the photo, it must be important. It obviously implicates George in some way. I wonder if James used it against George in the past as some kind of threat?'

'You mean blackmail?'

'It's possible. A small amount of blackmail over the years would mount up quite nicely.'

'Then maybe George did meet James last night after all! Perhaps he intercepted him in the front garden after Archie left and walked with him to the cliff… Emily, that's dreadful!'

Emily looked grim. 'You don't have to be Superman to give someone a slight push, and think of the temptation to get your own back after nearly 40 years! It wouldn't have taken long, and he could have been back in the music room well before their scheduled meeting. It could explain why it appeared to take him a very long time this morning to realise the body belonged to James. He would expect it to be washed away – or he was putting on an act.'

'That's true… but he's a solicitor.'

'That's why I can't believe it was George, even though it's just possible. He seems to be such a genuinely nice, normal man with a good home life, even if he's a bit vague. Perhaps this says more about James than George.'

Emily put the creased picture with its cutting next to the photo of Cassidy and picked up one of the remaining pieces of paper. It was a double-page spread, dated Wednesday 22nd May 2013, again from the local *Huddersfield News*. On the left-hand side was a wedding photo. A slightly slimmer Clara, arrayed in white, stood arm in arm with a young and gawky Archie in front of a church doorway, smiling happily at the camera.

'Stella, listen to this!' Emily bent over the article. '"Bride stood up by father",' she recited quietly, but with excitement. '"Miss Clara Wedderburn had to travel alone to St Francis' Church, Link Way, for her wedding last Friday, 17th May, after her father had been urgently called away on business. Her brother, who had taken on the role of best man (the latter having been taken ill after a celebratory meal the previous evening), had to leave the nervous bridegroom's side, and prepare to accompany the beautiful bride from the church door to the altar. However, it is to Mr James Wedderburn's credit that he found what he himself described as the fastest cab in Huddersfield, and was able to arrive at the church just in time to walk Miss Wedderburn down the aisle.

'"'It is unthinkable that I should miss my only daughter's wedding,' he told me, as the photographs were being taken after the ceremony. 'I was so proud of her.'

'"A smiling Mr Philip Wedderburn confided that he was most relieved to see his father hurry through the lychgate, as he would have had considerable difficulty in moving from one side of the church to the other, to perform the roles of both best man and father. Mr and Mrs Archie Braithwaite were obviously glad at the happy outcome.

"'Mrs Cassidy Wedderburn, the bride's stepmother, wore a brilliant turquoise suit and smiled happily. 'I never doubted my husband would be there on time,' she said. 'Clara's special day went just as we had planned and we are delighted with all the good wishes the couple have received. My husband has proved that he can deal with a crisis and still fulfil his duties as the proud father on the day.'"'

Stella grinned. 'I bet they weren't as calm as they made out. I'd be furious if my husband even thought of putting work before his only daughter's wedding. Well, he wouldn't even consider it. I wonder what was so urgent that James had to attend to it on that day of all days?'

Emily was not listening. Her eyes were scanning the facing page: more weddings, baptisms and a short column of deaths. Had James not bothered to tear the first page off, or had he kept this for a reason? Emily skimmed downwards till the print swam in front of her eyes, and then she lighted on the thing she had been unaware that she had been looking for: a brief article beneath a small photo, in a column alongside the dozen or so announcements of death. She moved the paper to where they could both read it.

The happy face of a small boy clutching an extremely large teddy bear laughed up at them. It was obviously a family photo, taken in a very ordinary back garden. Stella smiled. 'What a poppet! Though he's got a wicked grin, I'll give him that,' she remarked, before becoming more solemn as she read out the report which followed.

"'The funeral took place last Friday at 11am at St. Clement's Church, Back Street West, of Alistair Wharton, aged three years, two months. Many letters of condolence have been sent to Mr Wharton – a former commercial traveller, now working for the council – and Mrs. Wharton, a part-time secretary. Both the funeral and the following cremation were private, mourners being the family and close friends only.

"'The second son of Mr and Mrs Wharton died suddenly in Huddersfield General Hospital three weeks ago. The results of the post-mortem have not yet been made public. It is still possible to make donations in his memory to the Longhope Children's Hospice through Black, Eastward and Fife, funeral directors, 47 Upper Park Street.'"

Emily gazed at the photo. They'd had one taken of her nephew, Giles, at much the same age. He'd been hugging his pet rabbit. At least her nephew had had 45 years to live to the full before the crash which had killed him; to lose your life at the age of three was unthinkable.

A piece of folded white card was lying face down on the table. Stella turned it over. It was black-edged and in the centre of the front page, in old-fashioned script, was written:

Alistair James Wharton
14th February 2010–26th April 2013

Lower down the page in shaky biro were written the three simple letters: *RIP*. Along the bottom above the black edging was part of a Bible verse: 'Let the little children come to me.'

Carefully, Stella opened the card.

The order of service began with the words of the hymn, 'All Things Bright and Beautiful' and was followed by details of the readings, prayers, an address by the Reverend Clifford Randall-Forsythe, and a short eulogy by Alistair's uncle. The words of the commitment and final blessing were smudged as though they had got wet at some time. A small thank-you card was caught between the last two pages. Emily and Stella bent their heads to read the neat handwriting: 'Thank you so much for your kind gift of flowers, we really appreciate it. We miss our unique and special Alistair James so much. There will never be anyone else like him. Paul, Mary, Joshua and Sheila.'

The two friends stared in disbelief at the pieces of paper lying open in front of them. There was a long silence. Stella frowned at the evidence, obviously trying to make sense of it all. Emily put her head in her hands and groaned. 'Oh, the silly, silly man,' she breathed almost inaudibly.

'What man?' asked Stella, obviously still unable to link the facts in front of her.

Emily looked up. She suddenly felt unutterably weary and disillusioned with the human race. 'James,' she said simply.

'James?' echoed Stella.

Emily looked Stella squarely in the face, as she restored a stray hair to its former position. 'Stella, I don't want to tell you what I'm thinking. I may have made two and two come to ten, but just think about this evidence for a minute or two. We know that James was late for his daughter's wedding…'

Stella nodded. 'Business problems.'

'Would you allow business to come in the way of your daughter's wedding?' Emily asked.

'I wouldn't, neither would any mother,' Stella replied. 'Nor any father either.'

'In what situation might you miss the wedding, then?' Emily persisted.

Stella frowned. 'I suppose…' she said cautiously, 'if I'd been arrested I wouldn't have any choice in the matter, or if I was hurt or perhaps unwell…'

Emily waited.

'Or if someone I cared for a lot, my husband or another child were seriously ill, or…' her voice trailed to a whisper, 'or dying.'

Emily watched as Stella pulled the newspaper closer to her, consulted it and glanced at the order of service for the funeral of Alistair Wharton. 'They were both on the same day,' she said, almost to herself. 'You mean he went to the little boy's funeral first?'

Emily went on waiting.

Stella stared at the jolly little boy with his dark hair and square determined jaw, and Emily watched as a glimmer of understanding came in her eyes, followed by disbelief. Emily reached across the table, picked up the front-door key and put it quietly onto the order of service.

'Emily, no!' Stella stared at her friend. 'Do you really think so?'

Emily lifted her shoulders and sighed. 'Tell me what you're thinking,' she said. 'I don't want to influence you and, as I said, I'm afraid I've jumped to conclusions.'

Stella took a deep breath. 'It looks as though Alistair might have been our James' son...' She paused. 'Oh, Emily, the will. Didn't George read out James' full name?'

Emily nodded. 'I think it was James Alistair,' she said.

Stella frowned. 'And the baby was Alistair James... Named after his real father. You might call a baby by both his names to begin with, but by the time he's three you've decided which one to call him. It seems odd that the mother should put both on her thank-you card, unless it's a kind of message.' Stella looked again at the card. '"There will never be anyone else like him",' she quoted. 'That's true of every child, but maybe she's saying the little boy is uniquely theirs; that she and James can never be parents again.' Stella looked at her friend.

Emily bit her lip. 'I'm afraid I had the same thought. The husband was a commercial traveller, he must have been on the road quite a bit, but not away for very long, so the date of any pregnancy would not be questioned.'

'I wonder who Alistair looked like,' Stella mused.

'I expect they could find some grandfather to cite as a possible throwback,' said Emily. 'James had pretty average colouring, although the square jaw would be a bit of a giveaway.'

'So,' said Stella thoughtfully, 'you think James was prepared to be late for his own daughter's wedding in order to say goodbye to his son? He kept the order of service for the funeral in his pocket all through his daughter's celebrations... He invented the urgent business problem. He had no other option. Martin would have been invited to the wedding, so they would have shut the office anyway; he just needed a story to convince Martin, and it could all be behind them once the weekend was over.'

Emily nodded encouragement. 'And the key?' she prompted.

Stella picked it up and turned it over in her hand. 'All the keys I possess are on rings,' she said. 'The car and the door keys are together, the Seascape house keys are on another ring. The only key I've got that isn't on a ring is one I keep in the back of the kitchen drawer with the potato peeler. It's my neighbour's and is there for emergencies.' She paused and looked at Emily. 'James couldn't put someone else's key on a ring with his home or office keys – Cassidy or a colleague might query it. He kept it in his briefcase, so that if he went out on business in the daytime and Paul Wharton was away driving his lorry, James had instant access to the house...'

Emily sighed. 'Rightly or wrongly, those were my conclusions too,' she said. 'Either Paul has forgiven his wife or she's pulled the wool over his eyes. What a mess! Fancy having a child you can't acknowledge as your own and then to have him die aged just three! It doesn't bear thinking about. I wonder he got through the wedding at all.'

'Do you think James' own children knew? Or Cassidy?' Stella asked.

'I imagine not,' Emily replied. 'James seems to have been a workaholic – everyone would imagine he was at one or other of his shops or doing paperwork late into the night. The children had a predictable routine at school and work and Cassidy seems to be away from home a lot, as they had au pairs. It really would have been very easy to carry on a relationship – until the child became seriously ill and, of course, when the date of the funeral was announced.'

'If Alistair had lived,' said Stella thoughtfully, 'he might have had a claim on the inheritance; but presumably he would never have been told the truth, or not until his present father died.' She began to fold the pieces of newspaper neatly, using the knife and one fingernail, preparing to return them to the envelope. 'At least this is all past history and won't be of interest to the police.'

'What's that?' said Emily as another folded piece of newspaper fell to the floor. 'Did we look at this one?'

Stella didn't answer as Emily retrieved the paper and carefully unfolded the page. She put two smaller cuttings to one side. A headline shouted, 'Local doctor accused of failure to care'.

Emily read aloud: '"Following an anonymous phone call to this paper, one of our journalists has been investigating claims that a paediatrician at the local St Clement's hospital was slow to diagnose an unusually severe reaction to the chickenpox virus, with the result that local boy Alistair Wharton, aged three, died four days after being admitted to hospital. No doctor has been available for comment, and the hospital has repeatedly claimed that all complaints are always investigated thoroughly and objectively. We are aware of public interest and will continue to cover this story and make sure that the parents of the boy have justice and the full facts. They have asked that their right to privacy will be respected."' Emily paused.

'What was the date?' asked Stella.

'Just a few weeks after Alistair died.'

'And the other cutting?'

Emily picked it up and looked for the date. 'Four months later,' she reported. 'It says, "Dr Ian Matthews was found not guilty of any form of malpractice following the death of a three-year-old boy from chickenpox. The hospital will not confirm that the paediatrician has since moved to another part of the country."

'And this,' she said, unfolding the other cutting, 'is older – from 2010. It has a picture of James cutting the tape across a shop doorway. It's about his second shop opening in Huddersfield.'

Stella leaned forward to study a photograph further down the same page. 'Look! This photo shows a team of doctors presenting a cheque to the same hospital following a sponsored bike ride in 2010.'

Emily pulled the cutting from her hand. 'And someone has ringed one doctor's face,' she said eagerly, 'and written an address in the margin.' She counted along the row of heads. 'From the names underneath, it's definitely Dr Matthews.'

'I wonder why James kept those cuttings,' Stella mused. 'You'd think he'd want to put the whole thing behind him.'

'Perhaps he couldn't let it go,' Emily replied. 'Perhaps he was the anonymous caller. He may even have wanted to make this Dr Matthews pay somehow. He must have come across this old cutting about the shop, noticed the picture of the doctors and realised its implication.'

There was a prolonged silence in the kitchen with only the ticking clock emphasising the passing of time.

'Ian Matthews!' said Stella suddenly. 'Our leisure manager is called Ian Matthews!'

'It's surely not the same man!'

'It's a common enough name. It couldn't be, could it?'

Once again they bent over the photo. 'This was taken ten years ago, but it could be him,' Emily said doubtfully. 'The hairstyle is a bit different, but the rather long nose looks the same. What was it he said about himself at dinner?'

'He'd recently got involved in the leisure business, and that he'd benefited from it so much that he wanted others to gain from it too. Oh, Emily, what if it is our Ian?'

Emily again put her head in her hands, dislodging the comb from her hair. She shook her head until her long white hair fell around her shoulders; with practised ease she then began to put it back into place.

'We have the potential for blackmail,' she said at length, as she pushed the comb back into position, 'and the motive for murder. But I really don't think my mind is up to sorting one from t'other at the moment.'

Stella yawned and looked at her watch. 'It's no good; like you, I'm too exhausted to think it through; it'll have to wait. We must get to bed. If you'll put those pieces of paper back in the briefcase, I'll hide it till the morning, and then contact the police. Or I could give it to Edward, though perhaps it's better that he doesn't know – let's sleep on it. I won't take any action without consulting you.'

For once Emily was content to be told what to do. She suddenly felt very tired and emotionally drained. It wasn't often she got in touch with her feelings, and the fate of Alistair James and those involved with him had somehow stirred her a great deal.

She woke Fin, and Stella let them out of the back door; neither of them wanting to risk the loud creaking of the front door. Emily shivered. But though the air was cold and the wind was off the sea, it was the evening's revelations that chilled her mind and sharpened her thinking.

James himself was coming into clearer focus. A hard-working, driven man, but determined to gain wealth, status and control in his own little world by any means he could. Even the loss of his own small son did not move him to compassion towards others, and it was clear from his attitude at dinner on Thursday night that he had no insight into the lives of his grown-up children.

Insensitive, mercenary, bent on self-aggrandisement... When had it all started to go wrong? Had James, in effect, brought about his own death? Had he led George or Ian out to the Heath with murderous intent? Had either of them witnessed a fatal accident, as James had slipped on the wet grass, or taken part in a desperate struggle to defend themselves, delivering that final gentle push or trip that sent him over the edge? Try as she would, Emily couldn't imagine George taking part in a drama on the clifftop, but she could not discount the possibility that he was being blackmailed, and what effect might that have on a mild-tempered man?

Then there was Ian. After all the adverse publicity about his involvement with the child, it would make sense to move as far away from Yorkshire as possible. Presumably Ian had never known James' identity, nor his link with Alistair James, and in his wildest dreams the one-time doctor could not imagine being found in a busy south coast resort, where he was working as a sports coach.

It was a ridiculous coincidence that Ian Matthews should now be working for James. But coincidences did happen. When James had read his CV, Ian's name would have shouted from the page. Supposing all the candidates had been asked to attach a photo, showing themselves in action at their local leisure centres? Ian's response to such an innocuous request would have sounded his death knell. James would only have had to compare the picture with his newspaper photo, which he had presumably carried with him every day, hoping for revenge – though he would probably call it justice – and then begin to spin a very clever web indeed. Emily shuddered; it all seemed so cold blooded.

Emily's mind gained momentum with frightening speed. Had James organised the meeting with George in the music room as a sort of cover-up? Had he lured Ian out of the gym and walked with him to the clifftop, and all the time been determined to push him over the edge, to punish him for the premature death of his small son? Had James gloated as he revealed to Ian who he was? But had Ian then used his fitness training to turn the tables on James? The body must have been damaged by the fall. Would any signs of a struggle still show?

Emily was breathless: with the possibilities that invaded her mind at breakneck speed, and with the effort she needed to make to keep up with the hurrying dog, she began to gasp for breath. As she paused to open the little gate of the Lodge, she looked out into the blackness where the cliff edge gave way to the rocks and the pounding breakers below, and shuddered. Was it possible that Ian had driven out of these very gates just 24 hours before, with no intention of contacting anyone for help, leaving the wracked body of his employer to the merciless pounding of the sea? It looked that way.

Part III
Murky Waters

Saturday

Chapter 17

Detective Chief Inspector Simon Drummond accelerated towards the top of the hill and indicated left. In the rear-view mirror he caught a glimpse of Eastbourne in the morning light, where dolls' houses and miniature blocks of flats huddled close to the gentle curve of the bay. The sea was inky blue. Ahead of him was the wide expanse of green grass which topped the white cliffs of Beachy Head. The sheen of moisture which had clung to it was beginning to release its hold. He drove on past the nearly empty car park. The ice cream van was parked in the middle of it – presumably the driver had gone to the nearby café for breakfast. The litter bin had as much litter around it as in it. Black sacks abounded. At the far end of the car park a couple of cars were disgorging men and equipment.

'The micro-lighters and hang-gliders are intent on getting started before the Saturday crowds get here,' his companion remarked.

Drummond did not reply and they drove in silence for a mile or so before Lindsey Pollard ventured to ask, 'How do we play this, sir?'

'With care, courtesy and consideration – but observing every movement made by everyone.'

'Sir?'

'In this situation we have the advantage; we use it – we don't abuse it. A family is grieving, coming to terms with a death and the unfamiliar, but routine, things that follow. They are also facing the permanent and unhappy changes which result. There will be fear too: the members of staff are likely to lose their jobs.

This is a weekend which they will all remember for the rest of their lives; it is not for us to make it a worse trauma. We walk softly and we watch – they may still think it was suicide, or the action of a stranger. We now know this was altogether more calculated, so look for anything unusual: any action, any word, any glance out of place.'

'Right, sir.'

Drummond tapped his knee with his left hand and frowned. 'I think I'll tell them all together, and then we'll have to go over every statement they have given and see what they add or retract.'

'I see, sir.'

'At the moment we divide the job straight down the line,' Drummond continued. 'I ask the questions, you observe and take notes. Your impressions will be vital, but the notes must be totally accurate – no loss of concentration, understood?'

'Yes, sir.'

Drummond could feel himself changing the further they drove. On any morning he could go to the police station feeling fairly relaxed – until he saw again the amount of paperwork piled on his desk – and even be pleasant to colleagues, but once it became evident that a case was more than routine, he almost added another two inches to his six foot one. He became the calm, efficient and disinterested detective, who would not relinquish any challenge in front of him. Even as a child he had hated unfairness of any kind, and had been known to sort out infant playground squabbles with an amazing insight into what had really gone on. Now, as he flicked the right-hand indicator and turned into the drive of Seascape House, he knew he had much more than a playground squabble to resolve.

They found the drive blocked by three men and a woman armed with notebooks and cameras. As Drummond braked, the car was surrounded. Lights flashed. Voices clamoured:

'Is it true that James Wedderburn jumped to his death in Seascape Bay?'

'Why did he buy the house and then end his own life?'

'How are his family reacting?'

'Who inherits?'

Drummond leaned out of his window. 'I will confirm one fact,' he said, making eye contact with each of the pack in turn. 'The deceased was, as you rightly say, Mr James Wedderburn, who had recently moved to Seascape House from Yorkshire. That much was on the news yesterday.' He paused as pencils hovered, waiting to devour more information. 'An urgent plea for witnesses to any activity on the cliff here, during yesterday evening, from 8.30 onwards, would be of great help to us, and in return I will let you know when I have any further information. In the meantime, look Mr Wedderburn up on the internet – you will find plenty of fodder there. Now kindly leave before I have you for obstruction or trespass.'

Drummond's fierce tones dispersed the group; the reporters walking slowly towards the gates muttering among themselves.

Pollard chuckled. 'They think he's got a criminal record now, and all they'll find on the internet is a history of his pork sausage industry!'

Drummond allowed himself a slight smile. 'You never know,' he said, 'if they start talking to fellow journalists in the north, some useful facts might be uncovered. Our part is to ensure the balance between keeping them sweet and keeping them hungry.'

He proceeded to drive round to the back of the mansion. The pink limo was parked near the Old Barn, and the other cars at regular intervals in front of the stable block. He drew in by the furthest one and they walked in silence round to the front of the house.

Drummond briefly noted the daffodils, bright in the grey of morning, the spikes of crocus leaves standing sentinel over their decaying purple petals, a blackbird tossing dead leaves out of the flowerbed and scattering them on the beautiful lawn, the forsythia, an explosion of yellow among the evergreens and, in the background, he heard the pounding of the sea, relentless and determined. He stood between the stone pigs, resolutely turned his back on the garden, and focused as DS Pollard lifted the old iron knocker and allowed it to fall three times. Inside, a dog barked.

The door opened.

'Ah, Mr Chumleigh,' Drummond looked straight into the brown eyes. 'I wonder if we could come in?'

He didn't wait for a reply, but stepped onto the mat as Martin pulled the door wider. Drummond removed his coat and placed it on the settle in the hall. He turned to face Martin. 'May I speak to Mr Edward Wedderburn?'

Martin vanished in the direction of the dining room. The entrance hall was filled with the smell of bacon and a hint of percolated coffee. Drummond was glad he had had an adequate breakfast. He looked around at the pictures of men and women on the walls, all staring at him. Not for the first time he felt like an intruder.

From the kitchen regions, Grace came pushing the rattling trolley towards the dining room, followed by Jayne carrying the large teapot. Was it only one day since he had interrupted breakfast here? It all felt like déjà vu – except that he had to add a nasty twist.

Heavy footsteps heralded the appearance of Edward. 'Good morning, Chief Inspector.'

'Good morning, sir,' Drummond said, stepping forward. 'I am so sorry to disturb you at this hour of the morning. I wonder if I could speak to everyone briefly, then – when you have finished breakfast, of course – I would like to check everyone's statements.'

Edward's eyebrows rose a fraction. 'Er, yes,' he said looking around uncertainly as Grace and Jayne came back along the corridor from the dining room. 'Ah, Jayne,' Edward said, 'would you ring the gong now?'

'Right-oh,' said Jayne, with a quick glance at the police officers. They stepped back as she lifted the soft hammer and waited as the sound rose and fell and was completed by the final crash. She steadied the gong and replaced the hammer. Only then did the police go into the dining room.

DCI Drummond opted to stand behind James' chair, but accepted a cup of coffee as he waited for the family to assemble. Lindsey Pollard poured herself a cup of tea and stood a few steps inside the open door of the room.

Dame Emily came in and greeted the police politely, but without comment or question. She walked to the sideboard and collected a bowl of cornflakes, placed it on the table and returned for fruit juice. Martin, who was busy with his mobile phone, stepped to one side to let her pass. She had on what Drummond's mother would have called 'sensible' walking shoes, a jumper and pleated skirt. Some of her white hair had already escaped from the clasp at the back of her head, but the walk from the Lodge and the wind would have seen to that. Drummond wondered just how she had wheedled her way back into the family home and even seemed to be accepted – or were they putting up with her for some reason?

Archie and Philip arrived together. Drummond noticed that they got on well together, but guessed that they rarely saw each other, as they lived at opposite ends of the country.

Archie entered the room first and stopped so suddenly that Philip almost cannoned into him. 'You're not disturbing our breakfast again?' Archie glared at the police, like a guard dog protecting his territory from invasion. 'What now?'

Drummond was gravely polite. 'We just needed to have a word, sir, and then we'll leave you to have your breakfast.'

Archie muttered something inaudible, then, guided by prods in the back from Philip, went over to the hotplate and clattered the lids of the dishes in his hunt for food. Philip merely acknowledged the two visitors with a nod of his head before making for the muesli.

The two young wives came next. Samantha paused in the doorway and allowed Clara to come in first. 'Oh!' said Clara, staring at Drummond and then looking round the room. 'Do I need to get Cassidy?'

'Yes, please,' said Edward, putting his plate on the table and glancing longingly at his second full English breakfast in two days. 'I suppose I need to round up the rest?'

'If you would, sir.' Drummond was struggling to keep both his patience and the element of surprise to his announcement.

Edward glanced at Philip's bowl of cereal. 'I'll ring Ian and see if he's arrived. Philip, would you find George? He seems to be a bit vague about times of meals.'

Philip sighed and got to his feet. He looked at Drummond. 'I hope you're going to say we can go home now – we've had enough.' He didn't wait for an answer and left the room as Martin put his mobile away and helped himself to pink grapefruit.

Stella arrived, full of apologies that she'd had to ring the dairy over a misunderstanding about the amount of milk they required for the weekend. All heads turned to look at her. Drummond sensed none of them had thought of staying beyond breakfast. He wondered what he would do in their position. Run for the sanctuary of home, probably; try to blot out everything that had happened. But now he would have to imprison them indefinitely.

Stella suddenly became aware of the police presence and, covered in confusion, went to her place quickly. Edward returned and gave his full attention to demolishing his breakfast, simultaneously buttering toast, before helping himself to coffee.

Ian arrived and George shuffled in, with Philip in his wake, murmuring about queues and bathrooms, and finally Cassidy came in with Clara behind her.

'Good morning, Mrs Wedderburn.' DCI Drummond, having mentally ticked the register and checked his ability to remember their names, turned to face the assembled company as Clara and Cassidy took their seats.

'Well,' said Archie. 'Have you got it all sorted, so we can go home?'

Drummond looked at him and then back to Cassidy. 'I'm afraid buwe have met unforeseen complications.'

Even Edward paused with toast halfway to his mouth.

'I am sorry to tell you that we have reason to believe that Mr James Wedderburn's death was not an accident. He was killed elsewhere and his body was then taken to the cliffs.'

Philip looked shrewdly at the police officer. 'You mean he was attacked in the grounds and then taken to the clifftop?'

'No,' said Drummond slowly, torn between the need to be sensitive and the urge to be rather more dramatic, in the hope of provoking a reaction. 'The post-mortem shows that the water in his lungs was not seawater, but water from a swimming pool.'

Drummond and Pollard watched as very slowly in some cases, and more quickly in others, the significance of his statement dawned on their minds. One or two gasped, others looked bewildered.

'No!' The cry came from Cassidy and her hand flew to her mouth; again the frightened little girl look came into her eyes. Clara slipped an arm round her shoulders. Drummond's eyes scanned the company. Everywhere there was disbelief. It would seem they had not got further than accident or attack-by-a-stranger theories.

Sympathetic eyes turned towards Cassidy and the family, who looked at each other in horror and bewilderment. George looked the impassive solicitor who had seen it all before; Martin sat, statue-like, holding his dessert spoon in one hand and tipping his bowl with the other; Ian looked puzzled. Drummond caught a slight movement at the far end of the table as Stella and Emily exchanged knowing looks. So they, at least, were not surprised.

Having left time for the news to sink in, Chief Inspector Drummond resumed. 'I am sorry to bring such distressing news, but you will understand that we need to work quickly and thoroughly to discover the person or persons responsible.'

He looked up the table to Edward who was draining his coffee cup. 'You have a swimming pool?'

'Er, yes. I haven't seen it myself...'

'I could show you,' Martin offered.

'Thank you, sir. I'm afraid we shall have to treat that part of the estate as a crime scene for the moment, so I would be grateful if you would wait for us to tell you which areas you will be free to use. Our officers will be arriving soon.'

Drummond turned to Edward again. 'May we use the music room again for our investigations?'

Edward was looking much more concerned now. 'Yes, of course. I can go...'

'No, thank you sir, I can set up the room myself with the help of DS Pollard. Now, if you haven't any questions...'

He and his sergeant paused only briefly before putting their cups on the trolley and following Martin from the room.

Martin led them down the corridor to the kitchen, where he stopped. 'I'll collect the keys,' he said.

Drummond nodded. 'Perhaps you would like to show me where they are kept?'

Martin opened the door of the pantry on his right and Drummond followed him in. Martin partially closed the door and pointed to the rack of keys on the back of it. 'It's the set labelled "walled garden".'

Drummond held up a hand. 'Allow me, sir,' he said. Taking a biro from his pocket he carefully lifted the key ring from its hook and took it down. Keeping the five keys suspended on the biro, he followed Martin out of the back door.

'Now, if you can point me to the swimming pool,' said Drummond, looking at the huddle of old buildings in front of him, 'I need not keep you from your breakfast.'

Martin pointed to the old walled garden. 'It's in there,' he said. 'The long key is for the old gate, the one next to it on the ring is for the box with the light switches just inside the old wall, the key with the green tab is for the outer doors of the pool, the smaller one is for the supply cupboard, and the tiny one is for the drinks and snacks machines.'

'What's that used for?' Drummond asked, pointing to an old ramshackle building which seemed to provide one wall of the garden.

'It's the old laundry,' Martin replied. 'It's being renovated. It's not in use yet, though the new washing machines have been plumbed in. The two upper rooms are going to be...' he paused, 'were going to be bed-sitting rooms for the hotel staff.'

As he spoke, a police van turned the far corner of the building and parked tidily at the far side of the pink limo.

Drummond turned to Martin. 'Thank you for your help, Mr Chumleigh. I think we can take it from here.'

Martin opened his mouth, appeared to think better of it, and turned to go back into the mansion. Drummond waited briefly until he had shut the back door, and then he and Pollard walked quickly to the van, where several men were struggling into white protective clothing before collecting an assortment of bags and containers.

'Nice place,' commented one white coat.

Drummond glanced at him. He knew that in a job like theirs they had to keep cheerful, but already his mind was neatly filing the information he had just been given. If the keys had always been kept in the pantry, anyone could have had access to them, though how many people would have known about them he didn't yet know. He'd get them fingerprinted, but by now he was sure it would be too late.

He gathered the group of scenes of crime officers together – a small number for the size of the task, he thought. More cutbacks.

Briefly he summarised what needed to be done. 'Half of you start with the pool area,' he said, 'fine-tooth comb the lot. Then I need the rest of you out on the cliff, just in case we missed anything. Pollard will show you the exact spot. We're looking for any suggestion that wheels of some kind were used to transfer the body from the pool to the sea. And without any of you falling over the edge, see if there's any evidence at the bottom of the cliff. Low tide isn't till 3.30 this afternoon, so a thorough search will have to wait until later. The cars parked by the stables need to be searched – I'll get the keys for you – and compare the tyre treads with the marks in the mud on the front lawn. Then check all the outbuildings for anything unusual. I'll be in and out between interviews. All right?'

Taking the series of nods as indicating agreement and understanding, he went on, 'This is going to take time. I don't want it rushed. The trail has already gone cold. We can't afford to miss the slightest clue. I want the whole area sealed off, from the front gates to the area where we are standing, including the outbuildings and the pool, of course. Similarly the likely route from the gates to the cliff edge; the press are already sniffing around – keep them well away. Oh, and if you are in need of refreshment, see the cook – the kitchen's just inside the back door on the right.'

Drummond and Pollard led a group of SOCOs along the back drive and waited at the gate as one of them dusted all the keys and the old round knob, before opening the gate. The rest went ahead of him, like white bloodhounds, heads down, eyes keen, ready to do a fingertip search of this presumed scene of crime. Drummond stood in the gateway, surveying the investigation from a safe distance.

He hadn't known what to expect when the old gate creaked open. Certainly not what he saw. Ahead and slightly to his right stood what looked like an overgrown greenhouse with a turquoise-tiled pool, surrounded by the remains of what had probably been a prolific kitchen garden. He sighed; there was nothing he could do here until the SOCOs had finished.

He returned to the dining room, his feet echoing down the corridor. By the time he stepped through the doorway, any conversation had ceased. Heads turned. He looked at them surrounded by the debris of breakfast – could he clear the debris of their lives? It would cost.

With formal politeness he said, 'We shall soon be ready for you.'

'Do we have to stay here?' Edward queried. 'It would really be much more comfortable in the drawing room.'

'By all means. We'll call you from there.'

With obvious relief and much scraping of chairs, the whole company stood and made its way to the drawing room.

As Ian, in his tracksuit, passed him, Drummond held out his hand. 'Sir, we need to lock the gym. Are you expecting anyone to use it today?'

'I was asked to have it available for the family, and I was going to go to my office to finish the paperwork I began before breakfast. I locked up before I came across.'

Drummond nodded and said, 'I'm afraid I can't let you go there for the moment. May I have the keys, please?'

Ian handed over an assortment of keys, and followed the family into the drawing room, while Drummond continued on to the music room where George found him a few minutes later. It was then that George passed on the news – that Edward had inherited everything.

'Has he now?' was the chief inspector's only comment.

Chapter 18

By ten o'clock Simon Drummond was sitting at the large mahogany table in the music room. To his left was a list of those in the house, to his right the pile of signed statements that they had taken only yesterday. He took his pen out of his top pocket and laid it horizontally in front of him. For the moment his mind was perfectly clear. Soon it would be muddied by half-truths, lies, innocent speculation and biased opinion. In among it all would be the tiny pieces of truth, like segments of broken pottery found in an archaeological dig, waiting to be cleaned, identified and carefully positioned, so that the whole 3D genuine specimen would finally ring true and its story be revealed.

Lindsey Pollard was standing looking out of one of the music room windows. The four separate windows in its semicircular bay enabled the viewer to see both the converted Old Barn and stables to the left and the Lodge and main gate to the right, while straight ahead, behind the camellia covered in brilliant-pink flowers, the forest of evergreen provided the backdrop to the old boundary wall with its border of rhododendron and laurel bushes.

'They've taped off the entrance, sir, and there's a WPC on duty by the gate.'

'Good. I think we should start. Are you ready?'

Pollard patted various pockets in turn and eventually produced a notebook and a couple of pens which she put on the small table in front of her chair, which was set slightly back from Drummond's, by the window overlooking the stables. 'I am now, sir.'

They were interrupted by a knock at the door. The chief inspector's 'Come!' was followed quickly by the appearance of a slightly flustered Dame Emily, brushing strands of white hair out of her eyes.

'I'm so sorry,' she said, slightly breathlessly, holding up a battered briefcase. 'I completely forgot this. It belongs – belonged – to Mr Wedderburn. It had been left in the hall on the first evening, and we hid it in the cupboard under the stairs for safety.'

'We?' questioned Drummond.

'Stella and I; when she was seeing me out at bedtime.'

'Thank you, Dame Emily. We'll look after it.'

Emily seemed unwilling to relinquish the briefcase and clung to it uncertainly with both hands.

'Perhaps I should confess that I may have tampered with evidence,' she said, eyes fixed firmly on Drummond. 'I'm afraid I looked inside to see if there was anything that might be important. It has some rather sensitive information in it, I'm afraid. Stella was with me at the time, but you can be sure that we will say absolutely nothing about what we read.'

Drummond decided a slightly severe but polite look would be appropriate. 'I see,' he said slowly, wondering if Dame Emily had received her title for services to the acting profession. 'We'll see if it is pertinent to the case.'

Dame Emily looked at the beautifully polished table, and with a little difficulty stooped and put the briefcase on the floor by Drummond's chair. 'Thank you,' she said. 'I'm so sorry to disturb you.'

She nodded to DS Pollard and left the room.

Lindsey gave a little laugh. 'Dame Agatha rides again! She sounds as if she's solved the case and is handing it to us on a plate.'

Drummond was not amused. 'We really need to get on with the interviews, but I suppose I must appease your curiosity.'

Lindsey grinned. 'I'm just a big kid when it comes to mysteries,' she admitted. 'Let's see what's in it.'

Drummond tried to hide his own curiosity as he pulled on a pair of gloves, while Lindsey did the same. He tipped the contents of the briefcase onto the table, before checking the inner pocket and bringing out an envelope. Lindsey gently separated out the items.

'A diary, some invitations for this weekend, and this brown envelope's just got old newspaper cuttings in it,' she said, glancing at the dates on the top of each one. 'And there's an old key in among the other bits and pieces. Probably a spare one he forgot to hand over when he moved house.'

Drummond picked up the diary and opened it with the ribbon marker. 'Nothing down here for the night he was killed,' he remarked. 'Just "Family birthday bash! Retirement!" and earlier in the week some changes to the plans for moving down here.' He glanced at the empty sections of the following week. 'No meetings planned, except for Wednesday morning. "9.30 Silverlinks Lane", whatever that means. It could be something to do with selling one of his remaining shops, I suppose.'

Drummond shut the book with a slight bang and put everything back in the briefcase, and the briefcase back on the floor.

'Nothing that can't wait,' he said decisively, removing his gloves. 'We really must begin the interviews. I've made a list. I think we'll start with the people most affected by all this: James' wife, Cassidy, and his brother, Edward. After that I suggest we see Martin, who will know about the business side of things, and his children and their spouses. Then we'll talk to the other people in the house – Stella and Dame Emily, and the hangers-on like George and Ian. We'd better talk to the kitchen staff too, all right?'

Pollard scribbled the last name on the list and put down her pen. 'Shall I get Mrs Wedderburn?'

Cassidy looked very trim, sitting in her chair opposite Drummond. Neat navy slacks were topped by a pale-blue, low-cut shirt; blue and pink beads spilt from her neck. A thick cardigan was slung round her shoulders, and her fair hair was tied back in a pink clasp. She crossed one elegant leg over the other and let one of her pink shoes swing free from her toes. For all that she looked controlled, her hands were restless. Drummond leaned forward across the desk. 'I am so sorry to add to your distress at this very difficult time,' he said.

She looked at him, focusing her eyes on his face and almost seeing him as a person, he felt. 'I can't believe it's happened,' she said, shaking her head. 'I expect him to walk into this room at any moment. It's just all so strange. On Thursday night he was so alive, so real.' She stopped suddenly. Drummond knew the signs; after a shock people often had to repeat the facts many times, just to convince themselves that it was all true.

Drummond picked up the top piece of paper from the pile. 'If you don't mind, I'd like to go back to Thursday and fill in a few details. You said you arrived about four o'clock.'

'Yes, I flew in from Barbados and Martin – James' secretary – picked me up and brought me here. I suppose it was some time after four o'clock.'

'And were you in Barbados for a holiday?'

'No. I was out there on business – visiting my scuba-diving school.'

'Forgive me, Mrs Wedderburn, but that seems a strange occupation for the wife of the owner of a pork sausage empire and one who lives so far from the coast.'

Cassidy allowed herself a slight smile. 'I love swimming. When we married, James gave me a honeymoon present of scuba-diving lessons – then I was hooked. We met a man who ran a diving school, and he invited me to teach the holidaymakers and introduce them to the wonderful underwater world of Barbados. I went back many times. The numbers of English tourists increased and the school prospered. When the owner died ten years ago, I found he had left it to me. After that I set up two others – in Greece and Spain.'

'I see,' said Drummond quietly. 'Are you away from home for long intervals?'

'Not more than a couple of weeks at a time – I only go to check up on things. I have managers to oversee them all.'

'Do you think this business interest affected your relationship with your husband?'

Lindsey Pollard, who had looked faintly bored with the way the interview had been going, looked up sharply and glanced at Drummond before she focused more fully on Cassidy Wedderburn.

Cassidy's entwined fingers twisted in her lap. Her eyes fixed on some intricate detail in the patterned carpet. 'James worked long hours, so we only saw each other briefly, and at weekends, of course. It worked for us.'

Drummond smiled reassuringly. 'I'm sure it did. So let's return to Thursday evening. What was Mr Wedderburn's mood that night?'

Cassidy's eyes remained on the carpet and she bit her lip. 'He was excited, I suppose. It was his birthday and our anniversary and he had all his family around him; he enjoyed keeping us on tenterhooks, waiting to find out his plans for this house. He was going to tell us more on Friday morning.'

'And did he remain excited?'

There was a pause. Cassidy took a deep breath. 'Not to the same extent. He did drink rather a lot at dinner, and perhaps that's why he became thoughtless in the things he said.'

'For example?' Drummond prodded gently.

'He made an insensitive remark about his daughter's weight, and an unnecessary comment about his son's reluctance to earn a good income – but it was just the drink, I'm sure.'

'And they were upset?'

'Yes.'

'Had they provoked him?'

'I don't think so. I don't remember.'

'Did he upset anyone else?' Drummond could understand that Cassidy would be reticent about pointing the finger at her stepchildren, but this was a murder enquiry. He looked at her face, drawn and pale, eyes still on the floor, finger fiddling with a buttonhole on her chunky-knit cardigan. Was she protecting one of them?

'He did argue with his brother, Edward, who'd accused James of causing the death of a colleague of his, but his friend had actually taken his own life, so it wasn't true.'

'And you saw or heard nothing unusual after James had left the dining room?'

'Nothing. I went to unpack – for James as well as myself – he hadn't bothered. I think he would happily live out of a suitcase.' Cassidy smiled faintly. 'I got ready for bed about 9.45, I suppose – I was beginning to feel the effect of the flight – but later I felt cold and decided I needed a hot drink, so I went downstairs and Stella made me a hot chocolate. I saw Dame Emily in the hall, but none of the rest of the family. Then at about 10.30 I went back upstairs. I guessed James would be late – he had a meeting with George. I took a sleeping pill so I think I must have fallen asleep very quickly. I had no idea until the morning that James had not come to bed.'

'You heard no unusual sounds in the night? Voices, or a car engine?'

'No, nothing.'

'Do you know of anyone who might have wanted to harm your husband?'

'No. No one at all.'

Drummond decided not to press her further. 'Thank you, Mrs Wedderburn; I think that will be all for now. We may need to talk to you again over the weekend.'

Cassidy looked up; the blue eyes were pleading. 'Do you know what happened?' she asked.

'Not yet; it's rather too early. I only received the results of the post-mortem this morning.'

She nodded, stood, put a hand on the table to steady herself, and walked out of the room.

Drummond leaned back in his chair and looked at Lindsey Pollard. 'Any comments?'

Lindsey said, 'Cassidy is certainly a very attractive woman, even now. You can see why James fell for her. I thought she seemed to be the normal grieving wife, but very anxious about the questioning. Whether she didn't want to remember the events of the night he died, or whether she wanted to protect someone, I don't know.'

Drummond made a quick note. 'She mentioned three possible suspects, though,' he said, 'the daughter Clara, the son Philip, and the brother Edward. James seems to have upset them all. You would think they could've buried the hatchet for a special birthday celebration.' He relocated the statement to the bottom of the pile and glanced at the next one. 'Will you go and get Edward now? Oh, by the way, I had a quick word with George – the solicitor – just before you came into the room, and he says Edward is the sole beneficiary.'

Pollard paused in the doorway. 'Really?'

'I don't know the details,' Drummond said, 'but we shall find out.'

Edward arrived, calm and under control. When asked, he was happy to explain how he had arrived at Seascape.

'I was going to drive down to Sussex by car, but in the end-of-term chaos on Wednesday night, some careless parent backed into my car and managed to smash a headlight. There was no time to get it put right. A colleague gave me a lift to the station in the morning and I came down by train. I got to Eastbourne about 2.30 and found somewhere for coffee. When I eventually caught the bus, it rattled along at about 20 miles an hour. I think I arrived at about twenty past four in the end.'

'And what was your relationship with your brother? Was it close?'

Drummond had decided to go for the jugular. He could feel Pollard's eyes on Edward, and imagined her, pen poised. He had an uneasy feeling about Edward.

Edward looked him straight in the eye. 'We have not been close for decades,' he said. 'When our father died, James helped with my upbringing, but after our mother's death we gradually lost touch.'

'Was it just the passage of time, or did you not want to make contact?'

Edward shifted slightly in his chair. 'A bit of both, I think. I saw him at each of the children's weddings, but avoided speaking to him.'

'And why would that be?'

Edward leaned forward and clasped his hands together round one knee. 'I believe,' he said, 'that James cheated my friend's parents out of some money. His family suffered considerably as a result.'

Edward looked out of the window, avoiding Drummond's gaze. His face had become hard. He had told his story briefly, but clearly his emotions were only just under control. Drummond diagnosed deep-seated hatred. It wouldn't be difficult to bring it to the surface with some sharp interrogation, but perhaps he would learn more from other members of the family. He switched tack. 'When did you last see your brother?'

'At the end of dinner on Thursday evening. I left the dining room before James did, collected my laptop from my bedroom and went to the drawing room. I wanted some peace and quiet to send an email. I also had some schoolwork to do before term begins and intended to get on with it. I gather from the family that James went into the garden. I never saw him again – until I went to the mortuary,' he added, his face softening a little.

'I gather you had a disagreement with your brother at dinner. Did anyone else argue with James that evening?'

'James upset both his son and daughter. He wasn't particularly complimentary to anyone, and seemed very full of himself and his ridiculous plans.'

'Ridiculous plans?'

'To turn this place into a hotel using the family's spare cash… As if any of us had any! Oh, he'd pay us back when both he and Cassidy were dead. He'd write a new will and make it all fair.' Edward could not keep the sarcasm out of his voice.

Drummond looked thoughtful. 'In view of all that, can you think of anyone who had reason to dislike, even hate, your brother?' He watched Edward carefully. He was giving him the chance to turn attention away from himself.

'I should think all the family had something against him.' He stopped as if realising the implication of his words. 'No, of course not. It must have been an accident... I don't know. Nobody's gained anything.'

'Except you,' said Drummond softly.

Edward's head shot up. 'What? Being left this place and complicated investments? I don't want it – I just want a quiet life away from it all. Anyway, I had no idea what was in his will. And from what I hear no one else did either – except George.'

'What about the staff? Would any of them want to harm Mr Wedderburn?'

Edward looked bewildered. 'The staff? As far as I know, Stella has only been employed for a few months, and Ian four or five weeks. I don't think either of them had met James till this week. The same goes for the kitchen staff. Martin has worked for him for ages and was going to move down here with his family. I can't see why he'd suddenly turn against him. None of this makes any sense.'

Drummond secretly agreed with him – unless it was Edward himself who had killed his brother. The time of death was rather vague, but James had certainly died within a couple of hours of his final meal. Edward's statement had said that he was with the family and then Archie that evening. He had the motive and the opportunity if Archie had been his accomplice.

'Thank you, sir, for being so helpful,' Drummond said to Edward. 'I think that will do for now.'

Edward nodded; looking tired but a little relieved, he left the room.

Lindsey Pollard put down her pen and exercised her fingers. 'You didn't push him very hard.'

'I'm saving it,' said Drummond. 'I have a lot of evidence to gather before I put any pressure on him. There'll be many twists and turns before we get to the bottom of this.' He looked at his watch. 'I don't think we've got time for another full interview before elevenses; let's just see the two in the kitchen – we can do them together. That shouldn't take long.'

Grace and Jayne came into the music room ahead of Lindsey Pollard. They sat on two of the dining room chairs in front of Drummond. Grace had her hands folded, sitting bolt upright, clearly on her best behaviour. Jayne seemed almost excited by the novelty of being interviewed by the police; her eyes sparkled and she looked at the pile of papers on Drummond's table with considerable interest.

'Ladies,' said DCI Drummond, 'I would just like to know if you have any information which will help us in our investigation. For instance, would you tell me when you last saw Mr James Wedderburn?'

'When they'd all finished eating in the dining room. He wouldn't let us clear the plates – he said he wanted to talk to everyone, so we had to go back to the kitchen. We didn't see him after that,' said Grace. 'He wasn't there when I went back.'

'You saw or heard nothing unusual after that?'

Jayne put her head on one side. 'Well, I was in the kitchen. I think I can remember hearing the front door slam, but that's all.'

'I didn't hear anything,' said Grace thoughtfully. 'We did night-time drinks for the family, but he never appeared. We went to bed quite early.'

'Too early,' said Jayne with a grin.

'You'll learn, my girl,' said Grace rather forcefully. 'You need your sleep when you work full-time in a kitchen.'

'Half nine is far too early,' retorted Jayne.

'You managed to spin it out.' Grace seemed determined to have the last word.

Drummond felt the interview slipping away from him. 'Thank you both,' he said. 'Please let me know if anything occurs to you.'

Grace and Jayne left to take elevenses into the drawing room, and Lindsey shut her notebook. 'Not much help there, then,' she said. 'Shall I go and get the tea and coffee?'

'I'll come with you and we can take it out to the walled garden. I'd like to check on the progress of the SOCOs.'

Drummond paused in the gateway to the walled garden for his second visit. 'Can we come in?'

The senior scenes of crime officer was standing by the pool door with his paraphernalia. 'All done, apart from the changing-room area, so yes. I'm going there now. The news so far is that the box with light switches here in the wall has been wiped clean. We've given the whole place a good going over; there were some prints in the pool area, and a few hairs caught near the steps at the shallow end. They might just be the victim's, which would tie him into the scene, but I gather the family used the pool yesterday morning, after which it was thoroughly cleaned, so I fear you won't have any conclusive evidence. Even so, it might be helpful to have everyone's fingerprints.'

'The family has used the pool?' Drummond looked at his officer in disbelief. 'Are you saying the whole family went for a swim, hours after they had lost their father and husband, in late March, when we've hardly seen the sun for days?'

'The cook mentioned it, sir, when I went in for my coffee just now. She thanked me for appreciating her clean kitchen floor, unlike the young woman who came in with dripping wet swimwear yesterday, asking where the drying room was, and saying could they have their elevenses now as they'd finished in the pool.'

'That was when Edward and Martin were waiting with us at the mortuary,' Pollard said. 'The family wouldn't actually have known that the body belonged to James.'

Drummond glared at her. 'That's hardly a good reason,' he snapped. 'Dame Emily's identification at the scene was absolutely correct – she told them all at breakfast.' He frowned.

'Was someone trying to tamper with forensic evidence? I wonder who put them up to using the pool.'

DS Pollard had no answer; instead she said, 'Shall I do the fingerprinting, sir?'

'Yes, thank you,' said Drummond rather absent-mindedly. 'Do it later... I want to look at the murder scene – supposing it happened here, which seems the most likely scenario.' He walked down the left-hand path, Lindsey at his side, and stopped at the glass door. 'Now,' he said. 'Let's put together what we already know and see if the scene can reveal other facts. What do we know about the victim?'

'He'd had a large dinner, a considerable amount of wine – and some pills. We think they finished the meal about eight, but stayed in the dining room for another 40 minutes or so. The post-mortem indicates that Mr Wedderburn died sometime between 9.30 and 11.30pm. No watch was found on the body, so to pinpoint the time more accurately we need to find out the temperature of the pool area and water – although it's unlikely it would be warm at that time of night – and how long he remained here, as that would affect the onset of rigor mortis. We know the temperature of the sea would be a few degrees above freezing.'

'We'll ask Ian about the heating. Now, why did James Wedderburn come here? Was he going to meet someone? At their invitation or his? And does that someone follow him through the gate and jump him from behind, or are they here already, lying in wait?'

'There's nowhere to hide in the walled garden, sir, and it's unlikely they attacked him before he got to the pool. Anyway, he'd have switched the lights on at the gate, or found the place already lit. But it wouldn't be difficult for someone to hide in the showers or changing rooms and then surprise him.'

'So who did he come to meet? And why meet at the pool? There are plenty of spare rooms in the mansion.'

'That makes it sound secretive. Perhaps someone enticed him here, saying they wanted to give him money, and discuss it out of sight and hearing of the rest of the family. Didn't one of the statements say he wanted the family to talk to him that night about their contribution to the future of the hotel? Maybe the perpetrator wanted to create an opportunity to finish him off. On the other hand, it might have been a genuine offer, but with a demand to be put in the new will on their terms, which James refused and then things got a bit heated…'

Drummond frowned. 'So we're back with the "it could be anyone in the family" theory,' he said. 'Let's leave it and look inside.'

They went straight into the pool area. Training from school days prompted the chief inspector to take off his shoes, and Lindsey did the same.

'It's a good size,' remarked Lindsey, 'and that slope at the shallow end is sensible for children. I like the unusual turquoise tiles, too.'

'Never mind the aesthetics,' said Drummond, his eyes on the pool surround. 'We need to work out how our man was hit once on the back of the head and twice on the jaw before he was drowned. The pathologist has identified the other damage as having been caused by the fall from the cliff, after James had been killed…' He stared thoughtfully at the pool edge. 'Mm,' he said. 'I have an idea, but need to think it through.'

By mutual agreement they walked around the pool, each thinking their own thoughts. As they left, Drummond shut the door rather more forcefully than he had intended.

'I'm thwarted at every turn,' he complained. 'Yesterday the SOCOs found very little evidence on the clifftop. The body'd been rescued before we could look at it in situ; the grass was churned up by the wheels of the coastguard's vehicle, the ambulance, the police car and the mortuary van; the only two partial footprints we found have to be checked with the emergency services' shoes as well as those in this house, so that'll take some time. When we come to look at the pool we find it's been used by most of the family and goodness knows who else, and it's been thoroughly cleaned. Added to all that, all the switches in the light box have been wiped clean.'

Lindsey said nothing. Drummond knew he had that effect on her when he was annoyed. She followed him up the path and onto the back drive, and waited while he locked the door to the walled garden. She went back into the kitchen to return their mugs, while he went on to the music room to prepare for the next victim of his interrogation.

Chapter 19

Emily was very relieved to see the coffee trolley. The time since breakfast had passed incredibly slowly.

The family had seated themselves more or less in the centre of the drawing room, except for Edward, who sat in the further bay window and had his laptop open on a small table. He divided his time between studying the screen and flicking through a newspaper. He seemed to be fully absorbed.

George was buried in a low armchair, hidden behind one of the Saturday supplements, and Ian, in the furthest corner of the room, had picked up one of the other weekend magazines. Martin was also deep in a paper, while Stella and Emily sat in companionable silence.

The earlier buzz of conversation, mainly led by Clara, had died, briefly. Her eager questions had largely been ignored by Cassidy, who stared into space, keeping her emotions under control. The peace did not last long.

'Well, who could have done it?' Clara had demanded.

Philip had shrugged his shoulders and indicated with an outstretched arm every person in the room.

'You mean, someone in this room?'

Philip gave her a pitying look.

'But what about an outsider? Someone said a stranger might have pushed him over...' she swallowed, thinking more carefully about the possibility.

Emily watched as Philip glanced at Cassidy. Even in these dreadful circumstances he had some thought for his stepmother. Then he looked back at Clara and threw caution to the winds.

'Would someone from outside come and grab Dad, force him into the walled garden, which might have been locked for all we know, drown him, walk him back down the drive and propel him over the cliff into the sea? You're not thinking, girl!'

'Well, then, it was an accident. He fell in the pool and hit his head.'

'And then wandered back to the cliff and fell over the edge?' The sarcasm was becoming stronger in Philip's voice. 'Face it, Clara, someone wanted him dead, and for some reason it wasn't good enough to leave him floating in the pool as if it were all an accident.'

Cassidy pulled herself back into reality. 'Philip, Clara!' she said firmly. 'Please stop it! This is your father you're talking about and I don't want to hear it.'

The tears had begun to flow and hankies were passed to her, but now the truth of the situation had been spoken about in all its stark reality. Emily felt the movement of suspicious eyes, not only on her, but on each of them in the room. Soon mistrust would begin its silent, divisive work.

She turned and looked at Stella, her gardening magazine open in her lap. Stella was looking at her too, not in a wary kind of a way, but questioning. Emily gave the slightest shrug of her shoulders and shook her head. She really didn't know what to think. George had been blackmailed by James for years; perhaps Ian had been threatened by him this very weekend. Emily wondered what the police would say to Ian. He had every reason to kill James, who might have been about to ruin his life for a second time. At least she and Stella could be trusted with Ian's secret if he were proved innocent.

One or two of the family had strong motives, but Emily found it so hard to suspect them: artistic Philip with his deep resentment; emotional Samantha, desperate for life to become easier and to start a family; loyal and quick-tempered Archie, and the damaged Clara; they seemed like the offspring of any typical English family. Could they have joined forces? Perhaps linked up with Edward? There were too many unknowns.

Edward, with practised ease, folded his paper neatly and looked at the bottom quarter of the page.

'Anyone got a pen?' he enquired of the world in general.

Clara looked round the room as if one might be lurking on the bookcase or a table. 'Can't see one,' she said.

Martin got up and exchanged his paper for a supplement lying on the top of the piano.

'Martin! The very man!' Edward got up and went over to him. 'Can I borrow your pen?'

Martin patted the sides of his blazer.

'The one in your top pocket,' persisted Edward.

'Oh, that one. I thought I might need it – for my statement.'

'I'm sure they'll lend you one,' said Edward, holding out his hand. 'Come on. I need to keep my mind busy and I've just worked out 9 across.'

He waited as Martin pulled the silver pen from his breast pocket and handed it over. James' secretary was dressed immaculately, as he had been at dinner yesterday, and today wore a navy jacket over a mauve shirt with navy trousers. Emily wondered if he ever relaxed. Perhaps he considered himself to be James' representative now that James was no more? Certainly Martin seemed to know more about the plans for the hotel and the future than anyone else.

Edward returned to his seat and filled in his first answer. Briefly Emily wished there had been two copies of the paper. Right now her sister, Margaret, would be attacking the crossword with her usual enthusiasm, and if she went to visit later in the afternoon, would be required to report on how much she herself had completed. Only a couple of years ago they would have sat at opposite ends of the dining table, each with a paper and pen, competing fiercely to be the first to finish. Well, that time would not return, unless she too went into the Deanery, and Emily had no intention of doing that for many years to come. She had expected to come back from Australia to start a new, relaxed life, in a home of her choosing, and now she was inextricably involved with the tangled relationships of complete strangers. Bother James Wedderburn – he had a lot to answer for.

Emily sighed and had just turned her mind to George when the door opened. DS Pollard put her head round the opening and said, fairly cheerfully, like a receptionist trying to brighten a dull waiting room, 'Mr Chumleigh, please!'

Martin relinquished his supplement and followed her from the room.

Emily returned to her musings on James' solicitor. It was ridiculous, but she had a soft spot for George. She'd only met him at meals and watched him read the will, but somehow she felt he was the one reliable person present, a rock in the middle of a river in full spate; yet even he was under threat from the Deceased of Seascape House. Emily found it impossible to remain in her chair. There was just enough time, she guessed. She crossed the room.

'George?' she said, addressing the cover page of his newspaper.

George lowered the paper and peered up at her over the top of his glasses.

'Could you spare me a few minutes?' Emily asked him. 'There's something quite important I need to discuss with you. Perhaps we could go to the dining room,' she went on, as George looked doubtful. 'Someone can come and fetch us if we're needed.'

She glanced round the room. Philip had his eyes on her, but Edward was now fiddling with his mobile phone.

'Well,' said George, 'if it's really important.'

He rocked himself in the armchair a couple of times, in order to gain enough momentum to stand up and follow her from the room.

They sat at the dining table, Emily in James' chair and George next to her.

'What's so important?' said George. 'I know you want to talk about your furniture and so on, but I really can't deal with that just now.'

Emily fiddled with a serving spoon. 'I have something to confess,' she said.

George's eyebrows shot up, but he said nothing.

Emily felt her heart beating rather faster than usual; she told herself not to be stupid. 'Stella and I found James' briefcase, and I'm afraid I looked inside before we handed it to the police. It contained something about you.'

George frowned. He was clearly not following.

Emily took a deep breath. 'In an envelope, inside the briefcase, was a very old photograph of a group of young people. On the back it stated that you were at a disco while your wife was giving birth. I also noticed the words, "naughty George!".'

George's eyes never left Emily's face, but he relaxed a little in his chair. 'And the police have it now?'

'Yes,' said Emily.

'I am sure I can trust your discretion,' said George. He paused and straightened the place setting in front of him, before speaking. 'I think the cutting says a little more about James than it does about me,' he remarked, 'and yes, before you ask, he did use it as blackmail. I didn't kill James, but you have no idea of the relief I felt when I heard that he'd died. At first I just could not believe you when you said that you had found his body; by the time I left you after breakfast, I just wanted to dance all the way down the corridor to the music room!'

Emily waited.

George sighed. 'I'd better explain. The disco photo was taken the night my daughter was born. It was early evening. I'd taken my wife to hospital. They kept her in and said the child wouldn't come for many hours. I didn't fancy pacing up and down with other expectant fathers, so I decided to go home.

'Just as I reached the house, one of our neighbours caught me. She was one of those fun-loving, lively girls, always looking for a lark. There she was in her flowery skirt, longing to go to this disco, but her boyfriend, who'd been playing football that afternoon, had just landed in the local A & E with a broken leg. I went with her to do her a kindness, really. I'd rather have been at home with a cold beer and my feet up before my life changed forever, I can tell you.

'We went on my motorbike – I'm sure it was the bike she liked, not me! I took her for a spin first – she loved it. Then we went on to the disco and were together for most of the evening. Before we put our helmets on to come back she gave me a quick peck on the cheek. I can only guess that James saw us. That's all there was to it.

'Unfortunately the local press took that photo (which I managed to keep from my wife), and more unfortunately still, the baby surprised everyone and arrived prematurely that night. I missed the first call from the hospital; later I told my wife I must have been replacing some tools in the garage when they rang. It would have been disastrous if she'd found out. She's always been a very possessive woman; insecure, I suppose. She would have read so much more into a harmless good deed, and I might well have gone on to have a very rocky marriage.

'My wife had a very hard time during the birth. We nearly lost the child. I rushed to the hospital and after a few hours the baby turned the corner. She's coming with our grandson on Sunday to celebrate their birthdays and I badly wanted to be home for the family meal. Now James, even in death, has put a stop to that.'

George pulled a neatly folded handkerchief from his pocket and wiped his brow before continuing. 'At that time, I had just taken over all James' legal requirements from my father, and the old so-and-so soon trapped me. He got a copy of the photo and used it as blackmail. He said he would show it to my wife and say he'd seen me in the car park, wrapped in the girl's arms. I should have forestalled him and told my wife the truth, but I kept putting it off, and before I knew it we were expecting our second child. After that life was always too busy to have a serious conversation with my wife, and I dreaded the effect it might have, so I left it.

'I've let fear of James cheat me out of a great deal of money for the last 40 years. How pathetic!' George sat up straighter in his chair and ran his hand over his balding pate with its remnants of silver, wavy hair. 'So now you know. Is that a good enough motive for murder?'

Emily looked again at the little man in the chair next to her. How he had suffered for the best part of a life time – and all because of the greed of a bully.

'I think it is a motive for murder,' she said slowly, 'but not for someone like you. If you had felt strongly enough, you would have done something about it years ago. I can't see you contriving to drown a large man and transfer him to the cliffs, and you wouldn't have wanted to confide in anyone here and enlist their help. I don't believe you killed him.'

'Thank you,' said George.

He looked round the panelled room and put his hands flat on the polished wood of the dining table, preparing to stand. 'I suppose I should be grateful for your warning and for your support. At least I will be ready in case the police try to trap me – you never know which way they'll jump.'

Chapter 20

Chief Inspector Drummond was sitting upright in his chair when Martin entered. 'Good morning, Mr Chumleigh, please sit down.' His tone was informal but firm. 'You will understand that this is now a murder investigation and we will require more details about what happened here yesterday and during the night.'

'Yes, of course, I will be glad to help.'

'You have worked for Mr Wedderburn for how long?'

'For about 13 years.'

'Has that always been in your capacity as secretary and accountant?'

'I was his accountant first, but as his investments grew, he also valued my help in finding suitable shops for sale, so I gradually took over more responsibility. It also seemed to be sensible to become his secretary. It saved James the expense of a second salary and I was able to have an increase to cover the extra work. More recently I have been able to use my graphic design skills to create a logo for the company and to help with marketing.'

Drummond made a mental note that this man had a good interview technique. Swiftly he changed the subject. 'Now, perhaps you can explain to me how Mr Wedderburn came to buy Seascape House, when the building work was done, and how the staff came to be taken on.'

'Briefly,' Martin said, shuffling slightly in his chair, 'Mr Wedderburn came down last summer for a short break. His chauffeur had been asked to take him for a drive and happened to come past this house, which had gone on the market the day before. Mr Wedderburn was very taken with it and insisted that the agent should be called immediately to show him round. Then he sent for me and I came the next day.' Martin allowed himself to smile. 'We spent hours with the calculator and the accounts from all his shops and farms in front of us. We decided that if he could manage to sell his own home and all the shops, he would be able to buy the mansion and still have money available to turn the place into a hotel, restore the Old Barn and stables, and put in a leisure centre, laundry, adventure playground and shop. The sale went through sometime in August, as far as I remember; the two solicitors concluded all the business while Dame Emily was in Australia attending a wedding. She wasn't expecting the house to sell so quickly, but James wanted everything completed at speed.'

Drummond nodded and glanced at Pollard, who was bent over her notebook, writing quickly. 'That much is now clear to me,' he said. 'Perhaps you could explain the presence of the staff and how the previous owner appears to be staying here.'

'Some accident prevented Dame Emily from returning immediately from Australia, and it was agreed that she could keep the contents of the house in situ and, on her return, was offered a temporary new home while she found one of her own. Then there was some problem with the new place and she came back to the Lodge. Then... I think... the electricity failed – or something like that...' Martin's voiced faded a little and Drummond was aware that his eyes were on the window behind him. Drummond glanced round to see the police van reversing out of its parking space, turning and backing towards the parked cars outside the window. As he turned back to face Martin again, a very definite crunching sound was heard from outside.

'My car!' Martin leapt to his feet. 'The stupid man!'

In a split second he was out of the door and his feet could be heard running along the passage. Drummond and Pollard exchanged glances as the chief inspector turned in his chair to face the window. 'This may be an interesting exchange,' he remarked. 'Which idiot was driving the van?' As if in answer to his question, one of the white coats emerged and stood gloomily looking at the damage. Seconds later a distraught Martin came to a halt outside the window. His angry obscenities penetrated the old glass, as he waved and pointed and threatened the police officer.

'Take notes,' said Drummond briefly. 'Just in case he hits the man.'

Pollard moved slightly to get a better view, and they watched as the van was moved forward a little and Martin surveyed his car's damaged wing, newly crumpled and with flaking paint. Together the two men bent down, and Drummond could see Martin place his hand between the metal and the wheel. 'It'll hurt his pride to have a dented Mazda, but it looks driveable and the lights aren't damaged,' he observed.

After another brief exchange, Martin turned and went back towards the kitchen door, striding quickly, his head down. Soon they heard his returning footsteps on the wooden flooring. The door opened and Martin, resembling a thundercloud, marched in and sat like a ramrod in his chair. 'Inexperienced drivers should not be given the opportunity to drive vans of that size!' he proclaimed very loudly, glaring at Drummond as though he held him personally responsible.

Chief Inspector Drummond refrained from pointing out that the officer in question had been driving for several years without a problem, and did his best to calm troubled waters. 'I am so sorry that you have been inconvenienced,' he said smoothly. 'Will you be able to drive it?'

Martin scowled. 'Yes. No thanks to him.' He snorted and stared pointedly out of the window, where the van was gently moving backwards in the direction of the walled garden.

'I'm sure our insurance people will deal with the claim as quickly as possible.' Drummond was at his most diplomatic. 'Now, may we continue with the interview?'

Martin, with apparent and deliberate effort, relocated his gaze to Drummond's face. 'Of course.'

'Perhaps we could return to the time you came to Seascape House.'

Martin took a deep breath. 'Since August I've been down on several occasions to liaise with Stella on the refurbishment, to initiate plans for the future and to appoint staff. This time I came down at the beginning of the week to get the house ready for this weekend – again with Stella's help. She had ordered new beds and I took delivery of them; she found the cook and I interviewed her, but as the woman had worked here before it seemed sensible to take her and her granddaughter on.

'I was also here about six weeks ago. Ian Matthews was one of five who applied for the leisure centre manager's job. Mr Wedderburn went through the applications and shortlisted three, but he made it clear that he thought Mr Matthews was the candidate with the most potential. I came down and interviewed them and was happy to recommend Ian, so he was offered the job.'

Drummond glanced at his notes. 'Perhaps you could tell us about the progress of the building work here?'

Martin crossed his legs and leaned back, almost as relaxed as when he had first entered the room. 'Briefly, work began on the outbuildings almost at once, and the Old Barn and the stables are virtually complete. There is considerably more to be done to the other buildings. James' plans for the mansion are in abeyance. We just did not realise the problems involved in altering a listed building. Under Stella's guidance we have sent several hundred drawings to the Elizabethan Heritage Association, but we still haven't found something which pleases both parties. It's all taken more money and time than we anticipated.'

'So Mr Wedderburn was beginning to run out of money?'

'He had the money, but it had been carefully invested. He had been relying on the sale of two shops, but he hasn't been able to find buyers for them. He hoped that if the family would loan him some money, and the bank be persuaded to provide any finance still outstanding, he might be able to complete the work here and repay it all, once the hotel was up and running.'

'How did the family react?'

'James only touched on the idea on Thursday night – he was going to explain it fully the next day – but I think they were shocked, and didn't really appreciate being asked for money.'

'Would anyone have reacted sufficiently strongly to want to do him harm?' Drummond asked the question quietly, as if he were casually asking the time.

Martin glanced at him quickly – the implication of the question was not lost on him. 'Some members of the family reacted very strongly,' he said.

'And they were?'

'His two children; they seem to resent the fact that James expected their help. They even blamed their father for their own shortcomings. His brother accused him of foul play in the past, and said he didn't want to have anything more to do with him.'

Drummond looked at Martin, still sitting upright in his chair, neat and every inch the secretary. He considered carefully and then decided not to pursue the resentments for the time being. 'Anyone else?' he queried.

'The previous owner of the house, Dame Emily, was very upset with the way he had treated her.' Martin paused. 'The rest of us depended on him in some way for our jobs or for income; it wouldn't be in our interests to harm him. It's such a tragic business. I can't believe it's happened. I was going to move my family down here to join me in the autumn. I wonder if perhaps Cassidy and Edward might yet run the hotel together...' He looked at Drummond and shrugged his shoulders. 'Who knows?'

The chief inspector nodded. 'Thank you, sir, that's most helpful. Just before you go, is there anything you want to add to your statement, about the last time you saw Mr Wedderburn – or perhaps you saw or heard something unusual which you have since remembered?'

Martin paused and stared past Drummond at the roof of the stables, below which his damaged car was parked. 'No, I can't think of anything. Most of the guests were in the dining room when he left. I went straight to my office to make sure all the papers James needed for the next day were in order.'

'Can anyone verify that?'

'No, no one came into the room, but I did go to look for James, to clarify a couple of details. I checked with his solicitor in this room, and asked Dame Emily, but no one had seen him.'

'And what time was that?'

'Between about 9.45 and 10.15, I think.'

Drummond rose. 'Then that will be all, thank you. Perhaps you would ask Philip to come next.'

Chapter 21

DCI Drummond slid the next witness statement from the pile onto the polished wood in front of him and skimmed its contents. There was a knock at the door and Philip Wedderburn entered. Drummond looked at the tall young man dressed in pale-blue jeans, with a deep-pink hoodie over a white T-shirt.

The inspector waved to the chair opposite him and Philip sat, cleaning his glasses with a tissue before settling them on the bridge of his nose. He reminded Drummond of a shrew, quickly washing its face with its paw, nervous, twitchy.

Drummond began in relaxed, pleasant mode, thanking Philip for his previous statement and directing his thoughts once more to the last time the family had seen his father. Philip fiddled with the tissue in his hands and then, decisively, put it in his pocket. 'I told you – it's in my statement; I didn't see him after he left the dining room.'

'But you did argue with him at the meal?' Drummond leaned forward trying to make eye contact. Philip stared at his jeans. 'You realise there were many witnesses to your outburst?' Drummond persisted. 'We shall find out.'

'Yes!' Philip blurted out. 'Yes, I did argue with him. He wasn't much of a father and was rude to Clara and dismissed all my hopes. I couldn't contain it any longer. It's been years since I've seen him; I think I'd forgotten just how awful he could be.'

Drummond decided to change tack. 'You said you were in the drawing room for the whole evening. Do you wish to change that statement?'

'No.' Philip looked surprised. 'I was in there with the others till I went to bed.'

'And what time was that?'

Philip thought. 'It was about 10.20, I suppose. We'd been up since five that morning, and driving is tiring. I was longing to get my head down.'

Drummond glanced at the sheet in front of him. 'And your wife, Samantha, she went upstairs with you?'

'No, she went a little earlier.'

'You were both in the room until just before breakfast?' Drummond endeavoured to make it sound as casual as the weekly shopping.

'Yes –' Philip broke off.

Drummond fixed hawk eyes on him. 'Would you like to rethink your answer?' he asked. 'We have a witness who heard a door bang and then crying, and was sure it came from your part of the corridor. That would have been about 10.45. Is that not so?'

Philip's hand went to his glasses. 'Er, well, yes.' For the first time his eyes met Drummond's and they were pleading. 'We had an argument. The day before we came here, Samantha put in an offer for a house in St Ives – I knew nothing about it. She was really upset when she realised Dad wouldn't have any money to lend us, and then, that night, she confessed what she'd done. I was furious. She should never have gone ahead with the stupid idea without discussing it first. We argued for quite a time, and then it got really heated – I suppose people did hear, I didn't think about it at the time. We've been given the old nursery on the first floor. I grabbed the spare bedding from one of the single beds and went into the nurse's part of the room and banged the communicating door. I stayed there all night.'

Drummond's eyes had never left Philip's face; he probed delicately, 'Did your wife join you at any time?'

Philip dropped his gaze. 'No,' he said quietly.

'So either of you could have left your rooms at any time that night without the other knowing...' Drummond left the sentence unfinished.

Philip looked up in horror. 'You can't mean...? Neither of us wished my father any harm. In fact we'd wanted to talk to him about a loan. We did nothing, went nowhere – I swear it!'

Drummond changed tack once more. 'And when did you discover that your father was missing?'

Philip blinked twice. 'I think it was when I heard Cassi call out on the stairs, and then when you told us in the dining room.'

'You will understand, sir,' said Drummond, 'that we are very anxious to know the whereabouts of all the guests at Seascape from the end of dinner on Thursday to 7.30 the next morning, when Mr Wedderburn's body was found. Can you think of anything unusual that you saw or heard during those hours?'

Philip's eyes were moist. He shook his head. 'I know Sam was crying in the next room. I pulled the bedclothes over my head to shut out the sound. I think I fell asleep quite quickly. I'd set the travel alarm earlier. I didn't wake until it went off in Sam's room at about eight o'clock.' He twisted his long fingers in his lap. 'I just can't believe it's happened. I think I'll wake up and find him sitting in the dining room, smell his cigar smoke in the corridor...' Philip's voice cracked.

Drummond decided to have mercy on him and thanked him for his help. Philip left, his head bowed, his mouth set in a grim line.

It was Samantha who came into the room next. Quite striking, was Drummond's mental summary. She was a tall woman, probably not quite as tall as Philip, with a long delicate nose. The blonde hair had been swept back from her face and was fastened neatly at the back of her head; dainty metallic earrings set off the blue-grey eyes. Her jeans and blue top were warm and practical, as if she was used to hard work in cool conditions. She sat self-consciously on the chair in front of Drummond and glanced at Lindsey Pollard before looking at the chief inspector.

'Mrs Wedderburn,' began Drummond.

'Please would you call me Samantha?' she said.

Drummond smiled reassuringly. 'Of course. I don't want to make this any more difficult for you than it is already. Now, you told us in your last statement how you left the dining room before your father-in-law...' He paused.

Samantha nodded, the earrings swinging. 'Yes,' she said softly.

'Where did you go from the dining room?'

'To our bedroom.'

'When did you leave your room?'

'When Philip came to look for me – after about 20 minutes. He persuaded me to come down to the drawing room for a hot drink, because I was shivery.'

'And you stayed there all the time, till you went to bed?'

'Yes, Clara and I went up together sometime around ten o'clock.'

'Did you hear or see anything suspicious during that time?'

'No.' Samantha looked surprised. 'All I was thinking about was going to bed; it had been an exhausting day.'

'Was it long before your husband joined you?'

Samantha hesitated. 'I'm not sure, perhaps 15 minutes,' she said. 'I got undressed very quickly because it was freezing cold.' She stopped and looked at Drummond.

'And when he came into the room?'

'He's told you, hasn't he?' Tears welled and Samantha swallowed hard. 'He said he would sleep next door.'

'Did he look dishevelled in any way? As if he had been outside? Was he wet?'

The polite, rather self-pitying image vanished. 'No. Of course not! What are you saying?'

'We have to be sure of everyone's movements on Thursday night,' said Drummond.

'You mean someone could have killed Philip's dad while we were going to bed?' Samantha's eyes were wide with horror. 'I thought it was while we were asleep; then we wouldn't have known he needed help. But if we were all awake and moving around the house…'

'We can't say exactly,' Drummond said, with a grim expression. 'We have to look at every possibility. So, how did Philip seem?'

Samantha stared unseeingly through the window at the hills beyond the stables. 'Philip was just normal, except that he was tired from the journey and shocked by his father's plans,' she said. 'He came and sat on the bed. He said I shouldn't have set my heart on borrowing money from his dad this weekend, then I wouldn't have been disappointed, and it was silly to be so upset. Then I explained I'd already put in an offer for a house and he went ballistic. I showed him the pictures of the property, but he was absolutely furious and wouldn't even look at the house. I should've waited to tell him, I know, but I was so upset about his dad's attitude, I just wanted comfort and understanding. He went into the next room, slammed the adjoining door and I could hear him banging around. I cried myself to sleep. I don't think I would have heard anything else. And I didn't wake up till the alarm went off at eight.'

Drummond decided to reserve judgement. The two of them could have made a lot of noise as a smokescreen – then gone to meet James. Or Philip might have overplayed his anger and slipped outside after leaving Samantha, sure that she would not have dared to go into the nurse's bedroom after his outburst. But the timing seemed all wrong. James had been due to see George at 9.45. Several witnesses had heard him say so. Would Philip have had time to find him and delay him – say that he wanted to talk to him without Samantha there? And why meet at the pool, unless he already had an 'accident' in mind? Surely Philip wouldn't cold-bloodedly attack his own father? Yet it wasn't unknown. Drummond tried to stop his mind racing and forcing together facts which did not fit.

'Thank you, Samantha,' he said. 'Please do let us know if you think of anything at all that might help us.'

The blue-grey eyes fixed themselves on Drummond's face. 'It can't have been one of us; no one here would have hurt him,' she said. 'Why aren't you asking the people in the village up the road? They might have seen a stranger.'

Drummond smiled slightly. 'We are doing everything we can,' he said. He hated the stock phrase, but it was useful. 'Thank you for your help.'

Samantha responded with a polite 'thank you' and left the room.

Drummond leaned back in his chair, clasped his hands behind his neck, and yawned loudly. 'Sorry,' he said to Lindsey Pollard, remembering his manners. 'Any comments?'

'It's not a very good alibi for either of them,' she said. 'They had opportunity, if James was killed after ten o'clock, but I'm not sure of motive.'

'That's the trouble,' said Drummond, his eyes fixed on a painting of a wild sea in the middle of the far wall. 'I suppose it's fair to assume that as a son or daughter you will have a share in the estate. When James was ill he had the opportunity to make a new will in favour of his children. He chose Edward instead and never changed it. It would seem that no one in the family was aware of that.'

'So we could assume that they expected to inherit, so money could be a motive for both the children?'

'I think we could. Although all of them seemed to hate him to one degree or another and that might be a stronger motive.'

'But why kill him? Did they really want him out of the way? He didn't seem to play any part in their lives.'

Drummond, his left elbow on the arm of the chair, cupped his head in his hand and doodled with his pen with the other. 'There's revenge. Suddenly it's payback time – probably without thought for the consequences. There's passion too. Anger that is too strong to control – or an accident resulting from an emotional outburst.' Drummond sighed. 'Why are people made with so many complex emotions?'

'To make our job harder?' suggested Pollard.

Drummond grinned. 'You could be right. Well, I suppose we'd better tackle the daughter. Would you go and collect Clara?'

When Pollard had gone, the chief inspector got up from his chair. He paced the room, feeling the soft carpet under his feet, running his hand along the smooth surface of the grand piano and looking at the water colours on the wall. Three were signed 'Margaret Hatherley-Browne' and showed summer scenes in the garden: a tennis party, a study of the cedar tree and the portrait of a young man. It all looked so idyllic, and no doubt it had been, in those wonderful, snatched moments in life when, just briefly, happiness gives colour and a sense of fun to everything we touch. It was good to remember such times in his own experience...

In the passage he heard Lindsey Pollard's feet approaching, and scuttled back to his seat like a naughty boy about to be caught out for a minor misdemeanour.

Clara followed the detective sergeant into the room, accidentally slamming the door behind her. 'Oh, I'm so sorry,' she said. 'I think it slipped.'

Drummond indicated the chair she should take and smiled slightly. 'That's all right,' he said.

Clara must have the same sort of build as James, he thought, as he surveyed the broad expanse of red top and the dark-blue jeans with dirty white trainers half-hidden under the chair.

Clara looked him straight in the eyes. 'Are you sure?' she said. 'About the pool water, I mean.'

Drummond decided that directness was the best policy. 'That your father was drowned in the swimming pool and then taken to the sea? Yes, we are. He was definitely drowned in a swimming pool and this is the most likely one. We shall know more when we have the forensic report.'

He paused as Clara digested this information, although he guessed that she had not had much doubt when she asked the question. 'So, anything you can add to your previous statement would help us considerably,' he said. 'We do want to catch the person or persons who did this.'

Clara nodded. 'I want them caught too, but I don't think there's anything I can add.'

'Tell us about your husband's argument with your father that night.'

Clara looked startled. 'Archie wouldn't have hurt Dad!'

'Then tell us,' said Drummond quietly. 'The more we know the easier it should be to discount him.'

Clara looked at him long and hard. Drummond could feel her eyes penetrating his brain, but he was practised in shutting in his most private thoughts and his eyes gave nothing away.

'Archie was just defending me,' she began. 'Dad never really understood how I felt, especially about...' she looked down at her chest, 'about my size and things.'

Drummond nodded encouragingly.

'Dad said some dreadful things at dinner. Archie went after him when he left. I didn't see what happened, but Archie said he gave him a quick punch outside the front door – he was nowhere near the pool.'

'But he could have taken James to the pool and punched him there? Were there any witnesses?'

'Archie wouldn't do that!' Clara sat bolt upright and jerked her head, the tangled brown hair swinging across her back. 'He's an instant sort of person. He wouldn't go for a walk and then hit someone; he'd do it at once or not at all. He's the same with me. When he comes home at night he either gives me a quick kiss and a hug, or he forgets. His emotions don't last very long.'

Drummond decided to follow a different tack. 'How long was he in the garden?'

Clara looked blank. 'I don't know. Not very long. My hot chocolate was still warm when he came in and said he'd taught Dad a lesson.'

'He admitted doing it?'

'Yes, of course. He should never have done it, but he said Dad was still standing afterwards. Oh, and then he went to the gym before he came back. But even so, he hadn't been long.'

'Did you go up to bed together?'

'What?'

Drummond didn't reply. He waited. Clara glared at him. 'If you must know, we didn't. Archie played one frame of snooker with Uncle Ed and I was still awake when he came up.'

Drummond noticed a quick flash of alarm in her eyes. She had realised as she spoke that to give Archie the alibi of being with Edward did not free him from guilt; in fact, it could make things worse.

'And did your husband leave the bedroom at any time in the night?'

Clara almost squirmed. Drummond waited; did he have a fish at the end of the line?

'Not that I know of; no, of course he didn't.'

'Did you wake at any time in the night?'

'No.'

'I see.'

Clara opened her mouth, but Drummond went on quickly. 'Is there anything else that you think might help us? Anything unusual you saw or heard?'

'No. I was exhausted. We'd had a good meal and we'd brought our lovely warm duvet. I fell asleep very quickly and Archie was the one who woke me in the morning.'

'Thank you,' said Drummond, 'you've been most helpful.'

Clara shot him a glance and left the room. Lindsey followed her out, obviously intent on bringing Archie before the pair had time to compare notes.

Once Archie was in the chair, Drummond became every inch the inquisitor. He allowed his eyes to run down Archie's previous statement.

'Mr Braithwaite, in view of the fact that we are now conducting a murder enquiry, I would like you to go over your previous statement and ensure that it contains everything that you know of the events of Thursday night and the early hours of Friday morning.'

Archie swallowed hard. His shoulders were rigid.

Drummond, satisfied that his victim was ready to reveal what he knew, decided to begin with the encounter in the garden.

'I believe that after Mr James Wedderburn, your father-in-law, went into the garden on Thursday evening, you joined him there.'

Archie nodded.

'Pardon, sir?'

Archie cleared his throat, 'Yes.'

'Why was that?'

'He had been particularly rude to my wife.'

'Rude?'

'She has always been well built, a bit like her father, but he never realised how sensitive she was. When I first met her she was bulimic for several years. It took a lot of reassurance to bring her to the point where she was happy with herself and with life. She's hard-working and fun and...' for a moment fire came into Archie's eyes, 'her dad undermined her so badly that night. He also rubbished her mother, and that wasn't fair.'

'So you hit him.'

Archie winced. 'I was angry. I just wanted to warn him, to let him know he'd gone too far, to stop him ruining the whole weekend. It was just a quick right hook to his jaw, he staggered and banged into the sundial a bit – he didn't fall. I didn't hit his head as such. I didn't kill him.' The words poured out in a flood. 'Anyway, he was OK later.'

'Later?' Drummond glanced at Archie's previous statement; he didn't recall that Archie had seen his father after the punch-up in the garden.

Archie swallowed. 'I left him by the sundial and went round the back of the house to the gym. I was still a bit wound up and wanted to get rid of some energy.'

Pity you didn't do that earlier, Drummond thought. 'And?' he queried.

'I took it out on the punchbag for a while, then I heard James talking to Ian. There's a separate bit where Ian has an office, out of sight of the equipment area.'

'And you spoke to them?'

'No. I stayed out of sight. Ian said he was going to lock up soon, so I crept out. I didn't want to come face to face with my father-in-law again that night.'

'Did you hear any of the conversation before you left?'

Archie considered. 'I think James was telling Ian off for spending too much money, and Ian said he thought he'd got more to spend than James had said.'

'Did they argue?'

Archie made a face, as if to squeeze more energy into his memory. 'I don't think so. Ian was pretty polite really, and James was more like a particularly strict teacher, who lets you fear a punishment before he actually gives it. He said he'd see him in the morning, in a threatening sort of way.'

'I see; then what did you do?'

'I slipped out quickly, to avoid meeting James. I went into the mansion through the back door and had some hot chocolate in the drawing room. Then I went and waited in the snooker room for Uncle Ed. He'd promised to play one frame before we went to bed.'

'Did you see anyone when you entered the building?'

Archie looked vague. 'No, I don't think so. There may have been people talking in the kitchen when I came in.'

'And what time would you say it was when you left Mr Wedderburn in the gym?'

Archie's shoulders rose and fell. He shook his head and fixed his eyes on the pile of statements. 'Somewhere between ten or quarter past nine, I suppose. I think it was after ten o'clock when Uncle Edward came to play snooker. I was practising for a long time before he joined me.'

'Did anyone see the two of you together?'

'No.'

'And did you leave your room during the night, at all, Mr Braithwaite?'

Archie turned frightened eyes on Drummond. 'No, I swear I didn't.'

'And your wife can confirm that?'

'She was nearly asleep when I went in, but I was with her all night, really. She'd set the alarm – we had to be up early for breakfast and James was a stickler for punctuality. I didn't stir until it went off at eight o'clock, and then I had to wake Clara, and it was a rush to get ready, queues for the bathroom and all that.'

He looked helplessly at Drummond. 'I didn't hurt him,' he repeated. 'He was quite OK at the gym.'

'A fact you omitted to put in your statement,' Drummond reminded him. 'And now, is there anything else you would like to tell me?'

Archie shook his head, his hands clasped tightly into fists. 'No,' he whispered.

'Then thank you, sir, that will be all for now.' Drummond turned his attention to Archie's previous statement and waited for Archie to leave the room. Then he looked at Pollard with his eyebrows raised. 'Interesting. Neither Archie nor Ian mentioned encountering James later that night.'

'And the victim was hit on the head, wasn't he, sir?'

'Yes, the back of the head and the jaw. And the damage sustained to the jaw was consistent with a right hook, possibly two right hooks.'

'If his story is correct, Archie could have waited for James to leave the gym and lured him to the pool on some pretext – it's not far to walk. He could have drowned him and then got help to dispose of the body later.'

'Mm.' Drummond considered this piece of insight. 'And Edward is the obvious candidate. It looks as if he was in the drawing room for some time before going to play snooker. But Archie could have persuaded his father-in-law to go to the pool, drowned him either accidentally or deliberately and, while he was playing snooker, cooked up a plan with Edward to push James over the cliff later that night.

Pollard got up and perched on her small table, frowning at the carpet. 'But did Archie have time to do it and get back for his hot chocolate? The keys were readily accessible, but would he have known where they were? If he and Edward were in it together, Archie could have waited till Clara was asleep and then joined Edward. After that they had all night to dispose of the body.'

'Mm,' said Drummond again. 'I can see that they could have played snooker and discussed plans, but would Archie have admitted hitting James so openly if he had indeed killed him, and could he really have drowned his father-in-law in such a short space of time? I shall put the facts on the back burner and let them simmer.' Drummond shuffled the papers on his table. 'Will you go and tell the assembled company that we shall not need any of them until after lunch? We'll take a break.'

Pollard left quickly.

Chapter 22

Drummond and Pollard walked in silence to the unmarked police car. The inspector waited as Lindsey went straight to the driver's door, before he eased himself into the passenger seat with a quiet groan, his mind stretched and over-exercised as much as when his whole body used to ache from an early season's squash game.

Lindsey inserted the key in the ignition and turned to him, eyebrows raised. He blinked away the glazed look from his eyes and said, 'What about a snack and a quick pint on the top of Beachy Head?'

'At the Astonished Seagull?'

'I didn't mean the ice cream van!' Drummond snapped the answer back, startling himself by its forcefulness. He was obviously more stressed than he had thought. He was grateful that Lindsey pursued the subject no further, and remained silent for the whole journey. He guessed that she wanted to chatter, but he needed time to think.

He remembered the day in prep school when the teacher had given each of them a jam jar and instructed them to tip in six spoonfuls of soil, each from different parts of the grounds. He'd carried his solemnly and carefully back to the classroom, obediently added a cup of water, stirred the mixture, and then watched it over the coming days. Whatever the lesson, he would glance in the jar's direction, as if he expected a sudden movement, but he could never catch it out. Eventually he moved it cautiously to his desk and sketched the different layers of soil as they had sorted themselves in immaculate order beneath the gradually clearing water. So often his cases were like that, clearly identifiable characters, situations, settings abounded; but stir in murder, motive and opportunity and the water muddied instantly. And it took a long time to clear.

He deliberately relaxed his body, leaned against the headrest and allowed the calm of the Sussex undulations, populated with the occasional scattering of sheep, to give his mind the stillness it needed, before he prepared to examine the complicated layers of human relationships he had left behind at Seascape House.

Pollard swept the car neatly into a designated parking place and they got out, fighting to shut the doors against the bitter wind. They hurried through the pub doors into the heady mixture of cooking smells and claustrophobic warmth. Lindsey marched straight through to the little restaurant. A waitress was sweeping up the debris from under a table which had obviously been occupied by a large family with a small child. Drummond looked around – they had come at a quiet period.

'Let's go in that corner overlooking the fields,' said Drummond. 'We shouldn't be interrupted there.'

It was Lindsey who ordered the meals, paying with a note which Drummond produced from his wallet, and who returned with their drinks. Drummond took a long slow draught and then put his glass down. Mentally he switched to a clear blank screen in his mind. 'Well? First impressions?' he said, putting the ball firmly in her court.

Lindsey put her glass down, pushed it towards the middle of the table and slowly turned it with both hands. 'All the way here,' she said, 'I wanted to comment on one person after another and, now I don't know where to begin.'

Drummond smiled. 'It doesn't matter where you begin. There will be lots of impressions, some important, some insignificant, some downright inaccurate, but it helps to talk them through, to identify them, to sort them and decide which to discard and which to keep for the moment.'

Lindsey sipped at her drink. 'When we first came, they all seemed, well, so ordinary. A dreadful tragedy had happened, totally unfairly, to a family that were getting together for a special celebration and being – well, a family.'

Drummond smiled. 'And you were wrong?' he queried.

Lindsey considered. 'No, I think they are a family like other families, but they've drifted apart, sort of cracked, and the cracks seem to get wider and deeper the more you look into them. Put the label "murderer" round the neck of any of them and you begin to see all sorts of devious motives and relationships.'

'You've left out the key person,' said Drummond as the waitress plonked onto the table knives and forks wrapped tightly in bright-red serviettes, said, 'There you go,' and vanished into another area of the pub.

Lindsey looked at him. 'You mean the deceased?'

Drummond nodded. 'What do you make of him?'

Lindsey clearly found it hard to turn her mind to the still body on the stretcher on the clifftop. 'His room told us nothing,' she said slowly. 'It had twin beds, one made up immaculately, presumably never slept in, the other left unmade – but we did see it straight after breakfast. The room was bare, except for a few of Cassidy's clothes left untidily in a heap on a chair. Some of James' clothes were in the wardrobe and his weekend bag, lying in a corner, behind a chair, wasn't properly unpacked, so either he couldn't be bothered or didn't have time when he first arrived.'

Drummond interrupted, waving his glass in front of her before drinking some of its contents. 'Remember, Cassidy may have moved his bag. Once he'd died, I imagine she wouldn't want to see his things around the room.'

Pollard acknowledged his theory with a nod, but was clearly too intent on expressing her thoughts to pause. 'There was £60 in his wallet with five credit and debit cards – no photographs. Nothing. He didn't seem to leave a mark on the place at all.'

Drummond, who remembered the oversized body and had, possibly wrongly, drawn conclusions about excessive drinking, eating and self-indulgence, said nothing in reply. 'Who, of the people we interviewed, stands out most in your mind?'

'His wife, I think,' Lindsey replied. 'She's so mixed up, though I suppose anyone would be. She's distracted and distraught at the moment, but she must be a very capable lady, running businesses abroad and flying out to remote places.'

Drummond nodded. 'The station rang while you were getting the drinks. Until recently she owned scuba-diving schools in Barbados, southern Spain and Greece. She sold the Spanish one four months ago and the Greek one three weeks ago.'

'What sort of a man lets his wife flit around tourist attractions and run businesses without having any involvement himself?'

Lindsey's reaction sounded quite old-fashioned and Drummond smiled inwardly. He and his wife had talked things through soon after they were married, and had come to the agreement that part of their lives they would live independently. He had wanted this, aware that if something happened to him through the nature of his job, she would need her own friends and interests, but they had always made a point of being involved in some of each other's activities – she came to golf club dinners and he took their teenage girls to watch her amateur dramatics; whenever possible he joined the 'Walk the Downs' club on their monthly excursions and pub lunches. But their priority had been to give time and energy as a couple to bringing up their children, whenever his work permitted.

He forced his mind back to Cassidy Wedderburn. 'She's his second wife,' he pointed out.

'So what are you saying? That the first marriage was an infatuation that died?'

'It's hard to say when we know little about the husband,' said Drummond. 'What was the age gap between Cassidy and James?'

Lindsey fumbled on the floor for her handbag and produced her notebook and pen. She flicked a couple of pages and stared into space briefly, apparently calculating. 'Twenty-four years!' she said, gazing wide eyed at Drummond's face. 'That's indecent! He was old enough to be her father!'

Drummond looked at her. 'And old enough, at the time he first met her, to be tired of his current wife, to have found they were incompatible, or for her to have found someone else. Human nature is all too fallible.'

He watched as she digested the information. She'd had a certain amount of experience as a detective sergeant, but he wondered how much experience of life she'd had. He'd heard a couple of girls in the station canteen discussing how long Lindsey and her new partner would stay together. He guessed she would defend their love as permanent and indissoluble, but life wasn't that simple.

'So could Cassidy have done it?' he pressed.

'She seemed genuinely shocked,' Pollard mused, 'but would she really have wanted him dead?' She paused and sipped her drink. 'Did she hope to gain money from the will? I suppose she would have expected quite a large share, together with the children, of course. But could she have committed the crime on her own?'

Drummond leaned his arms on the table and linked his hands round the sugar bowl. 'The murder? Doubtful,' he said. 'Who would you pair her with?'

Lindsey frowned. 'She doesn't seem to know any of them very well; Philip and Clara moved away from home years ago. I suppose we would have to prove she had a link with one of them; I don't know how.'

'What about Edward?' Drummond asked. 'He seems to have lived completely independently of James and disliked his brother intensely. Killing him is extreme, but if the opportunity presented itself…'

Pollard was gazing unseeingly out of the window. 'Do you think Edward knew about the contents of the will, even though he denies it? Perhaps George dropped a hint? Edward would certainly have a lot to gain, and if he joined forces with Cassidy he could leave her to run the hotel, get a teaching job locally, and enjoy the profits of their enterprise – and have the bonus of a comfortable place to live.'

'It might well suit them both; Cassidy has more ready cash now.'

'You mean Cassidy has sold off her businesses with the intention of investing her money in the new hotel, but running it without James?'

'Just a thought,' said Drummond.

'I think it's very far-fetched. What about the children?' Pollard sounded more positive. 'Either or both Samantha and Philip could have left the house during the night, and Archie and Clara could have joined them. I think the back door key is always left on the back of the pantry door. It would have been much easier for a foursome to remove the body from the pool to the sea.'

'I think,' said Drummond, as the waitress carrying their meals came into sight, 'almost anyone could have got rid of the body in the night. We need to find out why James remained outside the house after he left the gym. Was he too drunk to move? Unlikely, as he'd already walked round the back of the building. Or did someone lure him to the pool – ensuring he couldn't get out, and then fix up an alibi which couldn't be broken? Afterwards they could go back and drown him. Or did they drown him first and go back to dispose of the body later?' He sighed. 'This one could be quite a challenge.'

The waitress arrived and plonked two plates on the table. 'Enjoy yer meals,' she said, and was gone.

Simultaneously the two diners unwrapped their cutlery and turned their minds to the needs of the inner person.

Emily was thankful when lunch was over. The long table had seemed to be divided into two by an invisible line separating the family from 'the rest', although Edward kept his place next to Emily.

At the 'family end' there had been a relaxation of nervous tension, and now that their police interviews were over, the group behaved like students set free from exams. There had been laughter and noisy chat, while at Emily's end her companions had remained subdued. Politeness covered an underlying anxiety, and even Emily found it hard to sustain a conversation with those around her.

Standing in the drawing room, swallowing the last of her coffee, she had spotted the returning police car and went out of the back door to meet Chief Inspector Drummond on his way in. Drummond and Pollard, however, had walked to the gate of the walled garden and were about to go in. Emily caught them up at the door to the pool, slightly breathless. 'Is it all right to come in? I just wanted a word.'

Drummond held the door open for her. 'It's fine; forensics have finished. Come into the pool area, it looks as if it could pour at any minute.'

Emily glanced at the sky; dark clouds were massing and it did look threatening.

'I wondered,' she said, as Drummond closed the pool door behind her, 'if I could go off to see my sister this afternoon? I'd be back soon after tea – if you don't need me before then. I don't like to leave her without a visit.'

Drummond nodded and looked at his watch. 'That should be fine,' he said. 'We won't be starting the other interviews just yet. We wanted to look again at the crime scene first.'

'You know,' said Emily, 'I've sat in court many a time with a youngster in trouble, but I still find it so hard to grasp that here, in the garden where we used to pick our vegetables, a man was deliberately killed. You're sure it wasn't an accident?'

Drummond looked at her shrewdly. 'Quite sure.'

Emily said nothing – he obviously wasn't going to give much away. She gazed at the pool. 'I suppose he could have been pushed in from almost anywhere,' she said, thoughtfully. She glanced at Drummond and as their eyes met, she caught the mixture of his trust in her judgement and the element of professionalism which Drummond had to show. It was enough to make her wait, sure that he would reveal something.

Drummond turned back to the pool. 'It is difficult to assess the injuries to the body,' he said carefully, 'since the fall from the cliff and his time in the sea may have masked some evidence of what happened earlier. A fact the killer was no doubt aware of. But the Seascape cliffs are lower than some others around here, so the damage was less.'

'He had a blow to the head,' said Emily. 'Archie told us about his right hook earlier that night.'

'There was a second blow to the jaw area,' said Drummond quietly, 'possibly another punch, and a third blow to the back of the head, consistent with falling against the edge of the pool.'

'Oh!' Emily was instantly alert. 'So he didn't fall straight forwards or backwards? He must have been standing sideways to the pool, perhaps near a corner, at the time he fell or was pushed.'

'We believe so,' Lindsey Pollard said, positioning herself near the edge of the pool and turning her shoulders experimentally, trying to work out the angle of fall, Emily presumed.

'But why go to such extraordinary lengths to get rid of the body? Couldn't it have been made to look like accidental death?' Emily spoke the thoughts aloud, and then answered them. 'But there was something on the body which would prove it wasn't accidental,' she said, 'so he or she or they had to push it over the cliff.'

'All right,' said Drummond, 'if that is the correct scenario, how do you get the body out of the water, and how do you transport it to the cliff edge?'

'A wheelbarrow,' said Pollard quickly.

Emily blinked. 'Could anyone lift the weight of that man, in sodden clothing, even in a wheelbarrow? We have one or two barrows around which the gardeners use. They're very grubby usually and they certainly squeak. Not a good mode of transport for the middle of the night.'

'Well, have you got a better idea?' Pollard's voice had a hint of spiteful sarcasm about it. Emily guessed she wanted to talk to Drummond on her own and resented the amateur detective. But Emily wasn't going to leave yet. This was far too interesting. She pondered Pollard's question.

'You need silent wheels,' she said, thinking out loud. 'I suppose if I were disposing of a body I might nip through the side gate near the summer house onto the golf course and borrow a buggy. My sister used to use one there up until quite recently; I went with her once.' She shut her eyes briefly and tried to picture the scene. 'There'd be quite a lot of room in the back. I don't think the body would fall out. But they're not silent – they sound rather like milk floats. It would have been very risky to use one, but it is a possibility.'

All three of them stared into the waters of the pool, but it reflected nothing. Above them the sky was getting darker. Emily continued her monologue. 'I suppose a car is a possibility, if you can move it without the engine on, so that it's silent. The steering wheel might lock, though; these modern cars have so many safety devices. The other possibility, of course, is one of those loungers with wheels. It could be used like a wheelbarrow. Difficult with a heavy body, though.'

Neither Drummond nor Pollard made any comment. She felt she must find another question quickly or she would feel obliged to go. 'I presume two or more people were involved?' she said.

'We're keeping an open mind,' said Drummond.

So that was it, thought Emily. The formality was returning and probably they knew little more than she did at this stage. But the possibility remained that she could solve this case before the police did. At the moment both she and they seemed to be caught in the starting blocks. Well, she would take up the challenge – but she would play fair; she would have to share what she knew and still beat them. Her eyes gleamed. Why not? Up till now she'd felt like a pawn in this complicated game of moves and counter moves.

Drummond interrupted her thoughts. 'There is just one thing,' he said. 'It would seem very likely that someone involved would have got their clothes wet. Would you tell us if there is some kind of drying room in the mansion?'

Blow, thought Emily. Why didn't I think of that? She would have to be sharper from now on.

'Yes, there is,' she replied. 'Under the back stairs there's a door that opens on to the cellar steps. One of the sections of the cellar houses the boiler. We've often used the big pipes in there for drying clothes after hikes and so on.'

'Excellent,' said Drummond. 'I'm sure Edward won't mind if we look in there.'

He nodded at Emily and she took her cue. 'Well, I must be going to my sister, or I shall never be back in time,' she said brightly. 'Thank you for letting me join you. Goodbye.'

Emily let herself in the back door and resisted the strong temptation to go straight to the cellar. She took the dog lead from the peg by the backstairs, put her head round the kitchen door and said, 'Come on, Fin. We're going to Margaret's. Let's go out through the front door, while we still can!'

In the entrance hall she met Stella, removing a couple of dead daffodils from a vase on the shelf above the gong. 'I'm just off to my sister's,' Emily said in passing. 'Margaret will want to hear the latest news and will, no doubt, have some useful theories about who did the dreadful deed! I must remember to ask the manager if they can send a van to collect the scooter. I've just had an interesting chat with the chief inspector – I'll tell you all about it later.'

Stella looked startled and glanced quickly up and down the corridor. 'Emily, not so loud,' she whispered.

'There's nobody around,' Emily replied with a shrug of her shoulders. 'Come on, Fin, Margaret might have the odd chew stashed away for you, and I need you to cheer the other ladies up.'

As it happened the 'other ladies' were fully occupied with basketball, while Margaret waited for her impatiently in the conservatory.

'Why aren't you joining in?' Emily demanded.

Margaret gave a disparaging snort. 'Basketball? It's a ridiculously grand name for throwing a sponge ball into a wastepaper basket! I said I didn't need the arm exercise. I want something to exercise the mind – I finished the crossword hours ago!'

Emily sat next to her sister on the none-too-comfortable wicker seat for three which graced one side of the conservatory. Four leggy geraniums in varying shades of red decorated the windowsill, and outside the leaves of the oak tree dripped rainwater onto the bare patio. In a couple of planters three or four daffodil buds showed some sign of life, one beginning to split and reveal the promise of yellow petals.

Margaret fiddled with the catch on her handbag. Eventually she opened it and offered Fin the morsel she was waiting for, before depositing the bag on the seat between them and saying, 'Now give me something interesting for my brain to work on.'

Emily did. It took her nearly an hour to go through all the events at Seascape House from the time her removal van had parked outside the Lodge, to her recent conversation at the poolside.

Margaret's eyes were wide with excitement. Whenever Emily took breath she would interrupt, 'Go on. Yes, yes, I got that bit, what happened next?'

Eventually Emily could remember no more. She leaned back in her chair. Just telling the story made her exhausted; how had she managed to live through it?

'This is far better than the crossword,' said the delighted Margaret. 'Now, which part do we need to tackle first?'

Emily knew she ran the risk of Margaret taking over the whole investigation; after all, her sister, older, taller and more dominant, had done it all her life. But now that she was becoming frailer, Emily felt rather more fond of her, and protective in a way. Margaret had been through a lot, and in the space of a decade had lost her husband to a heart attack and her son in a crash to a drunk driver. It had knocked her back badly, as it would anyone, but she had hidden her vulnerability until the Parkinson's disease had made itself more obvious. She was a courageous and sensible woman, and Emily knew it was more important to keep her sister involved and interested than to assert her own independence.

'I don't know,' she said honestly. 'There are so many facts, and plenty more possibilities, but I can't link any of them or draw any conclusion.'

'Well,' said Margaret briskly. 'Put yourself in the shoes of the murderer. Why do you want to get rid of this James and how do you dispose of the body?'

Emily flinched. Margaret was in full teacher mode – ask the child questions till they think they've found the answer themselves, when all the time the teacher could have provided the solution straight away... Infuriating.

Determined to humour her sister, Emily obediently thought it through. 'James has hurt me,' she said. 'That would be true of any of the family,' she said, coming out of character briefly. 'Edward loathed James, blaming him for the deaths and unhappiness in Jonathan's family, Ian had possibly just discovered James had driven him away from his family, George hated him for the blackmail, Clara and Philip felt he failed as a father...'

Emily tried to return a stray wisp of white hair into the clip at the back of her head. 'Right. James is hurting me,' she repeated, 'so I want to hurt him, perhaps very badly. Seascape is an ideal place. A fall from the cliff could be interpreted as an accident, a suicide, or a killing by a person or persons unknown. All I would need to do is to lure him onto the cliffs when no one was around, and night-time would be best, although if seen by a passing motorist might arouse more suspicion.' Emily paused.

Margaret nodded her approval. 'Fine so far. Why didn't you take him to the clifftop, then? Why drown him first?'

Emily stroked Fin's head absentmindedly. 'Either I tried to get him onto the cliff and he wouldn't play ball, or I had planned that for later in the weekend and a different opportunity presented itself.'

'Opportunistic rather than premeditated?' Margaret yawned.

Emily, not in the mood for in-depth role play, said grudgingly, 'I think so.'

She heard the rattle of cups and peered through the conservatory door into the sitting room. She was relieved to see that the basketball had finished and tea and scones were in evidence.

'I must go. Chief Inspector Drummond will be asking for me.'

Margaret rose with difficulty, reaching for her walker. 'I'll want to know more tomorrow, work on the opportunistic angle,' she said, the older-sister voice peremptory and sharp. 'And you mind out for yourself,' she went on, 'someone out there won't welcome you prying into what went on.'

Emily caught her breath. 'Oh, come on, Margaret! This is real life,' she said, scorning her sister's warning.

'I mean it, be careful,' said Margaret in a voice that reminded Emily of their mother's. 'Don't do anything stupid.'

Emily came to her senses and laughed. 'You've been watching silly crime programmes on the box!' she said. 'Anyway, I'm beginning to think it was James who was intent on murder, and he's not around to hurt anyone.'

Margaret sniffed. 'Just open this door for me, will you? I'm missing my tea. And I'll expect you here in good time tomorrow.'

Emily watched Margaret ease the walker over the threshold before she herself turned and escaped by way of the side door of the conservatory, and through the dining room. A member of staff waited as she signed the visitors' book and smiled goodbye as she let her out of the front door.

As her bright-yellow Nissan kicked into life, Emily began to have some misgivings that she'd told Margaret – but her sister's sharp brain could be a help in beating the police to it. She smiled. Just for the moment life looked a little more positive and very interesting indeed.

Chapter 23

For DCI Drummond, the afternoon involved the concentrated gathering of yet more evidence. The general public probably thought of the process like the solving of a simple jigsaw, where one had only to 'put the pieces together'. They envisaged the detective moving 'these clues' and 'those statements' around a board in the police station, just straightforward trial and error, until each slotted into place, the resulting picture sharp, tidy and irrefutable.

But this was a 3D puzzle and the unattached pieces would continue to thud around his brain for days. He knew there was no point in forcing them together at the moment, though instinctively he always wanted to hurry the process, to join two parts just because they had something in common – but that could be fatal, distorting the true picture and displacing other pieces. There were depths and unexpected angles which prevented the shapes fitting together in a seemingly obvious way. He just hoped for the magic moment when two parts would slide together naturally, even though he didn't understand why, and then, gradually, the other pieces might just slot in neatly to complete the whole.

He had been dissatisfied with his time at the poolside. Pollard didn't seem to have much insight into the mind of a criminal and Dame Emily wanted to know more than he was prepared to give her. Not that he thought she would keep back any important evidence, she was a pillar of society, but she might know things unwittingly. He'd check with her in her interview. In the meantime, there was Ian to see.

Back in the music room, Drummond read through the newspaper accounts from James' briefcase and Ian's previous statement very carefully. He had said nothing about meeting James that night. Had he judiciously left that fact out? Or had Archie invented the meeting, knowing it was his word against Ian's – the outsider?

The door opened and Pollard indicated the chair opposite Drummond. 'Mr Ian Matthews, sir.'

Considering it was a Bank Holiday, Ian looked very smart, but Drummond guessed he wanted to look the part to impress the family, especially if they were going to use the gym or pool. 'Personal trainer' was just visible, emblazoned on his T-shirt, and his well-cut lime-green tracksuit trousers and top looked as if they were new. His trainers were a stunning white.

Drummond glanced again at the details at the top of the statement. Aged 42, previously employed in a gym in Eastbourne, fully qualified for the job. For all Ian's smartness there was a limpness about his demeanour, which suggested sadness and anxiety, where Drummond might have expected defiance – but most people had a talent for acting when they needed it.

'Mr Matthews,' Drummond began.

Ian lifted weary eyes to his. The tidy brown hair was beginning to recede. Wasn't he just a little too old for this job?

'I would be grateful,' said Drummond, folding his arms, 'if you would tell me again when you last saw Mr James Wedderburn.'

'At the evening meal; he left before the rest of us,' Ian responded.

'And you didn't see him again?'

'No. I went straight out of the back door and then to the gym.'

Drummond searched the man's face with his eyes. Would a doctor ever want to kill a man? It had been known. Perhaps this one had been pushed too far… 'Are you quite sure?' Drummond paused for effect. 'I have your previous statement and wondered if there was anything you would like to add.' Drummond lifted the paper casually and replaced it on the table.

Ian shook his head. 'I don't think so. I only got the letter confirming my appointment about six weeks ago, giving me just enough time to work out my notice while helping with the initial planning for the leisure area here. I really didn't know Mr Wedderburn. After all, I only saw him for the first time just before dinner on Thursday night.'

'But,' Drummond leaned across the desk, his eyes fixed on his prey, 'you did speak to him later that night – in the gym – and may well have been the last man to see him alive.' He increased the volume slightly. 'We have a witness to the fact – so why didn't you tell us?'

Ian's hand went to his mouth. The hazel eyes were wide, alarmed. He said nothing. Drummond watched him carefully. Was he now compiling a new story, or mentally checking every detail of his last statement in an effort to prove it matched the witness' statement?

Drummond remained in his leaning position for a moment. 'I think you need to tell us everything, sir. You would probably prefer it to be here rather than in the police station in Eastbourne.'

'I was afraid,' Ian blurted out, and then paused, apparently searching for words.

'Afraid of what?'

'Of losing my job...' he paused, 'and of being accused of murder, when I'm totally innocent.'

Drummond surveyed the tanned face. He had been right, it would be difficult for a man of his age to find a similar job. He seemed to have left his training a bit late in life.

'Do you imagine that the gym and pool will continue to be used by the public after Mr Wedderburn's death? Don't you think you will lose your job anyway?'

'Of course I do, but I did hope I could go on running things till decisions were made about the house; it would bring in money for the new owner and I could earn while I looked for a new job – and I need a fair reference.'

Drummond made no comment. He moved a newspaper cutting from under the pile of statements, while keeping his eyes on Ian's face. 'I think you will find that we know quite a lot about you already, sir,' he said. 'It would be wiser to tell the complete truth.' Slowly he unfolded the paper, turned it towards Ian and rested it on the desk between them.

Ian glanced at the cutting and went white. He looked up in horror. 'I don't understand,' he said weakly.

Drummond fiddled with his pen for a moment and then looked Ian straight in the eyes. 'This would be your motive for murder. The article is about you, is it not? You did work as a doctor in St Clement's hospital in Huddersfield?'

Ian flinched. 'Yes, I did.'

'But then someone found out that you may have been the paediatrician who, through a basic mistake, failed to diagnose a disease which led to a child losing his life?'

'Yes, but the enquiry found that I was not guilty of negligence. I was cleared and allowed to continue to practise.'

'And were you guilty?'

'No, I'm sure of it!'

'But you left the hospital, nonetheless?'

Ian switched his gaze to the stable roof beyond Drummond's head. 'I had to,' he said simply. His voice shook.

'Please explain.' Drummond leaned back and waited.

Ian took a deep breath. 'I received an anonymous letter at home. It threatened to expose me to the press, and to have the case against me opened again, unless I left the area within a month. My wife saw the letter and she supported me when I resigned my post. I had no choice. I've always wondered if I could have done more to save the child, but I really don't think I could have. I still see him in my dreams.' Ian paused. 'The writer of the letter wasn't going to give me the chance to prove my integrity. I felt my name would be blackened for ever if the case were reopened. There are too many instances of injustice these days – I couldn't risk it.

'My wife and I agreed I would go into rented accommodation in Leeds and I got work as a locum for several months. We couldn't move the kids from school, they were settled and doing well. I came home when I had time off, but I felt guilty and I feared that I would be seen by the anonymous writer. Away from home I began drinking and it got worse. Eventually my wife said she wouldn't have me in the house until I'd stopped.

'A friend from medical school days suggested Eastbourne – he would let me share his flat while I sorted myself out. And I did. It took time, but I've done it, with the help of a specialist support group and a local gym. The gym gave me a new perspective on life; it kept me fit and gave me a framework to my week. Eventually I did courses to train as a fitness instructor and personal trainer. I proved myself in the leisure centre in town, and then I saw the advert for a fitness and activity centre supervisor for Seascape House in the local paper. It was worth a try, though I'm really too old for this sort of job now.

'I was so thrilled to get it. I just want to prove myself to my wife and get her and my kids back; to try to start again. I want to persuade her that I really am all right now. Can you understand how that feels?'

Drummond had kept his eyes on Ian for the whole of his long speech. He felt sure there was more detail which could have been slotted in, but it was unlikely to be relevant. He had listened to the story with hidden sympathy. It sounded plausible enough. He wanted to say that he understood with all his heart. He would do anything to remain with his own longsuffering wife and children. The poor man seemed to have been treated most unjustly. But he couldn't ignore the fact that Ian might be pulling the wool over his eyes.

'And do you know the author of that anonymous letter?'

'No. It's probably a good thing. At the time I was so angry – he or she took my career, prompted my wife to threaten to divorce me, and forced me from my home. For a long time I lived in fear that the writer would take it out on my family or pursue me, but it's in the past now, and I have new horizons – or did have until yesterday.'

Drummond produced another page from a newspaper, leaned across the desk and pointed with his pen at the left-hand side of the double-page spread. 'Perhaps I should tell you who unmasked you, who it was that forced you from the north of England to the south and made your life a misery. His picture is on that very page,' Drummond paused and repositioned the pen, indicating the death announcement of Alistair James, 'and he has kept a photo of the child and the result of the enquiry.'

Ian glanced down at the marriage photograph and the caption under it, then at the photo of the child. He looked up and stared in amazement at the detective inspector. He looked down again as if expecting the words to have changed, and ran a hand through his thinning hair. 'You mean it was the James Wedderburn in this photo, who threatened me, who contacted the newspaper, and possibly the hospital… He is the same man I now work for – did work for?'

Ian leaned back in his chair, blinked his eyes and exhaled. Drummond was reasonably satisfied that he was genuinely shocked and had not known who his betrayer was.

Ian shook his head. 'It's too much of a coincidence; it can't be true,' he said desperately. 'I knew Mr Wedderburn came from Yorkshire, but had no idea he had links with the child's family. Was he an uncle or something?'

Drummond ignored the question. 'There's no reason you should know who had written your anonymous letter. I imagine you didn't keep it.'

'Hardly. I threw it on the bonfire until it had turned to ashes – like my life.' There was a hint of bitterness now that the memories were returning. Suddenly Ian sat up straighter. 'How do you know it was him? You're guessing because it's with this wedding photo.'

'We know, sir, because we found the cutting in his briefcase, together with this photograph of a team of doctors.' Drummond put his final piece of evidence on top of the rest. 'Is it your face that is ringed? You will see there is an address in the margin – is it yours?'

Ian scanned the writing and nodded miserably.

'I think,' continued Drummond, being deliberately vague, 'James Wedderburn must have known the family. Perhaps they were customers in one of his shops. He had kept a copy of the funeral service in the same envelope.'

Ian shuddered. 'I wanted to go to the funeral, but no one would have welcomed someone from the hospital; feelings ran too high, and it might have been interpreted as an admission of guilt.'

Suddenly Ian leaned forward, his elbows on his knees, his head in his hands. His voice was close to breaking. 'Why did you have to tell me who wrote it? I had managed to leave it all in the past. Why did you have to bring it up?' His hands were interlocked over the top of his head now – a bony helmet, unable to protect his suffering mind.

'I think that should be obvious, sir,' was all that Drummond said.

For one moment Ian's body was totally still as the words seeped their way into him through his pores. Then his body jerked as he sat bolt upright. 'You can't think…' Briefly he was lost for words. 'I didn't have anything to do with the death of James Wedderburn. I had no idea he was the one who wrote to me, and falsely exposed me.'

Drummond held up his hand briefly to stem the flow of words. 'We had to find out, sir. Someone in your position might well have held a grudge for years until he or she had the opportunity to exact revenge.'

Ian glanced across at Pollard, who had her head down and was writing rapidly. He looked back at the inspector. 'Does anyone else have to know about this?'

'Only if we have reason to believe that you committed the murder. We are not in the business of damaging reputations; we shall keep it confidential if at all possible.'

'Thank you,' the words came out as a cross between a whisper and a croak.

Drummond retrieved the newspaper cuttings and sat back in his chair. 'We have a clearer idea of how you came to be at Seascape House, but now we need to turn to the events of the last two days. Would you like to begin at the beginning, sir? Tell us what happened from the time you left the dining room.'

It seemed to take Ian several seconds to refocus on recent events. He frowned slightly. 'Mr Wedderburn had been angry and left the dining room quickly. I decided against having any coffee and went straight to the gym. I wanted to make sure everything would run smoothly the next day, and I needed to check the numbers of local people coming to the pool next week. I ran a final check on all the machines in the gym, and I'd just gone into my office – well, large cupboard – when Mr Wedderburn came in. He wasn't very pleased,' Ian said slowly. 'I was sure I had been given £30,000 to stock the gym from scratch, and to provide some equipment for the pool. Mr Wedderburn said it was £10,000. I had already spent £20,000. It was a big worry.'

'One which you tried to solve that evening.'

Ian looked blank and then horrified. 'No! Of course not, I couldn't harm anyone!'

Drummond thought he saw fear in the eyes – fear of detection or fear of accusation? He waited.

'Mr Wedderburn said we would go through it in the morning. He sounded quite severe, but I was reasonably sure it was just a mistake, and Martin would confirm what I thought. Otherwise, Mr Wedderburn had seemed quite pleased with the progress of the leisure complex; at least, he didn't complain about any part of it. He only stayed a short time – five to ten minutes at the most – and then he left.'

'He gave no indication that he knew anything of your past history?'

'None at all.'

Drummond looked straight at Ian. 'And you never saw him again?'

'No,' said Ian and then changed his mind. 'Oh, yes, just briefly. He came back almost immediately. He said he wanted the keys to the pool. I took them off my key ring and gave them to him. Then I put my file away, switched the lights off in the gym and locked up. We agreed he would leave the keys in the pantry for me to collect in the morning. He went towards the back door of the mansion, and I went the other way – straight to my car, and drove home to Eastbourne.'

'Did he leave the keys for you as promised?'

Ian looked surprised. 'Yes, they were on the back of the pantry door with the other set for the gym and pool. I attached them to my gym keys on the way in to breakfast and didn't think about it again. I presumed Mr Wedderburn had left them there for me.'

'And what time did you leave on Thursday night?'

'I suppose it was about 10.20 by the time I'd parked the car and got into the flat. I put the ten o'clock news on and it was nearly over. I guess I'd left Seascape between 9.30 and 9.40.'

'Can anyone confirm any of that, sir?'

'No, I live alone. I didn't see any other occupant of the flats. They're solid old buildings and we don't usually hear each other.'

'And no one saw you leave Seascape that evening?'

'Not to my knowledge. I saw no one.'

Drummond looked thoughtfully at the man. 'You will understand that the whole leisure complex will be treated as a scene of crime, for today and possibly for longer? We are stopping people at the gate, so no one will enter the grounds. I would be grateful if you would make yourself available and remain on site for the time being. Should you wish to leave, you need to ask me. Is that understood?'

Ian's tanned face looked considerably paler. 'Yes,' he said shakily.

'Thank you, sir. That will be all.'

Ian glanced at him, paused and then left the room.

As the door closed, Pollard put down her pen. 'Well,' she said, 'that shook him!'

Drummond smiled grimly. 'It certainly seemed to.'

'Do you think Ian did know James was the anonymous writer, and took the opportunity to have his revenge?'

'My gut feeling is no,' said Drummond, resting his elbows on the table and cupping his lower face in his hands. 'It seems most unlikely, unless something happened when he met James that night. Perhaps James challenged him about his past, or hinted that he knew something. That could have been all it would take for James to ruin Ian's new life, which he has built up so painstakingly, and break his marriage for good. That's sufficient to turn Ian to murder. His mind must have had plenty of strains and stresses put on it over recent years – who knows whether one short conversation led it to crack? It wouldn't be difficult for Ian to take James to the pool on a pretext and drown him. He's athletic and strong. He also has the keys to the pool.' Drummond stared at the carpet and sighed. He lowered his hands and sat up. 'I think we need to check his qualifications for working here, and anything else on his CV.'

Pollard made a note.

Drummond wandered over to the window and looked across the car park to the gym. Police tape sealed the doorway. He sighed and returned to his chair.

'So, to summarise,' he said. 'Ian had opportunity and was the last to see James alive, apart from the murderer. He has a strong motive, if he had discovered who James was that evening. He could have grabbed the opportunity to take his revenge. He's already lied to us, but he still maintains that he did not know of James Wedderburn's identity before this weekend – he didn't even know of the Huddersfield link – and it was Martin who did the initial interview.'

'Could Martin and Ian be in it together?' Pollard suggested.

'Old school tie or something?' Drummond made a face. 'Martin would hardly want to lose his job. I imagine it would be quite lucrative to be a joint manager of a hotel, and could be still, if Edward goes ahead with the idea. Even so, it might be worth finding out if they did have any contact years ago. Would you see what you can do?'

Pollard made a note and then stood, exercising her shoulders. 'Do you think we could have a break, sir, and then go on interviewing?

The DCI stretched out his arms and yawned. 'You're right. I could do with an injection of caffeine. Would you mind doing the honours?'

Chapter 24

The tea break had refreshed Simon Drummond and Lindsey Pollard, but the day was not over yet. Soon the detective chief inspector was calling 'come in' to a polite knock, and greeting George.

'Good afternoon, Mr McFarland – please do sit down.' He waved to the chair and waited for George to be seated. He was a man of medium height. According to his earlier statement he was 69, but seemed quite sprightly. He was going bald, but the remaining hair was grey with tinges of white, neatly parted and with diagonal waves. He was smartly dressed in a dark suit with blue shirt and navy tie. His black shoes shone with years of polishing. Every inch the solicitor.

George settled himself and then looked up. 'This is a dreadful business,' he said. 'You're absolutely sure that this was no accident?'

Drummond wondered at the man's level of intelligence. 'I can't think of a way that a drowned corpse could travel a quarter of a mile and jump off a cliff,' he said with a trace of sarcasm. 'So, yes, I am sure, and there are no doubts about the findings of the post-mortem, before you ask.'

George remained silent.

Drummond was aware that he had gone a little too far. 'Had you known Mr. Wedderburn long?' he asked to break the awkward silence.

'Yes. I was his father's solicitor. Initially, James had been made a partner with his father, and then, when he took over the business on his father's death, I dealt with all the paperwork. I can't believe it's nearly 40 years ago.'

'And you've worked for Mr James Wedderburn all those years?'

'Yes, on and off, as I've been needed. Of course, it's really the firm which covers many aspects of the law, but he always came to me first. We dealt with his divorce from his first wife, a long time ago now, then we also saw to the conveyancing of several farms and shops. Recently we have done more, of course, seeing to the paperwork as he's been selling farms and shops across Yorkshire and Lancashire. His Huddersfield home, by some fluke, was sold some weeks ago and the new owners move in on Tuesday. It's a mercy that everything – except for the sale of the remaining two shops – was completed before he moved down. I don't have that paperwork here, naturally.

'Martin acts – acted – as his financial advisor and the two of us had discussed with James some possibilities for his finances in the future. The plans for the restoration and refurbishment of this place have eaten into the money he wanted to spend on it, and it worried him considerably, until he thought of an informal way of involving his family.

'His idea of repaying their loans on his or his wife's death meant drawing up a new will, which is my area of expertise. He was determined to make the hotel idea work – and make a profit for the family, using their money to start it off. I even got the impression that the next step would be to encourage his family to join him and to help run the hotel. He seemed sure of his powers of persuasion.'

'So, what sort of man was he?'

The solicitor made a face – Drummond wondered whether George's teeth had slipped a little and needed to be put back in place. Mentally he slapped his own hand and tried to wait patiently for the answer.

George was obviously not going to be hurried and clearly worded his answer very carefully. 'He was an entrepreneur – almost ahead of his time, really. His father had been a hard-working pig farmer and eventually bought and ran a shop as well. James managed to run both and in due time bought and leased more farms and opened several other shops. He knew how to manage people and to get them to work hard. It was a pity his father never lived to see how well he did. He was alert to new possibilities and, of course, the growth of the fast-food market made it essential for him to find a way to keep pork products popular. Locally he made himself well known, used the weekly papers to advertise, and insisted that a reporter was present at his annual fete. In those days, people would flock to see "The Crowning of Miss Pork Chop" each summer.'

'Local man made good.'

'That's about it.'

'Was he a popular man?' Drummond enquired innocently.

George's eyes narrowed. 'Reasonably popular as an employer – if you worked hard you got quite a fair wage, a summer works' outing and pork products at a reduced rate at Christmas. If you slacked, you were thrown out. As a person, I don't think he was liked very much. People would doff their caps, but no one would call him their friend. Older people turned against him when he divorced his wife and married Cassidy – and they were very concerned for the resulting effect on the children.

'Would you class yourself as a friend of his?'

George glanced at Drummond's face, which Drummond knew gave nothing away. 'My wife and I occasionally went to his home for drinks at Christmas, or when I had done some work for him we might go out for a meal together and James would pay. We were more on Christmas card terms – he would send one with a boar's head on it every year, and it was all I could do to stop my wife sending him one with a turkey on it!' A brief smile lit George's face. 'I tried to stay neutral, but my wife never liked him; she felt he took advantage.'

'What sort of advantage?'

'Oh, just made me work long hours, and would ring me at home about business; she didn't approve of that.'

'Had she any other reason to dislike him?'

The question had an arrow-like quality to it – piercing deep. George looked taken aback. 'Inspector, is this really necessary?'

Drummond, satisfied that he had hit home, retained his composure. 'I'm just trying to get a full picture of Mr Wedderburn's character, sir.' The detective chief inspector paused and tried again. 'So, she did have reason to dislike him?'

'When we married he insisted that we bought all our meat from his shop – although we did abscond for our weekend beef! He would deliver our order himself, and I felt he tried to become a little too familiar with my wife.'

'Did you try to put a stop to it?'

'Yes.'

Drummond looked up at George, who declined to reveal any more. He pulled a brown envelope from under the pile of statements and carefully removed a photograph from it and placed it in front of the solicitor.

George picked it up and stared at the picture. 'Where did you get this?' he asked, without looking up.

'We found it among Mr Wedderburn's personal effects,' said Drummond. 'I think the writing on the reverse is Mr Wedderburn's?'

George turned the photo over and nodded silently.

Drummond quoted the statement written on the back very quietly, '"George dancing with Gloria while his Doreen was in hospital giving birth – naughty George! 27th March 1978."'

Drummond leaned forward. 'Was he blackmailing you, sir? I'm sure it would be possible for us to find out, but I would rather hear it from you.'

George put the photograph back on Drummond's desk, the writing face down. 'Can this remain confidential?'

Drummond, who had to admit to himself that he felt considerable sympathy for George, said, 'If you are innocent of the crime we are investigating, there is no reason that anyone should know.'

George sighed. 'The girl next door begged me to go to the dance because she'd been let down by her boyfriend. My wife had just gone into hospital – we thought it was a false alarm, but they were worried about her blood pressure and wanted to keep her in. The trouble was that Doreen gave birth that night, a fortnight early. The next thing I knew was that the photo was in the local paper, but thankfully my wife never saw it.

'However, the next time I did some work for James, he showed me a copy of the photo and what he had written on the back. He threatened to tell my wife. I couldn't trust him not to add some juicy details of his own imagining, so I gave in to his demand to reduce every future bill by ten per cent. It was so stupid of me, but I was really afraid he would break up our marriage.

'I sometimes wondered if he still called at home and pestered my wife, but I couldn't ask, it would look as if I didn't trust her – and, in addition, I just had to pay for his silence – for nearly 40 years…'

Drummond allowed the silence to deepen before he said, 'You won't have to pay any longer.'

'I thought I'd already reached that point,' George said gloomily. 'I finally retired this last Christmas, but he insisted that I carry on until all the details of this house and its future were finalised – I suppose I shall, at least, be able to charge the estate the correct fees.' He brightened visibly.

'It also gives you a motive, sir.'

George sat up. 'No, inspector! Like you, I would never take the law into my own hands – and if I did do it, how would I have moved the body from the pool to the cliffs? No, I waited in this very room for him for nearly half an hour and then went to bed. I was not involved with his death.'

'Can anyone confirm that, sir?'

George paused, 'Martin came looking for James, sometime after he was due for our meeting. I saw no one on my way to bed that I recall, though there were the usual sounds of footsteps in corridors and bathroom noises.'

'Thank you, sir, you have been most helpful.'

Drummond had decided he would not achieve any more with further questions.

George McFarland got to his feet. 'And the photograph?'

'It stays firmly in its envelope, and at some point I hope I shall be able to give it to you to do with as you will.'

'Thank you.'

As George left the room, Drummond slipped the photo back in its envelope, stretched and leaned back, gazing at the ceiling. Above his head overfed cherubs cavorted, their tiny wings outspread and their little fingers clutching lilies. Drummond wondered at the mindset of those who had commissioned such decoration all those years ago.

He pulled his thoughts back to the present and checked his pile of papers. 'Just Stella Matthews and Dame Emily, then we'll pack up for the night and put all this on the back boiler and let it simmer. OK?'

'OK,' said Pollard with a grin.

Emily let herself in by the back door and took off Fin's lead. She was later than she had intended and guessed that the tea in the drawing room would be a little stewed.

As she hung up her coat, Grace appeared from the kitchen. 'Thank goodness you're back, Dame Emily. Could I have a word with you? I've been that worried.'

'Of course, Grace.' Emily eased herself onto a kitchen chair and rested her arms on the old wooden table, made pale beige by years of scrubbing brush and soap. She ran her fingers over the old ridges in the wood and remembered vividly how, as a child, their old cook had allowed her to measure out sugar, flour and butter. Lifting the correct metal weight by its ring, she would place it on the balance and then put the knob of butter, on a piece of waxed paper, into the pan, gradually adding more until the two sides moved to an equal balance. The scales of justice were harder to read.

Grace bustled around and, lifting a large teapot, filled a mug for them both. She sat down with a sigh. 'I don't know where

Jayne is – didn't appear to help me with tea. She's good, really, but the young don't seem to have much initiative these days.' She pushed a packet of biscuits towards Emily and stopped talking with a suddenness that surprised Emily.

'Grace, what is it?'

Grace looked at her and then got up and shut the kitchen door. Emily had never seen her look frightened before. She sat down again opposite Emily and leaned forward confidentially. 'It's this murder, Dame Emily.'

'Yes, Grace.'

Grace wiped her hands on her apron. 'It was the night Mr Wedderburn… well, disappeared. I was that tired, and not to say a little upset – we'd picked up bits of conversation as we went in and out of the dining room – I'd never heard a family like it.'

Emily nodded. 'I think we were all horrified, Grace, but go on.'

'As I said, I was tired and persuaded Jayne to come upstairs to bed early. She wasn't keen, but she has one of those things – a pad or a pod or something – and she could fiddle with that upstairs. Well, Jayne was in the bathroom and I was just taking off my skirt when I heard this noise,' she lowered her voice. 'You know, when a cow has had its calf taken away…'

Emily smiled grimly. 'They bellow all night; and the pain in the sound is agonising.'

Grace took a sip of tea. 'Well, it was like that, but just one bellow, as you might say, and then there was silence. I thought perhaps it was a fox and then forgot it. The country's got many funny noises at night.'

Emily looked at her, wondering.

Grace continued. 'Well, then Jayne came in, and I'd got into bed by then, and I asked her to draw the curtains back, because I'd forgotten. She stood there looking out and then said there was a pattern dancing on the wall of the old laundry. Well, I got out to look, and Jayne was right, but I didn't understand it. She said she thought it was moving water reflected on the wall. We watched for a little while and the movement slowed down and then stopped. Does it mean anything, Dame Emily?'

For a fleeting moment Emily felt like some biblical character asked to interpret a half-remembered dream. She was sure it did mean something. She picked up her mug and frowned at a knot on the kitchen table and tried to think.

'The light was coming from the old walled garden?'

'Yes, well, the swimming pool, I suppose.'

'And what time was this?'

'We went up sometime before ten, I think.'

Emily put her mug on the table and warmed her hands on its sides. She leaned forward and blew gently, watching the ripples made by her breath. 'Grace,' she said, quietly but slightly dramatically, 'I think you witnessed the moment when James Wedderburn was killed and hit the water in the pool.'

For a moment Grace looked terrified and her eyes went to the door. Emily leaned forward and patted her arm. 'This is something the police need to know. It sounds to me as if he went to the pool and someone surprised him there. Later they took him out to the cliff edge.'

Grace shivered. 'I've never been involved in anything like this, Dame Emily. And there's Jayne, she's too young to have anything to do with something as nasty as this.'

Emily thought of some of the dramatic scenes on television soaps and guessed Jayne had been all-too familiar with such things from her childhood.

'The young are resilient, Grace, and they take things in their stride. It's us oldies who see more clearly the ramifications and lasting damage which comes afterwards. She'll be all right.'

Grace took great gulps of tea, but stopped before she'd finished the mugful. She needed the comfort to last, Emily guessed. She put her hand on Grace's arm and squeezed it slightly. 'It's all right,' she reassured the cook. 'No one has heard us – not through that thick door, and I guess it still creaks badly…' Grace smiled ruefully. Emily went on. 'So we'll keep this under our hats. I've got an interview with the police soon, and I can mention it to them. I think it's important because it could help to fix the time of death. Now, can you be more exact about the time?'

Grace looked very doubtful. 'I'm not sure. If I say the wrong time, I'd get into trouble, wouldn't I?'

Emily ignored the cook's fears. This could be crucial. 'I think everything was running quite late that night,' she said. 'Didn't the dishwasher hose flood the floor, and then you took some hot chocolate to the drawing room? Did you go straight up to bed then?'

Grace looked relieved. 'Yes, of course. Once you'd gone, I went to the dining room. Jayne was just finishing laying up for breakfast. I told her I was going up and not to be long, we'd have to be up early in the morning. Then she looked at her watch and said she hadn't been to bed at half past nine since she was a little girl.'

'Well done, Grace!' Emily beamed as much at her own skill in prompting Grace, as in Grace's ability to remember. 'Do you think it all happened within the next half hour?'

Grace thought. 'Yes,' she said definitely. 'It's that cold upstairs neither of us hung around, and we only stayed by the window for a couple of minutes. You can't see much from up there, and anyway, it was very dark. The clouds hadn't cleared away – I think it sounded as if it was still raining.'

Emily smiled reassuringly. 'Then if I tell that to the police, all they will have to do is ask you to confirm it. Is that all right with you?'

Grace surveyed the last mouthful of drink in her mug. She took a deep breath. 'Yes, thank you, Dame Emily, if you say so,' she said, draining the tea.

It wasn't until the evening meal was over, coffee had been taken in the drawing room, and the family members and George had gone to bed, that Emily had a chance to catch up on the day's events with Stella.

Briefly they compared notes on their interviews with the police and found that neither of them had had anything new to divulge, although Emily had told them what Grace had said to her.

As Emily told Stella about Grace's statement, Stella shuddered. 'Somehow I thought it must have happened when we were in bed and asleep. To think that he might have been murdered while the family was discussing his life history... It's unbelievable.'

'It was also at a time when everyone was coming and going,' said Emily thoughtfully. 'Archie and Ian were unaccounted for originally.'

'You don't think...?' Stella raised her eyebrows.

'I don't know what to think,' said Emily, sipping her second cup of hot chocolate. Her mother would have called it prevaricating. She sighed deeply. 'Perhaps we're looking at it from the wrong angle. Not that someone murdered James, but that he wanted to murder someone else and it went wrong – from his perspective.'

Stella leaned forward. 'Go on.'

'Think about Ian. If you had been James and had loathed this man for the last however many years, your hate would fester. Suddenly, by an amazing coincidence, you have the opportunity to employ him. You could blackmail him, as James did George. Then, you find yourself with an opportunity for revenge – only you call it justice. His life for your son's life.'

The two friends were silent. Emily remembered how hard it had been to come to terms with the death of her nephew, and to see the man responsible in the dock for the days of the trial. Stella must have felt the same for the woman whose thoughtless driving had startled the horse her daughter was riding, moments before her accident. Hatred was a vicious emotion; it sucked at the lifeblood, and robbed its victim of joy and freedom of spirit. She had fought to refuse it entry into her emotions. Come to think of it, Stella had never been bitter, either.

Stella spoke very quietly. 'You think that James went to find Ian in the gym, persuaded him to show him the pool – not difficult, I suppose; as the boss he might want to see it was ready for the morning – and then, at the poolside, he told Ian that he was unmasked.'

Emily nodded. 'It sounds perfectly plausible. And if, in his anger, James let slip that the child was his, he couldn't let Ian live to tell the rest of the family, and certainly not Cassidy.'

'And Ian is fit and athletic,' Stella added. 'It wouldn't be difficult to wrong-foot an angry man who is driven by passion. He could have hit him or just pushed him into the pool. James could have hit his head, or the water might have been enough to finish him off.'

'The police said it was definitely foul play,' said Emily thinking back to her time with Drummond and Pollard by the pool. 'But if he had water in his lungs that was probably the final cause of death.'

'Could he have got James to the clifftop alone?'

Emily made a face. 'That's the really difficult part. I can't see how that was done at all. But we don't know where Archie or Edward were at the time – although they went off to play snooker together about then.'

'I suppose,' said Stella slowly, 'the body didn't have to be removed straight away. The killer could have come back later with an accomplice in the middle of the night and removed the body then.'

'Which puts almost everyone in this house under suspicion,' said Emily, lifting her hands helplessly. 'Who has an alibi?'

Stella looked at her in horror. 'You're right,' she said. 'Almost everyone had a room on their own. Archie and Clara were together, but from what I heard on the first floor that night, I suspect even Philip and Samantha slept in different rooms – and come to think of it, even Cassidy was alone, if James was already dead.'

'Well,' said Emily, getting up from her chair, 'as my nephew used to say, "my brain hurts". I think I need to sleep on all this.

I'll get back to the Lodge and we'll compare notes in the morning.'

Stella smiled. 'You're right. I'll just get your coat and let you out.'

Emily walked slowly down the front drive, while a newly revived Fin zigzagged among the flowers on the front lawn, pursuing rabbit smells with an eagerly wagging tail. Her white markings were just visible in the darkness and the rain had eased to a fine drizzle.

The weariness which pervaded the whole of Emily's body made it an effort to put one foot in front of another. The future seemed as dark as the night around her. Briefly the clouds parted and the full moon lit the garden, but she was in the deep shadow cast by the cedar tree, and she felt she was wading through liquid darkness. She realised she was feeling sorry for herself. Just because her body felt tired tonight did not mean she was old, yet. Inside she felt as young as ever; however complex the problems she faced, whether the mystery of James' death, or the way in which her own future was to be resolved, she would not give in to the inevitable.

A few yards from the gate she fumbled in her pocket for her keys and paused, balancing her stick over her arm, so that she could turn on the tiny torch she had attached to the key ring. The little gate in the Lodge fence had a small step beneath it and she was always careful. She opened the gate and gave a small whistle – she could just see the white of Fin's tail waving somewhere in the direction of the sundial. She tried again and was finally rewarded as the small dog pattered past her up the path. Emily followed her, key at the ready.

For some reason the dog had stopped at the bottom of the two steps which led to the front door and was sniffing appreciatively.

'Fin, get out of the way!' Emily said sharply, putting her stick at an awkward angle over the dog and briefly preparing to step over her. The dog did not move, but the stick seemed to have a life of its own, and slowly, but surely, it began a gentle slide to the right, pushing Emily's body to the left, while her hovering leg swayed desperately in midair. She remembered suddenly and vividly her fall in Australia, the months in hospital…

'No!' she gasped. 'Please, not again!'

She put her hand out towards the second step to save herself, as the dog, aware of her descending body, backed away quickly. Emily felt a shooting pain in her wrist and then found herself sitting sideways on the bottom step as the stick shot away from her grasp.

For a moment she sat nursing her hand, breathing heavily. 'You silly dog!' Emily complained. 'Why did you have to stop just there?'

Fin came to her side and began to lick the step.

'Fin?'

Emily felt gingerly for the dropped keys and the torch. The step was greasy to the touch. At last she found the torch and twisted it on. There was nothing visible on the red tiles, no wet leaf, no slug or snail. She gently ran a finger along the step where she was sitting, and then peered at it in the torchlight. She could just discern a thin film of fat on her forefinger. Emily frowned at it and smelt it. Bacon fat! She tested the top step with the same result. Unbidden, from the recesses of her mind, came the phrase, 'An enemy hath done this.' Anger rose in her. Someone had meant her harm, and if she didn't move quickly, Fin would consume more than was good for her and become ill.

Dame Emily slipped the keys into her pocket and reached for her stick. She planted it firmly on the ground and, pushing up against the side of the lower step with her foot, with as much strength as she could muster, and grasping a branch of the camellia which grew at the side of the front door with her free hand, she managed to regain her balance and stand upright, her breath coming in small gasps.

What now? She dared not use the steps. She pulled out her bunch of keys and looked at them. What a mercy she had kept them all. The key to the side gate and the back door were still there. She had a job to tease Fin away from the grease, but the emergency dog treats from her pocket did the trick. The back gate, which was in the side fence of the plot, was hard to open, but now Emily was standing firmly on two feet, she channelled her fury, summoning all her strength to shoulder it open and fight back the encroaching blackberry branches. She forced her way into the back garden, closed the gate and relocked it before letting herself into the kitchen.

It was so hard to keep her temper; she felt like throwing her heaviest saucepan through the window. She walked into the hall and stared hard at the phone. Would Chief Inspector Drummond be at the police station? Well, if he weren't, someone would be. She sat down heavily on the chair and dialled.

Background noise made it hard to communicate with the policewoman at the other end – a discordant choir of drunks singing a mix of football and rugby songs, she guessed. Gradually the noise faded. Perhaps they were being led away to the cells for the night. Patiently she explained to the woman on the phone about the state of her front doorstep. The officer was polite, repeated the message she had written for DCI Drummond and hoped Emily would have a peaceful night.

Emily replaced the receiver with a disgusted snort. Bacon fat did not rank as your average murder weapon, but she herself had no doubt that it had been used for that purpose – well, at least put her out of action for some considerable time.

Suddenly exhaustion swept over her. She returned to the kitchen and pulled the flask of hot water from her parka pocket, but then decided against using it – it would do for her morning cuppa. Dame Emily needed something rather stronger to help her sleep – if she could sleep at all.

Part IV
Plumbing New Depths

Easter Sunday and Monday

Chapter 25

Emily turned over in bed and groped for the button which switched off her alarm clock. The next minute she was wide awake, aware of unaccustomed aches and pains all over her body. Gingerly she sat up, reached for her dressing gown and winced as a pain shot through her wrist.

Suddenly the memory of her return the previous night came back to her forcefully. Anger propelled her into the bathroom and exploded as she realised, for the third morning running, that she would have to wash her face in ice-cold water.

She padded around and glared at her reflection in the mirror. Who had dared to sabotage her front doorstep? Did they expect to frighten her? Did they think she knew too much? If only she did. This was the last straw, and she would get whoever this was.

She let Fin into the back garden, reached for a mug and teabag and began to unscrew the top of the flask. But what about the step? If she poured hot water over it... No, she must not destroy evidence, though she doubted the police would find any. She swallowed a quick cuppa, collected her coat, handbag and Fin's lead, and prepared to call the dog in from the garden. Suddenly she stopped.

Here she was in her old clothes and she'd forgotten it was Sunday. She sighed. It wasn't just Sunday, it was Easter Sunday. That settled it. She went back to her bedroom and put on her glad rags. She couldn't miss church on Easter Sunday, and she suddenly felt a great urge to get away into some kind of normality. Grabbing a pair of secateurs from the kitchen cupboard, she prepared to tackle the offending blackberries still encroaching on the back gate.

Emily was longing to tell Stella the events of the night, but everyone was in the dining room when she arrived. They glanced up as she said, 'Good morning,' but no one indicated surprise that she was there. Was last night's guilty party in the room? she wondered, as she walked over to the sideboard. She was helping herself to some porridge when Samantha came to stand next to her. 'I just wanted to let you know,' she said very quietly. 'There isn't a baby.'

Emily continued to spoon porridge into her bowl. 'I'm so sorry,' she said.

'It's probably for the best,' said Samantha. 'I don't think Philip could handle it just at the moment. Edward has promised him – and Clara, of course – some money from the estate. Then in about a year's time we may be able to afford a new home and start a family.'

Emily smiled. 'That'll be lovely. I hope it works out for you.'

'Thank you,' said Samantha, picking up her bowl of muesli and returning to her chair.

Emily walked over to the table and slipped into her place between Stella and Edward. The mood in the room seemed much lighter this morning; then she realised why.

'You're so clever,' she said to Stella.

Stella laughed. 'We couldn't have Easter day without everyone enjoying a small Easter egg. It has brightened the atmosphere, hasn't it?' she said with a wicked smile, glancing down the table, where brightly wrapped mini eggs lay scattered in shiny abandon on the polished wood.

'Any police coming today?' Emily asked casually. Not that she would let them stop her going out. She almost surprised herself at her rebellious attitude.

'We haven't heard they are,' Stella said. 'I guess you're going to church,' she added. 'I wish I could join you, but there's just too much to do here.'

'Mm,' said Emily, putting her bowl to one side and reaching unceremoniously for the toast rack.

Stella passed the butter and marmalade. 'What time's the service?'

'10.30,' said Emily, tucking into her toast. 'I should just make it.'

She did make it and even managed to find a parking place. She walked through the old door of the parish church and paused for a moment to take it all in. It was the smell that came first. The glorious scent of pinewood polish heavily overlaid with the pure aroma of hundreds of spring flowers... Little arrangements adorned the tiny windowsills down the side aisles, by the choir stalls enormous vases on tall stands held a multitude of yellow daffodils and white narcissi, and by the font a small model garden, made by the children, showed the empty tomb and a single empty cross. This was what Easter was about. She felt better already.

She took her hymn book from Dorothy, who gave her a quick hug, and went to her usual seat. It was nearly nine months since she had sat here. Someone behind her tapped her on the back and said how good it was to see her, a couple in front turned round and smiled, and one of the little boys who was forever getting into trouble in the Sunday Club looked across at her, grinned and held up his thumb. She relaxed. She was home.

She looked around and mentally tried to name as many people as she could. All the children had grown, without exception. Old Mr Jacoby had less hair and poor Mrs Wilson had given up her sticks and come in a wheelchair.

The vicar came in and the service began. Emily sang with enthusiasm and lost herself in everything around her. It was only as she got her money out for the collection that she noticed Mrs Wilson had fallen asleep and had slipped sideways in her chair. For a brief moment Emily wondered if she had died. Died in a chair – a wheelchair. Of course! That was how you could transport a body – silently – in a wheelchair. Emily felt the collection plate prod her elbow; with a murmured apology she put in her money and passed it to her neighbour.

It was really hard to concentrate on the rest of the service. Where could anyone get a wheelchair in the middle of the night? But it fitted. She remembered the body in the water, slightly curled. He must have been sitting when rigor mortis set in. A wheelchair is silent. You can push it. The day Margaret had moved into the Deanery she'd pushed her up the path to the front door in a wheelchair. It was really hard work...

The solution hit Emily's mind with a resounding crash. She glanced around, wondering if anyone in the congregation had noticed her suddenly jerk upright, but they were all looking up at the pulpit, their faces smiling at a joke the vicar had made.

Now Emily knew. She had solved one part of the puzzle. She joined in the final hymn lustily, and at the end of the service spent a long time greeting friends and chatting to the now wide-awake Mrs Wilson.

As she drove back to Seascape, she sang the last hymn over to herself. She parked the yellow peril in her space next to the Lodge, collected Fin and walked round the back of the mansion. Blue and white police tape still stretched from the entrance to the gym to the little pathway leading to the dairy and the laundry. There was only one police car and the man inside was eating a sandwich and reading a paper. Reluctantly she refrained from asking him if he had taken a sample of fat from her doorstep. Perhaps DCI Drummond would be around after lunch.

The atmosphere in the dining room was surprisingly cheerful. Stella had worked her magic by getting Grace to cook turkey with all the trimmings and a 'nut-something' for the vegetarians. There were plenty of vegetables, and the apple pie and custard went down very well. Gradually Emily gleaned that the family had been out. Philip and Samantha seemed to have called a truce, had taken Edward on a tour of a few local villages in their car and had visited a small zoo. Archie, Clara and Cassidy had invited Martin to go with them to Eastbourne and had played crazy golf, Ian had jogged along the cliffs to the lighthouse and back, and George had gone to the golf club next door and fitted in nine holes. Stella had stayed in the mansion briefly to check on lunch arrangements, and then had driven to visit her daughter. Even she looked more relaxed.

After coffee the group dispersed again and Emily was left alone in the drawing room waiting for Stella. She looked around; it all looked so tatty now. Perhaps she would just get the house clearance people in – having seen other people use her furniture with no appreciation of its sentimental worth, it didn't seem to be her own any more.

She frowned. There was half a cup of cold coffee on the mantelpiece and a whole lot of untidy papers on a side table. She went and looked more closely. It was music – handwritten, pages and pages of it – neat, with little comments in the margin, and occasionally question marks. She could almost feel her fingers twitching. It wasn't like reading someone's diary, after all.

She went over to the baby grand piano, and, with an enormous effort, lifted the lid to half height. She sat and arranged the papers carefully, then placed her fingers in readiness, and launched. Her hands felt stiff, and her wrist ached, but the music was reasonably easy to read, and before long she was lost in the sound which filled the room. At times it rose and fell like the sea, changing from discordant and angry to soothing and calm, rising to great heights, dissolving into romantic and soft susurration.

Crash! The drawing room door had been flung open, had hit the door stopper and shuddered in its frame. Emily stopped mid-phrase and looked in amazement at a totally distraught Edward. 'How dare you?' he burst out and then stopped. 'Oh, it's you, Dame Emily,' he said more quietly, before sinking into a chair. 'I'm so sorry. Will you go on playing?'

'To the end?'

'All the way to the end. Please ignore me.'

Emily turned back to the manuscript. It was all very well to go on, but where should she start? She turned back a page to where there was the heading 'Act II' and began to play softly, and then moved into the fierce and frantic section she had been playing when Edward had entered.

Although the music absorbed her, she was also conscious of Edward moving somewhere behind her – perhaps looking out of the window? – and then to the other side of her. She heard the springs of the oldest settee complain and then, barely perceptibly, she heard the certain sound of sobbing. Immediately she turned her whole attention to the music, forcing her mind to concentrate and her fingers to stretch uncomfortably. Once again she tried to identify with the music's moods: loss, despair, fear, anger, a hint of hope dawning, joy and victory. She felt a sense of triumph for herself, too, as she played the final chord, lifted her hands and let them drop into her lap. It had taken as much emotional effort as playing in her first concert in the Brighton Pavilion when she was just 12. At least her playing was better than it had been then, but not now at the heights it had once reached.

Slowly, she looked round. It would seem that Edward had slipped from the settee to the floor and had been half-kneeling, half-sitting there; as she turned, he was just getting to his feet. He sat on the settee and blew his nose loudly.

Emily walked over and sat in the chair next to him. 'I didn't mean to upset you,' she said apologetically. 'There are times when it is hard to resist the call of the piano.'

Edward smiled weakly. 'That's what Jonathan used to say.'

Emily put her head slightly on one side as she looked at him. 'Would it help to talk?' she asked gently.

Edward blew his nose again. 'If you wouldn't mind. My family have no idea.'

Emily smiled; she didn't need to ask what it was they had no idea about. 'And Jonathan wrote it?' she said, with a sudden flash of insight.

Edward nodded. 'We hope to perform it at school this coming term. It's five years since he died, so only the sixth formers will remember him, but of course it will be special for the staff too.'

'You said you knew him a long time.'

'We met at prep school in Yorkshire. After my father died, my mother spent a lot of time helping James, who was just beginning to run the shop. They decided that boarding school was the best place for me, and, like Jonathan, I managed to get a scholarship. They'd put us in alphabetical order so we sat next to each other on the first day, and that was it. We were friends till we left for university. I went to Oxford and read Classics and English and he went to Cambridge and did Classics and kept up his music as well.

'We stayed in touch and continued to spend holidays together – camping all over Europe. We both got teaching posts, but at different schools. My first job was in Leeds and it was quite an eye-opener. I couldn't believe there were kids who didn't appreciate classical Greek tragedies – I was naïve then! I felt a complete failure and nearly gave up. Jonathan urged me to try an independent school on the edge of Leeds, where I got some of my confidence back, then I got the post of head of English at his school, where he was teaching music.

'Jonathan married Beth, one of the junior school staff. She was very beautiful with long, dark chestnut hair. I was always sorry he'd met her first! I was best man at his wedding and am godfather to his firstborn twin boy.

'What we didn't know in all this time was that James – who'd got to know Jonathan's parents when we were children – had persuaded Mr West to sell his pig farm. He wanted to retire and thought it was a very good deal, but somehow James fooled him and undercut the price. He and Mrs West were left with very little to live on, once they had bought a new home. He grew to hate the little estate of bungalows – no fields, no animals, no space. He got so angry, so worked up.'

Emily nodded grimly; she had good cause to understand. So this was how empires were built.

'A year later, James sold Mr West's farm to a developer, making an enormous profit. I'm sure the shock of the news caused Mr West's heart attack. It was a massive one and he died instantly. I wouldn't be surprised if all the stress hadn't helped to bring on his mother's cancer, though there's no scientific proof of that, of course; she only survived her husband by a couple of years. Jonathan was distraught. It nearly broke our friendship, although I know he believed deep down that I knew nothing about any of it – I'd never kept in touch with James. Jon and I still remained friends, but for a long time it was not quite the same. Eventually we managed to put it all behind us and in recent years I'd been on holiday with the whole family.

'That last summer we went to Kefalonia. Beth and her daughter would go off together, getting a taste of local life, while the boys enjoyed a local water sports club. Jon and I studied the classical links with the landscape. We'd heard a theory that Odysseus was in fact a real person, and that he lived on a nearby peninsula, not far from where we were staying. We would pore over the relevant passages for hours. This wasn't quite as eccentric as it sounds! At college I'd begun to write a play about Odysseus called *Penelope* and Jon had written music about a sea battle. We suddenly came up with the idea that we could combine what we had done and it would make a tremendous production. Beth had already done the costumes for a number of school plays and she became equally enthusiastic. After a couple of years, Jon had just one more piece to write – about Penelope sitting at home, waiting. Then suddenly the news of his mother's death came, added to which, the school principal wanted a production based on the main A level book, so the idea was dropped.

'I think that was the final straw and depression set in. One Tuesday, Jonathan had gone home early from school, saying he was unwell. Both Beth and I were very concerned. She asked me to come back with her and talk to him. We walked in the front door and there he was, hanging in front of us. The chair was lying on its side, so I was able to put it under his feet and between us we cut the rope and lowered him down. He was still alive when the ambulance came, and we sat on either side of his bed in hospital holding his hands, but it was no good. Within half an hour he had gone. There was no time to get the children. Their daughter still blames me; she was away doing her nursing training then, and now will only come home if I keep away. Amazingly, the boys are more realistic. I'd taught them in school and always got on well with them and that still continues – but we never talk about that afternoon.

'When it was over, and we went back to their home, we found Jon had left notes in the bedroom. To Beth he said how sorry he was he couldn't carry on. To me he said he didn't hold me responsible for James' actions, and asked me to put on our opera production, and look after Beth and the family.

'Beth and I have both found it a very hard project, but I think it will prove to be very cathartic both for us and for the school. We need to put it all behind us and I think this may be the way to do it.' Edward stopped and leaned back. 'I'm so sorry – once I start talking I don't know how to stop.'

Emily smiled. 'I'm so glad you did talk. It takes courage to tell someone else, and it takes a different courage to take on this big production. I really hope it is a tremendous success. I loved the part of it that I played.'

'Thank you.'

For several minutes they were silent. Emily was allowing the story to sink into her mind. She hoped that Edward was feeling a lifting of the burden. She imagined that he'd never let himself cry or really grieve for the loss of his 'adopted family', and had probably buried himself in his work. Did he still feel guilt for James' part in the horrific story? She was glad that he had at least been with his friend before the end came.

Then, unbidden, the nagging thought came. While all that Edward had said was probably true, was he trying to win her sympathy and turn her mind away from the fact that he might have murdered James? Had the tears been not just for the loss of his friend, but for the remorse he might be feeling for playing a part in his brother's death? She didn't want to entertain the thought.

The door opened slightly and Stella put her head round. 'Emily, you wanted to see me before you go to visit Margaret?' she said.

'Yes,' said Emily getting up. 'Perhaps we could take Fin for a quick walk before I go?'

'By all means. I'll get my coat,' said Stella, vanishing.

Edward walked over to the piano and picked up a few sheets of paper. 'There's one part I'm not happy with,' he said. 'Thanks again, Dame Emily, you've spurred me on to tackle it, while I have a little free time.'

Emily smiled. 'I'll see you at dinner,' she said.

Chapter 26

Stella was waiting outside the door with Emily's coat and an enthusiastic Fin on the end of her lead. They walked down the drive and out onto the Drift.

White, flat-bottomed clouds clung, limpet-like, to the intensely blue sky, and the turquoise and navy flecked sea was motionless, a smooth, polished walkway extending all the way to the horizon. A tiny tanker, balanced between the sky and the ocean, made its imperceptible way in the far distance, while nearer to shore a fishing boat, accompanied by noisy gulls, and disturbing the still water, went at greater speed towards Newhaven. The air smelled of the sea, and the damp ground gave under their feet. A cold breeze teased Emily's hair away from its comb and she suddenly felt exhilarated. As she described to Stella the events of the night before, she became quite animated.

'It had to be deliberate, Stella,' she insisted. 'Who would do such a thing?'

Stella was less excited. 'You could call that an attempt on your life,' she said. 'It could have put you in hospital, and if you'd remained on the ground all night then you could have developed pneumonia and then…'

'Curtains for me!' said Emily cheerfully.

Stella stood her ground. 'I'll bandage your wrist for you when we get back, but Emily, you've got to be careful,' she said. 'It shows that the killer is still at large, and that James' death was no opportune accident.'

Emily didn't reply. She didn't want to face the fact that Stella could be right. She turned to other events and described her eureka moment in church.

'Very clever, Emily,' she said. 'It's so obvious, but none of us had thought of it.'

'Except the killer – and how did he or she know that the transport they needed was so easily available?'

By the time they had come back from their walk they were no nearer the truth – or even a theory. Emily stopped at the Lodge and picked up the car while Stella returned to the mansion.

Margaret was waiting anxiously when Emily arrived. The planned activity for the afternoon obviously held no attraction for her, and she was sitting in the conservatory running her hands up and down the arm of a basket chair.

'There you are!' she said, the moment Emily appeared. 'I know how they got the body to the cliff.'

'So do I,' responded Emily quickly, determined not to be outdone. She sat down. 'It's so obvious, when you think about it.'

'Have you found it?' demanded Margaret. 'Has it got telltale bits of mud and grass all over it?'

Emily shook her head. 'I can't cross the police tape and there's just one minor officer sitting in his car, guarding the area.' She felt slightly guilty that she had forgotten to follow up her phone call of the night before, but shrugged it off. The ball was in their court now. It gave her a few more hours' advantage to try to solve the murder before they did.

Of course, in her haste to tell her sister about the bacon fat, she had forgotten Margaret's warning.

'I told you,' the latter said fiercely. 'It would have served you right if you'd ended up in hospital.'

Emily felt slightly peeved. After all, she was the innocent victim, and her back and wrist still hurt. 'I was careful,' she protested. 'And I always walk down the drive close to the grass, away from the bushes and shrubbery. I'd see anyone jump out with a knife – and Fin would bark,' she added lamely.

Margaret snorted. 'After they'd stabbed you.'

Emily felt they were getting nowhere. There must be something else she could talk about. She remembered Grace, and told her sister the cook's account of the events at bedtime.

'It was somewhere between 9.30 and ten o'clock,' said Emily. 'She heard this noise like the bellow of a cow whose calf has been taken away. It must have been when James was hit.'

Margaret laughed. 'I remember those cows, and you with your cold feet!'

'What do you mean?' Emily was on the defensive again.

'Remember when we were small and shared the nursery, and Nurse What's-her-name was in the room next door, supposedly looking after us?'

'Nurse Steadfast,' said Emily, with a smile.

'That's it,' said Margaret. 'The farmer whose land backed onto ours had just sent the calves off to market that day, and the cows were most upset. They bellowed all night. You said they were saying, "No, no!" and you cried and cried. Eventually you ended up in my bed. Your tears soaked through my pyjamas and your cold feet stuck into me all night!'

Emily laughed. 'I do remember, now you come to mention it. I felt so sorry for them, and the noise was so loud. Nurse had no sympathy at all. "It's just a fact of nature," she said, in that stuck-up voice of hers.'

'Well, so it is,' said Margaret, 'but I knew better than to say so as well. You'd never have gone to sleep at all. I think I managed to extricate myself in the end and slept in your bed. Dear Nurse Steadfast was quite surprised to find us in the wrong places in the morning. I seem to remember a telling-off.'

Emily sighed, 'Those were the days,' she said. 'But now I've got to cope with these days, and it's really hard. You would think knowing the likely time that James died would help, but it seems that it was the precise time that most people were out of sight of anyone else.'

'It makes the puzzle all the more interesting, dear,' said Margaret vaguely.

Emily realised that her sister was staring past her into the sitting room. 'I think it's teatime,' she said, giving up the conversation as a bad job.

'Oh, good,' said Margaret. 'It's hot cross buns and jam today. I won't keep you. Keep worrying at it – something will fall into place and then it won't be difficult to solve at all.'

Emily resisted the temptation to thump her sister for being so smug, and opened the conservatory door. Margaret didn't give her a second glance, but hurried towards her special chair, while Emily made good her escape.

Back at Seascape, Stella caught her as she came in the back door of the mansion.

'The police sent someone while you were out,' she said. 'They've taken a sample from your front step, and they said I could get rid of the rest of the fat, so you'll be able to go in by your own front door tonight.'

Emily rested her hand on her bandaged wrist. 'Thank you so much,' she said. 'I really don't want to fight brambles in the middle of the night again.'

That evening, after dinner, Edward and Archie decided to have another snooker match, while George and Martin remained chatting and playing cards with the rest of the family. Emily, remembering her eureka moment in church, borrowed Stella's mobile and, standing outside the back door, had a brief conversation with the duty officer at the police station, who promised to give her message to the DCI as soon as possible.

On the way back she stopped at the coat pegs and fiddled in her jacket pocket for a tissue. She glanced down and smiled. It would seem that Jayne had removed her offending flip-flops; there was just one pair of gardener's shoes in evidence. She yawned and went into the kitchen in the hope of an informal cup of coffee, and lowered herself carefully onto the nearest chair.

Grace added another mug to the two she was carrying. 'Decaf?' she asked, pausing on her way to the kettle.

'Please,' said Emily with a sigh, as she carefully stretched both legs out under the table.

Stella came in with a clipboard holding a thick wad of papers and joined Emily, who returned the mobile with the air of a conspirator. 'I've left a message for the inspector,' she said quietly. 'My chat with Margaret made me even more sure of my theory.' Then in a normal voice she added, 'I really must find my phone charger. I don't seem to have had a moment to myself since I moved back in.'

'Is there much more to unpack?' Stella asked.

'Just two or three plastic bags with the last-minute things I threw in: the books and bits and pieces I keep on my bedside table, bathroom toiletries, photos I brought back from Australia, that sort of thing.'

Stella glanced at Emily as Grace plonked the mugs on the table so that the coffee swayed uncertainly. 'You really need to rest your wrist,' she remarked.

Emily didn't respond. She lifted the mug and warmed both hands on it. 'And I'll have to move again before long. It's such an effort,' she said. She stopped as pain shot briefly down one leg.

'Now, Dame Emily,' said Grace as she brought her own drink and sat down with them. 'Please be careful. It looks as if that chair isn't doing your hip a lot of good.'

Emily was startled. She thought she had managed to disguise any reaction to pain recently.

'Thank you, Grace, but I think it's just the hips adjusting after the ops; it's all mending very well, really.' She paused and took a sip of coffee. 'Though my hurried trip out on the cliffs the other morning has set me back slightly.'

There was a brief, respectful silence.

Stella leaned forward and selected a chocolate digestive from the open tin. 'Emily, you never really said what happened in Australia. I know your stay was extended and Mr Wedderburn was distinctly annoyed by it, but I'm sure you didn't do it just to inconvenience him!'

Both heads turned towards Emily. 'I just broke a hip when I was about to go on holiday with my goddaughter, and then everything got delayed,' she said vaguely. She stared at the table and sipped her coffee in tiny prolonged sips, and tried to think of a way to change the subject.

Stella was too quick. 'That was dreadful! Was it an accident? Did you have other injuries? How did it happen?'

Emily the courageous, Emily the independent, Emily the forceful, felt herself shrinking and reddening.

'Emily?' said Stella.

Both Stella and Grace were staring at her now.

Emily decided to brave it out. 'It was all very embarrassing,' she said.

She waited, but no one said, 'Oh, well, we won't ask you for the details.' Both Grace and Stella wore faint smiles and their eyes were alight with interest.

'Go on,' said Stella, passing the biscuit tin to Grace. 'We're sitting comfortably and waiting for our bedtime story.'

Emily glared at her. 'Then,' she said, like a child who is all bravado, 'you shall have the whole story.'

'Last June, out of the blue, I received a letter from my goddaughter, Sandra, in Australia. She wanted me to go out for her daughter Imogen's wedding in August, and stay with her for a three-week holiday afterwards. It would be winter and not too hot.'

Grace dunked her biscuit, forgetting the chocolate on it. 'I've got a cousin out there,' she said. 'Wouldn't dare go, though, it's so far, and you never know with these foreign places... though I suppose it's not as foreign as some...' She left her thoughts unfinished.

Emily took a biscuit herself and nibbled it. 'I really wanted to go. I've been to most of the continents at some time or another.'

She paused for another drink of coffee and the other two settled back. Now that Emily had begun, she was determined to enjoy telling the story. 'I checked with my solicitor and the estate agent and they agreed that I should go. I needed a holiday after all the stress of getting my sister into the home so unexpectedly, and the mansion was hardly likely to sell very quickly. They would try for a buyer, rather than have an auction, they said. I was sure nothing would happen in the month I planned to be away. I arrived a week before the wedding and stayed with Rosemary, an old school friend who emigrated there 40 years ago.'

The other two at the table watched Emily with interest, tolerating her prevarication, waiting for the moment of the accident. Emily swallowed. 'Then came the day of the wedding. The church was in a suburb of Sydney, a beautiful cream-painted building full of flowers and dozens of lively guests. It was a fine day and the bride looked wonderful. Uncannily like her mother when she was that age. Sandra and her husband, Paul, were delighted that everything went so smoothly – well, until the end of the reception.'

She paused. Stella leaned forward. 'Go on…'

Emily gave her a despairing glance. 'It was all so silly,' she said. 'There must have been 80 or so people standing on the wide steps of the hotel, throwing confetti, shouting goodbye. I was on the third or fourth step from the bottom. Sandra and Paul were just below me, by the car. Imogen paused and kissed her parents and then turned her back on us and threw the bouquet…'

Emily paused, as the present moment of embarrassment mixed with the past memory of severe pain. 'It was so ridiculous, just a reflex action, but you know how you forget how old you are?' She paused; Stella nodded and smiled encouragingly. 'Well, it was as if I was 17 and playing lacrosse again. I lifted my stick and tried to catch the flowers with it…'

Grace's eyes were wide in amazement; suddenly Emily realised she had no idea how to play lacrosse. 'But of course,' she went on, 'I had no net at the end of my stick to catch them. At the same time, I felt an arm behind me reaching for the flowers, and one of the little page boys pushed past the back of my legs. That was all it took...' she said lamely, as Stella covered her mouth with her hand. 'I heard the car revving and drawing away from the kerb, and everyone calling goodbye, as I bounced my way down the steps and landed at Sandra's feet. The pain was intense and I think I must have passed out. They told me the ambulance came very quickly, and poor Sandra insisted on coming to the hospital with me, but as soon as I came round I sent her back again. She'd got a lot of old friends staying at the hotel and they were going to have a meal together. Once I was in the hospital there was nothing for her to do – I was in good hands.'

'And you broke your hip?' Stella enquired.

'I broke the good hip, not the one that was already due for surgery back here. Not very convenient!' Emily, having told all, felt a little better about the whole scenario. 'Once the broken hip was sorted out, Sandra insisted that I stay with them to recuperate, and then it seemed sensible to have the other hip done before I came home. She and Paul wanted to get me on my feet again – literally – and there would have been no one here to help. I'd have ended up in a home or some convalescent place. Then, of course, I got MRSA which delayed things further.'

Stella smiled. 'You never did things by halves,' she remarked.

Emily grinned. 'It takes a lot to keep me down, and I'm really making good progress; or was until this weekend!'

'Well, Dame Emily,' Grace said, gathering the empty mugs, 'I reckon your hips'll get better soon, what with you settled in the Lodge and walking Fin every day.' She glanced down at the sleeping dog, before collecting the newly washed tea towels from the scullery and taking them outside the back door.

Stella glanced at her friend. 'Joking apart, Emily, you've had a tough time and it looks as though things aren't going to get any easier in the foreseeable future.'

Emily made a face. 'I can't bear to think of the future. It's going to be even harder to leave a second time. I love the Lodge, the cliff walks and the sense of space. But, I have to face it; this place no longer belongs to the Hatherley-Brownes.'

Stella looked gloomy. She rang her finger up and down a groove in the old table. 'But will Edward keep it on? What about death duties and inheritance tax? I don't know if he can afford it.'

Emily sat straighter in her chair. 'Then some millionaire somewhere will. This house has survived the Civil War and two World Wars – it won't lie down and die. I have to let go.'

Grace came clattering back into the kitchen. 'I bet it's those workmen,' she grumbled.

'What have they done now?' Stella asked, almost picking up her pen and clipboard to record the complaint.

'Oh, I don't know. I've hung a couple of tea towels on the line outside and it's as slack as anything. I don't know if they've knocked it or what they've done. Don't worry – I have to admit it's easier to reach now.'

Stella smiled. 'For one who's vertically challenged,' she murmured.

'I don't suffer from vertigo myself,' said Grace comfortably, 'but my Gary does. Even has to sleep the other side of the bed from the window, when we're in one of them high hotels in Spain.' And with that she went back to the scullery.

Emily and Stella exchanged grins and slowly got to their feet.

'Bed,' said Emily.

'Bed,' said Stella.

Chapter 27

Emily hated being in limbo. There was a nothingness about it which defied description. It was like dreaming you were talking to a ghost and finding that you were one too, without substance, without influence – being, but not being.

Of course, it was the police who were at fault. If only they could solve this case, then everyone would know where they were. Surely they had found evidence by now? They were taking too long. She sighed; she knew it was really up to her to get to the bottom of it. What had Margaret said? 'Keep worrying at it.' She would. After all, she had one piece of the jigsaw, she could try fitting it to other parts in turn. She was sure the answer was staring her in the face, but she couldn't see it.

As she walked from the Lodge towards the mansion in search of Monday breakfast, Emily tried to retrace James' last steps in her mind. She was sure he had gone from the sundial to the side of the building, and then past the gym. Perhaps he hadn't passed the gym – perhaps he went in and met Ian, if Ian hadn't left by then. James would have had time to drop in before he was due in the music room.

Emily's mind went into overdrive. Had they gone to the pool together, James planning 'an accident' for Ian? And if Ian had killed him in self-defence and wanted the whole thing to look like an accident, he needed an accomplice – did he know someone else at Seascape? He always seemed to keep himself to himself, but there might have been someone; after all, they all came from 'up north'.

Who would have helped Ian? Emily tried to think through the possibilities. Martin? He had appointed Ian as leisure manager and worked with him over the last few weeks. Or could there be a school link, a common interest? Or perhaps Ian had treated one of Martin's children at the hospital? It was just possible... But surely Ian would not have divulged his own past history – there was too much to lose – unless, of course, he was facing a murder charge. Was Ian so desperate that he took the risk of asking Martin to help him dispose of James' body? Why should Martin agree? Emily shook her head. She couldn't link them at all; she filed the theory and tried again.

Archie had been around the gym that evening. Perhaps Archie had overheard some of the conversation between Ian and James – if indeed there had been one – and had followed them to the pool. Perhaps Archie was a witness to James' last moments in the pool and agreed on a cover-up. After all, if he grassed – was that the right word? – on Ian, he would be placed at the scene as a witness, and that would make him a suspect too. Perhaps, during the snooker game, Archie had persuaded Edward to help and the three of them disposed of the body later that night. But how to prove it?

Emily paused opposite the gym, waiting for the dog, and thought about Edward. He really hated James; his outburst at James' birthday dinner would label him as the person with the strongest motive. She couldn't account for his movements up to the time they had taken the hot chocolate into the drawing room. Had Edward managed to keep James outside? Even locked him in the pool area?

Who would have helped him? Of course, he did have a link with Martin – they had been at the same school. Was that enough for them to help each other out? Perhaps Martin had something against James. Had James treated him in a similar way to George and was holding back some of the money due to him? But James had bought Martin a new house, and his family was due to move down in time for the start of the autumn term. Emily suspected that James couldn't have built up his empire without Martin.

So that brought her back to Edward again. His emotions ran deep... but he seemed so genuine, and Emily couldn't see how he would have had time to capture or attack James. When she saw him in the drawing room he was with the family, busy with his laptop and mobile phone for quite a long time before going out to meet Archie for snooker. He didn't seem to be in the right place at the right time, though it was just possible he had got drawn in as an accomplice and helped to dispose of the body.

She turned her mind from motive to opportunity, but found no inspiration. The keys of the walled garden and the pool had been hanging in the pantry, and apart from time constraints, the opportunity had been available to everyone.

Fin came pattering past, heading for the back door. Emily sighed; 'worrying at it' didn't seem to be working. She had gone round in a complete circle and was none the wiser.

At breakfast, a large part of the discussion was about the possibility of going home. The inevitability of waiting for the police to succeed in their job was being replaced by restlessness, as individuals turned their minds to the work which lay ahead of them at home. They had all planned to leave on Tuesday morning and didn't want to be delayed.

Edward paused before helping himself to scrambled egg, and said to the assembled company, 'I'm going to be in touch with the police again today. I really don't think they can stop us going home tomorrow, unless someone is arrested, of course.'

'Really?' enquired Cassidy, holding her piece of toast in the air. She looked relieved.

'That's great,' said Clara, then she stopped. 'Oh,' her hand went to her mouth, 'but you haven't got a home,' she said to Cassidy. 'Didn't Dad move everything down here?'

Cassidy looked slightly confused. 'Of course he did,' she said, returning her toast to the plate. 'It still seems unreal – just as if this is a short holiday, and then we'll be back to normal,' she said.

Clara, with a quick glance at Archie, put a hand on Cassidy's arm and said, 'Cassi, come home with us. There isn't much room in the flat, but you'd be welcome, while you decide what to do.'

Cassidy gave a slight smile. 'Thank you, Clara, dear, but I can go to my parents', once the police give us the go-ahead. I'll have to think about all the stuff in storage later. I'm not ready to cope with that yet. If you'll excuse me…' She got up and left the room, pulling her mobile out of her pocket as she went.

Philip looked up. 'Poor Cassidy,' he said. 'She didn't deserve all this. Thanks for making the offer, Clara, but she'll probably be better staying with her parents.'

Samantha poured herself another cup of tea. 'What about you, Martin?'

Martin shrugged his shoulders. 'I wasn't due to move down here till late August, and we haven't put the house on the market yet,' he said. 'My wife isn't expecting me back immediately; James had asked me to stay for a week initially. After that I was going to live down here and return home at weekends. It will probably depend on whether Edward needs any help as to whether I stay any longer.'

Edward looked gloomy. 'Thanks, Martin, but I haven't even thought as far as tomorrow, let alone into the future. Anyway,' he added, with an effort at brightness, 'let's try to make something of the day, while we can.' He topped up his plate with scrambled egg and returned to the table, while Emily and Stella looked at each other. One minute these people were at each other's throats, and then behaving like a perfect family the next.

After breakfast Emily wandered into the kitchen. The dishwasher was still enthusiastically spraying its contents, and Grace was up to her elbows in washing-up liquid bubbles, tackling the burnt egg saucepan in the scullery.

'Hello, Dame Emily,' she said. 'No end to this terrible trouble, then?'

Emily propped herself up against the wall, disinclined to offer to dry any of the clean saucepans. 'No. It's all so civilised in the dining room, everyone talking, being polite and normal, I can't believe we have a killer sitting among us.'

Grace glanced over her shoulder. 'It gives me the shivers,' she said, lowering her voice. 'Especially when someone tried to harm you.'

'Who could have got hold of bacon fat, Grace?' said Emily.

'Anyone,' said Grace. 'I hardly go round locking it up! Sorry, Dame Emily, I didn't mean to be disrespectful.'

'It was a stupid question,' admitted Emily, gloomily watching Grace's deft movements.

'Come to think of it…' said Grace slowly.

'Mm?'

'It was Saturday, wasn't it?'

'Saturday night, yes.'

'Saturday morning I had this to-do with the milkman. He came straight after breakfast and I nipped out to catch him. He'd left us with the full cream bottles the day before, and I didn't want it happening again. Stella had said she wanted semi-skimmed.'

Emily stood a little straighter. 'Where was Jayne?'

'Well, she was up doing the beds, like she is now.'

'And the fat?'

'I put foil at the bottom of the grill pan, to catch it. It was still on the stove.'

'It was in full sight. Someone saw its potential,' said Emily thoughtfully, 'and all they had to do was to take the foil, fold it to keep the grease in, and secrete it somewhere to collect later – or after dark. They could even spread it straight onto the step from the foil.'

'Well, I wouldn't have noticed if it had gone,' said Grace, adding a second saucepan to the heap. 'Sometimes Jayne will clear things away before I get to them.'

'So that's how,' said Emily pensively. 'But it still leaves us with the problem of "who?"'

'There you have me, Dame Emily,' said Grace. 'As I said, just about anyone, I reckon.'

Emily agreed with her, remembering with shame her loud comments to Stella in the entrance hall, which could well have been heard by someone in a downstairs room or even from the upper parts of the staircase. She sighed as she continued to prop up the wall. She was restless and wanted to do something, but didn't know what.

Jayne appeared in the doorway with a wastepaper basket.

'Oh, Jayne,' said Grace. 'You'd do better to leave those until tomorrow when everyone's left, and we'll get it all done in one go.'

Jayne's face dropped. 'I emptied everything into this bin,' she said, 'so the rest are done.'

Emily smiled. 'You're too efficient,' she said.

Jayne made a face and, as she turned to go out of the scullery into the kitchen, she knocked the basket against the lintel. It fell out of her hands, scattering its contents on the stone floor.

'Well done!' said Grace without even turning her head.

Emily bent down to help. It was mainly paper: a couple of wrappers from bars of soap, a toothpaste box, several tissues, a number of cotton wool balls with evidence of make-up on them, three sweet papers and a screwed-up plastic bag. Emily picked up the bag and, out of habit, began to smooth it out. Two receipts fell out. Idly she glanced at them and then bent to inspect each in more detail. Her pulse quickened. Here, at last, was some key evidence, though she wasn't quite sure of its implications. She replaced the slips of paper and slid the folded bag into her pocket. She needed thinking time.

'I won't get in your way any longer,' she said to Grace. 'I'll see you later.'

'Right-oh, Dame Emily,' said Grace, drying her work-hardened hands. 'I think you'll enjoy lunch – and so will Fin.'

'You're dreadful, Grace,' retorted Emily. 'My dog will get so fat!'

Grace laughed. 'Not with all those walks you give her.'

Yes, decided Emily. It was a walk that both she and Fin needed – and some inspiration.

The walk did Emily good and she strode back down the drive to the mansion swinging her stick, with her head held high and her heart pounding. Had she really solved this case? She had been over it again and again, but all the pieces had suddenly fitted beautifully, she could almost hear them click together in her brain.

She must contact DCI Drummond before lunch. As she walked past the stables she spotted him. He was in the doorway of the dairy and, seeing her, invited her to watch the few remaining SOCOs searching the building. The accumulated junk of years, which had been taken from the coach house and dumped in the right-hand half of the dairy were being painstakingly moved, piece by grubby piece, to the left-hand half of the room.

Drummond looked thoroughly discouraged. 'Good morning, Dame Emily. I do apologise that I haven't contacted you personally about the bacon fat on your doorstep. We are taking it very seriously. I don't suppose you are any nearer to coming up with a suspect?'

Emily smiled. 'There wasn't a flicker of horror on a single face at breakfast. I confess I felt really mad last night.'

Drummond glanced at her. 'I was concerned. Please be very careful. I'm afraid we still have very little to go on: every car was clean; there were lots of fingerprints left by the family when they went swimming; and we haven't found any significant links between our suspects, prior to their arrival here. However, we have found some shoe prints. One superimposed on the tyre marks on the front lawn and the other near the cliff edge. One was of a size eight walking shoe and the other a small part of some sort of beach wear, like a flip-flop. Emily's eyebrows shot up, but Drummond's eyes were focused on the room in front of him. 'I wanted to thank you for yesterday's message. I was so sure you would be right,' he continued, 'but we've found nothing here. There's no sign that any of this has been moved in the last few weeks, let alone days. It's still covered in the dust which must have been there long before the Easter break.'

Emily sniffed. 'Why don't you try the other door?' she said.

'What door?'

He followed Emily's eyes to the diagonally opposite corner of the dairy, where a series of old shelves stood upright against the wall.

'Clever,' she said. 'Someone's placed those long planks of wood on end, along the far part of the wall, to disguise the fact that there's a second door to the outside. If you go round the back of the dairy into the field you can open the door from there. Remove those old shelves and I can almost guarantee that, under the pile of junk in that corner, you will find what you are looking for.'

Drummond's face was a picture – she dared not laugh – but she could just see in the far corner of the room, under a selection of brooms, buckets and brushes, a familiar shaped lump, covered in a tarpaulin, and was sure she was right. She decided to change the subject.

'Chief inspector, I have been thinking.'

The inspector turned patient eyes on her.

'May I tell you my solution to this case – try it out on you, perhaps, where no one can hear us?'

Drummond blinked. 'Of course,' he said. 'I'll just get a couple of SOCOs to start from the other door first, if I may. Then we can go to the music room.'

Emily breathed deeply. It was now or never.

Chapter 28

The steak pie was delicious but Emily was finding it hard to swallow. How stupid to be nervous at her age and with her experience.

She looked down the table – could it be only four days since she had first sat here with Stella and this group of complete strangers? In that time she had shared their intimate moments of tragedy, and now that she was party to the inmost feelings and past history of so many, she felt quite motherly towards them; well, nearly all of them.

Emily gave her thoughts a break as the plates of blueberry crumble were passed down the table. Stella was busy discussing with George what she should do with all the files of correspondence about house plans and restoration details, while Edward, only half-listening, was pouring an unending stream of custard over his crumble. Comfort eating? Emily felt sorry for him. He probably didn't bother much about eating if he lived alone. A slim man, he didn't appear greedy, but this weekend had certainly taken its toll. He looked greyer, older, and his face more lined.

Soon, perhaps, it would be all over. The one hope that Emily clung to was contained in the tiny scrap of evidence in Detective Chief Inspector Drummond's pocket, protected by a plastic bag – unless he had now found what he was looking for in the dairy. That could very well clinch things. Emily was glad she had talked to him, but her evidence was so flimsy; she didn't know if she could build a case on it. Might the culprit, or culprits, incriminate themselves? It was a lot to hope for.

The meal had been late and quite leisurely. No one seemed inclined to move, and they had even had coffee among the debris of lunch in the dining room. Energy had seeped from them – a kind of false calm before the storm.

Outside, the daylight was being sucked steadily away as dark clouds moved in from the sea. From her vantage point at the end of the table, Emily could see through the far window to the side of the dairy, and down to the gates of the rose garden. She would have to say goodbye to it all soon, this lovely place which had been so recently desecrated. She watched as the silhouette of the chief inspector huddled briefly with a few SOCOs until they walked together towards the stables and out of sight. It couldn't be long now.

Emily jumped violently as the knocker on the front door banged loudly, and her coffee cup fell from her shaking hand onto her saucer. She heard Fin's pattering feet and loud bark. DCI Drummond had said he would come to the front door and do things formally. This was the moment.

Martin went to answer the door and brought the detective chief inspector and DS Pollard with him. All eyes turned to Drummond's grim face. Emily swallowed hard. Had everything come together? Did he have any other evidence to support her theory? Did he know the identity of the murderer? His face gave nothing away.

Drummond scanned each face before saying, 'I am sorry once again to interrupt you all, but we have one or two matters which need to be cleared up straight away. Would it be convenient to meet now in the drawing room? The kitchen staff too, please.' He glanced at the empty cups and stepped back, indicating the door with his arm.

Lindsey Pollard left the room followed by Martin, who had offered to get the kitchen staff.

Chairs scraped and the whole group headed for the drawing room, Stella and Emily bringing up the rear.

'Are you all right?' whispered Stella.

Emily nodded and paused, putting a wisp of hair back in place and adjusting her skirt. 'I think I know,' she said in a very low voice. 'Back me up if you can.'

'Of course.'

The group settled in chairs and settees which had been quickly moved into a wide semicircle. Drummond indicated a chair for Emily, from which she would be able to see everyone in the room. Emily sat, ramrod straight.

Clara wriggled to get comfortable in her armchair. 'Can we go home tomorrow?' she asked the inspector. 'I have to be back at work on Wednesday.'

'You're not the only one,' Samantha snapped. Everyone turned to look – it seemed an unusual outburst. Samantha reddened. 'Well, all of us, then,' she added lamely.

Drummond, standing near the door, leaned on the back of the chair in front of him. 'I think I will be able to tell you with a little more certainty when we have cleared up a few more details.' He cleared his throat. 'This has been an unusual case, in that, for a long time, we were unable to collect very much evidence from the crime scene, but in the last couple of hours we have been able to piece together a reasonably complete picture of the events of Thursday night.'

Having got the undivided attention of the group, he continued. 'I don't know if you fully appreciate the lady who has been your guest over the past few days...' He turned to smile at Emily, who immediately wanted to shrink back into the cushion of her upright chair. 'She has a sharp eye for detail and has probably been our key witness.' He paused, but no one seemed inclined to believe him. Emily wondered if 'the old witch' image lingered at the back of some minds. Drummond resumed, 'I would like to ask her for her theory on what happened on Thursday night. Dame Emily.'

Emily glanced at the familiar carpet and told herself to be courageous – after all, she had the advantage over everyone in the room, apart from the detective chief inspector, who was clearly taking her theory very seriously and generously allowing her to explain it.

There was a hush as Emily began. 'This is a long story,' she said, 'and I'm quite sure that from time to time someone will think or say, "That's ridiculous!" or, "That's not true!" It's the sort of thing an accused person would say, so, before anyone makes such a comment, I am asking you to give me a fair hearing because, however strange it may sound, this one solution to the crime does fit all the facts.'

Emily looked at the intense faces in front of her. So far, so good. 'It seems to me,' she said, slowly and carefully, 'that the most difficult question of this whole mystery has been: "Why did James remain outside on Thursday night?" We know he was in the garden when Archie punched him, but Archie said he did not fall. This was borne out by the fact that I have seen the evidence. Archie, did your father-in-law light a cigar that night?'

Archie looked startled. 'Yes,' he said after a pause. 'He was trying to light it and juggle a bottle of wine at the same time.'

Emily made no comment. 'I found the stubbed-out cigar end near the sundial, and the wine bottle in the bushes outside the music room. I presume James threw it there. The police have confirmed that it had no other fingerprints on it. I therefore conclude that after his encounter with Archie, James walked round the east side of the house. Maybe he thought the front door would be locked, or more likely, there was someone he wanted to see in the interval between dinner and his late meeting with George. Two witnesses agree that James went to the gym and talked briefly to Ian. Ian told DCI Drummond that when he left, James appeared to be walking towards the back door, but he returned and asked for Ian's keys to the pool. Why was that?'

Heads shook. Even though he was sitting quite a way from her, Emily was conscious of Ian's tense body. With Drummond in the doorway there was no means of escape. Lindsey Pollard was standing by the fireplace and a uniformed police officer was sitting at the back of the room by the bookcase. Emily felt more confident and continued briskly. 'If James had planned to meet someone at the pool, it is likely he would have taken the pantry keys with him and not asked Ian for his set. No, I think James saw something in the darkness as he walked to the back door of the mansion, something that surprised him – a stream of light coming under the gate to the walled garden. So he returned for Ian's keys and then went to investigate.

'This theory is borne out by Jayne's evidence. When she drew the curtains back in the end bedroom on the top floor that night, she saw moving light reflected onto the wall of the old dairy. She could not see any part of the pool itself, but the lights were obviously on and the water moving.

'There was another piece of evidence supplied to me, this time by Grace. At some time before ten o'clock that night she heard what she described as a long bellow, like that of a cow deprived of its calf.'

'You mean she heard someone murdering Dad?' Clara said, horrified.

'No,' said Emily. 'If he had cried out at all, it would have been a quick, short sound.'

She glanced at the inspector, who nodded and added, 'The forensic evidence suggests that he was hit on the left lower jaw, and then overbalanced backwards, knocking the back of his head on the edge of the pool as he fell in.'

'So who made the noise?' Clara asked.

Emily opened her mouth to answer, but was disturbed by a loud knocking on the front door. Fin shot from her resting place by Philip, and preceded Stella out of the room.

The whole company, who had listened riveted to all that had gone on so far, eavesdropped unashamedly on the conversation in the entrance hall.

'Yes, can I help you?' Stella's polite tones reached them easily.

'I've come for Mr James,' responded a male voice. 'I'm driving him to St Albans tonight, and then home tomorrow.'

Drummond frowned slightly. Emily, forgetting that she was a guest, called loudly, 'Stella, bring him in.'

Stella returned to the room, and the whole company gazed on the bronzed figure of a young man, with a closely shaved head and a small wedge of upturned reddish-brown curls where his middle parting should have been.

'Fraz!' exclaimed Emily, as though welcoming a long-lost member of her ancient tribe. 'Just the person we need! Sit down.'

For a moment Fraz stood motionless in the doorway, surveying the assembled group. His boots were covered in mud and the lower part of his jeans had turned brown. Stella pointed to an empty chair next to Emily's, and returned to her seat.

Dame Emily looked at the confused faces in the room. 'This,' she said, indicating the newcomer, who was lowering himself into the chair, 'is Fraz, who drove Mr Wedderburn down from Huddersfield. He's been to some gigs in Brighton over the weekend.' She felt quite pleased with the phrase, although she wasn't quite sure if she had used it correctly. Emily didn't even glance at the inspector, but turned and said quite gently, 'Fraz, I'm sorry that we have some sad news. Mr Wedderburn died a few days ago, in unforeseen circumstances.'

Fraz uncrossed his legs and blinked. 'Poor old Uncle James. Sudden, was it?'

'Yes,' said Emily. 'I'm afraid...'

'"Uncle James"?' said Philip, sitting bolt upright. 'Who are you to call my father "uncle"? I've never seen you before in my life!'

'Neither have I!' said Clara, glaring at Fraz. 'You've no right coming in here to a private family conference!'

'Whoa!' said Fraz putting both hands in the air.

For a split second Emily thought that he looked like some convict in a western, suddenly finding himself looking down the barrel of a gun. She pushed the image from her mind. Despite the fact that she, too, had been a little shaken by the word 'uncle', she stepped in quickly. 'I think you'd better explain, Fraz,' she said. 'How did you come to be working for Mr Wedderburn?'

'He was mates with my dad,' Fraz told her. 'He was Dad's best man or something. Me and my brother helped Dad in the garage, and we often cleaned Uncle James' cars for him.' He paused, and glancing round, became aware of the antagonistic faces around him. 'I've always called him "uncle", ever since I was small. We live next door to the garage, and Uncle James often used to pop in and give us some sweets, while Dad serviced the car.'

Emily felt slightly sick. In her mind, little red lights were flashing on and off. Could this be yet another sibling? With considerable determination she focused on the problem in hand. She needed to steer Fraz towards the present; but it was Stella who spoke next. Emily suspected she was similarly disturbed and realised the urgency of changing the subject, to give Emily time to collect her thoughts.

'So, how is it you come to be here?' Stella asked, smiling reassuringly at Fraz.

'My older brother used to act as chauffeur for Uncle James, when he was going to a "do" and wanted a car. Pete wasn't free this weekend, and as I'm old enough now, I jumped at the chance to drive Uncle James down in the pink limo. Brilliant!'

'He's right,' said Martin, relaxed in an armchair. 'I was here when he arrived with James and, as he left, I paid him some of his fee in advance.'

Fraz grinned. 'There isn't much of that left. Anyway, Uncle James wanted me to take him back tomorrow; he had to sort out the last two shops he was going to sell, so here I am. Now it looks as if I'll be going back on my own.'

Having justified his presence, Fraz sat back in his chair and crossed one muddy boot over the other, seemingly quite content to await instructions.

Having taken advantage of the break Stella had given her, Emily decided it was time to take control of the situation once more. Drummond was leaning against the wall by the door, his arms folded, apparently preferring to watch than take action. Or was he watching for one final false move?

'Fraz,' she said, 'I have something to ask you that is very important. I'd like you to think very carefully before you answer.'

'OK.'

'You remember I showed you the bus stop for Brighton on the day you left here?' For a moment Emily couldn't remember which day it was.

'Yeah.'

'I presume you stood at the bus stop and waited. You didn't decide to walk off anywhere?'

'Nah.'

'Did you, by any chance, notice a car leave Seascape before your bus came?'

There was a pause. Fraz screwed up his face in an attempt to recall the moment. 'Yeah,' he said eventually.

Emily thought it was a bit like getting blood out of a stone, so concentrated hard on wording her next question carefully. 'Can you remember anything about the car and the direction in which it went?'

Fraz relaxed his head against the cushion as if he had been asked to add two and two together. 'Oh, yeah, blue Mazda, MCC 66, going towards Eastbourne.'

Bingo! Emily wanted to jump and laugh and cheer. The faces around her were blank, but she pursued her line of questioning.

'Are you sure it was MCC 66?'

'Yeah,' Fraz grinned. 'They're my dad's initials, Michael Charles Cooper. He's always going on about them having something to do with cricket. I saw the car go out of the drive and caught sight of the number plate. I thought, if I do really well with my gigs and get famous, I could buy a number plate like that for my dad. I'd have the number one though, sounds better.'

'I believe,' said Emily carefully, 'that that is the number of Martin Chumleigh's car?' She raised her eyebrows at James' secretary.

'What if it is?' asked Martin.

'You were going to collect Cassidy, I believe,' persisted Emily, beginning to enjoy reeling in her catch.

'Yes. She was flying in to Gatwick.'

'But you drove to Eastbourne.'

'She wanted to buy some warm clothes. There's a direct train line from Gatwick.'

Emily turned to Cassidy. 'And can you confirm that Martin picked you up in Eastbourne?'

Martin glanced at Cassidy, who looked steadily at Emily. 'Martin met me with the car just before three. He put my luggage in the boot and I did my shopping. We got back here sometime after four o'clock.'

Martin leaned back in his chair and crossed his legs very deliberately. 'You see?' he said.

'In court,' said Emily stiffly to Cassidy, 'you will be expected to tell the whole truth. Both Fraz and I saw Martin leave at one o'clock.'

'I had business to attend to first.' Martin maintained his relaxed attitude.

'I see,' said Emily, unruffled. 'What is strange is that, among the price labels that Mrs Wedderburn cut off and left in the wastepaper basket, was a receipt from the Princess Grace hotel, Eastbourne, dated for last Thursday.'

There was total stillness in the room as Dame Emily continued addressing Cassidy.

'We know that the plane from Barbados actually got in at 6.20 in the morning. You will have arrived in Eastbourne at sometime after 8.00am. You clearly had plenty of time to do some shopping before meeting Martin. The receipt is for the use of a room, breakfast for one, and a champagne lunch for two... It was paid at 3.30.'

Shocked faces turned to look at Cassidy. 'I needed to rest after a bumpy flight, and wanted a safe place to leave my luggage,' she said firmly. 'Anyway, what's that got to do with James' death?'

'It proves you lied – and why would that be necessary?' Emily countered, aware that the odds were now in her favour. 'However, the answer to that will become clear very soon. First,

I'll go back to the point I'd reached when Fraz arrived, and then everyone will see how this fits.'

'You were going to explain the stream of light under the gate, and say who made the noise like a cow,' Clara said. 'Go on from there.'

'I believe,' said Emily slowly, 'that your father, having unlocked the gate to the walled garden, probably ran down the path to the pool, and the sound Grace heard was an agonised, protracted cry of "No, no!" such as one might hear from a man finding his wife in the arms of his secretary.'

There was a gasp from the family and Martin looked horrified. 'That's…' he said before stopping.

'Ridiculous?' prompted Dame Emily. 'Perhaps it is, but let's consider the lies we have just uncovered. Were they not to ensure that no one knew how close you and Cassidy really were? To give the two of you time to make your final plans to go away together? I doubt any of us guessed over the weekend, but you probably communicated via your mobile phones whenever you needed to confer.'

Martin gripped the sides of his chair until the knuckles showed white. He was breathing quickly and stared at Emily in disbelief.

Cassidy, too, had her eyes fixed on Emily, and held onto her necklace as though it were a talisman.

Dame Emily continued unperturbed. 'To go back to the night in question… Imagine James, running down the path to the brightly lit doorway of the pool shouting, "No, no!" As he stumbled in and ran towards the couple, he was met by the second right hook of the night, which threw him off balance, making him hit the back of his head on the corner of the pool, as he splashed into the water.'

'That's when the reflected light from the pool was moving on the wall of the old dairy?' Edward asked.

'Precisely,' said Emily.

All eyes moved between Cassidy's face and that of Martin.

'That's not true!' said Martin. 'I was nowhere near the pool that night. You saw me yourself, Dame Emily. You were standing by the stairs when I asked if you'd seen James. I would never compromise Cassidy's position.'

Cassidy looked bewildered and there was a hint of tears in her eyes. 'Of course it's not true!' she protested. 'That evening I unpacked, got my hot chocolate from Stella and went to bed with a sleeping pill. I didn't see James from the time he left the dining room.'

'You're trying to poison everyone's minds!' objected Martin. 'You have done nothing but interfere ever since this weekend began.'

Drummond cleared his throat loudly and delivered his *coup de grâce*. 'The forensic evidence shows that Mr Wedderburn hit his head on the edge of the pool. No doubt he could have been saved but, according to the pathologist, marks at the base of his neck indicate that he was held under water until he drowned.'

Shock registered on every face as the group suddenly faced the precise details of James' murder.

Cassidy jerked forward, her eyes suddenly wide and wild. 'He was drowned by someone? He didn't drown on his own? But Martin, you tried to save him!'

Martin's face went white.

Drummond moved in for the kill. 'Mrs Wedderburn, did you see Mr Chumleigh hold your husband under the water?'

'No, I'd fallen…' Cassidy stopped. The twin horrors: that she had implicated both Martin and herself, and that her husband really had been murdered, showed on her ashen face. She shook visibly, clinging to the arms of her chair. For a fleeting moment, Emily felt sorry for her.

'Perhaps you would like to tell us what really happened?' Drummond pursued his quarry relentlessly.

Martin turned to her. 'Say nothing!' he urged. 'They'll only twist it.'

Cassidy looked at him and then at the inspector. 'Are you sure someone drowned Weddy?' she whispered.

Emily held her breath; she could feel the electricity in the air.

Drummond looked Cassidy straight in the eyes. 'Without any doubt,' he said. 'The marks showed clearly on the neck. They were inflicted before death and were not distorted by the fall from the clifftop, as no doubt the killer intended they should be.'

Lindsey Pollard moved a few steps closer to Martin, and the uniformed police officer at the other end of the room stood, as Cassidy sat with tears pouring down her cheeks. 'You said you loved me,' she said bitterly, as Martin put his head in his hands, avoiding her gaze. 'You said we would be together for always.'

'I did love you, I do love you,' he said. 'I was prepared to give up everything for you: that's not a crime!'

'But you killed Weddy!'

'I tried to save him. He's got it wrong!'

Drummond intervened. 'Mrs Wedderburn, will you please tell us what you saw that night?'

Cassidy sniffed. 'I didn't see anything. Martin and I were standing by the pool. When James came through the gate I had my back to him. There were running footsteps, then the pool door opened and I heard a loud cry. James was shouting, "No, no!" The sound lasted a long time and echoed round the pool. It was a sort of desperate wail.'

Cassidy stopped and shivered. 'Then I turned my head to see what was going on. I remember Weddy rushing towards the pool, and Martin trying to prevent him from colliding with us. Then, in the confusion, an arm hit me in the stomach. I doubled over and I fell on my side, hitting my head on the floor. I remember half-lying on the tiles, gasping for breath. Then, I think, I passed out. When I came to I felt really dizzy. I was sprawled on the ground. Everything was a blur. I could hear splashing and Martin's voice, but it all seemed a very long way off. My head didn't feel right. I was shaking and the whole of my side was bruised. I couldn't see into the pool from where I was lying and I remember wondering if Weddy had fallen in. But Martin's a good swimmer, and I knew he could easily help him. I lay on the pool side until the dizziness lessened.'

'So it is likely you were unsighted and on the ground for several minutes,' Drummond summarised. 'Did Martin tell you to get up, or did you do that on your own?'

Cassidy considered. 'He called out, "Are you all right?" Then he said, "Don't hurry; I can manage." When I got up I could see that Weddy was in the pool and Martin was trying to revive him. Then he towed Weddy through the water and I met them at the shallow end, but we were too late. Martin kept on trying to revive him, but he couldn't, and I tried, but it made me dizzy again.

'We couldn't bear to leave him there, so we decided the best way to get him out was to use one of the loungers with wheels. We slid it under Weddy while he was in the water, and after a lot of struggle, we managed to pull it up the little slope onto the poolside. We raised the back of the lounger so that he looked as if he was just sitting by the pool.' Cassidy's voice wobbled and the tears began again.

The family sat motionless, sculptures, petrified by horror and disbelief.

Drummond pressed the truth home. 'That account would fit the facts as we know them. An overweight man, who had taken several pills, after eating and drinking rather too much, arrived at the scene. He was then punched for the second time that night, and fell, fully clothed, into the water, cracking his head on the side of the pool as he did so. Such a man would put up little resistance. But,' Drummond paused and looked severely at Martin, 'he could well have been saved. It would seem that you, Martin, chose to save your own future instead.'

As the inspector paused, Emily spoke gently to Cassidy. 'Why did you move the body, when this could have been mistaken for an accident?'

Cassidy's bottom lip quivered. 'Martin said if Weddy was found at the pool there would be lots of questions asked; people might even think it wasn't an accident. Now I know why.' She looked accusingly at Martin. 'He said it would be better if it looked like suicide from the clifftop. His body would be washed away and not be found for days. Later we would be free to leave, as we'd planned.'

'So you came back into the mansion,' said Emily, 'quickly took off your wet clothes and put on your night things, and then came down the main stairs, making sure you asked someone for hot chocolate.'

Cassidy said nothing.

'Martin did the same,' Emily continued, 'but he came down the back stairs and came into the hall to enquire if I'd seen James; when I asked him if it was raining, he touched the back of his head, which was damp; he didn't automatically touch the top of it where the rain would have caught him.'

'Hang on,' said Edward. 'How did they manage it with so many of us walking around the mansion at that time of night? Surely one of us would have seen them in their wet clothes.'

Emily smiled slightly. 'Some of you complained of feeling cold that night.'

'Yes,' said Samantha, 'it was freezing on the top floor.'

'And on the floor below,' added Archie. 'We thought some idiot had opened a window.'

'They had,' said Emily, 'on to the fire escape, I would suggest. It runs down the building from the staircase next to Martin's room, past the window of Cassidy's room to the ground. They probably left that way, so that they could meet at the pool unseen. After that the two of them could come and go unseen all night.'

At last the irrefutable truth began to dawn on Emily's listeners.

'You callous...' Archie stood and took a step towards Martin, his fists ready, before Clara pulled him back.

'Wait, Archie. We need to hear the full story.'

'And we haven't found Martin's wet clothes,' Pollard added. 'Nor the gardener's shoes and pair of flip-flops you both borrowed for the walk to the cliff edge.'

'My flip-flops?' said Jayne, disbelievingly.

'I told you,' said Grace. 'You should never have bought those flip-flops. You couldn't even remember to put them upstairs once they were dry. There they were, under the gardeners' coats, all ready for Mrs Wedderburn to wear when she walked to the cliffs. A lovely way to disguise her footprints, and no mistake. You've only yourself to blame if they've been used to try to hide the identity of a criminal.'

'So,' said Pollard, trying to ignore the interruption. 'Did the clothes and shoes go over the cliff, too? It would also appear that James' watch is missing – where might that be?'

Cassidy looked at Martin, who studied the carpet with great intensity.

Everyone's mind seemed to be working overtime. Then Edward spoke. 'I remember, the next morning Martin checked with me if he could go to the off-licence. He certainly took some time.'

'There isn't one in the village,' said Emily.

'So he'd go to Eastbourne,' said Pollard, watching Martin shrewdly. 'With a black bag, no doubt. Probably one which had been taken from the flip bin at the pool. When we passed the car park above Beachy Head lighthouse on Saturday morning, the bin was full to overflowing with black sacks, but I'm sure we can count on the cooperation of the refuse collectors to locate it, wherever you may have hidden it.'

Martin didn't move.

Edward was sitting bolt upright, obviously anxious with another question. 'So how did they move James' body to the cliff?'

Emily, feeling that the group were now with her, began to feel more confident. 'My sister had one of those mobility scooters before she went into the home. They have no room for it there at the moment, so it was left in the old coach house to be dealt with on my return from Australia.' Emily glanced at Martin, who was still staring at the floor. 'My guess is that Martin, who was responsible for clearing the coach house, to give the workmen access to prepare the new gym, spotted it when it was transferred to the old dairy, and later remembered where it had been stored – near the far door.

'I imagine he drove it alongside the low platform in the pool area – we always left the key attached to the handlebars. With Cassidy's help, Martin would have got the lounger up the slope onto the platform, and positioned it on a level with the scooter seat. It would have taken a great deal of effort, but after that they only had to slide James' body from one to the other. If he were already in a sitting position, that would have helped.'

'Thanks to Dame Emily,' said Drummond, 'and despite attempts to disguise its hiding place, forensics have found very small traces of grass and mud on the scooter, but no fingerprints, of course. However, we may yet find DNA from Mr Wedderburn's body.'

'But we didn't see or hear it going down the drive,' said Edward.

'They are very silent,' said Emily, remembering how Margaret had nearly knocked her down once, when overtaking her as she walked down to the Lodge.

'And Mr Wedderburn had the old gravel replaced by tarmac,' added Stella. 'There would have been no sound at all.'

'I don't know if you found rope marks on the body,' said Emily to Drummond, 'but I wouldn't be surprised if Martin used the washing line by the back door to keep the body upright against the seat. It wouldn't have taken long to replace it when they came back.'

'That's why the line's been slack!' exclaimed Grace. 'Well, I never!'

'I believe that this was an opportunistic killing,' Emily summed up. 'If Martin and Cassidy had not arranged to meet at the pool that night, and if James had not gone to investigate why a light was shining under the door of the walled garden, he would most likely be alive today. I imagine that Martin and Cassidy had planned to leave in the early hours of Tuesday morning, or possibly wait until James was on his way back to Huddersfield, then drive to Gatwick and flee to Barbados. It would be some time before James discovered the truth.'

Drummond interjected. 'No wonder you were worried, Martin, when your car got damaged! You needed it urgently and no repairs could be done over the Bank Holiday weekend.'

As Martin squirmed silently, Emily continued the story. 'Once Martin and Cassidy were safely away, they would no doubt contact their families – unless they had decided to disappear for good, without a thought for those who loved them, nor a backward glance at the house James had built for the Chumleigh family near Eastbourne?' Emily gave Drummond a quick look.

'A very likely scenario,' Drummond said. 'Certainly when I contacted Mrs Chumleigh earlier today, she was worried about what she had seen on the television news, had only had the briefest of texts in reply to her calls, and she had no idea of any plans for the family to move to Eastbourne.'

'You *contacted* her?' Martin rounded on him, fury darkening his face.

Drummond remained impassive. 'Upsetting as the news may have been,' he said, 'I think the complete truth, when it is revealed, will have a far more devastating effect on your wife and children.'

Martin put his head in his hands once more.

Emily resumed her story. 'I don't know what time the body was taken to the cliff,' she said. 'I would guess that it was sometime after the house was silent and my light in the Lodge had gone off. Martin and Cassidy could have waited in Cassidy's room, planning what to do. Anyone hearing a man's voice would have presumed it was James' voice.

'They must have worked extremely hard to get the body to the Heath, but unfortunately for them,' she went on, 'they hadn't planned for the tide, which was too far from the cliff base to sweep the body away, otherwise it could have been missing for days. As it was, it fell into the large pool between the landslips, and James' clothing caught on the surrounding rocks.'

At this point Drummond interrupted. 'We know that Mrs Wedderburn has sold two of her businesses abroad, but has kept the one in Barbados. We have, of course, just presumed that the two of you were going to Barbados, but we are sure that Mr Chumleigh's computer will reveal some interesting facts.'

Cassidy looked at Martin, clearly not understanding the implication. He ignored her. 'You will find nothing on my computer,' he said, leaning back in his chair once more. 'You can search it.'

Edward suddenly sat upright. 'Don't bother, inspector! Search his top pocket instead!'

Martin suddenly put a hand over his breast pocket. 'I have just a pen here,' he said, 'no plane tickets.' He glared at Edward.

Edward addressed the inspector. 'I borrowed that pen the other day. It's very heavy and half of it is, in fact, a memory stick – I think it will hold all you need to know.'

Drummond held out his hand and waited until Martin reluctantly placed the pen in the upturned palm. 'I expect we shall find the details of an e-ticket – oh, no doubt it's just for you – but then I'm sure Cassidy has a return ticket for the same time, on the same plane.'

'I'm just going for a short trip to help Cassi with the financial details of the scuba-diving school – it's nothing more,' Martin blustered.

'We shall soon see if you have a one-way ticket,' Pollard commented.

Martin was silent.

'Martin brought three suitcases with him!' Clara elbowed Archie forcibly in the ribs. 'Remember, we saw them in his room that first night.'

Archie frowned, thinking. 'Yes! He did.'

'Perhaps,' said Emily softly, 'he bought them in Eastbourne. He could hardly let his wife see how much luggage he was taking with him for a brief stay in Sussex.'

Archie half-rose from his chair. 'You're despicable, Martin!'

Drummond held up his hand in warning and Archie sank back.

'Martin might have something interesting to say about bacon fat, as well,' Emily heard herself saying, causing heads to turn in her direction. 'On Saturday night I discovered that someone had smeared bacon fat on my front doorstep. I slipped on it as I was going to open the door. Thankfully I didn't break anything, and didn't have to spend the night in the front garden of the Lodge, as no doubt this man had intended. He obviously wanted to put me in hospital, at the very least, where I couldn't continue to investigate this case.' She paused to glare at Martin. 'However, I think the police have plenty to go on for now.'

'Thank you, Dame Emily,' said Drummond. 'As you say, I think we have heard enough.' He moved to stand in front of Martin. 'Martin Chumleigh, I am arresting you...'

'No, wait!' Cassidy held up her hand and Drummond paused. Suddenly she was assertive, alert. 'Martin, the money!'

Martin's eyes widened. 'Be quiet!' he shouted. 'Be quiet, you silly fool!'

'Chief inspector,' Cassidy turned to him, 'there's something else.'

'No!' Martin tried to move towards her, but found himself held down in his chair by the uniformed police officer.

'I want everyone to know,' Cassidy said, her voice trembling, but strong. 'Yes, it's all true, and it happened just as you said, Dame Emily. Clara, Philip, I'm sorry. Your father and I just drifted apart. Martin and I have been planning to live together for some time now, and this weekend seemed the perfect opportunity to slip away. Martin told me all about the mansion and your father's plans long ago. James himself never consulted me. Both Martin and I would have been trapped here, servants constantly being made to do James' bidding. It was the last thing either of us wanted. We are still young and had so many plans for the future.'

Stony faces greeted Cassidy's impassioned speech. No one challenged her, but Emily, for one, wondered at Cassidy's ability to have acted her part so well over the weekend, lying, conniving and fooling everyone. It was second only to Martin's cool performance, calculated, polished, cruel and totally dedicated to self-indulgent luxury – even to the extent of permanently damaging his own family.

Cassidy turned to Martin. 'Even up to ten minutes ago I loved you; but how can I ever forgive you for killing Weddy? He gave me a good life and – yes, I was still fond of him, for all his faults! Now you've killed something in me, too, and all I want is for you to get what you deserve! And yes, I will tell them how you went to visit Weddy in hospital, without telling me at the time, and how you slipped some extra papers in with others he had to sign, so that ever since, money has been diverted to your offshore account in Barbados! Yes, we needed that money to start our new life, because Weddy would have cut me out of any future will he drew up, but why should you have it now? How *could* you, Martin? It was going to be so wonderful and now it's all so terrible!' Her voice broke and she collapsed in anguish, curling into a tight ball in her chair and weeping uncontrollably. Her audience remained unresponsive.

Edward looked aghast. 'That means that Martin, who was so supportive last Friday, actually drove me to the mortuary in a car which he had bought with money he had stolen from my brother, in order that I should identify that same brother whom he'd killed the night before! I...' He stopped, lost for words.

Drummond moved forward, his face impassive. He thanked Cassidy formally for her information, turned back to Martin and once again began the familiar words: 'Martin Chumleigh, I am arresting you on suspicion of the murder of James Wedderburn. You do not have to say anything, but it may harm your defence if you do not mention when questioned anything which you later rely on in court. Anything you do say may be given in evidence.' He turned to Cassidy. 'Mrs Wedderburn, we would like you to accompany us to Eastbourne Police Station for further questioning, and where we would like you to make a statement.'

As the uniformed police officer led the sulky-faced Martin away, DS Pollard took Cassidy's arm, and the little group moved solemnly into the hall.

Drummond paused at the drawing room door. 'Thank you, Dame Emily, for your invaluable help. All of you are now at liberty to leave here. We will be in touch, Mr Wedderburn.'

Edward, who now seemed to be in a complete daze, half-rose from his chair. 'Thank you, Detective Chief Inspector Drummond,' he said politely, before sinking down again.

No one else stirred as Drummond left. It was as though the whole group was holding its breath, unsure of the true nature of reality around them. As the front door shut with a final clang, an almost audible sigh filled the room.

'Well, I never,' said Grace.

Part V
Clear Water Ahead

Chapter 29

Emily wheeled the trolley into her little dining room and put the final dishes on the table. She nodded in satisfaction. Now that the power points were working, she was poised for action. The casserole (cooked by Grace and stored in Emily's freezer) with dumplings, fresh vegetables, a large dish of mashed potato, washed down with a rather delicate vintage wine she had kept for a special occasion, followed by rhubarb crumble, a chocolate gâteau and fresh Kenyan coffee with cream, should serve her purpose well.

She walked over to the mantelpiece and picked up the postcard of Fountains Abbey, which had arrived that morning. Turning it over, she read it again.

> *Had a wonderful time with the wife and kids. Beginning to make plans for the future. Thank you for everything. Ian.*

She smiled and put it back, glad that she had confessed to Ian that she had read James' newspaper cuttings, and relieved that he bore no ill will towards her. Good news was welcome just now.

Suddenly the letter box clattered and Emily went to the front door. She bent down to pick up her copy of the local paper and saw her own face reflecting back at her. She sat on the chair in the hall and scanned the headline and following columns. 'Murder mystery solved by the Dame of Seascape' it shouted, and in smaller letters, 'by Mandi Jones'. Emily smiled, she'd read it later, and if that Mandi had misquoted any of their interview she'd be for it! Inwardly she was pleased; forget that Mandi had never done her piano practice as a child, she had been very personable last week, when they had chatted over the whole saga of James' death. She deserved a good start up the journalism ladder, but Emily would have preferred not to be the one to give her the necessary shove...

Emily put the paper out of sight in her bedroom, went back to the dining room and glanced out of the window. Edward was on his way. He was clearly weary, his hair hanging limply and his eyes on the ground. Emily decided he was in limbo between all the activity and anxiety of the past few days, and the long summer term ahead with the prospect of Jonathan's production at the end of it. Well, perhaps that state would not last too long if her little plan worked. The stage was set, if only she could play her part inconspicuously and to perfection. There were times when Emily enjoyed being devious.

'I've come on ahead,' Edward said, as Emily opened the front door. 'I've just been showing Beth and the twins round the mansion and outbuildings. I've left them to go for a short walk along the cliff. Beth said they'd be here at one o'clock.'

Emily nodded. 'Come into the dining room,' she said. 'We can see them come through the entrance gates from here. Did you manage to find somewhere to stay when the Bank Holiday was over?'

Edward sat sideways on one of the dining room chairs, looking out onto the drive. 'Yes, I've got a room in one of the pubs in Alfriston. Beth was glad of some help yesterday when we moved her mother from the family house into a local nursing home, a couple of roads away from the pub. Last night the twins arrived back from their Outdoor Activity week in Cornwall, and tomorrow they'll celebrate their twenty-first birthdays with Beth's mother. I'll go back to Yorkshire in a couple of days, and Beth and the boys will follow just before term begins. But I will be in touch with you as soon as I know what will happen to the mansion. '

'That's fine,' said Emily, as she went to check on the vegetables. So she had only the next hour and a half at the most in which to talk to Edward. Her heart sank together with her hopes.

Emily put the knife down on the table. The vegetables needed five more minutes. She had no time to do more as Edward went to answer the knock at the door and returned, all smiles, bringing a laughing Beth into the kitchen. She was slightly taller than he, slim, and her dark chestnut hair, drawn back from her face, fell in natural waves to just below her shoulders. Under her jacket she wore an olive top with black trousers. Her hands, Emily noticed, had the long slim fingers of a musician. Emily suddenly realised she hadn't combed her hair and she still had her slippers on. She reached out a hand. 'I'm so pleased to meet you. Please do come on through. You don't want to stand here in the kitchen.'

'The boys are coming. They decided to race each other to the far side of the golf course and back, so I left them to it and came on ahead. They won't be long,' Beth said, by way of explanation. 'I'm delighted to meet you. I've heard so much about you.'

'Not all bad, I hope,' responded Emily shooing them with her hands out of the kitchen. 'Come on, Edward, take the lady's coat!'

Five minutes later she was opening the door to the twins, tall, dark-haired and full of life. Emily glanced at the knees protruding from their jeans and reminded herself that they were young. 'Come in!' she said. They slipped off their jackets and threw them on to the hooks on the hallstand as if they had been coming to the Lodge all their lives, and followed Emily into the dining room.

'Sorry to be a bit late,' said the slightly broader one. 'I'm Tim, by the way, and this is Chris.'

'Don't worry,' said Emily easily. 'Excuse me; I need to be in the kitchen. Edward, will you deal with the drinks?' She left them to it. She had the vegetable dishes ready, but she must strain the broccoli. How silly to be so nervous.

'What can I do to help?' Beth was standing in the doorway, smiling.

'Oh,' said Emily uncertainly, her oven glove trailing from her hand.

Beth came over. 'I'll drain the broccoli, shall I? Which dish would you like it in?'

Emily pulled herself together. 'The round one,' she said. 'The oval one is for the peas and carrots.'

Soon everyone was round the table, glasses filled, eagerly anticipating the food. The boys were full of news about their varied activities over the last ten days, and even Edward had lost his tired-old-man look.

Emily dished up. How many years was it since she had done this for her sister and nephew? It was a treat to feel a family atmosphere just once more.

Tim and Chris fell on the food with enthusiasm. 'This is great,' said Chris. 'The food in Cornwall's been pretty basic.'

'You enjoyed the odd pasty and pint!' teased Tim. 'You had two on the abseiling day!'

'I deserved it! You should have seen the height of the cliff, Mum. I came down a good 50 feet.'

Beth smiled. 'What else did you get up to?'

Chris began to count the days off on his fingers. 'Wednesday – windsurfing, Thursday – water polo competition, Friday – a vicious assault course, Saturday – cross country, Sunday – sailing and Tim was sick!'

'What about you?' Tim chipped in. 'You went a funny green colour yourself at the top of the abseiling cliff.'

'That was after that awful fish lunch…'

'OK, boys!' Beth held up her hand. 'You had a brilliant time and I'm proud of you, but you'll have to tell me the rest later.'

She turned bright eyes to Emily. 'I'm sorry. The boys only got back late last night and it was all I could do to wake them this morning and drag them here in time to look round Seascape House, before coming to meet you!'

Emily laughed. 'I'm all for those who make the most of it when they are young. So what are you doing when you're not bouncing down cliffs?'

Chris finished his last mouthful as Tim contemplated the strange qualities of the dumpling in front of him. 'We're both in our last year – I'm doing Media Studies and Tim's doing Music.'

Beth looked at Emily. 'My daughter, Jessica, is a nurse and she lives with her young man in Manchester. I don't see much of her at all these days.'

Emily caught the pain in her voice and decided to move on. 'And how is your mother settling in?' she asked.

'She's happy in the home. It's in a beautiful building in Alfriston, so she will still see her old friends. She's glad to give up the responsibility for the house and garden: it was all getting too much and she's quite frail now. That's why I feel I must leave school in the summer and move down here to be nearer her.' She glanced at Edward's gloomy face and then continued. 'Sadly, we shall have to sell her bungalow in the long term, to pay for the cost of the home, but I'm sure I shall find somewhere to live – and a job too, hopefully.'

Emily nodded and indicated the vegetable dishes. 'Please do help yourselves to more,' she said, eyeing the boys' empty plates and hoping she had made enough for second helpings – at least the rhubarb crumble would be filling.

Tim put three more potatoes on his plate and declined the broccoli. 'Did you really live in that mansion all your life, Dame Emily?' he asked.

Emily grinned. 'I was even born there. Life was very different in the late thirties; there have been so many changes, some for the worse, but at least the role of women has improved.'

Beth put down her knife and fork. 'So you must have had some links with the suffragette movement. Forgive me, Dame Emily,' she said, 'but that doll on your sideboard, it's been fascinating me ever since I came in the room.'

Emily turned her head. 'Oh, the one made out of sackcloth. Please do look at it more closely.'

Beth got up and brought the little figure to the table. The elegant lady wore a long skirt and carried a placard with the words, 'Votes for women' written on it.

'This looks original,' she said.

'Yes,' Emily acknowledged, 'our family had strong links with the suffragette movement. Emmeline Pankhurst came to the mansion a couple of times, and gave the doll to my grandmother. My mother was born not long after and named Emmeline – though not everyone in the family approved – and in due course the name came to me.' Emily smiled. 'It was quite a name to live up to. I've kept the doll to remind me of all the changes those women fought for, to challenge me never to give in, and to fight for what is right and fair.'

'You certainly did that over the Easter weekend,' Edward said with feeling, 'and I for one am enormously grateful.'

'Is that your motivation for giving so much of your life to helping and guiding young people?' Beth asked.

Emily leaned back in her chair. 'I think it probably is. I care about the young, especially those who have a tough time; they've got so much vitality and potential. Still, enough of that, it's time to get the pudding.'

'We'll clear away,' said Tim, beginning to stack the plates.

Beth stood up. 'I think I saw the puddings on the kitchen work surface?' she said.

'Yes,' said Emily. 'Do bring them in.'

The crumble and gateau disappeared almost as fast as the first course had done. Emily was glad that she would not need any supper; there were certainly no leftovers.

Beth brought in the coffee and everyone seemed very much at home. Emily relaxed a little. Tim was fiddling with the foil from his chocolate, smoothing it and trying to remove the creases, while Chris was folding his unused paper serviette into the shape of a paper hat.

Gradually the conversation turned towards the future of the mansion.

'It's a great building, Uncle Edward,' said Tim. 'But what on earth are you going to do with it?'

The shadow returned to Edward's face. He sighed and shrugged his shoulders. 'I guess I shall have to sell it,' he said dismally. 'There'll be death duties and other taxes to pay, I expect, and I have no interest in running a hotel – and I doubt the Elizabethan Heritage Association would let me make the necessary changes anyway. I love it as a building and its sense of history, but really I can't live in it. If I had my way, I'd lock it up until this coming term is over and then think again.'

'Oh,' said Chris, 'the production of *Penelope* – how's it going?'

Beth spoke quickly, preventing Edward from saying anything. 'Ed's done so well, the rehearsals are going amazingly smoothly – only a few hiccups, and that's to be expected – and the music is brilliant. The orchestra is very good this year. As soon as the exams are over, Ed will have a few full rehearsals to get it all polished, and we shall be ready to go. We're going to go into Eastbourne tomorrow to get the material for the last few costumes, so that I can get them completed in the next six weeks.'

'It's a pity school isn't near the sea,' said Chris. 'I could really imagine Odysseus landing on this beach,' he nodded towards the main gates of Seascape, 'and walking up to the mansion to find his wife.'

Edward's face lit up. 'I wish we could create that sort of atmosphere, but it's hard in a school hall.'

Emily's eyes gleamed. 'Edward,' she said. 'What is it about teaching that you really love?'

Edward looked startled, as if he had never thought about it before, just accepted the package as it was.

'If I'm honest, I suppose it's the dramatic and literary side of English. I'm happiest when I'm with the school drama club, seeing the young people learn to act, to relate, to work as a team, to produce something that comes fully alive, and feel they've achieved. I can do without the marking and the exam work. Why?'

Emily ignored his question. 'Try to suspend disbelief for a moment,' she said. 'Supposing you could put on another performance of *Penelope* here at Seascape, and invite local schools to be the audience. Would you enjoy that?'

Edward stared at the lacy cloth on the table; he appeared to be struggling with the idea.

'If you could guarantee the weather,' Beth said, 'it would be wonderful. The orchestra could be under the cedar tree, we'd have the sea in the background, the front of the house as a stage…'

'And if it were wet,' butted in Chris, 'you've got the gym. You could easily erect a stage there, even stage blocks would do, and we could make some very simple scenery.'

'There are all those rooms in the stables where people can change,' added Beth, getting enthusiastic.

'And you'd charge for admission…' Tim put in.

'And they could pay extra for a swim,' Chris said eagerly.

'It's an impossible dream,' said Edward, his eyes still on the cloth.

'Edward,' said Emily softly, waiting till he lifted his eyes to hers. 'Have you heard of Glyndebourne?'

'I have,' interrupted Beth. 'It's a large house and garden, where they invite people to come with picnics of wonderful wine and amazing food, and they put on operas in the open air, and… Oh, what an incredible idea!' she said and stopped.

Edward looked from Emily to Beth and back to Emily. 'What are you on about?'

Emily pushed her coffee cup further away and fiddled with a spare serving spoon. 'This would take courage,' she said slowly, 'but I think you have that. You believe in the value of drama and of making a production together. You want to motivate young people, bring out their potential. What about resigning your job, moving down here and having a young version of Glyndebourne – not for opera, but for drama? Run week-long seminars, culminating in productions to which families and friends could come!'

Edward frowned; he looked as though he were trying to translate the words into a language he could understand. He had obviously not got the message yet.

Beth's eyes had lit up. 'Edward, don't you see? We used to go on school journeys with the kids – they stayed in a hotel, studied the local history and geography, did projects. You could use the mansion in the same way, but purely for drama projects. The kids could stay here, or in a local hotel and come every day. You could run the drama and perform it in the gym or the grounds, you could even get the parents to come and pick them up at the end of the week and be the audience!'

Tim leaned forward. 'Members of staff might be willing to be responsible for music, or scenery or props. It's a great idea! Think what it would be like to work surrounded by that architecture and those amazing portraits.'

Beth laughed. 'It all sounds wonderful. Ed, you don't need to stay on at school if you're not really happy – you've a ready-made home here in the Old Barn.'

Emily took a sip of cold coffee. 'I'm sure Stella would run the mansion for you.'

Edward ran his fingers through his hair and shook his head in disbelief.

Beth smiled. 'I'll be living just a few miles away. I might be able to help out with costumes for any productions you put on. We can do it on a budget. You only need simple shifts and then you add hats or sashes or something to give a flavour of the period. Or they could bring some things of their own that would suit.'

Edward looked round at the excited faces. 'It sounds wonderful, but the money… It wouldn't work.'

Emily took a deep breath. She'd challenged Edward to be courageous, but this took enormous courage on her part. Could she trust someone she'd met only recently?

'Edward,' she said quietly.

Edward looked at her. Emily moved a stray wisp of white hair and lodged it behind her ear. 'Edward, I gained a lot of money

333

from the sale of the mansion. Apart from providing for my sister, and my own care later on, I have no one to leave it to. My friends are my age and really don't need money. I still believe passionately in young people, and today they desperately need goals they can reach, and the opportunity to work as a team and succeed together. I think it might be possible to set up some kind of trust fund to tide you over and to establish this.

'There are plenty of local schools that would be interested – just one visit from one class from each would spread the news of what you are doing. They wouldn't need to stay overnight. A local coach could bring and collect them daily and parents could see their work at the end of the week.

'Use the house for lectures; I can leave the furniture there for you if you like. Then put bunk beds in the present bedrooms, sound-proof the attic rooms for music practice and rehearse the orchestra in the music room. I might even come and accompany them myself, if you'll have me.'

'Then Dame Emily could still live here in the Lodge, couldn't she?' Beth interjected.

Edward looked overwhelmed. 'Of course she could; I'd be delighted, after all she's done for us.'

Emily tried to hold on to her emotions and failed. 'If I did stay in the Lodge,' she said slowly, 'I wouldn't have to buy a new house. That money could be invested, added to the trust.'

Edward looked from one eager face to another and ran his fingers through his hair. 'It's a wonderful dream, but it's such a big project, I don't think I can do it…'

Chris glanced at his twin, who nodded.

'"… without the woman I love",' Tim quoted.

Edward jerked his head round to face him. 'What?'

Chris reached for his back pocket and produced a small rubber band. He placed it in Edward's hand. 'It's time you made an honest woman of her,' he said.

'Go on,' said Tim.

'What?' said Edward again.

'Propose to our mother, now!' said Chris.

'But she doesn't want me. I'm not half the person your father was!' Edward protested.

'Will you stop talking about me as if I weren't here!' Beth burst out. 'And anyway, didn't Jon ask you, the person we both chose as our best man, to take care of us?'

Edward looked at her. Her eyes were bright and she was smiling at him. She nodded very slightly.

Emily held her breath – things were going far too fast, and in public too!

In the silence, when even the clock seemed to have stopped ticking, Edward took a deep breath. 'Beth, will you marry me?'

'Yes, of course I will!'

'Come on,' said Chris. 'Put the ring on her finger, then!'

Beth held out her left hand and allowed Edward to ease the elastic band on to her third finger.

'A beautiful, blue, expanding ring,' she said, showing it to the assembled company. 'What more could a woman ask?'

Laughter filled the room.

'Come on, boys,' said Emily firmly. 'It's time to do the washing-up.'

She led the way into the kitchen, where the Cavalier King Charles spaniel woke and looked up expectantly from her basket. Emily gave her the small piece of meat she had put to one side and with great satisfaction announced, 'Finlandia, the war is won!'